Donald Thomas and The Murder Room

››› This title is part of The Murder Room, our series dedicated to making available out-of-print or hard-to-find titles by classic crime writers.

Crime fiction has always held up a mirror to society. The Victorians were fascinated by sensational murder and the emerging science of detection; now we are obsessed with the forensic detail of violent death. And no other genre has so captivated and enthralled readers.

Vast troves of classic crime writing have for a long time been unavailable to all but the most dedicated frequenters of second-hand bookshops. The advent of digital publishing means that we are now able to bring you the backlists of a huge range of titles by classic and contemporary crime writers, some of which have been out of print for decades.

From the genteel amateur private eyes of the Golden Age and the femmes fatales of pulp fiction, to the morally ambiguous hard-boiled detectives of mid twentieth-century America and their descendants who walk our twenty-first century streets, The Murder Room has it all. ›››

The Murder Room
Where Criminal Minds Meet

themurderroom.com

Donald Thomas (1926–)

Donald Thomas was born in Somerset and educated at Queen's College, Taunton, and Balliol College, Oxford. He holds a personal chair in Cardiff University. His numerous crime novels include two collections of Sherlock Holmes stories and the hugely popular historical detective series featuring Sergeant Verity of Scotland Yard, written under the pen name Francis Selwyn, as well as gritty police procedurals written under the name of Richard Dacre. He is also the author of seven biographies and a number of other non-fiction works, and won the Gregory Prize for his poems, *Points of Contact*. He lives in Bath with his wife.

By Donald Thomas

Mad Hatter Summer: A Lewis Carroll Nightmare
The Ripper's Apprentice
Jekyll, Alias Hyde
The Arrest of Scotland Yard
Dancing in the Dark
Red Flowers for Lady Blue
The Blindfold Game
The Day the Sun Rose Twice
The Secret Cases of Sherlock Holmes
Sherlock Holmes and the Running Noose

As Francis Selwyn
Sergeant Verity and the Cracksman
Sergeant Verity and the Hangman's Child
Sergeant Verity Presents His Compliments
Sergeant Verity and the Blood Royal
Sergeant Verity and the Imperial Diamond
Sergeant Verity and the Swell Mob

As Richard Dacre
The Blood Runs Hot
Scream Blue Murder
Money with Menaces

The Day the Sun Rose Twice

Donald Thomas

An Orion book

This edition published by
The Orion Publishing Group Ltd
Orion House
5 Upper St Martin's Lane
London WC2H 9EA

An Hachette UK company
A CIP catalogue record for this book is available from the British Library

ISBN 978 1 4719 0445 5

www.orionbooks.co.uk

For Menna

Contents

1

The Pale Criminal

1

With its steel-frame butt folded down, the Skorpion VZ 61 machine-pistol would fit into a large handbag. The matt silver of its steel barrel is ten inches long, the magazine and hand-grip extending six inches downward. When a silencer is fitted the effective range of the Skorpion is halved to a hundred yards. Beyond that, the spraying effect of the silencer causes the bullets to fan out too widely to be accurate. When the frame butt is folded down, accurate fire is reduced to fifty yards.

To most of those who use the Czech-made pistol these reductions in range are not important. The Skorpion is a weapon of assassination, seldom used at a distance of more than ten yards. It is also a favourite instrument of the executioner. Aldo Moro, the Prime Minister of Italy, and Francesco Coco, Chief Prosecutor of Genoa were two of the victims put to death by the Skorpion following clandestine trials by 'people's courts'. Though the gun is no longer manufactured, the Czech arms agency Omnipol has a stockpile of the pistols which are supplied to urban guerilla groups and to resistance movements in southern Africa.

Western governments are quick to denounce Omnipol and its traders. Yet the Skorpion VZ 61 represents a supreme collaboration between the communist and the capitalist systems. Its design owes everything to the Czechs but the format of the twenty rounds in the metal crescent of its magazine is American.

The three men who came to Ezeiza on a dull winter afternoon at the end of May were each armed with the satin steel of the Skorpion. They wore the well-cut suits of the professional class, their leader in grey chalk-stripe, the other two in blue and in flecked brown. Their documents bore photographs which were their own and names which were not. These were no urban guerillas but servants of the existing order. Their authority came from 'The College', the Naval Mechanical School, in whose cellars the enemies of the state wept and died. It had been so in the old days and now it was so again. Behind its smart iron railings the red-roofed Spanish-colonial building was neat with black inlay on white stone. Its trim lawns and oleander bushes had the tranquillity of a funeral home.

The three gunmen obeyed the orders of their immediate superior. He, in turn, took his commands from another. None of the three men knew the identity of that other person. In this ignorance lay their own security.

Silver-grey, the Ford Falcon approached Ezeiza across the miles of flat alluvial soil. Behind them, the broad flow of a brown river caught the glimmer of winter afternoon, cold and neutral as glass. Grey and white, the grandiose blocks of the vast, impoverished city receded in a chill ocean haze. Lights were coming on in the suburb of San Martín. Metal shutters were closed in its narrow shopping streets, the 'En Venta' signs betraying the decay of commerce and currency. Beyond the suburbs, red funeral lamps flickered in the cemeteries of Moreno.

Presently the car entered a complex of new highways, curving, dividing, intersecting, among tall signs and the harsh whine of aero-engines. Only the language on the signs distinguished this from a dozen international terminals: the wooded terrain of Moscow, the rainy fields of Charles de Gaulle, the mud flats of Kennedy or the damp Virginian grasslands of John Foster Dulles.

The airport was not their destination. The car turned off through woods and weekend parks, the litter of summer visitors strewn in the cold afternoon. They stopped at a gate more heavily fortified than any part of the air terminal. Guards in jackboots and leather tunics looked on as the three men's papers were presented to a computerised scanner. A pair of handlers stood close, their alsatians on short chains looking simultaneously cowed and vicious. Each visitor was then given a lapel plaque. The inner gate of steel swung open and the car was waved on.

They walked in silence, unescorted but observed, from the car park to the airless hum of the research block. It had been built several years before, when the reprocessing facilities yielded their first plutonium-239. Now there was no further barrier. The television scanners overhead were motionless, the red activator lights off.

On a door at the end of the passage was the triple red segment of a radiation warning and a glass observation panel. The leader of the group, in grey chalk-stripe suit, unbuttoned his jacket and looked through the window-panel. His hand disengaged the barrel of the machine-pistol, strapped to his waist under the cloth's concealment. The laboratory with its frosted glass and grey tiling held no interest for him in the banks of dials or the glove-boxes where men handled fuel with their arms sheathed for safety. He knew only as much of such things as his job required. When it was done, he and his companions would go to the shower-room opposite, discard their suits, and put on the clothes provided.

Through the panel, he could see a man whom he knew from photographs to be Walter Vogel. In the partial safety of a glass-fronted glove-box, Vogel sat at a laboratory bench under the cold glare of fluorescent lighting. Perhaps because the work upon which he was engaged had not been authorised, he disregarded the more elaborate precautions. So far as the watcher could see, Vogel was assembling a miniature fortress wall, like a child with toy bricks.

He worked with a device resembling retractable forceps, his hands and arms sheathed in white rubber. To the man who watched, Vogel might have been operating a bran-tub claw at a fairground. When the steel spider-grip picked up a brick of heavy metal, dull as brass, he would lower it slowly to the centre of the existing assembly, too engrossed to realise that he was spied upon. Each time the tarnished brick neared the structure, he paused, waiting for a directive.

Shifting his angle of vision, the man in grey chalk-stripe saw a metal screen and the white-coated technician beside it. From another photograph he recognised Reinhard Nunvar. Nunvar was monitoring a red light-pulse, the neutron counter at the centre of his instrument-panel. The pulse beat faster when a metal brick approached the assembly, diminishing again as it was drawn back. A metallic chatter rose and fell in time with the light.

The leader of the executioners satisfied himself, so far as he could, that the two men were alone in the room. Opening his jacket again, he lifted the curved steel of the loaded magazine from its concealment, clipped it into place and heard his two companions do the same. By screwing on the gas-silencer, he knew that the shots would spray a little more than usual. At such close range, it would scarcely matter.

At that moment an incoming jet passed low over the building in the last mile of its approach to the airport runway. The man hesitated, hearing in the breathless whining thunder of the engines a cover more effective than any silencer. But he was a professional and knew that a first successful temptation to disobey the rules would be followed by others that were more dangerous. With a final twist he secured the heavy muzzle of the silencer.

He opened the door gently, as if from habitual courtesy, and stepped into the room. Vogel spoke without looking up, unable to take his eyes from the precarious balance of another metal block.

'Close the door behind you, please, and stay just where you are.'

Slowly he lowered into place the rough and tarnished brick. The red eye of the counter winked faster and the dry chatter of the mechanism rose to a pitch of frustrated energy.

'Stand up,' said the man in grey. He kept the barrel of his

pistol towards the floor and spoke with an instinct of quiet courtesy. 'Stand up and turn round. Dr Nunvar will please come from behind the screen and stand beside you. Leave everything just as it is.'

'You have no right to enter without the director's permission.'

Only after he had spoken did Vogel twist on his stool, ignoring the order to stand up. He saw the satin grey of the pistols in the hands of the intruders, and then he understood. The man in the chalk-stripe nodded to one of his companions, who moved quickly behind the screen, searching the laboratory for other occupants. When he reappeared, however, he had found only Nunvar, now walking slowly in front of him. Nunvar was a man in his late fifties with a face which seemed a good deal younger. He stood beside Vogel, his eyes moving from one to another of the three gunmen.

Vogel's gaze wavered from the face of the leader.

'I should still like an explanation of your presence in this laboratory. An experiment was in progress. The red warning light was on the door and the electronic lock should have sealed it. Why have these devices been tampered with?'

The man in the grey suit touched the identity plaque on his lapel.

'Military security,' he said, as if the words had just occurred to him. 'Two experiments in this laboratory were unauthorised and must be investigated. Do as you are told, please, and co-operate with the inquiry. No harm will come to you.'

It was surprising how readily, even when faced with men whom they instinctively knew to be their executioners, the victims would grasp at any lie which was told them in order that they might still hope. The leader with the machine-pistol was grateful for this. He took no pleasure in the abject terror, the loss of manhood and self-control on the part of some of those who were to die in a few minutes more. Within the limitations of his profession, he was merciful. Yet as his eyes met Vogel's, he knew that the grey-haired German was not deceived.

'Do as you are told and no harm will befall you!' He looked steadily into Vogel's eyes as he spoke, willing him to believe. 'Step back behind the bench, away from the window. Dr Nunvar as well, if you please.'

'If there are allegations of unauthorised experiments, that is a matter for the project director!' Nunvar flurried the words, as if he too were well aware of what must follow. With Vogel, he now stood on the far side of the bench which was between the condemned men and their e ecutioners.

'The project director will be here in a few minutes,' said the man in the chalk-stripe suit gently. He brought the flat snub barrel of the machine-pistol up and fired at Nunvar, four shots reduced by the gas-silencer to a popping of corks. As he did so, the breathless roar of another trans-ocean jet passed low above them. Nunvar's body, arms thrown wide, was lifted and thrown backward by the muzzle velocity of the gun, crashing down amid fragments of glass from the front of a storage cabinet behind him.

The executioner turned to Vogel, his voice quiet and reassuring.

'You have no more to fear now. The project director has known all the time that Nunvar deceived you as well as the rest of us.'

As he spoke, he brought the muzzled barrel of the Skorpion pistol up again to fire. But he was so accustomed to his victims accepting the lies by which he soothed their last agony of waiting that he had overlooked Vogel's trained scepticism. Vogel put his arm across the bench, as if in a gesture of intercession or even in the hope that he might be able to deflect the bullets at the cost of shattering his hands upon them. The executioner was used to such desperate irrational acts by men in their last moments, when the greatest need was to find a promise, however insanely based.

He raised the flat gun barrel a little more and, in that

moment, Vogel's hand tilted the lead hod above the bench. As the executioner's finger tensed upon the curved steel of the trigger, he saw a small pile of the bronze-coloured metal bricks begin to slide. One after another they slithered into the centre of the assembly which Vogel had been building.

In the seconds which followed the first bullet hit Vogel in the ribs, spinning him aside. The shots that followed brought a blossom of blood from his neck and shattered his skull. He fell across the wreckage of the cabinet-front and lay dead, the flow of blood from the wounds ebbing as the heart stopped. On the bench itself, as the metal bricks piled into the assembly, there appeared a sudden aura of blue ionised light. As it brightened to an intenser glow, the chatter of the neutron counter became a constant high-pitched whine of alarm. The pulse of the red eye quickened until it was soon visible as a steady glow.

Of the three gunmen, only the executioner himself had some inkling of what had happened. He pumped the remaining twelve shots from the magazine of the machine-pistol into the assembly of metal bricks, trying to scatter the fuel of a conflagration without touching the hot metal himself. Several of those on the top of the structure clattered on to the bench. He had no chance to see whether it was the heat of the metal or the penetration of bullets into the wiring ducts which brought the first yellow fingers of flame.

Terror at the blue aura of lethal radiation was compounded in the three gunmen by the sight of the fire which leapt and spurted upwards across the ceiling tiles of white polystyrene. The first of the killers reached the door, the back of his coat already exuding wisps of smoke from the rain of burning ceiling debris. His last words came as a shout, rising to a scream. The bulbous metal of the handle was firm as rock and without movement. In the few minutes which the three men had spent in the laboratory, the electronic lock had been activated again.

While one struggled unavailingly with the lock and beat on the heavy door like a demented child, another clawed at the thick armoured glass of the windows. It was only the leader of the group who surrendered to a death more cruel than any he had forced upon others. As the scorching heat and smoke entered his lungs with every breath, he fell to his hands and knees, knowing that even to escape the fire would be to die in a few days more from the falling blood count which such radiation had caused.

It was not the agony of flame but the pain in his chest which he struggled to put from his mind in the last moments. Who had re-activated the lock? Was it possible that Vogel had the means to do it from within the laboratory? Had it been done by the men who planned Vogel's death and those of his executioners as well? Had it been done by Andor? Andor!

The sound of his own breathing came to him now like the crying of a wounded child.

Andor, the conspirator who should have been lying with his body blown apart like the other two. Why was Andor not there with Vogel and Nunvar? It need not have mattered . . . Andor could have been trapped in his office and dealt with . . . Tracked to his apartment . . . But Andor had escaped . . . The oldest man in the conspiracy of old men, but also the leader . . . Andor was alone, but a lone genius . . . Some portion of the human remains, too dangerously contaminated for close examination, would be gathered from the detritus of the fire and buried under Andor's name. Irony and failure possessed the gunman's mind. Blood welled up in his scorched throat. Coherent thought eluded him. With an instinct of childhood he began automatically and half-consciously to pray a long-known prayer for his own salvation.

2

Dr Andor closed his eyes and folded his hands on the grey webbing of the seat-belt. A thrust of engines gathered behind him, the aircraft jolting across tarmac that seemed flat and vast as an Atlantic calm. The force at his back redoubled, as if the pilot sensed that the power of the jets might fail him. In that moment of half-acknowledged danger, when the wheels left the ground, Andor remembered the burning horses.

The memory returned often to his mind on such occasions. Sometimes the animals were little more than a thought. This morning they streamed across his inner vision like the proud beasts of an apocalypse.

The greater part of his lifetime now separated him from the reality, a momentary glimpse of the creatures of flame. In that period the sequence of images had become stylised and unvarying, like a filmed record.

Andor's recollection began, as the reality had done, with a direct hit on the riding stables at the Tiergarten end of the Kurfursten-Damm. For more than a week the centre of Berlin had been an open target for the Red Army's Katushka rockets. As the siege grew tighter, the missiles were fired from the very suburbs of the city, somewhere to the south beyond Wilmersdorf. The force of the explosion in the riding stables shook the ruined structures of the Kurfursten-Damm. It flickered on the flame-coloured pall of smoke, stagnant as a thundercloud over the broken buildings.

In forty years Andor had never understood how the four horses survived the impact of that explosion. They had appeared almost at once between the ruined walls, moving at a gallop in the smoke-darkened morning. The street was a mere canyon between bomb rubble piled on either side by the labour gangs of children and old men.

At first Andor was merely astonished by the sleek grooming of the horses' flanks in the smashed and dying city. They were smooth and unblemished as pale brown satin. He supposed that the stables and their owner were under the protection of a party official from the Luftwaffe building or even from the Chancellery. Not until someone pointed it out to him did he see the quivering fire in every tail and mane. The uneven flames seemed to falter and then fluttered out behind as the animals reared and charged towards the Uhland-Strasse crossing.

Their pace slackened only once, where a gang of civilian volunteers had turned a cream-coloured streetcar on its side. Filled with rubble, it was to be a makeshift barrier against the advancing Soviet tanks. With the precision of ballet dancers, the doomed horses divided into pairs and passed surefooted on either side of the obstruction.

After that they were briefly lost to sight among the riven trunks and branches of the Kurfursten-Damm lime trees, the wood charred by bomb and shell. Andor had seen them last on a mound of rubble, bucking and thrusting against their backdrop of firecloud, falling and rolling among the jagged stones, where fashionable shops and elegant apartment buildings had lately stood.

The horses remained a mystery to him. Did they feel pain from the burning manes or was it only fear which drove them on? Did the fire consume them or would the flames gutter as soon as the hair was destroyed? Had they escaped the explosion only to shrink and die, uncomprehending, in the famine which was soon to have Germany in its hold? Or had they, like Andor, been among the creatures who survived the inferno and prospered?

With their passing a stillness had returned upon that darkened avenue where the boarded windows of the cafés were splashed with new blood. In such a place, even the burning horses had been an unimportant spectacle. Across the hastily filled bomb craters of the Uhland-Strasse, nurses from the damaged Charité hospital had improvised a casualty station in an abandoned bus. From two adjacent lamp-posts the bodies of a pair of hanged boys turned in stiff half-circles. They wore dusty uniforms and had been convicted by one of the Flying Courts-Martial instituted by the SS when the siege of Berlin began. Their blank and bulging eyes stared down upon the crudely printed placards pinned to their tunics by the executioners. 'I was a traitor to my people.' 'By my cowardice I sold my country.'

Then the sounds had begun again. An irregular crack

and thud of anti-aircraft guns from the Flak Tower near the Tiergarten was a prelude to the next assault. Clear above the grinding howl of the Katushka rockets rose the shell-screams of the Russian batteries. They came with such frequency now that the civilian volunteers of the labour gangs had learnt to ignore all but the impact of the missiles. Even the stone skeletons of the cafés and cinemas offered little protection. At every burst of a shell or a rocket, the ruins blazed anew, the masonry itself burning with the intensity of the heat.

Dr Andor opened his eyes again as the plane began to steady into level flight. The vision of flame under a sky of burning smoke was now replaced by a reality of white sun and infinite azure. Below him, as the plane pulled away from the airport pattern of runways, he could make out the shabby little station of Howard Beach, the grey derelicts of subway cars, the white clapboard houses of Queens where the smell of the Atlantic was sharp and cold among tall reeds and grasses.

Higher still, the oval glass of the window looked down on mud flats stretching towards Long Island, cut by rivulets and tiny bays, like sand uncovered by a receding wash of tide. There was movement in the cabin of the aircraft again, the moment of danger past. A rattle of glasses and a quick exchange among the uniformed hostesses caught Andor's attention briefly. Then he looked away towards the little window, limitless blue above storm and weather, his thoughts still imprisoned within scenes of that other life.

After another week of the bombardment, the rockets and shells ceased. Under the eyes of strangers who were now its conquerors, the city stirred cautiously to life again. Andor remembered the yellow-amber cloud which veiled the spring sky, a mist of tiny particles from the smashed stone and plasterwork of the old buildings. At every breath of wind during June and July the fine grit which had settled again was blown into the faces of the vanquished, making the eyes smart and forming a rough powder between the teeth.

He had stood where the heart of Berlin had once been, on the Potsdamer-Platz. A landscape of flattened rubble, empty as the moon, extending on every side to the horizon with scarcely a landmark remaining. Looking up, Andor had seen beyond the yellow veil of dust the mallards flying in formation through the clear sky of north Germany, as though that spring had been no different from any other.

The shells and the rockets were silent by then. Only the sporadic stutter of rifles and the occasional boom of an explosive charge reminded the conquered people that the justice of the victors had yet to be completed. The terror of retribution was longer and less predictable than the bombardment had been.

It was a time of ancient stoicism, brave and reasoned advice among lovers and families. His father had ordered that Sybille, Andor's sister, should sit nearest the door of the cellar in the ruined house at Schoneberg. Stories from East Prussia and Pomerania described how the Red Army scoured such ruins with their flame-throwers. The men therefore put the women nearest the doors so that they might be mercifully consumed at once, spared the nightmare of seeing their families burnt before the jet of fire was turned upon them.

The stories carried all before them, though the terrors had rarely been substantiated. Death and violation, such as Andor had seen, appeared more casual and even banal. He thought of the words of Stalin to Djilas, the imperial victor now jovial and voracious in his triumph.

'Can't you understand that a soldier who has crossed thousands of miles through blood and fire will enjoy himself with a woman or make free with a rifle?'

Beyond that voice, in its jocular cruelty, there could be no further recollection. Andor roused himself and looked down through the narrow oval of the window at his side. Below him the sunlit sea was a steel reflection, between grey and blue. He supposed it was the Canadian coast ahead, Nova Scotia or Newfoundland. The contoured snow lay smudged here and there by oyster-coloured earth and the marks of man-made tracks. It was desolate as any ruined city. Further still, the cold sea was deeper blue, as the coast fell away behind the dull metal fin of the plane's wing. Scattered bergs of ice, like a litter of broken plastic, spread northward over the vast surface of the Atlantic.

Presently he looked up, aware that someone had been speaking to him without acknowledgement on his part. A man of natural courtesy, Andor gave a quick apologetic smile. His round pale face, the grey hair-wisps of a man approaching seventy, had an unnatural smoothness and a fullness of curve. He looked like a man being treated for a tumour by cortisone, yet he was not. The pale criminal. That was how he thought of himself whenever he faced his mirrored image, remembering Nietzsche. He held just the right balance of humility and arrogance. *Behold, the pale criminal has bowed his neck: from his eye speaks the great contempt.*

He smiled again at the girl who was leaning over the seat, looking down at him through the clean painted mask of her face.

'No thank you,' he said in his gentle voice. 'Nothing to eat thank you.'

There were several hours of sleep as the plane rushed headlong towards the darkness of the eastern Atlantic. Andor slept easily, untroubled by memories of the past or by fear of what he had begun to do. Only in his conscious mind did he recall the images of the other life, the horses burning, the streets on fire, the silent wastes of rubble in spring sunshine. It was rare for him to dream at all and even in the destruction of forty years ago he had found sleep a refuge. His waking memories exorcised the horrors. With that accomplished he enjoyed the repose of a man armed in righteousness. He was alone, and in his loneliness able to defy the world. It was the beginning and end of a survivor's mission. The thought pleased him. Whatever was important to him, Andor had done alone. To have no allies in these last days made him invincible.

He woke unprompted to find the cabin busy with preparations of descent. The world outside was black, except for a few clusters of distant light on the ground below. Darkness obscured little from Andor who had travelled this way so often. He knew that the narrow brown and green strips of the Dutch fields lay below by dark patches of water, where in summer the sunlight flared on the hothouse roofs. The German fields were larger and broken up by geometrical shapes of woodland where the western armies tried ineffectually to conceal their rocket launchers. Then he heard someone mention Osnabruck and knew that they were over the jagged brown scar which ran like the zig-zag incision of a lunatic surgeon across the belly of Germany and Europe, cutting woods, fields and villages with its sandy minefields and wire fences.

Magdeburg and the other towns of the East marked the route of the air corridor. Berlin itself appeared as a mass of brilliance against the flat plains of night, unlit patches mapping the woods and lakes. Through light and darkness ran the angular line of the dividing wall, a gash of green-white lamps illuminating the death-strip.

The sight of the city where he was to fight his lonely battle left him unmoved. War had become impossible in a nuclear age, such was the gospel of friend and enemy alike. Victory was to be won with as little bloodshed as in a game of chess. The conqueror was he who could show by a diplomatic note that an enemy's resistance would be futile. To Clausewitz, war had been the extension of diplomacy. A new satanic technology relegated such wisdom to the world of the playground squabble.

Losing height, the aircraft crossed the garishly illuminated cordon round the western city. Unlike the swarming lights of the Stadtring traffic, the zonal boundary resembled an autobahn where nothing moved. Observation posts and machine-gun towers rose on concrete stilts at precise intervals, like a stranded regiment of Martians in their bright islands of light. Andor glanced down with distaste. He was unmoved by the enormity of what he would threaten. It puzzled him only that a conquered race had been docile for so long.

In a wide sweep the aircraft curved out over East Berlin to begin a westward approach to Tegel. Even in this manoeuvre Andor saw how easily and conveniently his own people had made their peace, accommodating their destroyers and legitimising the very destruction. City landmarks swept away beneath. They were lower now than the top of the Fernsehturm, the thousand foot needle of the DDR television tower with its bulbous revolving restaurant, the mast which beamed the message of collective autocracy to west and east.

Red warning lights flickered past on the tall industrial chimneys of Siemenstadt. The plane skimmed a road of bright little shops and cafés in the French sector of the city. Then the thud and judder of tyres brought it to earth on the dark tarmac of Tegel, almost at the heart of Berlin.

Andor sat still until the young woman in her air hostess uniform came to help him to his feet. She gave him a brisk and empty smile, blank as the blue Atlantic sky, looking down at his round pale face. Andor gathered his thoughts and apologised again.

It was not infirmity which kept him in his seat, though the long flight had wearied him. He was thinking with relief that he had made the last journey which would ever be required of him. He had come to Berlin for the last time. Even if he was victorious, his enemies would not spare him. From the beginning he accepted that his own death was as certain as those of Vogel and Nunvar. His enemies? Perhaps he had none in the usual sense. They thought of themselves as protectors and allies. It mattered no longer to Andor. Sacrifice, not victory, was uppermost in his mind.

He looked up at the young woman, warding her off with a smile of his own, hiding his contemplation. In his pocket lay a final message, addressed to Brigadier Henry Bonnell-Thornton, commandant of the British garrison in the beleaguered city. Its words had come first to Oppenheimer, recalling the *Bhagavad Gita* on a brilliant summer morning in 1945.

'I am become Death,' Andor said to himself, too softly for the air hostess to catch the words, 'the destroyer of worlds.'

Ten minutes later he dropped the envelope into a mailbox by the forecourt cab-rank.

3

From his eye speaks the great contempt. The words came aptly and spontaneously to Andor's mind as the doors of the Hotel Excelsior slid open before him and he walked into the hazy Berlin morning.

The great contempt. Once he had been disturbed by the division in his mind and feelings between a natural courtesy towards humanity and a savage disgust at what humanity had done to his city, his country and itself. Now he was used to this civil war in his soul, as if the battle-lines fell quiet. An armistice of ease and hate existed within him as surely as it did in the divided city. Even so, he might have failed in his determination, except for his sure moral refuge. It was unnecessary for a single man or woman to die, except perhaps himself. Whatever blood was shed would be the responsibility of his adversaries. It was the one article of faith which he shared with the urban guerilla and the freedom fighter.

He turned into the broad tree-lined Hardenberg-Strasse where the sun-withered leaves were scuffing and flying up in warm gusts of wind. The night before had been clear but the morning promised a day when the mist lifted late from the city streets. To the east, nothing but the onion-bulbed needle of the DDR television tower was visible by the red pattern of its aircraft warning lights. In the avenues of the west, a solitary glimmer of distant sun touched the gilt of the winged Victory, high on its imperial column among the Tiergarten trees.

Unhurried now, Andor walked down the broad pavement towards what would have been the city centre, if the city any longer had a centre. For the first time he noticed that the clean new buildings of Amerika Haus and the British Centre were protected by armed West Berlin police with alsatian dogs from the very citizens whom the two allies purported to defend. This travesty of the brave world promised by the victors in 1945 gave him a new sense of the logic upon which his cause rested.

In defiance of the guards with their brown bullet-proof jackets a group of the radical young had crept to a length of adjoining wall and worked unobserved with their spray cans of red paint. The lettering had been scrubbed but not obliterated. Andor could still make out '*West Deutschland*' set between two swastikas. A more ambitious slogan ran the length of the wall. '*Ami Söldner Mörder und Faschisten Westzonen Polisten!*'

He did not share the uncalculating hatred for authority, though he understood it. He had seen its cause when swift and vicious justice was dealt by the clubs of patrolling pickets in the green and white Polizei vans. Summer was the worst. The young from the packed apartment blocks of Moabit or Charlottenburg, or the derelict squatters' tenements of the Bulow-Strasse, roamed brightly lit streets round the Zoo station and the Europa Centre like wolf-packs, caged in a tiny island of lurid promise. Power and resentment confronted one another under the bland neon gospels of the grille-protected banks and the locked department stores.

Andor walked under the broad iron bridge which carried the railway tracks over the street and into the terminus. The paving outside was gaudy with the banked carnations of the flowerstalls. Already the music moaned from a discotheque under the iron arches built out across the pavement. The euphemistically named Peep-Show shops were open, watched over by impassive young women and depressed looking Turks with moustaches and scowls.

Pleasure. He glanced at a window case lined with the baby-faces of inflatable rubber dolls, each mouth pouting in dumb childlike invitation. In their flaccid state the rubber skin and features were curiously withered and shrunken, like those of mummified corpses. Was it a peculiar sickness of this city, the love of a man for a doll, the desire of the living body for a corpse? He knew it was not, and yet he shuddered at the sight.

Berlin bleibt Berlin. Berlin remains Berlin. The absurdity of that boast was visible all about him. To a man of his age, it was merely a fairground encampment of concrete and steel, mean and meretricious. The fact that it was set up in the ruins of a place he had once known gave it no claim on his loyalty or affections. Much as he loathed the cold military autocracy of the east, he would not have spent a single bullet to defend the brash and squalid commercialism of what he saw around him. It was a supreme irony, he thought, that the rulers of the two halves of the city presented each as a 'capital'. In truth, each was the worst possible advertisement for the political system it enshrined. In that respect, he had chosen the ideal place for what must be done.

Under the pink-shaded verandah of the Terrassen am Zoo, the poorest of capitalism's children had gathered. Middle-aged men and one or two women lounged with their bottles on the stone plinths and wooden benches where they had slept the night. A few were much younger. Andor noticed a boy of sixteen or seventeen sitting against the wall of the station entrance, legs splayed on the pavement, a crudely chalked appeal between his knees. *Ich habe Hunger* . . . "I am hungry. Help me." The poor came out by day. At night the streets for a mile around were bright with neon, a visual oratorio in praise of banks and automobile showrooms, blue movie houses and cosmetics. Then the poverty of Berlin would draw back into the shadows again, as if ashamed of itself.

At the street level the concourse of the station was a windowless limbo of shabby yellowed tiles and bleak passageways. Somewhere overhead an announcer's voice intoned the departure of the Amsterdam express. Andor found a phone booth and dialled the number. Punctilious as always, he had chosen the commandant of the British sector, for that was the sector he was now in. A woman's voice answered him in English.

'I am calling the office of the British commandant to speak to Brigadier Bonnell-Thornton,' said Andor meekly.

'The commandant is not available to callers.' Her voice was so flat and precise that he thought at first it might be a pre-recorded announcement. 'If the matter is official, you may call the command post at the Fusilier barracks in Spandau, or the Royal Military Police post at the Entlastungs-Strasse in the Tiergarten. I can give you the numbers if you do not already have them.'

'I will speak only to the commandant,' said Andor patiently. 'Since that is not possible by telephone, I will call upon him later today.'

'If you have good reason to see the commandant, you must go first to the garrison offices at Spandau and make a request in the usual manner.'

She was harsher now, as if with an awkward child.

'He will see me,' said Andor gently. 'Please tell him he has received several letters from me recently. Each was headed by a quotation from Nietzsche's prose-poem *The Pale Criminal*.'

He heard her draw breath to reply and then he hung up the receiver.

Going down the steps to the darkened platform, Andor waited for the custard-yellow U-Bahn train to draw into the station with a soft swish of its rubber tyres. He rode a single stop to Wittenberg-Platz and changed there to the line which ran out to the city's more affluent southern suburbs. It was unlikely that he had been followed as yet. However, by changing trains and platforms he assured himself that no one who travelled the single stop was also on the second stage of the journey.

Several years ago, Vogel and he had rented a Dahlem house, in the American sector. The area was one where the last comforts enjoyed by the Berlin bourgeoisie half a century before still lingered. Yet even in Dahlem the square white concrete of the Free University, the pizzeria and filling station on the wooded corners opposite the Botanical Gardens marked, for Andor, the inexorable encroachments of barbarism.

He came out of the U-Bahn entrance at Dahlem Dorf, where the booking-hall was disguised as a thatched and gabled hunting chalet. With the satisfaction of seeing a familiar landscape, he began to walk down the wooded avenue of the Konigin-Luise-Strasse, the solid villas of imperial Germany still set in gardens of fir trees, the outlines of museum buildings rising obscurely in the misty parkland beyond.

The physics department of the Free University was a complex of single-storey buildings made of prefabricated panels of grey concrete. Nearby on the other side of the broad suburban highway was a cul-de-sac. Here the houses were more modest, the white modernistic boxes of the 1930s which had survived the ordeal of siege and shell. Andor had not regarded it as his home, preferring to stay in hotels on his visits to Berlin. Yet it had been his base of operations. The woman from whom they rented it assumed that he was in some way connected with the physics department of the Free University. Andor had never bothered to correct the misapprehension. He encouraged her to think that he had several times been the department's guest. For all practical purposes the house had become a private laboratory, though the term seemed too pretentious for the little work which was carried out there. However, he thought, the good Frau Kenner judged it quite reasonable that a man of science should devote part of his home to the purposes of study.

Glancing at his watch, he saw that there was only just time to complete all the tasks he had assigned himself before calling on Bonnell-Thornton. Yet he had planned everything with such meticulous care that he knew the time would be enough.

After the freshness of the day outside, the house was

warm and musty from several weeks of being closed up. In his absence no one was encouraged or permitted to enter it. He went down the steps to the basement with its boiler and concrete floor. All the seals of sticky paper or thread across the doors were still unbroken. No one had been there.

It was a very rudimentary laboratory, he thought, if that was not too grand a term anyway. In its present disordered state it might have been the repair shop of a television retailer. Perhaps the assembly room of computer circuitry. In one corner, however, stood the exhibit to which so much of his hope was attached. Because of its shape and weight it was encased in tubular laboratory scaffolding, though a mere child would surely have guessed what it was.

In appearance it resembled two hemispheres of steel, each the size of a sink or a kettledrum, sealed together. To Andor it mattered nothing that the steel was tarnished by time and stained in patches the colour of bronze. The two halves of the sphere had been cast by metallurgists of the Auer company at Oranienburg, now in East Berlin, during 1944. It had been the spring of Karl Wirtz's development of the uranium pile at Dahlem which was intended to produce a German nuclear bomb by the end of that year. The bombing of the city had caused the evacuation of the pile from the Kaiser-Wilhelm Institute to Hagerloch in Bavaria. The special steel casings had been left behind.

After a perfunctory examination of the sphere, the switches of its inset control-panel and the harness of detonator wires by which it was surrounded, Andor ran the main lead across the room and plugged it in. At once the green digital figures on a timer, standing on the table close by, began to flicker, until the seconds became minutes.

Andor patted the cold smooth roundness of the sphere and smiled. A child would guess what it was, of course – but the child would be wrong. It was merely his toy, perhaps no more than his joke. For all that, the beautiful mechanism within must work precisely and convincingly. If it failed him, then his adversaries would not believe in his threat. In their disbelief lay the worlds of his dread and agony.

He went to a white metal cupboard, opened its door carefully, and took out what appeared to be a very large vacuum flask. It was two feet in length and round in proportion. Even so, it was far heavier for its size than any Thermos. The smile left Andor's face. The flask and its contents were not part of his joke. By the time that they were found, he would have won or lost.

Lowering the flask into its canvas carrying-bag, he went round the room once more, checking leads and switches, watching the movement of the green figures on the digital timer. To have done so much to ensure that not a man, woman nor child need come to harm! That was the supreme achievement to him. At the thought of it, Andor experienced a thrill of joy which other men felt in the sublime Sanctus of the B Minor Mass.

His plan had been laid with the precision of logic, the sublime perfection of a mathematical proof. Those who confronted him would surely operate by the same laws. Ten years before, Andor had heard a lecture by Dr Feld of the American Academy. The lecturer had supposed that he, as a nuclear physicist, was called upon by the Mayor of Boston for advice. A terrorist group had planted a nuclear bomb in the city. Ought the Mayor to submit to their demands or defy the blackmail? 'I would have to advise surrender,' Feld had said.

Surrender. But only, as Feld pointed out, on being convinced that the device would work. In such a game of bluff it was the one moment where logic was not enough, where even the perfection of mathematical proof might be flawed. Therefore, Andor had taken care to be believed. Great care.

Looking round the basement room for a last time, he went up to the main door and let himself out. The mist had cleared now and the heat of the summer day was dry and intense.

In his formal coat and hat he was indistinguishable from ten thousand elderly clerks and businessmen. Yet he was cautious, varying the route on his return, waiting for the bus by the iron railings and brick pillars of the Botanical Gardens. Under the full-leaved spruce trees, the petrol pumps and kiosks on the edge of the woodland stood silent in a noon calm.

Andor had planned this final journey six months before, following the route until he knew it like the landscape of childhood. At the Zoo station he changed to the 92 bus which took him west along the Kant-Strasse, the humbler grocers and fruiterers besieged by the midday crowds. Beyond the commercial heart of the city, the bus crossed the housing estates of Spandau and came at last to the quiet and deserted terminus at Staaken. Its final buildings were brown stucco maisonettes with concrete balconies.

The wasteland of tall grasses and reeds was silent as the remotest country. Beyond this nothing moved. It was the western edge of the Berlin enclave where the grey slabs of the roll-top wall divided the city from East German fields. No checkpoint, no guard-post here. The wall cut across the road and ran into the distance on either hand, rising from the rough grassland belt on the Berlin side.

In the silence and stillness of the summer day, Andor could see the concrete observation tower on the far side, a movement of field-glasses in the firing-slit. Further still rose a few roofs and a church tower of the village of Staaken, which he had known as a boy between the wars. So close to him now, it was as unattainable as his own infancy.

The Vopos in their watch-tower were no impediment to his plan. What he had to do would be done close to the foot of the wall, where he was out of their field of vision. He picked his way across the deserted weed-cracked tarmac of the road beyond the bus terminus. A litter of barrier poles and trestles, the tools of crowd-control, had been left unattended after an anti-DDR protest of some kind. They looked like the relics of a gymkhana.

A narrow path, passing between the litter of shacks by the roadside, followed the wall at a distance of several yards. On Andor's previous visit, during a December Sunday, it had been busy with West Berliners from the maisonettes walking their dogs through the overgrown waste. Now, on a working day in summer, it was deserted.

Between the path and the wall itself ran a ditch, just visible under grass and thorn-bushes before it disappeared into a concrete culvert. As Andor looked round, there was not another person in sight between him and the white blocks of the Heer-Strasse on the level, foreshortened horizon.

The concrete tunnel of the ditch-culvert was about two feet across. He stumbled down the bank to it, a buzz of insect colonies rising round him. Thorns caught and snapped in his jacket. Lifting the canvas bag again, he slid it into the dark tunnel as far as he could reach. The culvert was dry, the earth of Berlin baked to a pale brown dust.

A thorn tore flesh between his thumb and forefinger as he climbed the bank and felt his breath come with a little pain. At last he stood again on the waste land, under the colourless glare of sky. So often he had imagined the drama in which he would confront his adversaries. A man who might blow the last trumpet for a city's death or a world's end. In reality, he walked to the road and saw the driver smile as he boarded the bus. Andor thought of himself now as Death in a medieval morality, greeted by revellers who did not recognise him for what he was.

In the tiled hotel bathroom, he destroyed his documents and the identifying marks on the little luggage that he carried. He kept only his keys and a small lightweight case.

Following a familiar procedure, he sat on the bed, opened the case and took out a keyboard with an upper row of coloured tabs. When he plugged the lead into the hotel computer socket by the television panel, a flickering light appeared on the monitor screen in the corner of the room.

Sitting on the bed, the keyboard on his lap, he tapped out the first signal. In a moment the Ezeiza terminal responded and the interrogation began. *Enter name and password.* Patiently he tapped them out on the keyboard. The reply ran across the screen in neat electronic print. *Identity verified.*

The final lock opened before him. Even before Vogel and

Nunvar died, he had taken meticulous care to retain access to the IBM 38 complex. Those who hunted him – if anyone did – certainly thought they had prevented him. Now he had beaten them. The machine had been taught two languages. Andor was fluent in both of them.

Enter operator code. Like the peremptory demands of a spoilt child, the letters began to flash on the screen. He gave it what it wanted. *By pressing F4*, came the reply, *you will exit to ADA Modum.*

He was through. The last fragment of the complex mosaic lay in place. Gently he tapped out his final instruction, the warm lamplit room sounding dully to the clack of the keys. When it was over, he pulled out the plug from the socket, turned the television over to a broadcasting channel, and sat on the bed watching the coloured fictions of another world.

A previous guest had left the set tuned to the DDR-East channel, which broadcast to east and west alike at half-past seven. Andor had seen the newscasts from the east too often to be irritated any longer by the performance of the young announcer with his neat military haircut, his cold and unsmiling courtesy.

Preoccupied by his own thoughts, the old man gave only half his attention to the panorama of the day's events. He watched a fraternal Soviet delegation – the major news-item – file down the steps from a blue and white Aeroflot plane at Schonefeld. They paused for the camera, a stairway of tubby anonymous men, uniformly dressed in dark lounge suits and trilby hats, which seemed little altered since the days of Molotov and Vishinsky. Then an indeterminate number of women was shown struggling against a police cordon outside an American air-base in England. West German riot police dispersed a protesting group of young men near Stuttgart. An American professor addressed a Prague peace conference on the dangers of his country's military ambitions. Castro reported to the Cuban national assembly on the achievements of industrial production.

Despite the clean, earnest zeal of the young announcer, Andor saw no more hope in his eyes than in those of the boy who sat begging outside the Zoo station that morning. *Ich habe Hunger . . .*

When the bulletin was over, he took the portable computer keyboard in its neat case and checked out of the hotel. The remnants of his luggage had gone into one of the waste trolleys in the hushed and softly-lit bedroom corridors.

Berlin in the warm twilight was softer and quieter, the lamps among the paths and trees of the Tiergarten recalling an older imperial opulence. He walked through the parkland as far as the industrial skirt of Moabit, where the Moltke-Strasse Bridge crossed the dark waters of the Spree. While the traffic sped and screeched at his back, he held the little case with the keyboard over the iron balustrade, released his hold on it, and saw the faint feather-splash in the night river below. Then he turned back and began his last journey.

The white flat-roofed guard-house of the British Military Police post stood on the eastern edge of the Tiergarten trees, midway between the Brandenburg Gate and the Reichstag building. It adjoined the railed-off area of the Soviet War Memorial with its pair of World War II tanks and white marble temple. By a quirk of the sector boundaries, the memorial was isolated in the British zone, two hundred yards from East Berlin. The Royal Military Police had been stationed close by to prevent clashes between West Berliners and Soviet guards who marched from the east to take up duty there every day.

Andor looked across the parkland road and saw that there were lights in the guard-house. The complex was surrounded by iron railings, a notice on the main gate forbidding entry without the permission of the British commandant.

First of all, Andor went into one of the Tiergarten phone booths, dialled a long series of numbers, held the phone for a moment, then put it down. Prometheus. Fire from heaven. A fuse smouldering. The images jostled in his mind. But now there was no going back.

He crossed the road to the guard-house, where the Union Jack hung limp in the warm dusk above the Royal Military Police insignia. A jeep with a blue lamp clipped to its hood was waiting for the hour at which the western allies took it in turns to exercise their right of driving through the streets of East Berlin.

Andor glanced back once at the phone box by the far pavement. Then he turned to the door of the guard-house, opened it, and stepped into another world.

4

Major Elliott felt the back wheels of the Ford Sierra slide ominously as the staff car took three sides of the Theodor-Heuss Platz at speed. The windows of the Westend department stores flew past him, the wheels slewing again on the wet tarmac. Then the car turned into the long, dusty switchback of the Kaiser-Damm.

'For God's sake,' he said softly.

The car swung back into line on the long axial road which ran through the heart of West Berlin. It narrowly missed the side of a white garrison bus, drawing into Edinburgh House on its return to Montgomery Barracks from a shopping trip.

'For God's sake!' said Elliott monotonously.

'Sorry, sir,' said Private Lucas brightly. 'It's that kraut behind the wheel in front, sir. That little one. Too clever for his own good, sir.'

'Then slow down and make him wait for us.'

Ignoring the instruction, Lucas pressed the accelerator hard and sent the staff car twisting after the green and white Mercedes of the West Berlin police which cleared the way for them with flashing lights and siren.

'The town's not on fire,' said Elliott sharply. 'Slow

down!'

He glanced aside through the window. They were in the broad rebuilt thoroughfare of the Bismarck-Strasse. Crowds gathered on the pavement outside the stark modernism of the new opera house with its long plate-glass windows. Ahead of them, where the buildings ended, the floodlit imperial victory column of the Siegessaule towered among the park trees.

Elliott put his hand to his throat, checking that his shirt was buttoned and his tie straight. When the call came from the commandant's office, he had been aligning the wings of his bow tie before a mirror. It was the evening of the Pinchas Zukerman and Marc Neikrug recital at the Philharmonie. As the staff car slackened speed a little before the Siegessaule roundabout and then accelerated once more, the limpid melody of the *Regenslieder* from the Brahms G major Sonata rose in Elliott's mind like a taunting spirit.

A widower at fifty, the wall of serene melody with which music enveloped him was one layer of the protective shell by which he surrounded his solitude. The other was his work. Of the two, it was the tranquil romanticism of Brahms or Schumann which had proved more dependable.

There had been time to change into uniform again. On his tunic the medal ribbons marked him as a post-war soldier. The Korean campaign and the mauve with green flash of the Malaya 'emergency' were chief among them. Hitler's war had been no more to him than an extension of schoolboy heroics, a game between professionals to be followed with the same partisan enthusiasm as football or cricket.

Youth, to Samuel Elliott, was neither his schooldays nor the three years of reading modern languages at Cambridge. It was a memory of that conscript army of the 1950s, the Joint Services Language School and the hectic acquisition of colloquial Russian in a remote camp on Bodmin moor. It was an army of school-leavers who seemed still to have their eyes set on self-improvement and education. Elliott had run the camp music circle during his first posting, a long hut crowded by young men who sat through the evening to listen to Rossini or Beethoven.

Despite its heartless novelty, Berlin suited him. Now that he dwelt so much in his own thoughts, shaping memories to a pattern, there was welcome solitude in a city where other men were said to be lonely. The wistful placidity which they had found in views of lakes and mountains came easily to him among iron railway bridges over city streets, the expensive glitter and shine of Ka De We or the other department stores of the Tauentzien-Strasse.

Rousing himself from his thoughts, he resumed the mask of the senior intelligence officer on Bonnell-Thornton's staff. Berlin kept him busy and interested in his professional occupation. That was another benefit to him. He had seen the three anonymous letters with their quotations from *The Pale Criminal*, and thought them unremarkable. Every week, somewhere in the world, a government received a message announcing that a weapon of mass destruction was hidden and ready. Its detonation could only be prevented by conceding a United Ireland, a Basque homeland, the release of Red Brigade leaders, justice for Palestine, an independent Armenia, or merely a sum of money. All had been the work of cranks or opportunists, the limits of their abilities represented by plastic explosive or the Soviet-made RPG rocket-launcher. But sooner or later all that would change.

Elliott doubted that the Pale Criminal represented such a change. As the police escort swung left from the parkland statues of imperial Prussia, he thought that such cranks, opportunists, or blackmailers were not likely to surrender to the authorities first.

His driver brought the car to a smooth halt at the Royal Military Police post. The green and white Polizei Mercedes waited long enough to see Elliott's arrival, then took off in another burst of acceleration, screaming past the deserted Reichstag and vanishing in a tail-light glow over the river bridge towards Moabit.

'Wait here,' said Elliott tersely. He slammed the car door and went round to the rear of the guard-room. Corporal Craig saluted in the shadows.

'Well?' Elliott peered at the corporal in the gloom.

'Brigadier's not here yet, sir. Said for you to carry on.'

It irked Elliott that Craig, capable of the Queen's English, cultivated this ungrammatical argot, as if merely acting the part of a military policeman.

'Where's the prisoner?'

'Point of fact, sir, he isn't a prisoner as yet. No arrest and no charges. Corporal Hoskins's duty relief. I left the guard-room in his charge for the time being.'

'So that by now our visitor may have changed his mind and walked off into the night,' said Elliott savagely.

'Not likely, sir. If he's half as keen to see the commandant as he cracks on, he won't go anywhere.'

There was no reproach in Craig's voice, merely a suggestion of indifference as to what Elliott might think of his conduct. The major walked in through the rear door and stood listening in the passageway. There was no sound from the room beyond. He put his hand on the door handle, almost expecting to find that Corporal Hoskins was alone once more, reading the newspaper.

When he opened the door, however, the visitor was still sitting on the small wooden chair. Elliott glanced at him as Andor got to his feet, taking in the main features of his appearance for future identification. A small man of about seventy by the look of him. A thin bridged nose and a pale round face. The eyes were blue and rather small. Elliott saw in them a precise, neurotic intensity.

This was no challenge to Elliott's professional skill as an intelligence officer. Looking at Andor he felt only a gloom that overcame him at parties when strangers insisted upon telling him the stories of their lives or confiding to him jokes of elaborate tedium. Despite his profession – or perhaps because of it – Elliott kept a fastidious distance from all but a few members of the human race.

'Now then,' he said briskly, 'what's all this about?'

Andor came forward and Elliott noticed that he limped slightly, as if from an injury to his right leg.

'I have come to see Brigadier Bonnell-Thornton. It is imperative that I speak to him tonight.'

Elliott's gloom weighed more heavily upon him. Andor's voice betrayed the quiet pitiless tone of the obsessive. Yet the major knew that the next few exchanges would decide the success or failure of interrogation. His subjects always prepared themselves well for the opening encounter, like fencers who had rehearsed the initial passes to perfection before a mirror. If the blade could once disconcert Andor's practised attack, the rest would be easy. If not, then the man would retire behind his guard and yield nothing more.

'The commandant is not available this evening.' Elliott was suave as a head-waiter disposing of a late arrival for whom there was no table. 'Perhaps I may be of assistance. Major Elliott, Intelligence Corps.'

'I must speak to the commandant himself. Tonight.'

Andor spoke mournfully as if anticipating the next refusal.

'Even if he wished to see you, the commandant is not free.'

'I have written letters to him. Letters . . . '

'I know about the letters, Herr Andor. I have read them all. You may quite safely talk to me about them.'

Andor sat down again, making this seem an act of defiance. The major hitched himself on to the edge of the guard-room table, laying down his brown kid-gloves and cap.

'To put it bluntly, Herr Andor, a man of your age has no business to be writing foolish letters. If you continue to do so, then you may find yourself in trouble with the authorities.'

'Continue?'

Elliott ignored the interruption.

'As the matter stands, you have come forward and admitted your responsibility. Taking into account your age and social position, I shall recommend that the matter be dropped. If there is anything further you wish to discuss, you may discuss it with me.'

Andor shrugged at the impossibility of discussion with such a man.

'You are a subordinate. What authority have you for this negotiation?'

The major slid his feet to the floor. He picked up his cap and gloves.

'If my authority does not satisfy you, Herr Andor, I must send you about your business.'

'You will not send me away?'

From long experience, Elliott knew that the blade had passed under his opponent's guard. With his slight shrunken figure the old man glowered up from the chair like a sullen child.

'You cannot send me away!'

'I can and will, Herr Andor. This post is responsible for frontier security. Its duty personnel have more important things to deal with than the delusions of irresponsible old men.'

'I will not go!'

Though the major had no intention of allowing his visitor to leave, the alarm in Andor's words was unmistakable. Elliott took one more cautious step.

'If necessary, I shall put a call through to the city police in the Pank-Strasse. You belong to them, not us. I imagine they will remove you to an observation ward in the geriatric wing of the Turm-Strasse infirmary.'

He looked down at his prisoner, as if for the last time, before turning and leaving the room. The words of capitulation which he hoped to hear did not come. When Andor spoke, his voice was quiet but not subdued. There was, in the slow speech, a neurotic tone of triumph. Elliott heard it and thought of the gentle, plaintive logic which belonged to total insanity.

'If I am put under observation in the Turm-Strasse, Major, you would be well advised to begin evacuating the city tonight. In fourteen days neither Berlin nor its occupying powers will exist. The timer on the warhead was activated half an hour ago.'

Despite the absurdity of it, Elliott felt a momentary chill.

'You have the letters,' the old man continued gently. 'Ask your own experts in weapons research if what I have written is possible.'

The blue eyes were round and still, as if in anger. Elliott pulled on his gloves. He touched the old man's shoulder.

'Cities are destroyed by bombs, Herr Andor, not by theories. And such bombs are always preceded by demands. Your letters make no such demands.'

Andor looked past the major at the guard-room paraphernalia of fire bucket and coiled hose on the far wall. He spoke as if the world could hear him, in the same self-absorbed quietness.

'I want only what was promised to this city and to my people. The promise freely made at Potsdam by your own government, by the leaders of the United States and the Soviet Union. I ask the removal of a frontier which divided my country against the terms of the treaty. At present, I demand only the beginning of that. Freedom of access must be restored between the two halves of Berlin. The four powers must end their illegal division.'

'A third world war over Berlin?'

'No!' Andor's voice rose, impatient yet persuasive. 'By my demands, it may be conceded without war. That is the point.'

'You imagine that the Russians or the East Germans will open the frontier?'

'They will have no alternative.' Andor looked down at his hands. 'I leave them no alternative. Neither they, nor you. It will happen, Major Elliott. You will see. Once you know that I am speaking the truth. My life is almost over. If I am not strong enough to do this, who else will? I am ready to die at any time.'

It seemed that Elliott had not heard this last remark. He turned to Corporal Hoskins, who stood behind the reception counter meticulously avoiding the gaze of either of the two men.

'Keep an eye on him,' said the major casually. 'I'll be back in a few minutes.'

He spoke with sympathy in his voice, as if confiding a patient to the care of a nurse.

Closing the door behind him, Elliott raised his eyebrows inquiringly at Corporal Craig who stood in the passageway. Craig nodded.

'In that case,' said the major, 'go and give Hoskins some moral support. See to it that our German doctor of physics stays just where he is.'

Without waiting to see this command obeyed, Elliott tapped on the door of the next room and entered even before the invitation to do so was uttered.

The British commandant of the Berlin garrison, Brigadier Henry Bonnell-Thornton, had turned from the observation mirror through which he had seen and heard the major's conversation with Andor. He sat now behind the desk usually occupied by the duty officer of the Military Police post.

In his well-cut blazer and flannels, concealing the paunch of too many diplomatic dinners, Bonnell-Thornton looked like a youthful fifty-year-old. He wore the brown and gold tie which was the insignia of the Cambridge University Hawks Club, its membership reserved to those men who had won a double blue. Rowing and rugby had been the commandant's sports. Both had built him into a fair, wavy-haired Adonis at twenty-five and left him a soft and balding fat man by thirty. To his credit he had now contrived an appearance of height and virile smoothness.

Bonnell-Thornton was bowed over a memorandum on the desk. With punctilious courtesy, Elliott saluted the top of the commandant's head. Bonnell-Thornton spoke without looking up from the paper.

'I've sent for the senior medical officer on duty at the Military Hospital. I don't think our man is the sort to be wearing a cyanide capsule. All the same, I'm not prepared to risk an elderly lunatic giving us his Heinrich Himmler farewell on the carpet. The death of a German in British military custody is bad news nowadays. Worse still if he turns out to be well known.'

'Yes, sir.' Elliott had his reservations about Bonnell-Thornton but there was no doubt that the commandant, during years of peace-time soldiering, had become adept in safeguarding his position and those of his subordinates.

'What do you want to do next?' asked the commandant suspiciously.

'I'd like custody arranged, sir. We shall have to check him.'

'But not at the military prison,' said the brigadier quickly. 'Not with the Yanks, the Ivans, and the Frogs on the premises. Worst of all, it's the Russians' turn to guard our remaining Nazi leader this month. Out of the question.'

'I'd rather have the military hospital, sir. One of the psychiatric rooms on the top floor. A guard on the room and a guard on the corridor.'

'Done,' said the commandant, returning to his paper. 'What else?'

Elliott took a deep breath.

'I suggest we take him seriously, sir.'

'Out of the question,' said Bonnell-Thornton casually. 'That would mean evacuating the whole of Berlin every time a man with a bump in his skull picks up a phone and makes mischief.'

Elliott retrieved the initiative with infinite patience.

'All I had in mind, sir, was that the three letters should be read by a scientist capable of evaluating their contents.'

'That means telling the tale to Aldermaston and half the government,' said the brigadier, folding the paper. 'Sorry. Not a chance.'

'There is another way, sir.'

'Is there?' Hands clasped behind his back, the brigadier went across to the observation window again and peered through. 'Go on talking, Sam. You have my full attention.'

With passing irritation, Elliott addressed the commandant's back.

'You have a direct line, sir, to the Co-Ordinator of Intelligence in the Cabinet Office. You can bypass the Foreign Office and the Joint Intelligence Committees. Go direct to Oliver Jupp. At the most, he will tell the Prime Minister. He may not even do that. But Jupp can get you the man you want from Aldermaston. Beside ourselves, only two other men need know. Three, if you include the Prime Minister.'

'I'd rather not,' Bonnell-Thornton turned back towards the desk. 'On these occasions, his lordship is about as much use as a eunuch at the rape of the Sabine women.'

'We shall also have to decide who, among the occupying powers in Berlin, is to be told anything at all, sir.'

The brigadier wrinkled his nose.

'The Americans will laugh. The Russians will make trouble. The Frogs are only here by grace and favour anyway. As for the others, this is none of their business – legally or ethically.'

Elliott was preoccupied by other thoughts.

'If the story becomes public, Andor may have a lot of friends. The western world wants the same as he does. I wouldn't put it past some of our leaders to take the opportunity of rushing the barricades.'

Bonnell-Thornton brooded a moment more on the possibility of excluding the Prime Minister from the chain of intelligence.

'If we can keep Lord Fumblebum out of it,' he said at length, 'that leaves only two people outside this office.'

'And the two MP corporals, sir.' Elliott nodded at the glass, beyond which Craig and Hoskins sat with the prisoner.

Bonnell-Thornton made his decision.

'Keep them here tonight and reassign them tomorrow. I suggest the guard of the Military Mission in Potsdam. They won't find many opportunities for conversation in the DDR. By the time they come back, the problem of Andor will be solved.'

The phone rang. Bonnell-Thornton answered and listened without comment. Then he put the receiver down and looked across the desk.

'Nothing about Andor on our files, nor on Interpol's. The Berlin police have a booking for him at the Excelsior. Last night. He gave an address in Leipzig.'

'*East* Germany?'

The commandant nodded.

'The street was bombed in 1944 and never rebuilt. Still, that tells us something. However he travelled, it wasn't under his own name. Not as Andor. If Andor is his true name.'

'The Pale Criminal.'

Bonnell-Thornton's mind was on other things.

'We can't tell the allies at this stage,' he said at last. 'There's a one-per-cent chance that he's telling the truth – and a ninety-nine-per-cent chance that he's a clown. I don't see that we need be in a rush to join the circus. It's not the time for frankness.'

Elliott believed him. Four months short of retirement, Bonnell-Thornton was the first garrison commander for some years who had neither a knighthood nor a major-generalcy. Twice he had been passed over and the next chance would be his last. Though he bore his disappointment like a sportsman, the hunger for recognition and official commendation was almost visible in his bland features. Prudence rather than energy inspired him now.

5

Corporal Hoskins had no intention of waiting to be posted to the military mission in Potsdam or to anywhere else of the kind. In the previous half hour he had seen and heard enough to know that his opportunity had come. The time when he should have finished duty at the Entlastungs-Strasse guard-room was already past. Craig was duty NCO from now on. He had only to wait until Craig and Major Elliott were occupied with their prisoner in the other room. Then he would take his chance. Unless his luck turned against him, no one would report his absence for a few hours.

He heard Elliott, Craig, and Andor go out through the rear door into the transport yard at the back. From the few words that he overheard he guessed they were waiting for whatever vehicle would take the old man to the British Military Hospital on the Heer-Strasse, or perhaps even the military prison at Spandau.

Hoskins listened again. Then he snatched his canvas grip from under the counter and went quickly into the little wash-room. Like the other duty corporals, he had kept his civilian clothes to hand so that he could change and go straight from guard into the concrete and neon fairground which was the centre of West Berlin.

By the time that he came out, a few minutes later, he had changed his khaki for a corduroy jacket and trousers, his uniform now rolled up in the canvas grip. He turned the handle of the door which opened directly on to the lamplit woodland of the Entlastungs-Strasse. Between the dark Tiergarten trees only a single car passed, its tail-lights glowing beyond the Reichstag lawns as the driver braked at the river bridge and the junction for Alt Moabit.

In the past months Hoskins had often wondered how he would feel when the moment came – if it ever came – for the single irrevocable act of disloyalty. To his surprise he found that it excited him less than the meetings with Schroeder at which trivial items of information about military police duty were passed on for the benefit of the East German SSD. For the consequences of what he was about to do, he felt no apprehension whatever.

He stood in the open doorway and listened, a florid and round-faced man of thirty with his wavy hair cut short and neat. At the back of the guard-room a car engine started. Hoskins closed the door behind him, walked round the RMP jeep with its blue police lamp clipped to the hood, and went over to the park trees on the far side of the wooded avenue. It had crossed his mind to take the jeep with him but he knew it would be missed as soon as the driver reported for his patrol of the East Berlin streets.

Hoskins walked quickly towards the Tiergarten-Strasse, the brightly lit shops and cafés of the Budapester-Strasse and the Kurfursten-Damm. He felt not the least inclination to turn back, having a better idea of his status than most other soldiers of the garrison. Standing in the guard-room in civilian clothes he had been improperly dressed. Out on the streets, he was now a deserter. Unlike most men of that class, he carried with him a valuable commodity. Something to trade.

He crossed the Kurfursten-Damm by the shattered tower and walls of the Kaiser Wilhelm memorial church, lights glittering blue and mauve through its modern stained glass. Its illumination was a perfect foil for the green and yellow alphabets of neon which inscribed the elegant shopfronts. Blumen Exclusiv . . . Tanz Eden . . . Pelze . . . Salamander . . . Exquisit . . . Chic-Chic . . .

Beyond the Berlin Palast cinema and ornamental pavement pavilions selling newspapers and tobacco were the souvenir shops and the old corner cafés in white and cream with their advertisements for Cafe Möhring. Hoskins stopped outside one of the little shops, its interior a clutter of souvenirs made in the Far East and, with few variations, despatched to all the major cities of Europe. Debby was sitting behind the counter on a tall stool, reading a book. At twenty she had a fragile immaturity of figure which was almost childlike, her jeans worn tight enough to be drawn into sheaves of wrinkles. The blonde hair was pinned in a top-knot, revealing a dark-eyed face of elfish moodiness.

This was the worst part, Hoskins thought, the only likely obstacle. He went in, closing his mind to their conversation, and left the canvas grip under the counter. He had his passport and military identification card. There was nothing else he would need. Leaning forward he kissed the girl.

'Peep-Show Kino,' he said quickly. 'Soon as you can, love.'

'I'll be off in about twenty minutes.' There was a doubt amounting to distrust in her eyes.

''s all right, love!' said Hoskins, teasing and kissing her again. 'It's good news this time. Honest!'

He went back across the broad boulevard and into the cinema with its modernistic black glass and bright lettering. A twelve mark ticket entitled the holder to three drinks while he watched the two hour-length films. Eight marks entitled him to two. Hoskins handed over twelve marks.

'Ich mochte drei whisky,' he said, smiling at the girl while scarcely noticing her. Ignoring the smile, she handed him a little tray with three miniatures and a plastic cup.

The Peep-Show Kino was a favourite rendezvous for Schroeder and presumably others of the SSD. It was large, often ill-attended, and its programmes ran continuously from mid-morning until after midnight. Under cover of the film dialogue and music it was easy enough to hold a conversation without being overheard or seen.

At this hour of the evening the seats were almost empty. A dozen solitary men were scattered round the auditorium, their feet resting on the seats in front. There were a few men and women sitting together, holding hands as they stared earnestly at the pink flesh-patterns on the screen. The amplified sighing of the soundtrack died beneath the rock-beat of music at each approaching crisis of the film.

He sat near the back, in the usual place. If Schroeder and his colleagues operated so easily in West Berlin, the western allies were themselves to blame, Hoskins thought. They imposed no check at all on travellers in either direction at the frontier, for fear of destroying the fiction that Berlin was an undivided city occupied jointly by the four powers. Any East Berliner – or any other national – could come and go freely, checked only by the border control of the DDR.

The film being screened was almost at its end. Shot in white Californian sun it appeared to be the story of a baby-voiced blonde kidnapped by two men and a girl to extort a ransom from her millionaire father. Finding more in common with each other than with their companions, the two girls shot the men and drove off together with the ransom money.

As the titles faded and an orange flush lit the screen, Hoskins poured the three miniatures into his plastic cup. He let the warm spirit touch his tongue, wondering if it would be the last time. He was, after all, going to a place where genuine scotch was a rarity.

He saw the girl walk in during the long interval of peach and orange light. She came and sat beside him. Taking her hand, Hoskins stroked it gently.

'Listen,' he said, 'listen, Deb, I'm going over. I've got to do it now. Tonight.'

She twisted her hand away from him and he listened to her protests, knowing in advance what they would be. Debby was not ready to go. Schroeder had promised something, but not yet. The flat, the privileged shopping in tourist stores on the Unter den Linden or the Karl-Marx Allee, the well-rewarded job with the MfS evaluating western military broadcasts. All that was to come as a reward. Like everything else it had to be earned and there was a good deal of earning still to be done. Hoskins took her hand again, kissed it, and smiled at the pinched and hungry little face in the flickering light.

'It's got to be tonight, Debby. And in any case I'm not going to see Schroeder. This is too good for him or anyone else in the SSD. It's going to Colonel Rubin. Russian military intelligence.'

'But you don't know him!'

''Course I do!' said Hoskins scornfully. 'I've seen him a dozen times, coming over to talk to Elliott.'

Debby watched the film for a moment with a scowl of doubt.

'But what is it?' she asked at length.

Hoskins smiled in the darkness.

'Whereabouts of nuclear warheads in Berlin,' he whispered. 'I think Colonel Rubin will be ready to talk about that. I'd say it's our ticket across, Deb. A ticket out of all this!'

'And what about me?' She had turned away from him now and spoke as if to herself.

'Come with me,' he said.

'I can't!' Her voice was shriller now, unimpressed by stories of nuclear warheads. 'Not tonight! How could I?'

'Then go home and wait.' After his first attempt to woo her with the invitation, Hoskins' tone was harder. She must have known quite well what would happen to him if he stayed in West Berlin, a deserter. By her refusal, he thought, she was betraying him to that fate. Or telling him to go alone. In either case there was but one course of action.

He stood up and saw, in the pale reflected light of the screen, that she was crying with the uncertainty of the new situation and the impossibility of what was demanded of her. All that had been promised, the new life away from precarious drudgery and a Potsdamer-Strasse slum, was snatched from her as toys taken from a disobedient child.

'Go home,' he said quietly, gentleness masking his distaste. 'Wait there. I'll come back for you. Perhaps tonight. If not, I'll send you a message and tell you where to find me.'

He forgot the remains of his whisky in the anger which possessed him as he left the cinema and went down the stairs into the street. It was for this he had left Angie and their child. For this he had incurred the lifelong deductions of maintenance money, the debts and the petty dishonesties – in order to be let down, betrayed when the moment came.

Hoskins was a realist, knowing that life might be worse but never better than it was just now. A man who is a corporal at thirty is a corporal for ever – or rather for as long as his engagement runs. He had no difficulty in imagining the civilian future, the years of unemployment or the ex-soldier's menial jobs. He, a man who had passed every examination needed for promotion to sergeant – who was the equal of most warrant officers in that respect – had been passed over by his commanders. Somewhere, though none of them could quite locate it, there was a flaw in Corporal Hoskins. In his eyes or in his movements they saw that he was not their type.

The thought of them made him so angry that he almost had to blink back a tear as he went down the steps into the Uhland-Strasse subway and rode to the shabby little crossing at the Koch-Strasse, just within Checkpoint Charlie.

6

Above the stretch of roadway which had once been part of the Friedrich-Strasse, the tall concrete lamp-posts directed a light bright as magnesium on to the tarmac below. Here and there a grimy office block of the pre-war period had survived, but between the western police-post and the tall white observation tower on the eastern side, the buildings had been demolished. The tower was manned by East German VPD guards at their observation platform and at the gun-embrasure fifteen or twenty feet above the road.

Hoskins walked past the white concrete cabin on the western side. The first of its three rooms contained a British sergeant, his feet on the table, reading a book. There were two US military police corporals in white helmets, and three French NCOs in dark blue. None of them looked at him as he passed.

Ahead of him the white wall across the road was pierced by a single narrow entrance for cars, next to a walkway with high wire fencing either side and a roof of yellow corrugated plastic. A middle-aged East German sergeant stood by the gap in the wall, wearing a fur cap as a concession to age or perhaps the colder air of night. He took Hoskins by the arm, as if to reassure him, and led him across to the duckboards of the caged pathway. After the busy streets of West Berlin, Hoskins heard his own footsteps echo in the silence of the frontier zone.

At the far end of the passageway were the white-painted huts of the visa control, the customs and the obligatory currency exchange. At this time of the evening the passport control with its bare fluorescent light and white distempered walls was empty. A blond young lieutenant of the VPD with white piping on his field grey sat behind a glass screen, like a bank teller.

Hoskins stood before the glass screen and handed in his military identity card. The lieutenant scrutinised it and then looked up, neither impressed nor dismayed. The blue eyes seemed never to blink or waver.

'Was wunschen Sie?'

Hoskins' German was good enough to recognise common forms of question and to answer a few of them.

'Ich mochte sprechen mit Colonel Rubin. Sowjet Generalkommando.'

The lieutenant laid aside Hoskins' identity card and spoke in English.

'You will not find Colonel Rubin here. Why do you wish to see him?'

'I have information for him. I must give it to him tonight.'

The lieutenant shrugged and continued in his slow, precise English.

'You are a corporal in the British military police, are you not? Why do you wish to speak with Colonel Rubin?'

'I have information for him,' said Hoskins stubbornly. He saw the lieutenant press a button at one side of the counter.

'You are a deserter?' the lieutenant asked. 'We have no use for deserters here. You will be sent back.'

'I have information.' Hoskins was getting angry now at the slow indifference of his interrogator. 'I know Colonel Rubin. I have met him in West Berlin.'

This was not true, he thought, but it was close enough. He had had occasion to salute Rubin several times on the colonel's visits to Major Elliott.

'Then you may speak to him when you next see him in West Berlin.'

In the moment which followed, Hoskins was uncertain whether to explain, to plead with the lieutenant, or to lose his temper. Only with Rubin would he find safety now.

'If my information does not reach Colonel Rubin tonight, it will be of no use to him. In that case, you'll be the one who answers to him.'

Not a movement in the lieutenant's eyes betrayed his contempt. He spoke in the same slow and deliberate manner.

'This is the sovereign territory of the DDR, Mr Hoskins. Neither you nor Colonel Rubin gives orders here!'

For the first time Hoskins realised that the lieutenant had memorised his name from the identity card. Or was it that he recognised it from some link of his own with Schroeder and the SSD? In the present situation Schroeder was the one man who could ensure that he never saw Rubin. Hoskins prepared to apologise and conciliate. Before he could begin, the internal door opened and two vopos, conscripts in their teens, came in. The lieutenant gave orders which were beyond Hoskins' understanding of German. At a gesture from one of the two guards he went through the internal door. Beyond it was a room with opaque glass and barred windows. Its walls were bare and distempered. A small wooden table with a chair at either side made up the furnishing.

One of the guards took a chair and sat just inside the door. The other went out, turning the key after him, locking the prisoner and his escort into the room together.

Hoskins' imprisonment lasted for half an hour. He heard cars come and go but supposed that they were part of the traffic between the two halves of the city. When the door was opened at length he was led out to a black Volga limousine with a civilian driver and a second man in the back. Neither was Colonel Rubin.

The car turned into the Leipziger-Strasse, immediately

on the eastern side of the wall, the former boulevard derelict on one hand and lined with tall white blocks of workers' flats on the other. He tried to speak to his escorts, first in English and then in German, but there was no answer. Hoskins' geography of East Berlin was sketchy. Yet at one moment he saw down a dark road a wide and brightly-lit space which he recognised as the Alexander-Platz. Further on they passed a broad waterway with warehouses, dockside railways and barges moored to the quays. He saw the name Ost-Haven and knew that they were travelling south-east, just within the frontier. Soon after this the car stopped and he was led into a new office building overlooking parkland and a sports stadium.

Within this building the uniforms were the khaki and scarlet tabbed kind of the Soviet army. Hoskins caught the scents and sounds of Russian communal life, the reek of green tobacco, the hair oil and tallow-smell of soap. He was taken by lift to the second floor and brought to a large office, furnished with old chairs and velvet cushions. It was not in the least the clean functional room which he had imagined.

Colonel Rubin was a heavily built and sallow man in his early fifties, a dark southerner who would easily pass as being Spanish or Italian. He was wearing formal uniform and had the air of having returned from dinner to receive his guest. With one hand he took Hoskins' arm and led him to a chair.

'Sit down,' he said genially, 'I shall not keep you a moment.'

But it was half an hour before he returned to the room and when he did so Hoskins was more glad to see Colonel Rubin than he could have believed possible. In the cold autocratic world which he had entered, Rubin was the only man who spoke to him as if he might be a friend.

'I am so sorry to keep you waiting.' Rubin sat down and his dark face seemed on the verge of a welcoming smile. 'Now, tell me, you are one of Major Elliott's policemen, are you not?'

'Yes, sir,' said Hoskins uneasily.

'I have known Major Elliott well for several years,' said Rubin. 'He is my idea of what an English gentleman should be. Do not be surprised at that, Mr Hoskins. The English gentleman is much admired in Russia, not for his class but for his bearing and good manners.'

Hoskins nodded, eager to get the subject out of the way. His interview with Colonel Rubin was not going at all as he had expected.

'Now,' said Rubin amiably, 'what brings you here to East Berlin?'

'I want to come over, sir.' Hoskins took it as quickly as he could. 'I've thought it over a long time. It's what I want to do.'

'Oh, Mr Hoskins . . .' Colonel Rubin sounded as disappointed in him as Elliott or Bonnell-Thornton might have been.

'I know there's no reason why you should want me, sir,' said Hoskins rapidly, 'but I've got a good working knowledge of British military intelligence . . .'

'So have I, Mr Hoskins. So have I.'

Rubin was laughing at him now, there was no doubt of it. Hoskins decided to put an end to that.

'But what's most important of all, sir, I can prove my good faith. Do you know of a man called Andor?'

Rubin frowned.

'No. No, I don't think so. Who is he?'

'Do you know that there is a nuclear warhead in West Berlin? That Andor is the head of a terrorist organisation which controls it? That in fourteen days' time that bomb will be exploded, taking both halves of Berlin with it?'

'And how did you come by this story, Mr Hoskins?'

'Andor surrendered himself to the RMP post this evening, sir. I was in the room the whole time he was talking to Major Elliott. There's no doubt of it.'

'But suppose your Mr Andor is a joker, Mr Hoskins. What then?'

'Then you'll know in fourteen days, sir. Give me

temporary asylum for that long. Andor says he's got proof of what he can do.'

'Then,' said Rubin, smiling once more, 'I'm sure my good friend Major Elliott will share it with me. After all, if your man Andor can destroy both halves of the city, we shall have to work together shall we not?'

It was impossible that Rubin's loyalty to Elliott, the servant of a hostile power, could override his duty to a willing defector. Hoskins clung to the truth of that. Like the wall dividing the city, Rubin's imperturbability could be pierced if only one knew where. But Hoskins tried a blind rush at the defences.

'I want to come over, sir. That's the beginning and end of it. I only hoped this information would show I meant well. For the rest, you can ask Captain Schroeder of the SSD. I've been helping him for over a year.'

Rubin seemed puzzled by this outburst.

'But what would you do over here, Mr Hoskins? What is the great attraction?'

'I could analyse intelligence, sir. Listen in to military radio communications from the west and interpret them. You know as well as I do there must be a hundred men on this side who've crossed over from the British army.'

'And many more, alas, who had to be turned away for lack of skills,' said Rubin gently. 'We are not as rich as our friends in the west. We cannot afford to feed all those who come to us merely because they prefer socialism to capitalism. Do you speak Russian, Mr Hoskins?'

'No, sir.'

'You see! Are you fluent in German?'

'I know a little, sir. I could learn more.'

'No, my friend,' said Rubin gently. He leant forward, laid a hand on Hoskins' arm like a benevolent father, then sat back again. 'You would not be happy here. There is nothing for you.'

After his meetings with Schroeder and all that had been promised, Hoskins could scarcely believe that he would be turned back. But though Colonel Rubin was smiling again, there was no doubt of his intention.

'Besides,' he said, 'what should I say to my friend Major Elliott? He would begin to think that I was luring his young men across the border to live in a workers' paradise. Is that what you think the DDR is, Mr Hoskins?'

He stood up and Hoskins followed his example.

'It's where I want to live, sir. Where I want to work.'

Rubin bowed his head a little so that he was not obliged to look the corporal in the eye.

'That is not quite an answer, Mr Hoskins. I can imagine you would prefer to live somewhere where English law does not run. Forgive me, but I have taken the liberty of reading such information about you as is in our files. Captain Schroeder too is one of my friends. You are not a rich man, Mr Hoskins. Whatever you earn is reduced by money which you must pay for your wife and your child, with whom you no longer live. You have a *petite amie*, do you not? How convenient if you could leave behind you all your financial obligations and debts to begin a new life here with the young lady. Is that not it, Mr Hoskins?'

Hoskins stood in the middle of the stuffy over-furnished room. His despair was so complete that just for the moment he could not even feel resentment against Rubin. The colonel came across and put an arm round his shoulders. Hoskins, who had not eaten for several hours, was aware of food and drink on the other man's breath.

'I am sorry I cannot help you,' said Rubin gently, 'but I will tell you a story to make you feel more cheerful. A story to make you glad that you need not live in East Berlin. One day there was an East Berliner who died and went to hell. When he arrived there, he found two gates. One was marked "Capitalist Hell", and the other "East German Socialist Hell". The man was not sure through which gate to go. So he went up to the keeper of the gates and asked him. "Oh," said the keeper, "I shouldn't go into the capitalist hell, if I were you. They cut you with knives. They scald you with boiling water. And they burn you with fire." So the man asked about the East German Socialist

Hell. "You'll be much better off there," said the keeper. "The knives are blunt and they won't cut you. The hot water is always cold. The fires are never lit because the stoker spends his time attending workers' demonstrations." '

Rubin paused to chuckle at his own story.

'You see, Mr Hoskins? There are some things we should envy you.'

He went across to the desk, picked up the phone, and gave instructions in Russian. Then he returned to where Hoskins was standing.

'Now, my young friend,' he said gently, 'I have arranged for a car to take you back as far as the checkpoint. Go home. Perhaps no one will know that you have played this little game. If my friend Mr Elliott mentions it to me, I will put in a good word for you – never fear. As for your adventurous assignations with Captain Schroeder, they cannot amount to much. That is a matter between you and he, is it not?'

As they went down to the entrance where the same black Volga was waiting, Hoskins said nothing. It was Rubin who remained cheerful and self-assured at their parting.

'Go home, Mr Hoskins. Whether you return to Major Elliott or elsewhere is a matter for your own conscience. If you wish to disappear, do so somewhere in the west. A place where you will not be found. That is much better for you than here. Believe me, I advise you as a friend.'

He slammed the door and watched the dark car drive away towards the border. Then Colonel Rubin went back to his office and opened the door which communicated with the next room. He raised his dark thick eyebrows at the Soviet captain who sat in the flickering grey reflection of a cathode tube from which several lines of lettering had just vanished.

The captain shook his head.

'Nothing,' he said dismissively. 'Nothing at all for the name of Andor. Neither here nor in the data bank at Moscow. Perhaps it was a hoax.'

Rubin shook his head.

'Mr Hoskins was no hoax,' he said thoughtfully. 'Perhaps we shall persuade Major Elliott to enlighten us a little further.'

As though meditating on this, Rubin crossed to the uncurtained window and stood there, staring out across the dark river towards the coldly lit strip of the frontier wall.

'You know,' he said for the benefit of the captain, 'there was a farmer's wife in New Mexico on 16 July 1945.'

'New Mexico?' The captain looked up at Rubin's back, not seeing the point of his remark. Colonel Rubin enjoyed telling stories. Even his jokes were invested with a heavy philosophical significance, generally at the expense of the East German regime. The captain found it wearisome. He consoled himself by thinking that one day the colonel would go too far. One day there would be talk and complaints. For all his gifts as an intelligence officer, Rubin would find himself back in Moscow sorting files.

'New Mexico,' Rubin continued to gaze across the darkened city as he spoke. 'The good woman got up to make her husband's breakfast early, before dawn. Presently the sun came up. It stayed for a minute or two and then it went down again. She was a little puzzled by this but she went on preparing breakfast. Then, quite a while later, the sun came up again. This time it stayed. When she talked to the newspaper reporters she called it "The day the sun rose twice". Her first sunrise was the Trinity test at Alamagordo. The first explosion of an atomic bomb.'

The captain looked up from his papers and emitted a hum of comprehension, seeing the point of the story at last. Rubin turned to face him.

'Is the man Andor a *farceur*? He may be. Did our friend Mr Hoskins concoct the entire story to beg asylum here away from his wife, his debts, and his failures? Was it all an attempt to find a warm bed in the DDR for himself and his *petite amie*? It is possible.'

'It seems likely,' said the captain gently.

Rubin turned to the window again as if he might be

looking at the view outside for the last time.

'If not,' he said thoughtfully, 'then you and I and all the good burghers of Berlin may be next to see a day upon which the sun rises twice.'

2

The Prisoners

7

The briefing-room of military intelligence adjoined Bonnell-Thornton's own office. Its windows looked down on the cement-rendered apartment blocks of Smooth Barracks. A summer storm had darkened the drab buildings in the early evening. Rain shone black on the broad arterial road running north through Spandau. The lights of the new shopping centre, fashion stores and discotheques, were fogged in the damp twilight like a work of misty impressionism.

In company with Elliott and Dr Grimshawe, flown in by RAF transport from Aldermaston, the commandant stood at the central display-table with its map of the Berlin area. Yellow streets, the grey outlines of buildings, the major installations painted in red, made up a familiar enclave.

'I'm a terrorist.' Bonnell-Thornton stubbed out his cigarette in the metal dish. 'I call myself the Pale Criminal and I write the letters you have seen. If my claims are true, what sort of device would I possess?'

Elliott watched Grimshawe, waiting for the reply. The man from Aldermaston was in his middle fifties. His dark hair, moustache, and the uneasy movements of his eyes gave him the air of a sombre and humourless Groucho Marx. As Elliott had already discovered, Grimshawe had all the sociability of an oyster.

'What sort of device?' said the commandant again.

Dr Grimshawe shook his head.

'I don't suppose anyone can tell you that. The letters contain information which would not be available to anyone outside a weapons facility. But the writer of the letter may have got it from another man. Some of the details are also curiously antique.'

'Antique?' Elliott looked up sharply as if suspecting frivolity.

Grimshawe nodded.

'I suggest to you that the man who wrote these letters is probably in his sixties or seventies.'

'Why?'

'Because,' said Grimshawe, 'he talks of methods not used in nuclear weaponry since the 1950s. High-explosive lenses made of graphite! Even third-world bombs don't use them. In any modern warhead the neutrons are reflected back into the central mass by lenses of uranium-238. The non-fissionable kind. He knows a secret or two, I grant you. But the bomb described in these letters would be a primitive device. Home made. I doubt if he could do it at all.'

Elliott looked up at the moustache and spectacles, his first antipathy towards Grimshawe strengthened by the man's indifference.

'How would he get the plutonium?'

Grimshawe shrugged.

'At the last audit of the General Accounting Office in Washington, there was between twenty-five and thirty thousand pounds of plutonium unaccounted for in United States facilities.'

They looked at him, waiting for the explanation.

'Plutonium is lost in processing,' said Grimshawe simply. 'One never knows how much. It's not like keeping a bank account. You can't pick it up and weigh it. Sixteen pounds would make a bomb.'

'Thirty thousand pounds?' said Bonnell-Thornton cautiously.

'That's right.' Grimshawe seemed pleased at the dismay. 'Some was lost in processing, but it's scientifically impossible to say how much. Some of it certainly went to Israel with the connivance of the government. If all the missing plutonium was in the wrong hands, it would build a nuclear arsenal equivalent to that held by the armed forces of the United States. Don't worry. Most of it has certainly gone up in smoke. But we don't know how much.'

Bonnell-Thornton looked down at the map of the city again.

'If the technology is out of date, would the weapon work?'

'The principles remain the same,' said Grimshawe pedantically. 'If you had the tenacity, you could destroy a modern city with a battery of Renaissance artillery.'

He went across to the chair on which his briefcase lay, took out a folder and handed copies of a report to the other two men.

'*Towards a People's Bomb*, gentlemen, published by a London group in 1972. It describes how to construct a simple warhead with crystals of plutonium nitrate. Not a sophisticated weapon, of course. Exploded at Victoria Station, it would take out Whitehall, the Houses of Parliament, Buckingham Palace, and the main Thames bridges. In Washington, it would flatten the Mall and destroy the centre of government. Left in a luggage locker at Grand Central Station, it would lay waste the southern half of Manhattan and bring down a lethal nuclear rain on Brooklyn and Queens. By nuclear standards, that is small-scale.'

The twilight grew darker and colder. On the far side of the Wilhelm-Strasse were the buildings of red brick Gothic, built as a military prison in the Kaiser's day. In the hospital block of the central yard, the last of the Nazi leaders dwelt in fading senility. Elliott watched the guards on the gun-platforms. It was the turn of the Russians this month with their steel helmets easily recognisable by the more open rims.

'It's public knowledge,' said Grimshawe triumphantly. 'The French weekly, *Express*, published the same information with pictures. January 1975. You'll also find I've copied details from the 1976 Royal Commission report. The scientific skill required for a bomb would be no greater than that already used in the criminal refining of heroin. You see?'

Elliott and Bonnell-Thornton looked at one another. Grimshawe gave them a moment. Then he said, 'Your man *could* do it. The odds are in favour of a hoax, of course. But the Pale Criminal letters make it a possibility.'

Bonnell-Thornton stood under the main light, the broad dome of his head bowed and his powerful frame immobile. He was looking at the map of the city.

'If he has the means of destruction,' he said, not raising his eyes to Grimshawe, 'I want to know the best and the worst that might happen.'

'The worst,' Grimshawe touched the red oblong of the Zoo terminus at the centre of the western shopping zone, 'a device in the luggage lockers here. More or less complete destruction over a five mile radius. Fire storms perhaps spreading beyond that.'

Elliott watched as Grimshawe's white, narrow fingers traced the frontier of catastrophe. In that simple movement of the hand, the centre of East Berlin as well as West was torn apart by flame. The Soviet headquarters at Karlshorst would be annihilated in the same instant as those of the western allies.

The thin pale fingers moved outward, describing the area on which a lethal rain of radiation would fall. It included the whole of Berlin and the first towns and villages of the dark East German plain. Potsdam and the other ancient towns of the east might escape the fire and blast of a centrally exploded bomb. Yet the old imperial spa would die just as surely under the nuclear rain.

Bonnell-Thornton nodded.

'All right,' he said, 'what's the best to be hoped for?'

Grimshawe straightened up and stood back from the table.

'A crude device with much less explosive power. Suppose it were concealed in the airshaft of the Europa Centre. It would destroy the building and everyone inside it. There would be contamination for several hundred yards in the vicinity.'

'Is that a likely hiding place? An airshaft?'

'Oh yes.' Grimshawe spoke as if in reassurance. 'The only case of nuclear blackmail on file occurred in 1978. A terrorist group planted plutonium nitrate in the airshaft of such a building. Fortunately they were already under surveillance by the security services. The plutonium and the explosive were found long before the deadline.'

The commandant nodded.

'I'm afraid we've put you to work without much ceremony,' he said gently. 'There's no reason for you to be at beck and call again tonight. Before you go to your quarters, are there any other facts we should know immediately?'

Grimshawe stood in silence and relished his new authority.

'The letters and the threat are very likely to be a hoax,' he said presently, 'but if you have the least trouble in getting resources for this investigation, I should make the following submission. A bomb exploded at ground level – which would be the case here – is a dirty bomb. It sucks up earth and debris in a deadly radioactive cloud. A prevailing wind might carry the contamination up to two hundred miles. In this case, it would fall principally on the major cities of East Germany. It might reach Poland and even Prague. Western Europe would be little affected. However, the Soviet army in eastern Europe would find itself under a nuclear attack which emanated from Berlin. You can work out the consequences of that as easily as I.'

Bonnell-Thornton gave this a moment's thought. He said, 'What significance do you attach to the name Andor in your science?'

'Andor?' Grimshawe closed the folder which he had taken from his briefcase. 'None. I haven't heard of anyone by that name in the past twenty years. Mind you, some of the third-world governments are extremely jealous about the identity of their nuclear personnel. Even so, you can discount Andor as a big name.'

It was left to Elliott to escort Dr Grimshawe to the waiting car with its RMP driver and security officer. No one would be churlish enough to mention it, but Grimshawe was as much a prisoner during the present visit to Berlin as Andor himself. His quarters in the garrison mess were under the most discreet surveillance.

Just out of earshot of his guards, Grimshawe stopped.

'One thing, Major Elliott,' he said thoughtfully, 'your man knew how to pick his target.'

'Berlin?'

'Precisely.' For the first time that evening a gleam appeared in the restless eyes. 'The one city in the world where evacuation is virtually impossible. The air corridors will be filled with military traffic. How many trains could be run on a single railway link to the west? That leaves two million people to be evacuated on the autobahn. I'd say half a million vehicles at least. A dozen breakdowns and the lanes are blocked. Either side of the road is hostile territory. Forbidden. London, Paris, even New York, you could evacuate if you had to. Not Berlin. This is the true poker game. Two million lives on the table.'

The same thought had occurred to Elliott in the briefing-room but he had reserved it for the commandant. He nodded as Grimshawe got into the car and the driver closed the door. As the engine started, the visitor lowered the car window.

'By the way,' Grimshawe said, 'I'd like to see the Pergamon Altar and the Miletus Gate while I'm here. One and a half wonders of the ancient world.'

'That's out of the question.' Elliott was conscious of an unworthy satisfaction in denying Grimshawe his wish. 'The Pergamon Museum is in East Berlin. I'll arrange for an escort to take you to the Egyptian Museum at Charlottenburg. You'll find the head of Nefertiti well worth a visit. Very beautiful.'

He stepped back and watched the car turn towards the officers mess, near the broad axial road of the Heer-Strasse.

Ten minutes later Bonnell-Thornton tapped the outline of the Zoo terminus on the display map.

'He's right about evacuation anyway.' The finger now traced a contour of the western sectors of the city. 'It can't be done. To get two-and-a-half million people out, on the transit routes across the DDR, we'd have to start now. We'd have to take every threat seriously from the start. Can't you imagine the fun that the Red Army Faction and their friends would have with us? We'd have an evacuation alert every fortnight!'

Elliott nodded.

'He said it was the one city in the world you can't just walk away from. It appears an entire population has to sit tight and take its chance on these occasions.'

Bonnell-Thornton plunged his hands deep into his trouser pockets and stood at ease with his back to the window. He had the manner of a stout Victorian commander warming himself at the mess-room fire.

'If it looks like the real thing . . .' He came back to the table and stared down at the map. 'If we think he means it, I'd like some of our people out of married quarters. We could arrange an air-lift of families from the strip at Gatow. By that time I suppose the cat would be out of the bag and we should have pandemonium everywhere else.'

'When do we tell General Page and the Americans?'

'We don't,' said the commandant shortly. 'Not yet. Not on evidence like this. If the time comes, they'll hear from London. As it is, we've got nothing but a dotty old man and a collection of Grimshawe's fantasies.'

Elliott conceded this. As he was about to go, the brigadier said: 'What about the wretched Corporal Hoskins?'

The major pulled a face, as if the matter scarcely merited consideration.

'We opened a file three months ago on his association with the East Germans. Captain Schroeder was his contact. Since then, Hoskins has done guard duty at the RMP post and the RTO office at Tegel airport. He could tell

Schroeder who's going on leave and who's coming back. He could give him details of the duty rotas at the RMP post. That's about all.'

'Poor old Schroeder,' said the commandant laconically.

Elliott shook his head.

'When they had their shake-up at Lichtenberg, the SSD transferred Schroeder from Intelligence to Subversion. The aim is to get a string of low-level contacts like Hoskins, and then to blow them. The allies will assume that we're a nest of spies and the American friends won't trust us with the time of day. That's Schroeder's operation. I wouldn't call it promotion but it might be a neat sideways move in his scramble up the promotion ladder at Lichtenberg. He needs something. Rubin and the Russians loathe him. Schroeder's father was in Kharkov in 1941–43. After the liberation they stood him on top of a lorry with a rope round his neck attached to an army crane above him. Then they drove the lorry away. Him and six others.'

'Do we know why Hoskins bolted now?'

'Woman trouble,' said Elliott contemptuously. 'He guessed we'd want him out of circulation for a while and that his girl might be gone by the time he came back. He hasn't gone to Schroeder. If he tries, we'll know soon enough.'

'Find him,' said Bonnell-Thornton gently. 'Even if it's only the duty rotas and RTO movements at Tegel, I want him under our roof. Reel him in as soon as you can.'

'Two or three days,' Elliott said. 'It shouldn't take longer than that.'

8

Driving alone, in the sports slacks and singlet of his civilian clothes, Elliott followed the flat westward highway of the Heer-Strasse from the centre of Berlin. Detached suburban villas on its southern side stood among spruce trees which marked the wooded area of the Grunewald. The flat width of the three-lane axial road and the openness of the sky suggested that at any moment he might reach the slight crest of a rise and find the sea extending to a distant horizon.

He turned off to the north where the Heer-Strasse was overlooked by the British garrison compound. Its streets were dominated by the block of grey and white tiles which housed the eight-floor Military Hospital. Following the Dickens-Weg he drove through the little roads of utilitarian houses in brown stucco, built thirty years before when the occupation of Berlin had become a long-term necessity. It was the area of the garrison school, the board neatly covered with padre's notices, a grass playground for the use of children of authorised personnel only.

The entrance to the hospital grounds was unobtrusively guarded. Two of the Nazi leaders held in the military prison had been transferred here in the past for medical treatment. Since then, the building had been modified for use on such occasions. Among the signposts to the ante-natal clinic and the officers' mess were more familiar notices. 'Military Installation . . . Photography Forbidden.'

Elliott parked the car and rode up in the lift to the top floor, above the gaily decorated wards for children and pregnant wives who made up the majority of the patients. At this level the rooms were secure. An RMP sergeant in a glass-walled office guarded the end of the main corridor. He saluted, checked Elliott's pass, and saluted again.

'He asked for you about half an hour ago, sir,' the sergeant said helpfully. 'Commandant was informed. Thought you should see the prisoner first.'

Elliott nodded. He watched Andor for a moment through the observation panel. The prisoner sat by the hospital bed in the brown shirt and grey trousers issued to him as regulation wear. No external windows pierced the walls of the room and its temperature remained constant, whatever the season outside.

Prisoners in the first phase of their confinement were

generally restless, giving an impression of energy contained. They would pace the cell in obsessive patterns, try to see what lay beyond through windows or judas-holes, examine the walls and fittings of their little world. Then came the apathetic stage. Men would sit, as Andor was doing, stand with hands on hips or against the walls, for hours at a time. It was the moment when interrogation became more productive. Having fretted so long over the ordeal of questioning, the victim seemed at last to welcome it.

The sergeant was standing at Elliott's shoulder.

'He was made to clean the room and fold his blankets first thing, sir. No breakfast until he did. Not much trouble with him.'

'Good.' Elliott listened, still watching his prisoner. 'Obedience in little things first. The rest will follow.'

'He's had his chaplain's bible, sir. No padre's visit, of course. Hasn't read much, though. Talks to himself a bit. Reciting. German. He's been made to talk English if anyone goes in.'

Elliott logged the time of his visit in the sergeant's book. Then he unlocked the door of the room and went in. Andor looked up with a momentary surprise, seeing the major dressed as if for casual recreation rather than in his uniform. The blue eyes stared, moist and accusing, as Elliott closed the blind of the observation panel.

'Stand up!' Sharp as a parade-ground order, the words rang on the flat surfaces of stone and metal. Andor's blue eyes seemed wider and moist as he pulled himself to his feet.

'So long as you are a military prisoner, you will stand up when an officer enters the room!'

The old man's fingers touched and rubbed along the seams of his trousers. He spoke with quiet pedantic accuracy.

'You are not dressed as an officer should be.'

Long ago, in Malaya, Elliott had learnt the subtle art of hitting suspects. It would never do for this elderly German to appear, even before the commandant, with the bruises of a blow upon him. However, he raised his hand and lashed it at Andor's head, just hard enough and close enough to cause his victim to stagger back into the chair confused and fearful.

'Stand up!'

Andor touched his mouth with the back of his hand to stem the saliva gathering on his lips.

'You should not have done that,' he said gently, his voice now trembling a little with anger as well as fear. 'There was no need for you to do that.'

'Get to your feet!'

The old man hesitated, then looked at Elliott's face and obeyed. He was no stoic nor hero, pain and fear moved him as easily as any other subject under interrogation.

'What is your name?'

Elliott walked round him, standing at his back and repeating the demand closer still.

'Your name? *Wie ist Ihr Name?* The name you were born with?'

Andor's face was lowered, as if to hide his mouth and eyes from an anticipated blow. Now his words were mumbled.

'I have told you my name. I have answered your questions.'

'You will tell me now! If I ask a hundred times you will answer at each one! Understand that!' His hand smacked down on the hospital table. He saw Andor quiver at the sound of the impact. He walked round in front of his prisoner, moving silently to increase the air of menace.

'Look at me!'

Andor raised his blue eyes. The fear had dwindled to uncertainty. Now even that seemed to have gone, like a fire dying. There was a quiet self-assurance, blank and impenetrable as a prison wall.

'I am not your enemy, Major Elliott. You have enemies, I know that. But I am not one of them. You make a bad mistake.'

Elliott drew back his arm and pushed the old man into the chair again. Yet this time Andor's gaze scarcely wavered. In several years of such encounters, the major had dealt with fugitives, sullen fanatics, even a few men who sought petty martyrdoms. They had been easy to break. Andor was not a fanatic of their kind but a fatalist. How did one threaten with pain and death a man who looked so closely upon them in any case?

'You will not defeat me by force, Major Elliott.' There was no reproach in the voice, only a great weariness. 'What I will tell you now, I would have told you anyway. You are not my enemy, though you are not yet my friend either.'

'If you suppose, Dr Andor, that I am here to play games with you . . .'

But the old man shook his head, waving away the protest.

'Before you call it a game, Major Elliott, you may see for yourself. Go to Dahlem. To the house which stands at number 8 Sommer-Allee. You will find it easily enough. A little cul-de-sac off the Konigin-Luise-Strasse, near the Botanical Gardens. Go down to the basement and see for yourself. I am too old to play games, Major, and in any case the time is too short. Fourteen days yesterday. Thirteen today. Believe me, the clock has begun to tick. When all this is over, you may kill me or do as you please with me. But before you use force beyond the limits of my capacity to bear it, remember that mine are the only hands which can stop that clock.'

9

The two unmarked Sierras moved slowly through the traffic which converged on the broad Berlin ring-road near the Palais am Funkturm. Above the stadtring rose the bunker-like fun-palace of the 1930s, its steel-girdered radio mast a diminished Eiffel Tower.

Bonnell-Thornton and his driver were in the first car. Elliott followed with Dr Grimshawe and a military police private in civilian clothes. Beside the driver lay the wrapped and cased geiger-counter.

The two cars gathered speed on the broad ring-road with its overhead directions to the cities of the Federal Republic. A long grandstand, used on days when the lanes of the stadtring became a racing circuit, stood shabby and deserted in the strong sunlight. Presently the trees of the Grunewald, in pale green leaf, flashed by on either side. On narrow forest paths, parties of cyclists were riding towards the lakeside at Wannsee. The cars turned into the American sector on the suburban artery of the Potsdamer-Strasse, turning beside the Botanical Gardens and drawing up in the tree-shaded avenue of the Konigin-Luise-Strasse. Bonnell-Thornton slammed his car door and led the way down the unpaved cul-de-sac of the Sommer-Allee.

While Elliott and Grimshawe followed the commandant, the RMP drivers were left with the cars. An expensive calm settled on the villas and gardens in the warm day. The resinous odour of pines rose behind tall fences. In this quiet woodland road, the prosperity of West Berlin seemed more than a political myth.

The key found in Andor's pocket after his surrender fitted the front door of a white modernistic little house. It also opened a door inside, leading to the basement steps. Elliott went down first and turned on the lights.

As the fluorescent tubes lit the concrete basement room, his first reaction was one of irritation. It was impossible that the steel sphere, the size of a domestic water tank, could be the angel of annihilation. It was old and tarnished, held in place by laboratory scaffolding. Wired to it was a timer, whose green digital display flicked through the forty-seventh hour of its programme.

Grimshawe activated the flat metal box of the geiger-counter with its round dial at the rear. When he ran it over the room's surfaces, the needle remained at zero. Even the steel sphere registered no response. He shrugged with professional indifference, went across and turned off the timer switch. The green figures faded at forty six hours and nineteen minutes. Then he turned the main switches off.

'It won't explode.' Grimshawe patted the smooth metal flank affectionately. 'Not without a power source. Still, I should like the protective clothing brought from the car.'

When this had been done Grimshawe put on the protective suit of padded white cloth and the mask with its eyepieces and intercom. Elliott and Bonnell-Thornton did the same, like Alpinists about to engage in high altitude sports. Grimshawe began to wind the manual jack which raised one half of the sphere clear of the lower section. He eased the antennae of the counter into the gap. Elliott waited for the harsh crackling of a radioactive report. There was nothing. Grimshawe took a long-handled mirror from his case and inserted this, watching the reflection closely. Then he took off the headpiece of the protective suit.

'You can call off the alarm,' he said smugly. 'This contraption may blow the fuses – but that is the limit of its destructive power.'

He wound the two halves of the sphere further apart as the other two men stepped forward to look. The upper hemisphere was empty. Only in the lower half was the map of a nuclear hell laid out.

The concentric circles of hell in the theology of Elliott's own childhood perfectly matched what he now saw. Red and green fuse-lights glowed in the intricate vortex of wiring and metal wedges. Silver bubbles of dried solder were, perhaps, Andor's own contribution.

Enclosing this nuclear universe was the steel casing of the sphere with its intricate harness of detonator wires. Immediately inside the casing lay the black, polished wedges of graphite explosive mirrors. By means of these, the escaping neutrons were driven back to fuel the havoc of the central sunburst. Grimshawe smiled at last.

'You see? Graphite mirrors! A modern device would use non-fissionable uranium-238. Still, the wiring looks good.

Whoever put this together certainly knew his stuff.'

'But it's a dummy?' the commandant asked.

Grimshawe chuckled.

'Oh, yes. It's a dummy all right. Look.'

He touched the fourth circle with its mass of circuits and fusing conduits. Each was wired to an inner circle of wedges, shaped of soft butter yellow substance. Elliott winced. Plastic explosive, likely to become unstable in the present weather, would demolish the entire house and most of the Sommer-Allee. But Grimshawe dug his finger into the viscous mass and held a blob to his nose.

'Putty and fat!' he said with a chuckle. 'The real thing smells of almonds. Your man is a very clever faker. Probably.'

The sixth circle of wedges had the look of raw gold, as had the central core.

'Brass,' said Grimshawe contemptuously. 'Not a bad match for plutonium, if it had a duller look to it. You can do what you like with this contraption. Nothing will make it explode. Now if this were plastic explosive and this were plutonium, it would be a different matter. The wedges would blast inward on the central core. You'd attain a critical mass and the chain reaction would begin. Something like this would certainly remove Berlin from the map.'

'Could the man who built this build the real thing?'

'Oh yes,' said Grimshawe reassuringly. 'If he could get the weapons-grade plutonium. Yes, of course. A man who knows enough about circuitry to build a television set could probably do the rest – with a little guidance. But if your man could build the real thing, he'd hardly waste his time with this. Presumably this is the strongest bluff he's got. And it's not good enough.'

'We don't even know that Andor put it together,' Elliott said.

Bonnell-Thornton had lost interest in the possibilities. His mind returned to the easy ways of military administration.

'I'd say that Aldermaston was the best place for this. Our main problem is getting it across Berlin without telling the world. I'm not sure I can send marked trucks from the motorpool into the American zone without causing a stir. I daresay the military intelligence people could arrange something.'

He was interrupted by footsteps on the stairs. The RMP private in civilian clothes appeared with a flush of embarrassment on his fair cheeks. Behind him Elliott saw the brown uniform of the West Berlin polizei. That was not the worst. Bringing up the rear was a figure in the distinctive olive green of the United States military command in Berlin.

Whatever his feelings in the matter, Major Patrick Corrigan saluted Brigadier Bonnell-Thornton punctiliously. If the dismantled sphere of the weapon caused him any surprise, he concealed it flawlessly.

Bonnell-Thornton acknowledged the salute by a self-conscious nod of recognition. When Corrigan spoke, there was not the least irony or triumph in his voice.

'Good morning, gentlemen,' he said courteously. 'Welcome to the US sector. May I be of some assistance?'

10

The storm broke upon Elliott that evening in a private dining-room of the Kempinski Hotel, overlooking the gaudy neon patchwork of the Kurfursten-Damm. The sun-flush of the long summer evening faded to grey against the shimmering colours of the city. Massive and white-tiered the Europa Centre flickered and blazed with light, the neon alphabet of ITT . . . Cinzano . . . the yellow gash of the Berliner Commerzbank.

'Who the hell does he think he is?'

Corrigan put down his glass then picked it up again. He still spoke without anger, as if sincerely seeking information.

'It was difficult, Pat,' said Elliott hopelessly. 'Very difficult indeed. No one knew . . .'

'But it's our sector, Sam. Our sector, for God's sake!'

Unmollified by the dinner which Elliott had bought him at the brigadier's expense, Corrigan persisted with the quiet resentment of one who has been struck an unexpected blow by a friend.

'It was a mistake, Pat. If I'd been in a position to do so, which I wasn't, I would have been in touch with you first. It was a mistake. The situation developed so fast.'

Corrigan sat back in his chair, as if partly accepting Elliott's contrition. Far below them the lights of the New Eden discotheque flashed and swirled. Young women in tall boots and sham-leather trousers were taking up their nightly sentry-duty, lounging patiently against the display-cases of the avenue on their stone pedestals, among jewellery and porcelain, cameras and objets d'art.

'Fast?' said Corrigan thoughtfully. 'You'd had Andor in your hands for two days. On the whole, Sam, I'd say this wasn't the most professional performance I ever saw.'

From the shattered tower of the Kaiser Wilhelm Memorial Church, the xylophone tones began to chime the hour. Elliott refilled Corrigan's glass from a bottle of Remy Martin cognac. The American major was prickly at the best of times, even his amiability tempered by the phrases and timing of a Wall Street corporation lawyer. Looking at him, the wide-boned face, the eagle-beak nose, and the angular rimless spectacles, Elliott saw a rejuvenated John Foster Dulles.

Elliott turned the brandy in his glass. His companion went across to the window and then walked back.

'Who else is being told?'

'No one,' Elliott said. 'Not for the time being.'

Corrigan sighed.

'That's not very bright, Sam. You'll have to tell the Soviets. It's different with the French. No one gives a damn about them. But General Konstantin and his gang are going to find out, one way or another. They'll be twice the trouble if you've kept them out of it. You'll have to tell them – and soon.'

Elliott shook his head.

'I don't see why.'

Corrigan sat down, paused, then looked at him.

'I'll tell you why, Sam. Because if you don't tell them, we're going to. To be precise, they will know in forty-eight hours from now. That device was found in our sector and it's our decision. Your brigadier can behave like a horse's ass if he chooses – he's had the practice. But no one else is following his procession.'

'I can't very well put it to him like that, Pat,' said Elliott wearily.

Corrigan spread out his hands.

'Then let him find out when it happens. That's all.'

There was a knock at the door. It was one of the Kempinski's page-boys calling Elliott to the phone. The major came back a few minutes later.

'Bonnell-Thornton,' he said for Corrigan's benefit. 'He tried cosying up to Andor to see what might be gleaned that way.'

'And?'

'The conversation on the phone was oblique.'

'Come on, Sam!' said Corrigan impatiently. The light on the lenses of his spectacles gave him the look of an aggressively intelligent child.

'It seems,' Elliott said reluctantly, 'That Andor has begun to talk about his plutonium. Very large quantities. Enough to blow this city off the map.'

11

Dove sono i bei momenti . . . The mellow aria of the Countess soared and subsided again with controlled Mozartean perfection. *Di dolcezza e di piacer* . . . Words mattered nothing. Flawless as a pure melody of birdsong the sounds rose from the stage bedroom and hung in the plain simplicity of the auditorium. A dim reflection of stage-light caught the white shirt-fronts of the stalls, bare brown shoulders in the pale formal dresses of a summer evening. The low swoop of necklines at the back laid bare the fine shoulder-blades, fragile as fins.

From his box in the side gallery, the Prime Minister divided his attention between the sublime modulations of the Countess's aria and the half-lit vision of the women below him, grateful simultaneously for both.

Settling back further in his seat, he savoured the gratitude that stamped his mood for the evening. Arriving for the first act of *Figaro* at just after five in the afternoon, he had been noticed at once by some of the Glyndebourne audience as he took his place in the box. Row by row, they had stood, turned, and applauded him. Scattered clapping and proletarian bravos were displays he was well used to and now affected to despise. Yet to be applauded with such sense of performance by the English bourgeoisie was deeply gratifying. To his certain knowledge, the visit of the leader of the opposition to the opera had been greeted by no more than a few glances and whispers. In his mind he began to hum the aria to himself. The thought of the intimate opera house among the sunlit folds of the Sussex Downs and fields on a summer evening warmed his spirit, as one might warm a fine vintage.

When the aria drew to a close, he decided that he enjoyed such occasions more than he had allowed himself to acknowledge. In the present political climate there was no harm in being known as the son of a collier who could put on an evening suit and savour Mozart with the best of them. The coalition of equals – he winced at the banality of the nickname which he had affectionately bestowed on his administration – depended a good deal on the support of minorities. The Prime Minister at Glyndebourne's *Figaro*. More than a press-office release. Good enough for a feature, appealing to what he used to deride as the 'colour supplement vote'.

While he was fixing in his mind a resolution to speak to Jenny Roscoe about it, the Countess brought her aria to a splendid conclusion. He held his hands high, clapping with vigour so that those below should see him. To his annoyance they seemed unaware of him now. All their eyes were on the young singer who stood, frozen in mid-gesture on the stage as the eager applause broke into huzzas and cries of 'Encore!' She was very, very good. No doubt of that. They were beginning to drum their feet on the uncarpeted wood of the floor.

'England's middle classes stamping for more pudding!' he said sourly and quietly enough for Peacock, the Special Branch escort, not to hear. Just then, Peacock's hand rested lightly on his shoulder. The young officer had been taught that one does not tap royalty or government on the shoulder on such occasions as this. One lays a hand on the shoulder, increasing the pressure as necessary.

He looked round. Peacock said nothing. The raising of his eyebrows and the slight movement of his head sufficed. One of the ushers was holding the door of the box open and a thin dust-laden beam of sunlight fell across the darkened seats. The Prime Minister got up, his movements concealed by the dying storm of clapping below, and followed Peacock out. They went down the stairs into the loggia of the opera house, open to the sunlit gardens on two sides. The bare brickwork, the plain meal-coloured wood, gave it an air of expensive tranquillity.

One of the cabinet aides, a smooth young man whose immaculate grey flannel gave him the look of a school prefect, was waiting for him with a white cordless phone. The earpiece was equipped with a short aerial, tuned to the prime-ministerial helicopter which had been parked in a field on the far side of the country lane.

'Cabinet Office, sir,' the young man said. His fair, downy cheek coloured slightly and self-consciously. 'Sir Oliver Jupp. There's a lot of stuff coming in on the line from Berlin.'

The Prime Minister swore, in order to show that he was still the son of a collier, a man of the people despite his newly acquired patrician tastes and his private portfolio of directorships. He took the phone and listened.

'Quite right,' he said presently. 'Best not to. I'll come back at once.'

He handed the phone to his aide. Under his appearance of irritation he was not sorry to be going back. A little Mozart on a summer evening was most agreeable. *Dove sono i bei momenti* . . . The sublime melody ran teasingly in his brain. All the same, he had just about had enough.

They went out through the dim light of the organ room, the dark oil paintings, panelling, mullioned windows, and so into the gardens. In the last warmth of the sun, the terrace was alive with blue flowers and the scent of tobacco plants. He took a final glance at the full-leaved trees of the copses, the fields of cows, the champagne picnic dinners set out on the lawns. Already the light was turning yellow on the Sussex downland where the sheep grazed in scattered flocks.

'All right,' he said, falling easily into his familiar role. 'Let's get on with it.'

With a clatter of rotor blades, the Westland Executive swung upwards from the concrete pad provided by the opera house for its more ambitious visitors. The sunlit downs wheeled away beneath them, a glimpse of Brighton to one side, the two piers stretching distinctively into the sea, and the flat Norman battlefields of the Pevensey levels at the other extreme.

They rode in silence, the others waiting for the Prime Minister to begin the conversation – and waiting in vain. As it happened, he had nothing to tell them. Whatever it was that had come over the line from Berlin was evidently not suited to the airwaves. It was not supremely important – a threat of war – or else the more secret procedures would have been used. Short of war with Russia, there was nothing much to be regarded as urgent in the modern world.

The trees of the Ashdown forest gave way to the long pale sprawl of south London suburbia: Purley, Croydon, Wandsworth, Battersea, the cold grey strip of the Thames under a bank of evening cloud, and then the heliport.

Thanks to the foresight of Sir Oliver Jupp, the co-ordinator of security, the airport police had kept the way clear. In ten minutes more, the official car with Inspector Peacock swinging open the door had stopped outside the modest eighteenth-century doorway of the official residence in Downing Street.

Like so many of his predecessors, the premier had his office on the top floor, near his private rooms and well above the cabinet room and those used for entertaining. Sir Oliver Jupp was waiting, a small man with sleek black hair and a habit of taking breath through his teeth for no apparent reason. In consequence of this he seemed to surround himself with an aura of difficulty, surprise, and alarm.

'I suppose it's Bonnell-Thornton,' said the Prime Minister wearily. 'Surely we don't need an argument with the Americans over who has charge of the toy bomb?'

'It's not quite that, sir,' said Sir Oliver crisply. 'We were apparently wrong in assuming it to be a toy.'

'Well,' said the Prime Minister impatiently, 'it wouldn't work, would it? And if it won't work, it's a toy.'

As Sir Oliver Jupp prepared to shatter the immaculate sphere of political self-satisfaction, the pleasure of doing so glimmered in his eyes.

'Andor has talked,' he said quietly. 'They've found plutonium.'

Elliott stood back and surveyed the floodlit screen of dark green polythene. The erection of the polythene wall had transformed the bushes and scrub round the Staaken culvert into the semblance of an exhumation. The headlights of the RMP Land Rover added to the brilliance.

Beyond the concrete slabs of the sector frontier the East German guard-commander had evidently ordered a local alert. In addition to the white glare of the tall lamps illuminating the sandy 'death-strip', there was a searchlight beam moving slowly up and down on the far side. From time to time, as the beam played on the rolled-top of the wall, the light splashed over to fall, pale and diffused, on the brown stucco of the maisonettes in the British sector.

From where he stood Elliott could just see the binoculars behind the guard-tower windows on the East German side. The Vopos made no attempt to conceal their curiosity, yet the culvert itself was too low to be in their area of vision.

Bonnell-Thornton had left the staff-car parked on the roadway and was now watching the efforts of two frogmen from the Royal Engineers to probe the narrow tunnel of the dry culvert. The flask had been found easily enough, exactly in the position which Andor described. The problem, as the commandant had repeated several times since their arrival, was that there might be another flask further in. It would only require two more of the same capacity to hold enough plutonium-239 to constitute an effective warhead.

'Where the devil did he get it from?' Bonnell-Thornton's voice had been fraught with the unfairness of it all. Only Corrigan seemed to relax. It was as if he recognised that the game had at last become one with whose rules he was familiar.

'A workman in a processing plant who could smuggle one grain of plutonium a day would have enough for a warhead in less than a year.'

'Smuggling isn't that easy!' said the commandant petulantly.

Major Corrigan turned his head away as if to avoid looking at his companion as he spoke. The quiet voice had a professional's disdain for the amateur. A cool and even distaste.

'You think not? In 1974 a young woman called Karen Silkwood died in a car crash. She worked at the Kerr-McGee processing plant in Oklahoma. When the security officers examined her apartment, it was alive with plutonium. Smuggled or carried out unwittingly. Losses are often small, of course. Put them together and there's enough weapons-grade plutonium unaccounted for in the world to build a dozen warheads. We don't yet know that Dr Andor's stuff is weapons-grade. It may be nothing more than nuclear fuel. Even that, scattered as powder over Berlin, would contaminate east and west heavily enough to make the centre of the city uninhabitable.'

Elliott considered this as he watched the activity behind the polythene screens. By good fortune, Staaken was on the remote western fringe of the Berlin enclave and it was now after midnight. Anywhere else, by day, these activities would have drawn a crowd. Apart from the occasional movement of a curtain in the maisonettes he had seen nothing on this side. The East German side was another matter.

One of the frogmen had worked his way into the tight cylinder of the culvert with an inspection lamp and a long magnetised probe. The space was too narrow for the oxygen cylinders to be strapped to his back. Instead they stood outside the opening, connected to his mask by a long tube. Though the culvert was dry, the air was too foul to breathe.

As they waited for the frogman to emerge, Elliott was aware of a sound in the distance, shattering the stillness of the night as it approached. The chatter of helicopter blades. Looking up he saw the navigation lights of the Russian-built craft on the far side of the wall, the flashing amber of the cockpit lamp and the red glow of the underbelly. The pilot followed the line of the wall, curved away and came back again. For several minutes the helicopter hung above the concrete guard-tower, relaying to its occupants an account of the scene at the culvert. The down-draught from its blades stirred the tall browned grasses where Elliott stood. After a moment longer, Bonnell-Thornton turned to him.

'Go back to the car, Sam. Phone your friend Colonel Rubin in Karlshorst. Ask him to call his dogs off.'

'He'll want to know why, sir.'

The commandant nodded.

'The child of a British soldier is missing,' he said. 'Cries have been reported from the culvert. That should do it. They must have seen by now that we're not trying to tunnel under their wall!'

Elliott saluted and walked back along the rough path to the staff car. Using the radio phone he called the garrison exchange and put a priority call to Soviet Military Intelligence which, along with the KGB, had its headquarters in Karlshorst, near the East Berlin sports complex. He waited until the voice of the Russian interpreter answered him in American-accented English.

'This is Major Elliott, British garrison. Is Colonel Rubin there?'

'Colonel Rubin is not here until tomorrow.'

'A Soviet military helicopter is patrolling the sector boundary at Staaken. We are searching the culvert on the Berlin side for a missing child.'

'The child's name, please?'

Elliott guessed that the question had been prompted by a more senior officer sitting at the interpreter's elbow. In a moment of inspiration, he said, 'Karen Silkwood. She is the daughter of one of our men.'

There was another pause. Then the voice said, 'The frontier is the responsibility of the German People's Republic. You should speak to the Volkspolizei.'

It was no use showing anger, Elliott knew that by experience.

'The helicopter has the markings of the Soviet army.'

'It is a routine patrol.'

'Listen to me,' said Elliott patiently. 'The helicopter has been positioned overhead for almost ten minutes. So long as it remains there we shall not be able to hear a child's voice above the noise of the rotors. Do you understand?'

There was another pause. Then the voice spoke again.

'We understand. However, we do not have the authority to cancel military patrols. It is a matter of frontier security.'

'May I please speak to the duty officer?'

'This is an administration building. We do not have a duty officer. There will be someone here in the morning.'

'By that time it may be too late.'

'One moment, Major Elliott.'

The pause was much longer this time. Who was being consulted and to what purpose? At last the interpreter spoke again.

'We have a record of a Miss Karen Silkwood, Major. She was a United States citizen who died in 1974. It seems she had suffered contamination by plutonium.'

A chill passed through Elliott's heart. There was no humour in the interpreter's voice. Only Colonel Rubin, sitting at a little distance, would be chuckling. Mentally he tipped his hat to the speed and efficiency of the KGB computer-system. To Moscow Centre and back in little more than a minute.

'May I tell Colonel Rubin that you will talk to him in the morning?'

The tone of the voice was more relaxed now, warmer and encouraging.

'Yes,' said Elliott wearily. 'Yes, you'd better tell him that.'

He walked back from the car to report his failure. Bonnell-Thornton was coming along the path towards him. The commandant brushed aside Elliott's account.

'They'll have to put a guard on it tonight and dig it out tomorrow. Too dangerous to do it now.'

'It's not empty?'

'That's a matter of opinion,' said Bonnell-Thornton gloomily. 'There's nothing in it that you could weigh – no atomic fuel. But the structure of the flask itself is jumping with plutonium contamination. Whatever was in that flask could irradiate the entire centre of Berlin. We'd all better start taking Dr Andor very seriously indeed.'

'Including Colonel Rubin,' Elliott said thoughtfully.

This seemed to lighten the brigadier's gloom.

'Yes,' he said with a sardonic satisfaction. 'Him too.'

12

Colonel Rubin left the carriage of the overhead railway, the S-Bahn, at the lakeside terminus of Wannsee, in the West Berlin enclave. The underground railway, administered by West Berlin, ran under East Berlin, though never stopping at any of the stations. The S-Bahn, with its clean wooden seats and bare carriages, was administered by East Berlin but ran unimpeded through the entire city.

It was rare for the western allies or city police to make any check of travellers coming from the DDR on the elevated railway. Occasionally there was a search for illegal immigrants, Turks or Yugoslavs who sought an elusive prosperity and settlement by entering from the east. On the whole, however, Rubin still found this the best way of moving unobserved through the sectors of the west.

The grey suit that he wore had been a purchase from one of the hard currency shops in the Karl-Marx Allee which stocked the produce of capitalist Europe. Rubin excused the indulgence on the grounds that he would appear less conspicuous than in one of the loose, square-shouldered suits of the Moscow department stores.

He walked through the broad underpass of the old imperial station. Wannsee had been a fashionable resort in the Kaiser's day and its Italianate villas remained, white and balustraded on the bluff, above the glitter of the broad lake. Rubin came up into the fierce light of the summer afternoon. Though the lunch hour was over, the shaded café tables in the station forecourt were still crowded. Then he looked more carefully and saw the girl. Debby was sitting alone at a table which was separated from the others by a terra cotta urn on a pedestal. He recognised her easily from her photographs, though she had now exchanged the jeans and singlet for a cheap black dress with red shoes. Her fine blonde hair was once again put up into its coquettish little bun. Rubin had wondered whether Hoskins might also be waiting, but he saw no sign of him.

He walked across and stood so that his shadow fell upon the table, a burly outline with his heavy domed skull and saturnine face. Even now he inclined his head in an instinctive embryonic bow.

'I am Mikhail Yuri Rubin,' he said gently, taking her hand. 'My secretary tells me I am to meet you here.'

Her dark eyes responded in a widening look of gratitude, the wan little face animated at last.

'I thought perhaps you wouldn't come,' she said quickly, watching him sit down opposite to her. 'I wondered if I ought to have come to East Berlin.'

Rubin's smile grew broader in his reassurance of her.

'Mr Elliott and his friends do not mind,' he said. 'We understand each other well enough for that. If I choose to take a drink by the lake in such charming company, why should they mind? I would welcome them to the bar of the Unter den Linden Hotel whenever they wished.'

He turned and gave the waiter the order for their drinks. As he looked at Debby again, his eyes narrowing in the same smile of reassurance, he saw the hard young features soften under the influence of his charm. Rubin knew perfectly well that her experience of men could seldom have gone beyond the graceless and selfish passion of such vulgarians as Hoskins. It was Rubin's duty to flatter her femininity, yet it also pleased him to see the awkward delight she took in this.

He waited until the drinks had been brought.

'I was sorry,' Rubin looked down at the glass in his hand, 'I was sorry that I could do no more for your friend. How is he?'

Debby lowered her eyes and the first sign of resentment showed itself in the movement of her mouth.

'He's all right,' she said. 'He needs to think. Now that he's burnt his boats.'

Rubin sighed.

'He should have gone straight back, mademoiselle.

Before he was missed. If the story was discovered, I would have spoken for him with my friend, Major Elliott.'

'But you're on the other side,' she said simply.

Rubin smiled again and laid his large hand on her own as she touched the table by her glass.

'Mr Elliott and I do the same job. I like him. He is an English gentleman. Oh, of course we do not tell each other all our secrets. We belong to different armies. But, my dear young lady, it would suit neither of us if our young men were constantly being enticed from one side to the other. Do you see?'

Debby nodded without speaking. Then she opened her bag and took out an envelope from which she drew a dozen sheets of photocopy.

'You didn't want him,' she said calmly. 'He could have given you all this for a start.'

Rubin raised his eyebrows, as if truly impressed by this cache of documents.

'Did he keep these secret from me, then?'

'He thought you'd rather have the other information,' she said. 'Now he wants to show you what else there is. He means to come over. Really.'

'And what are these?' He picked up the papers.

'Records of the police post near the border,' she said. 'Notes of conversations. And there's the lists from the RTO at Tegel. All the leave movements, and the baggage, and the cargo handling. You couldn't ask for more. He knows all about both places.'

'But surely this information was collected for Captain Schroeder. Was it not?'

Debby lowered her voice as if talking with earnest confidentiality to an awkward child.

'Jimmy doesn't want to go to Schroeder. He wants to go over to you. There's nothing he can't tell you about the RMP post and Tegel.'

Rubin shook his head slowly and doubtfully.

'You ask me to make enemies of Schroeder and Mr Elliott. That is not easy.'

Debby sat back in her chair, the hopelessness returning to her dark eyes.

'You don't trust us,' she said wearily.

Rubin looked disappointed, the lines of his broad face changing easily from bonhomie to melancholy.

'On the contrary, mademoiselle. I trust you so much that I have come here to receive these papers. At this moment, Mr Elliott and his policemen might step out from behind that tree and take me into their custody. You see?'

'You'll take the papers and read them?' Her eyes brightened.

'I will do that,' he said. 'But I promise nothing. Yet.'

He sipped his drink.

'If we both came over,' she said, 'I could work for you. Even if there wasn't much for Jimmy, I could work for you.'

'How? You speak German or Russian?'

'No,' she shook her head energetically, 'But even speaking English there are things. The sort of things you read about.'

Despite himself, Rubin was shocked. That Debby should sell herself to be an agent provocateur in the beds of western visitors – on behalf of Corporal Hoskins – was grotesque.

Rubin spoke as a man of her father's generation.

'Such things are impossible. Even if they were possible, I would not permit them. You should not believe all the slanders that you read in the western press.'

'I don't!' she said, angered a little at last, 'I don't. But there must be something. I don't care what it is.'

'There is always a market-place,' Rubin said gently. 'But one should not pay the price of extortion.'

'I don't understand.'

He looked across the lakeside road to the pleasure launches which were loading with passengers for the Havel cruise.

'The good wife of Odessa,' he said thoughtfully, 'lost her gold wedding-ring. She went to the priest and begged him for a miracle that the ring would be restored to her. More than anything she wanted that miracle. She gave money to the priests and they promised her that the ring would be restored.'

Debby looked at him uncertainly but Rubin continued with his story.

'The ring had, in truth, been taken by a thief who thought it was brass and threw it in the river. In the river, it was swallowed by a fish. That fish was caught in the net of the good wife's husband. She cooked it, never guessing what was in its maw. That night at supper, she took a spoonful of the fish stew and choked to death on the ring, which had been restored to her so miraculously. You see how it is with these priests?'

He paused and watched her. Then he said gently, 'You think you want to come over, to savour the joys of socialism? Believe me, mademoiselle, the treasure you seek would choke you as surely as the gold ring choked the poor woman in the story. There is nothing for you there. I speak as a friend.'

'What else is there for us?'

For all his professionalism, Rubin was moved by the despair in the wan young face.

'I will see what can be done,' he said in the same gentle tone, laying his hand paternally over hers again. 'I do not promise. You must not expect. But I will see.'

'You'll take the papers and read them?'

'Of course,' he said.

It had not been Rubin's intention to offer her money for the photocopies. Yet he remembered the four notes of fifty West German marks in his wallet. He took them out and gave them to her. It was possible, after all, that she might be of use to him later on.

'Now we shall take our leave.' He stood up and helped her from her chair. 'I will read the papers carefully and then perhaps we will talk again.'

As they stood together, Rubin seemed like the generous uncle parting from an impoverished niece. He turned and walked to the broad underpass of the old imperial station again, holding the envelope. Ten minutes later the S-Bahn carried him above the streets of West Berlin to the DDR checkpoint at the Friedrich-Strasse station.

The man who had been standing on the little bluff with the other sightseers at Wannsee, staring out across the lake to the Potsdam shore, detached himself from the crowd. Rubin's arrival and departure had stirred no interest in him. It was Debby's face and figure which came into focus through the telephoto lens of his camera. The automatic winding-mechanism gave out a series of dry rhythmic squeals as he took a dozen photographs of the girl who stood forlornly, waiting for the bus which ran to the Hardenberg-Platz and the city centre.

13

The ambassadorial limousine with its outriders provided by the District of Columbia Police Department, swept down the broad lane of Massachusetts Avenue, across the busy commercial crossing of Dupont Circle. The cherry blossom was over now but the tall mansard roofs, the iron grilles and round baronial towers of the smaller legations marked the calm in the lower fringe of Washington's diplomatic quarter.

Fedor Anatoly Malkin, envoy of the Union of Soviet Socialist Republics, fidgeted in the back of the long, oversprung car. Chairman of Sovnarcom, the Council of People's Commissars, the Washington embassy was not an honour which he had actively sought. In preferring him before a more experienced diplomat, his superiors had shown how little latitude they proposed to allow him. Press comment in the west had marked his appointment as a downgrading of relationships between the two great powers.

He winced as the outriders turned on their sirens and cleared the way across the green space of Scott Circle with its bronze equestrian general riding against the blue heat of the capital's summer sky. 16th Street with its solid expensive hotels and clubs ran down to Lafayette Square and the White House. To be invited for so direct a discussion did nothing to ease the suspicions which proved native to Malkin's own Georgian personality.

Next to the prosperous brick towers of the University Club stood the older more elegant building of the Soviet embassy itself, a Second Empire pastiche which seemed to have been snatched up from the Faubourg St Germain and planted among the fast food and threadbare parks of the American capital. The embassy roof was a forest of masts and transmitters. As he glanced at them, Malkin could only see in their presence the final denial of his own usefulness. Moscow was no further away now than a tug upon his sleeve. How revealing, he thought, the report on the diplomatic service which the praesidium had commissioned two years ago. Its confidential conclusions had shown, incontrovertibly, that the likelihood of defection increased as the efficiency of communication with the Ministry of Foreign Affairs improved. The thought lightened his mood and he saw himself smiling in the mirror above the driver's head.

Skirting the central gardens of Lafayette Square, already hidden behind the parked lines of tourist buses, the ambassador's car came to the private entrance of the White House, between the residence itself and the Old Executive Building. The gates were already open and the car passed through, scarcely slackening speed.

Malkin's unease returned. He disliked such private and informal meetings as this. He had disapproved of them even in his own country and among his own people. Nothing of consequence was ever decided. No record was kept. Not a single thing which could be called substantial. In that respect, Malkin was a substantial man. Talks with the President, under such circumstances, were no more to him than the tail-wagging of two dogs. Warm and vague promises to understand one another better and to be friends. It offended his sense of logic, this pretence of friendship with men for whom – by the nature of their roles – such a thing was impossible.

The Marine guards opened the door of the limousine and saluted. Nodding self-consciously, Malkin got out and walked up the steps. With a face bland as cheese, the Secretary of State was waiting.

'The President thought we should be more comfortable in the library.'

The handshake. The hand always so cold, even in a Washington summer. Malkin supposed it was the man's circulation. There were rumours of a stroke two years ago, strongly denied upon his appointment to office.

The two men walked together along the low, vaulted corridor, the pale woodwork scrubbed and waxed, the bulletproof glass in the deep window recesses further protected by Venetian blinds. Through the steel slats Malkin glimpsed the south lawn. A gardener from the secret service detail was weeding the rosebeds, a gun visible in its holster as his jacket hung open. The low box-hedges of the Jacqueline Kennedy garden were clipped and trim in the French style of Versailles or the Bagatelle.

In the east wing of the building, the presidential library was an intimate room with a cool light. Its Venetian blinds were used to subdue the glare of the Washington summer, as well as to reinforce security. When Malkin entered, the President was standing up, hand outstretched in long-practised cordiality. That smile was offered equally to party financiers and ambassadors, to pretty women and beer-bellied cronies. Malkin wondered why, after so much use, it still failed to light the dark, shrewd eyes. Indeed, it seemed that the smile had shrunk with the passage of time until it was little more than a wry distortion of the mouth.

The President retained Malkin's hand a moment longer as if to impress upon it his sincerity.

'Mr Ambassador!'

Malkin gave a slight bow and then took the chair assigned to him. The President talked briefly of the weather and the garden, leaving Malkin to glance along the books in the alcove shelves. The brightness of the latest leather bindings suggested how recently their owner had become a convert to culture.

The topics of the garden and the climate dwindled and died.

'Mr Ambassador.' Now the voice had all the softness of integrity. 'I have to request the cooperation of the Soviet government in a matter which concerns both our nations as occupying powers – as guarantors of peace – in the city of Berlin.'

Malkin waited, promising nothing.

'A sealed flask has been found near the zonal border,' said the President, keeping his eyes upon the Russian's. 'An empty flask of the type used to transport nuclear fuel in reprocessing plants.'

The ambassador's first reaction was one of vindictive satisfaction. It was an article of his faith that the gangsterism of the urban terrorist was a symptom of mortal sickness in capitalist societies. A malignant growth. A terrorist's slogans of socialism married to fascist methods.

'May I know what material the flask contained, and what quantity?'

The President hesitated.

'We still await a final analysis. The quantity cannot have been more than between two and three pounds.'

Light glittered on Malkin's spectacles as he relished this discomfiture of the President and the Secretary of State.

'Why was the Soviet military command in Berlin and its government not informed directly?'

'A report has been drawn up,' The Secretary of State glanced up from his notes. 'The contents of it will be sent to Moscow on the direct-line teleprinter within the hour. A copy will be available to you before you leave this building.'

'Am I to assume that the loss of the material is related to the demands of a terrorist group?'

The President tried to look as if the idea had scarcely crossed his mind.

'So far as we are aware, Mr Ambassador, there is no such link.'

'Then why do you seek the cooperation of the Soviet Union? If the material has merely been misplaced, how can that be of interest to us?'

The Secretary of State intervened.

'In such a situation, Mr Ambassador, it is prudent to assume that we may all be involved. If some form of political blackmail were later attempted and we had not informed you of the possibility from the outset, you would be the first to criticise us.'

Malkin nodded. He took off his glasses and polished them with a piece of tissue, formulating his reply. Across the Potomac from the Pentagon, an olive green military helicopter swung in a wide arc beyond the Lincoln Memorial and hovered above the south lawn. Only the distant chatter of its blades carried through the thickness of the armoured glass in the windows. Malkin watched the wheels come to rest on the landing pad behind a grass covered rampart.

'I am bound to remind you, Mr President, that the Soviet government has warned constantly of the dangers to peace and security presented by United States nuclear policy.'

The Secretary of State gave a sigh of irritation, but Malkin was not to be deterred.

'The United States has repeatedly violated the terms of the 1968 Nuclear Non-Proliferation Treaty. It has done so both alone and in collaboration with its allies.'

'May we please return to the matter in question?' The Secretary of State turned his leather chair on its swivel as if to stare out across the lawn while Malkin's tirade lasted.

Malkin ignored him, addressing the President directly.

'The full-scope safeguards and inspection insisted upon by President Carter as a condition of supplying nuclear fuel were abandoned by the Reagan administration. The supply of heavy water to Argentina in 1983 was permitted without conditions. With the encouragement of the United States, the Canadian government has sold nuclear facilities throughout the world without control over their subsequent conversion to military use. The government of the Federal German Republic has been permitted to supply the means of reprocessing to Argentina since 1968. The plant at Ezeiza was entirely supplied by the West German government with a capacity to produce twenty or thirty nuclear warheads annually.'

'Germany is a sovereign state, Mr Ambassador,' said the President coaxingly. 'The plant at Ezeiza is constructed solely for reprocessing spent fuel for nuclear power stations.'

Malkin knew that his position was unassailable, yet there was one more point to be scored.

'Such processing, Mr President, renders plutonium as a by-product. The power stations of Argentina do not require plutonium. Your own security advisers will confirm that.'

The Secretary of State spun his chair round to face Malkin again.

'Are we to understand, Mr Ambassador, that the government of the Soviet Union refuses to cooperate with the other nations occupying Berlin if there should be a threat to security? Does the Soviet government suppose that the effects of nuclear contamination are going to be held back by the Berlin wall?'

The pencil between his fingers became a weapon of accusation with the last words, as if he might lean forward and jab Malkin's coat button with it. But Malkin's answer was ready even before the question was finished, a well-rehearsed statement of policy for all such occasions.

'The Soviet Union will hold the United States government and its allies solely responsible for the consequences of nuclear piracy in any territory under their control. An attack upon the Soviet Union or the other nations of the Warsaw Pact from such territory will be regarded as an act of the United States or its friends. If the positions were reversed, you would follow the same logic. In the event of such an attack, the Soviet Union will make an appropriate response.'

'That way madness lies,' said the Secretary of State bleakly.

Malkin looked up, not quite sure of the import of these words. Beyond the window, the gardener of the secret service detail had finished clipping the roses. Seated like a lone charioteer behind the rattling motor of the lawn mower, he was cutting the warm grass in long and accurate paths. A fragrance of the cut turf entered the air ducts and brought a memory of spring to the library where the three men sat.

For another half an hour the conversation in the room was volleyed to and fro like a close-fought and inconclusive game of tennis. Malkin took his leave after a copy of the promised report had been brought by a presidential aide. The Secretary of State accompanied him to the car port facing the Old Executive Building. At the last moment, Malkin turned to take formal leave.

'Dr Stenich of the Academy of Sciences will be our guest during the Scientific American conference next month. He shares your enthusiasm for bridge. I should be pleased if you and Mrs Whitworth were free to dine with us while he is here.'

'We should like that,' said the Secretary, still rather stiffly. 'Thank you.'

As he watched Malkin get into the car, the Secretary of State thought how hard it was to accustom himself to the idea that fate had made Malkin doyen of the diplomatic corps in Washington. The two countries had laid meticulous plans for one another's annihilation. Yet if the President should die tomorrow, it would be the Soviet Ambassador who concerted and led the grief of the world's embassies, walking or riding at the head of their representatives in the funeral cortège.

The car and its outriders turned from Lafayette Square and moved quickly towards the tall buildings and shops of Connecticut Avenue. In the warm June sunshine the Secretary of State turned away. He now contemplated the absurdity with which plans were made for dinner parties and games of bridge in a world that might cease to exist before the date of the meeting.

Dr Andor's clock had eleven more days to run.

14

The stranger came on to the Kurfursten-Damm from one of the quiet, affluent side-streets, a tree-lined avenue of expensive apartment blocks below whose balconies the ground floors were occupied by antique galleries, coiffeuses, and old-fashioned tobacconists. When she thought back on the incident, there was no doubt in the girl's mind as to the direction.

He stood by the glass of the window looking in at her as she sat behind the counter with its plastic souvenirs which were moulded to give the appearance of metal or wood. Though Debby was used to men who stared at her in passing, their eyes taking in the slim underdeveloped figure in the tight jeans, there was something in the stranger's eyes which was calculating and dispassionate. He looked, she thought, as if he might be measuring her for her shroud. Despite the warmth of the day, she shivered.

For ten minutes he waited there, watching her as she served the tourists from Swabia or Holstein who had come to glimpse the Sodom and Gomorrah of their Federal Republic. Once or twice she glanced in the man's direction. There was nothing lascivious in his cold admiration, his eyes were those of the pathologist rather than the libertine.

When she looked again, he was gone. At first Debby expected to see him in the shop itself, but he was not there. It was much later when he came back and then, of course, she understood that he had been waiting for a moment when the shop was empty of customers. This time he came in and walked slowly up to the counter. He was not young, she thought, the dark hair was greying and the black rimmed glasses gave him the look of a senior clerk. When he spoke there was only the trace of an accent.

'Your friend Mr Hoskins has caused his friends a good deal of concern. Captain Schroeder has been worried about him. Is he all right?'

'Yes,' she said, the dark eyes moving evasively in the suspicious little face. 'As far as I know.'

'You do not see him?'

'I might do,' she said.

The stranger smiled, as if with difficulty.

'I do not mean to pry,' he said quietly. 'Captain Schroeder is worried about our friend. Now that Mr Hoskins has – left – his military employment, how will he manage for money?'

She undid the pins of her bun to let down her hair. Then she shook it into a blonde veil across her shoulders to show her indifference to such things.

'Couldn't say.'

'Captain Schroeder is most anxious that our friend should not be driven to gangsterism or some other dishonest means. It is a great pity that Mr Hoskins did not inform us of his intention to visit East Berlin when he did. At the best he can only live here as a deserter.'

'I daresay he'd go back,' she said, 'if you wanted him. As I heard it, he was turned away.'

Now the stranger smiled more readily.

'Ah, Colonel Rubin! That was your friend's mistake, you see. He should have come to us.'

'I'm sure he would if he was asked!' Her voice rose in a wail of exasperation with the man and his questions.

'But Captain Schroeder does not even know where Mr Hoskins lives. Can you give me his address?'

'No,' she said, her mouth pouting at the unfairness of the question.

The stranger nodded and seemed not the least put out.

'Would you do me the service of passing on a message to Mr Hoskins?'

Debby was too quick to be caught by such a snare.

'I haven't seen him in weeks.'

'Could you telephone him or leave the message with a friend? I promise you no harm is intended to Mr Hoskins.'

'I daresay I might be able to.'

She turned her sharp little nose and dark eyes, resentment at the stranger's intrusion tempered by helpless cupidity.

'Will you just tell him this? Captain Schroeder will be shopping in West Berlin on Thursday. At two o'clock in the afternoon he will go to the big cinema, the Metropol. He will sit in the usual place. If Mr Hoskins will meet him there, he will hear something very much to his advantage.'

'I'll see.' Resentment faded from her wan little face to be replaced by a cowed compliance. 'I'll try and tell him.'

'Please,' said the stranger gently, 'please do. Your friend is highly thought of by his acquaintances in East Berlin. He was unwise, of course, to go to Colonel Rubin but that will not be held against him.'

'I don't know anything about that,' she said miserably.

'Do you not? Perhaps, then, you should ask Mr Hoskins. The Russians recruit only for themselves, not for the DDR. I do not think you or Mr Hoskins would wish to live in the Soviet Union when you might have a place found for you in Berlin. It is more agreeable in Berlin. Please tell your friend. You may be sure that Captain Schroeder has his interests at heart.'

'I'll tell him,' she said, glancing round as a middle-aged couple came into the shop. 'I'll tell him if I can.'

The stranger ducked his head in what was partly a nod and partly the beginning of a chivalrous bow. He turned from her and walked quickly away.

Debby watched him cross the broad boulevard of the Kurfursten-Damm, pausing on the broad central reservation with its fine leaved lime trees lit by the sun. She had known from the first that it was useless to ask his name. As she watched him go, she impressed on her memory as many details of his appearance as she could.

He reached the far pavement and was hidden in a moment by the moving tide of shoppers. She glimpsed him once more as he turned into the quiet street of antique galleries and salons. After that, she did not suppose that she would ever see him again.

15

Soon after one o'clock on the afternoon of the following Thursday, Corporal Hoskins left the girl's room in the dark brick apartment block off the immigrant shopping quarter of the Potsdamer-Strasse. It was the hiding place to which he had gone as soon as the black Volga car brought him to the checkpoint after his meeting with Colonel Rubin.

It was not the first time he had left the apartment but even in a few days his confidence had risen. The beard which he had begun to grow had done scarcely more than darken his face. Yet at a distance, he thought, it would give him the appearance of being bearded rather than clean-shaven. The brown suit which Debby had bought from the pavement-rails of the secondhand stall in the Friedrich-Strasse was rather long and too baggy. That, too, disguised his customary outline. He looked older and fatter. If they knew where to look for him, he would be caught. But no one cruising in one of the RMP jeep patrols would pick him out from the pavement crowds. If he had begun to frequent bars and cafés, he would have been in danger at once from random visits by the military police. But Hoskins had no intention of taking such risks. Despite his setback with Colonel Rubin, his plan remained essentially what it had always been.

Most of his time in the past few days had been spent in the little apartment, watching television, reading the English papers which the girl brought back from the kiosk near the Europa Centre. It did not surprise him when the message came from Captain Schroeder. He had expected something of the sort. Sooner or later.

Hoskins turned into the busy clamour of the

Potsdamer-Strasse and began to walk to the Metropol. It was about a mile away. Subways and buses were more dangerous to a deserter than the crowded pavements. He had learnt that from his experience as a hunter.

The streets through which he walked, with their square blocks of brown stucco, their drab cafés and kebab houses, formed an area of squatters and immigrants, dispossessed Turks and the 'guest-workers' of Italy or Yugoslavia. Pressed between the commercial heart of the city and the derelict areas close to the Berlin wall, the dingy streets bred their own despair and resentment. Under the signs for Charlottenburger Pilsner the bored middle-aged prostitutes waited in their short skirts and long boots. Appliqué lettering on café windows promised 'Bar – Film – Club – Thai Girls.' Young women with sallow, acne-marked faces stared out at him as he passed, the figure of their pimp just visible in the shadows of the room.

At the Bulow-Strasse crossing where the elevated railway ran into the station, whose glass-walled rooms had been converted into a Turkish bazaar, boarded fronts of derelict shops were painted with the slogans of international revolution. 'Palestina Vengera . . . We Support the Hunger Strikers.' But even the Bobby Sands Pub was boarded up and closed.

To Hoskins the battles whose slogans appeared around him seemed remote as the conquests of imperial Prussia. They belonged to a world in which there could no longer be a place for him. He walked as far as the heavy and prosperous façades of Wertheim, Ka De We, and the other department stores of the Tauentzien-Strasse. Then he turned about and walked back to make sure that no one was following him. The Metropol stood at one end of the shopping avenue where the road opened out into a square and the grey iron arches of the elevated railway ran eastward from Nollendorf-Platz.

With its towers and arches of grey rendering the Metropol looked more like a temple or a synagogue, abandoned at the heart of the city's decay. Its advantage to

Captain Schroeder was clear. The cinema was less than half-an-hour's walk from the frontier crossing at the Friedrich-Strasse checkpoint, closer even than the blue movie house which had been their alternative rendezvous.

Hoskins was under no illusion, as he entered the foyer and bought his ticket, that he had escaped the observation of one of Schroeder's men. The cluttered square outside the cinema was overlooked by the U-Bahn station and corner blocks on every side. Under the railway arches groups of squatters and their girls sat on the pavement with their backs to the support, watching the passers-by for one who might be tempted by an offer of cocaine or women. Among any of these Schroeder could have placed his accomplice.

In the softly-lit auditorium, among the candy smells and disinfectant, he walked slowly up to the back row and found his place, one seat in from the gangway on the right hand side. There was a murmur of music and a purr of ventilation as he sat down. In the rest of the auditorium, at this time of the day, he counted seven other people. All of them sat alone. None of them resembled Schroeder.

The lights dimmed and the film began. Hoskins had not noticed what was advertised outside. *Der Geschichte der Piera.* The title meant nothing to him and he began to fidget almost at once. His knowledge of German was far too slight to make the dialogue comprehensible to him.

Presently he saw one of the men in the seats in front get up and turn. In the flickering light of the film he could tell from the silhouette alone that the man bore no resemblance to Schroeder. But the stranger walked slowly up the aisle towards him and paused by the empty seat next to which Hoskins was sitting. Hoskins put his arm across the seat.

'Nein,' he said firmly. *'Das ist leider besetzt.'*

The stranger stood and looked down at him for a moment longer.

'Mr Hoskins?' The accent was slight, the voice not unlike Schroeder's.

Hoskins drew his arm away from the seat and the stranger lowered himself into the place.

'Where's Captain Schroeder?'

The stranger drew back his coat a little and settled himself.

'He will be here in ten minutes, perhaps less. There was some delay at Lichtenberg just before he was due to leave. We could not take the risk that you would think we were not coming after all. My name is Raasch. Joachim Raasch. I have been one of Captain Schroeder's staff for several months. It was not hard to recognise you, Mr Hoskins, despite your beard.'

'What does Schroeder want exactly?'

'He will tell you when he arrives, Mr Hoskins. It may be necessary for you to remain in West Berlin for a day or two more with your young lady. After that, arrangements will be made. I am authorised to give you this in the meantime. Count it please. You will find five hundred West German marks in all.'

He handed Hoskins an envelope and watched him slide out the wad of paper. Then, as his victim had both hands occupied in sifting the notes, the stranger took from his breast pocket a blade, no broader than a nail file. His hand went up behind Hoskins' neck as the corporal counted the notes with bowed head. At the moment that the soundtrack of the film rose in volume, the stranger's hand moved in a short and powerful movement, driving the blade home at the base of the cerebral cortex. Corporal Hoskins died without a sound. The stranger took the banknotes, which were in danger of sliding from the dead man's lap on to the floor. Then, standing up, he altered the angle of the torso a little so that it leaned against the corner of the seat, the head to one side on the shoulder but the eyes open as they watched the film.

Turning away casually, the killer walked down the length of the auditorium, raised the bar of the emergency exit doors, and stepped out, blinking, into the strong July light of the Berlin afternoon.

At seven o'clock that evening, Hanne Rune came out of the

Bulow-Strasse turning. She walked up the Potsdamer-Strasse and crossed over to the dingy little side-street with its apartment block of grimed brick.

The lift with its dark-stained wood and worn linoleum was large enough for only three or four people at a time. Its cracked mirror reflected the wan adolescent weariness of Hanne Rune's young face and the fineness of her mane of fair hair.

As she was about to press the button of the lift, a man stepped into it, holding the gate until two companions had followed him. They were strangers to the girl. One of the men pressed the button for the top floor. Another stood with his back to the gate of the lift, as if to prevent it being opened from outside. Hanne Rune looked up, the first pang of terror in her heart.

It was as if she had given the signal for her own destruction. One man seized her from behind, pinning her arms together. The second man forced something into her mouth. The third man, who stood with his back to the lift gate, took no part in overpowering her. The girl twisted and struggled to cry out as the lift passed the fifth and sixth floors. Only the widening of her eyes expressed her panic at what was to happen next.

When the lift stopped at the top of the building, she was still twisting and bowing her body in a vain attempt to break free. The men carried her bodily along the short passage and up the steps to the well-head. Her foot kicked and caught a fire-bucket of sand on its wall-bracket.

In the last moments that remained to her on the flat roof of the apartments, Hanne Rune began to scream wildly through the cotton which packed her mouth. Her vision was of blue evening sky and a geometry of office blocks, broken here and there by weed-grown wastes near the frontier wall.

Her feet were clear of the ground and her mouth was free of the gag at last. As she drew breath to cry out, the three men threw her clear of the parapet, far out above the vacant lot at the rear of the building. Without waiting to see the frail body spin down and smash on the rubble below, they ran to the well-head and the lift with its gate wedged open.

By the time that the first child playing in the street responded to the fracturing impact, the three killers had disappeared into the shopping crowds among the greengrocers and stalls of the Potsdamer-Strasse. Yet there was one witness.

Debby, crossing from the shops through the slow traffic, saw the three men walk quickly from the apartment block. Though they were strangers to her, she thought instinctively of the man who had brought the message from Captain Schroeder. As she walked slowly towards the building, she saw the children gathering at the rear, looking at a girl who might have resembled Debby in type and appearance.

For ten seconds or so, Debby stared at the broken body with its fair hair, sprawled on the rubble, and saw that her own death had been enacted there. Knowing only that she dared not go near her room and with no idea of where to hide, she turned and crossed the street again, weeping with shock and fear.

16

Major Corrigan stood up and laid a hand on the old man's shoulder. He said something which was inaudible to Elliott beyond the glass of the observation panel. As soon as he had entered the ward to begin his gentle questioning of Andor, Corrigan had exercised his right to turn off the audio communication with those outside. Andor sat on his little chair as if he had not heard a word spoken to him. The major turned and came across to the door.

If he felt surprised to find Elliott waiting as he closed the door behind him, Corrigan showed no sign of it. He was buttoning a pair of gloves which he wore with his uniform even in summer. Without looking up, he said, 'It seems that you got your man.'

'Not unless your little *tête à tête* just now produced something fresh.' Elliott watched Corrigan expectantly. 'The files at Ashridge had nothing on him. Nothing at all. As far as MI6 is concerned, he never existed.'

Corrigan glanced at him innocently.

'Not Andor,' he said. 'I was thinking of the late Corporal Hoskins. I won't say the method was particularly subtle but, I grant you, it was effective.'

Elliott stared through the glass panel, watching the old man who sat on the chair, shoulders drooping a little, apparently too apathetic to move.

'Save your congratulations for Schroeder,' he said. 'I was at Ashridge when it happened. In any case, we don't deal with a breach of the Official Secrets Act in that way. Hoskins could have told us more about Schroeder than he could have told Schroeder about us.'

'You think so?' The mask of innocence on Corrigan's face had scarcely slipped. 'Then if you didn't settle the account with Hoskins . . .'

'I was in England, Pat. At Ashridge.'

'My apologies. Then, if your people didn't settle the account, you are the most unfortunate man alive.'

'Why?'

'Because the death of Hoskins is booked to you by the fellows at Langley – and even by Colonel Rubin and his friends. Don't be modest about it, Sam. They admire you for it.'

'Why?'

'Because it means you've screwed Schroeder. Who else would gain from the elimination of Hoskins but you? It shows the other side that you were on to him from the start. It raises doubts about any two-bit agent of the kind under their control. It wipes out the credibility of Schroeder and every operation with which his name is associated. I should think Rubin will be grateful to you. To make his East German comrades take a long walk off a short plank seems to be one of the few pleasures left to him in life.'

'British intelligence had nothing whatever to do with Hoskins after he disappeared.'

Corrigan shrugged.

'You'll never duck the credit for it, Sam. Mind you, the business with the girl was nasty. Even the boys at Langley don't care for that sort of thing. Not that you'll hear any complaints about it from them. The way they see it, she was probably one of yours, after all.'

Corrigan was exercising his most cherished talent, that of an advocate with a well constructed case who cuts and pierces his adversary's defence effortlessly. It was not true contempt which Corrigan showed towards him, Elliott thought, but the professional duellist's pleasure in the exercise of his skill.

'Have you finished with Andor?'

'For today,' said Corrigan more equably. 'He's had about enough. When they're young you can get good results as they tire. You can't push a man of Andor's age like that.'

'I've got a couple of things for him.' Elliott glanced through the glass panel again. 'Things that should have been put right a long time ago. Better late than never.'

Corrigan sat down on the chair by the glass panel.

'Don't hit him,' he said coldly. 'He says you hit him a couple of times in the first interrogation. That was a dumb move, Sam, at his age. Really dumb.'

'I pushed him into a chair, that's all.'

'And if he'd fallen?'

'He didn't.'

'No,' said Corrigan quietly. 'And, by the way, the mark he's got is on his face, just below the cheekbone. Left-hand side from a right-hand punch.'

'Be your age, Pat.' Elliott paused, his hand on the handle of the door. 'I'm not likely to damage him until – or unless – I must.'

'I hope not.' Corrigan spoke quietly, as if to himself. 'I hope not. For all our sakes.'

Andor looked up as his second interrogator entered the

room. He showed no apprehension nor much interest. Elliott wondered if he had been sedated and made a mental note to check the chart outside. He drew up a chair and sat opposite the old man. He switched on the audio connection. Unlike Corrigan, he wanted to share the moment that was coming. Andor's secret, revealed by the files at Ashridge, was about to become common knowledge.

Andor watched him, the blue eyes wide and moist, wandering a little like a man with a fever.

'I am tired,' he said plaintively. 'I will answer no more today.'

The major's mouth moved, as if in a slight smile of reassurance.

'I have only two points,' he said gently. 'Two very small details. Perhaps you know nothing about them. If you tell me so, I shall believe you. If you will answer, I promise that you shall not be disturbed again tonight. I will even arrange for you to have a copy of today's *Berliner Morgenpost*. It doesn't do for a man to be cut off entirely from the events around him.'

Andor's round pale face seemed more animated by this promise.

'What is it you wish to know?'

For the first time since he had surrendered himself, he appeared willing to talk of whatever his captors wished.

'I want you to tell me about Clerk Maxwell,' said Elliott gently. 'Anything at all that you may know about him.'

'I know nothing.' The old man's face fell again, a look of ill-controlled disappointment at not being able to earn the reward held out to him. 'Who is he?'

'Who *was* he?' The major corrected him gently. 'He's dead now.'

'I am sorry the man is dead. Is he anything to me?'

Elliott shook his head.

'He died a long time ago, Herr Andor. In 1879 to be precise. James Clerk Maxwell.'

'I know nothing of him,' Andor said quietly. 'Do you suggest any reason that I should?'

'No,' said the major quietly. 'None at all.'

He waited in silence until Andor, shifting with uncharacteristic impatience in his chair, asked, 'Is that your only question, Major Elliott?'

Elliott made a reassuring movement of his hands.

'There is one more, a very minor detail. Would you be so good as to remind me of the subject-matter covered by the first law of thermodynamics?'

On the far side of the observation mirror, Major Corrigan's pulse quickened. He knew by the question, as much as from the change in Andor's expression, that the initiative had at last passed from the old man to his interrogators. Andor forced a scowl.

'There is no purpose in such questions,' he said gruffly. 'Why do you ask?'

Elliott leaned forward a little, as if in great confidentiality.

'Because I want you to tell me, Dr Andor.'

'I will not answer foolish questions.'

They sat in silence for a moment. Then Elliott spoke, as if beginning a long explanation.

'You wish me to believe that you possess certain power. In order that I may believe you, I have asked one or two questions. If you will not answer them, how can I be persuaded?'

'The questions are foolish.' Andor was now clinging to his reiterated defence.

Elliott nodded.

'Then I will ask a different question. What is the principle of the conservation of energy when applied to heat?'

There was no doubt whatever now, Corrigan thought, that the old man's eyes and mouth conveyed utter confusion and incipient panic. Something had happened to destroy his composure and leave him, for the first time, at a greater disadvantage than his adversaries.

The wooden chair scraped the floor as Andor got up and walked away with his back to the major.

'Let me tell you what it is,' Elliott continued in the same quiet and unrelenting tone. 'That principle is the first law of thermodynamics, as enunciated by Clerk Maxwell.'

The old man said nothing. He stood with his back to Elliott and his head slightly bowed, tense as if expecting a blow. The major got up, drew a folded copy of the *Berliner Morgenpost* from his pocket and laid it on the bed.

'I promised you this, Herr Andor, whether or not you were able to answer my questions. I hope you will now believe that every promise and every warning given to you in this place will be fulfilled.'

As his visitor withdrew and the door closed, Andor fell upon the newspaper, turning the pages rapidly, then settling down to read it from the first word to the last. Elliott was not unaware of the dependence which could be induced in the prisoner upon the one man who brought the news of the world outside to the place of solitary confinement. He went back to the adjoining room and confronted Corrigan, revealing his discovery after all.

'Congratulations,' said Corrigan laconically. 'Game, set, and match.' The two officers were at last confident and at ease in one another's company. Elliott smiled.

'A physicist who can't recall the first law of thermodynamics and wasn't even able to recognise it when it was described to him. Does that make it better or worse?'

Corrigan had no doubt.

'Better. Unless our friend Andor has confederates, which so far doesn't seem to be the case, he's put up nothing but an elaborate trick.'

'The plutonium flask was genuine enough.'

'But insufficient. That gadget in the house at Dahlem was nothing. Scrap metal left over from the German A-bomb programme of World War II. He'd have needed a heavy engineering works to finish the metalwork. As for the rest . . .'

'The plutonium flask was real enough.'

'Opportunity,' said Corrigan thoughtfully. 'Who knows?

If there's no more than that, we're safe. You can't fuel Armageddon with an empty flask. If that's all there is.'

17

Elliott locked the car door and turned towards the outer stairway leading up to the maisonette, the quarters allotted to him as a single officer. In the long summer twilight of central Europe, warmth and stillness settled over the wooded gardens. The British military quarters were on the northern edge of the Grunewald, among woodland groves and forest paths. Yet the spruce and evergreen, the firs and monkey-puzzle had an incongruous air of suburban Camberley or Aldershot. Even the English voices and the children's laughter from the nearby windows seemed to give the lie to this military enclave surrounded by Soviet power.

With the passage of time, Elliott thought less and less about the pattern of his own life. It was at this moment, taking the key from his pocket and returning to the empty house or flat, that its memories were present. Other men thought of him as one whose life had been shattered by his young wife's death and the five years of a widower's solitude. The truth was different. His life had been cut, rather than shattered, into two distinct existences. The break had been clean and precise. A police message and the bald details of her car's collision with a lorry. They had not even asked him to identify her body. From time to time he felt guilty that the break had been so easy to him, that resignation rather than grief remained uppermost in his thoughts. He had no doubt whatever that men who saw the truth of this deduced from his conduct the callous professionalism of the interrogator. Their judgment was wrong, he believed. Elliott had only the self-assurance of one to whom life had done its worst and who was not easily moved by its future threats. He did not complain. If this was indeed the worst, he felt that he had got off lightly.

At the foot of the concrete stairs he paused to select the right key from several on the ring, putting the past and the present of Dr Andor from his mind. At that moment he heard the girl's voice.

'Major Elliott.'

It was a statement, not a question, and Elliott knew even before he turned round who she must be.

Debby stood by the tree behind which she had been waiting. The coquettish little bun of her blonde hair had fallen in a dishevelled mane, the fashionably threadbare look of jeans and sweater was crumpled and askew. Streaks of brown dust showed on her feet and on the pallor of her face. Yet there was a crude nobility in the slope of her brow and long nose, a last reserve of anger in her dark eyes.

'I want Jimmy Hoskins,' she said quietly. 'I want to know where he is.'

Elliott felt no alarm or anger at her arrival. Unexpectedly the sight of Debby stirred a remote sense of despair.

'You'd better come in,' he said, and led the way up the concrete steps to the door. He unlocked it and they stood in the long room of the maisonette with its square comfortable armchairs and neutral carpet. Debby faced him again, implacable for a moment longer.

'I want him!' she said more shrilly. 'Where is he? What have you done to him? You, and Rubin, and Schroeder?'

Her voice trembled at the last syllable and she burst into tears, weeping gently but without any attempt to control it. Elliott, the accuser and interrogator, found himself the recipient of her anger and grief. In the security ward of the hospital, in the garrison offices at Spandau, in the prisons of Malaya where the Chinese 'bandits' were held, he would have reacted instinctively. Tired and depressed by hours of talking to Andor, he faced her in different circumstances. Samuel Elliott confronted by a girl's misery in his own drawing-room and shorn of his customary authority. With the natural instinct of humanity, he put his arm round her shoulders as she bowed her head and wept with her hands over her face.

'He can't be found,' Elliott said evasively.

'And me?' The words were a little muffled as she continued to hide her face. 'What about me? They killed that other girl. I saw her. They thought it was me.'

She feared for Hoskins but she was terrified for herself. The cold certainty that her own death had been planned by men who were expert in such matters checked the luxury of her sobs for a moment.

'They'll kill me,' she whispered. 'I know they will. I've got no one. Only Jimmy Hoskins . . .'

And then the tears began once more.

Elliott stared at her uncertainly, almost with distaste. To see and hear the sufferings of those who deserved to suffer at his hands moved him not the least. Now he was like the bomber pilot who sees the burnt flesh of children peeling from them, the old weeping for the young, and the survivors burying their dead. In that moment, the cold zeal of the east, the braggarts of capitalism in the west, Schroeder and Rubin, Corrigan and Bonnell-Thornton, Andor himself, seemed equally repugnant. The reality was a girl of twenty, fearful for her lover and terrified for herself, weeping without hope.

Against every rule of his profession, Elliott put his arms round Debby and held her to him as if trying to reassure an inconsolable child. They held one another in a strange asexual embrace, the need of one body for the comfort of another.

'Jimmy Hoskins,' Elliott said gently. 'He's dead. We think Schroeder killed him because he went to the Russians. It wasn't our people. So far as I know it was no one on our side at all.'

As he expected, the shock of it stopped her tears. With her cheek still resting against his jacket she became calmer and more sensible. Presently, she began a hesitant explanation.

'We talked about it,' she said distantly. 'We always knew it might happen. But he said there was no other way. Only going over to get away from all this. To be together there.'

'He should never have begun it,' Elliott held her lightly. 'It ends like this more often than the papers tell you.'

'Colonel Rubin,' she said thoughtfully. 'He wanted to tell Rubin about the man who gave himself up. The one with the bomb.'

'Colonel Rubin knew anyway. It was pointless.'

She moved away from him and sat down in one of the square comfortable armchairs. Elliott poured some whisky from a decanter, added a little water, and handed it to her. He sat on the arm of the chair and talked to her, warding off the return of her grief.

'You'll be safe,' he said, taking her hands in his to emphasise his sincerity. 'That's a promise. You'll be safe now.'

Even as he spoke he thought of the absurd boast of safety in a city which might be destroyed by blast and fire-storm in a few more days.

Debby got up and, as if by instinct, found her way to the bathroom. Without asking or insisting, she ran the water into the bath. Elliott wondered if she knew the layout of the maisonette from familiarity with another of the officers' quarters in the garrison complex. She returned in a little while, still wearing the shabby jeans tight on her thin legs and hips, the blouse with its marks of dust. The blonde hair was now pinned up again as it had been when Elliott once saw her with Hoskins. She sat on the carpet by his chair, waiting.

'I'll get you something to eat,' he said. 'You must be very hungry.'

He went into the kitchen and began opening tins. Debby followed him barefoot and stood watching and silent, like a child. The awkwardness of strangers thrown together in this domestic routine began to grow between them. It was as Elliott took a saucepan of boiling water from the ring that Debby said, 'I could work for you. Here.'

'You don't have to,' he said gently. 'You'll be taken care of.'

She continued to watch him in silence. Then she found

the plates and glasses in the cupboard and carried them through to the other room.

'What's going to happen to me?'

Her voice came from beyond the kitchen door.

'I don't know,' Elliott said. 'You'll be all right, though. Safe from Schroeder and his kind.'

That seemed to satisfy her. When the meal was ready, he had little appetite. While the girl ate, Elliott watched. Though she had probably gone without food since leaving the apartment block off the Potsdamer-Strasse, she ate with a self-conscious gentility. He had not the least idea of her expectations. In the world of Corporal Hoskins, it might be supposed that Debby would pay with her body for the kindnesses done her. Yet to Elliott she had qualities which were superior to anything that world offered. Hers was the nobility of humble fortitude.

'If you want to go to garrison headquarters tonight,' he said, 'I'll drive you there when you've eaten. Or you can sleep here in the spare room tonight. Then we'll make the arrangements in the morning.'

'I don't mind staying,' she said simply, 'I'll be safe here. It's the last place that Schroeder would come to.'

She spoke without innuendo and without presumption. What arrangements, he wondered, did she expect on the following day?

When the meal was over, he turned on the Tagesschau and they watched the news of the day. There was nothing to suggest that the mystery of Andor had been revealed to the press. In twenty-four hours or so all that would change. It had to. Elliott knew that in a little while the public media must be brought into the uneasy alliance of the city's occupying powers.

It was just after eleven when he turned off the television, put the lights out in the main room, and went to bed. The door of the other room was slightly ajar. Debby, in her blouse and pants, lay on the cover of the single bed, sleeping in total exhaustion.

As Elliott turned on the light in his own room and began

to undress, he knew that he was guilty of a misjudgment which his profession never forgave. Personal involvement. He smiled at the absurdity of it, the memory of the lecture received in Malaya. The jovial major with his knowing advice, not quite able to tell the trainees the whole truth. 'Your subjects may often be attractive or pathetic. You will be tempted to take their part, in one way or another. It is the one temptation to which you must never surrender. The face of the enemy appears in many guises.'

Personal involvement. It was, as Elliott had learnt, the flaw of the interrogator who had lost heart for his role. As he thought of the past two hours, he knew that the comfort which he had offered Debby was, in truth, the consolation he sought for himself. The simple act of holding another living creature. For the first time he could admit how far the routine of the beleaguered and assertive capital had corroded his own self-sufficiency.

He woke twice, soon after going to sleep, and thought of the girl in the other room. Then he slept more deeply. It was not movement which woke him but the sense of her being there, as if she might have been watching for a long while. With her hair spread loose, Debby was lying on the other half of the bed still dressed in the same clothes. She had been asleep, but woke as she felt him stir. Half-consciously, he held back the blanket and drew her to him. As he began to sleep again, it crossed his mind that it was the embrace one gave to a child who was in fear of the dark. Yet his own fear of the darkness was perhaps greater than hers. Without bothering to debate the matter in his own mind, he knew that his life for the next few weeks, or days, must be one of divided interests and loyalties.

He got up in the morning, while she was still sleeping, and went into the kitchen. Though it was full daylight, the sun striking through the pine trees outside, it was earlier than his usual time. Debby woke when he went back with coffee and toast. After the events of the night there was a complicity between them. By such simple acts they had united Bonnell-Thornton and Corrigan with Schroeder and Rubin as hunters of the prey.

This time it was Debby who put her arms round him. Elliott kissed her lightly, went out with the tray, hesitated, and came back. Only then did they make love for the first time.

He stayed with her until it was time for him to go to Spandau.

'Wait here,' he touched her face. 'Don't answer the door or the phone. No one can get in. If there's any trouble, ring me at this number. Give any name you like but remember the call may be recorded. All right?'

She nodded and he went out to collect his briefcase and begin his journey.

For two days their routine worked well. To divide his life so completely into its two halves was something Elliott had practised for periods in the past. When his wife had been killed, he had lived the life of a professional intelligence officer to the exclusion of everything else, and his work had been salvation. This time it would be easier. Andor would make it easier. Either the old man would be proved a fraud or the city would be destroyed next week. The simplicity of it suited Elliott's present mood.

The first warning came from Corrigan. Despite the differences between the two men, their relationship lacked habitual antipathy. Now it seemed that Corrigan, with the beak-nose and angular glasses of a caricatured attorney, spoke in genuine friendship. They stood together in the transport yard after one of Bonnell-Thornton's ponderous briefings.

'Do you have guests, Sam?' Corrigan asked casually.

'Guests?'

'Yes. House guests, in your quarters.'

'No,' said Elliott shortly. 'It's hardly the time for that.'

Corrigan nodded, as if satisfied.

'I thought so. Intruders, perhaps?'

Elliott looked at him, still not understanding what Corrigan could have discovered.

'What exactly, Pat, are you talking about?'

'You were over here last night with Bonnell-Thornton

until about eight?'

'Yes.'

Corrigan nodded again.

'Right. I went by your place and thought to have a private word. I didn't know you were here. I rang the bell. No answer.'

'So?'

'Just before I rang the bell, I heard water running down the drainpipe. It seemed you were in but not answering. But, of course, you weren't in at all.'

'Some of us occasionally like to have our quarters cleaned by the daily help,' Elliott said smoothly.

'At half-past six in the evening?'

Elliott dropped his voice a little.

'Do I understand from this, Pat, that you have your allies under surveillance?'

Corrigan glanced round to make sure that no one else was in earshot.

'Be your age, Sam! If you want to screw the help, that's your business. But it just looked as if someone was in your apartment during your absence. If it's an intruder, you're dumb not to say so. If you've started picking up women at this stage of the game with Andor, then you're even dumber.'

'As it happens, Pat, you're wrong on both counts. Still, you're right on one thing. It is my business.'

Corrigan smiled.

'That's why I came to you, Sam, rather than to the good Bonnell-Thornton.'

18

With ten days of the fourteen still to run, Bonnell-Thornton conceded Elliott's demand that an attempt to identify Andor should be made through a carefully vetted television appeal. It went out on the Tagesschau of the SFB network with photographs and a bland commentary. The confused old man who had wandered into the British hospital was known only as Andor. The telephone number for callers was that of the 'outer office' of British military intelligence at the Olympic Stadium complex.

By the following evening there had been a dozen calls. Most were from cranks. Two were pathetic inquiries after long-lost husbands. Not one of them had the least reference to Andor. Nothing had been said of the prisoner's surrender at the military police post, nor of his present place of custody. Twenty-four hours after the appeal, Elliott admitted to himself that the brigadier had been right. Nothing had been gained and a story had been spread which, in the long run, would do no good.

Andor, alone in the observation ward and under constant surveillance, asked for nothing and volunteered no further information.

As the long twilight of the summer day began, Elliott stood at the window of his office and stared across at the old red brick of the military prison. The Soviet guards with their machine-pistols still guarded the last senile Nazi. He was thinking of Debby, the secret places of his life, his own imprudence in keeping her. The phone rang. It was the duty officer.

'A call coming in, sir. Will you take it?'

'Who else is likely to if I don't?' said Elliott irritably.

'This one's different, sir.' The lieutenant spoke reprovingly. 'I think you ought to hear it.'

There was a pause, lasting so long that Elliott thought the connection must have been broken. Then he heard a woman's voice. She was young rather than old, he thought, but not very young. Her English was accented by native German and acquired American, suggesting that she had learnt it in the east rather than the west.

'Who is that, please?' she asked. 'To whom am I speaking?'

Her voice had the pedantic accuracy of a teacher or a propagandist.

'This is Major Elliott, British Military Hospital,' he said, using the description he had prepared for his callers. 'Will you give me your name, please?'

'Martina Hansen.' Elliott thought she spoke with the softness of one who fears being overhead. 'Are you the doctor who has a patient by the name of Andor?'

'We have a patient of that name,' said Elliott evasively. 'He appears to be suffering from loss of memory.'

'It is he whose photograph was shown on the television?'

'Yes.'

'What more do you know of him?'

'Only that his name appears to be Herr Andor. Can you confirm that?'

In the darkened window glass he confronted his over-dressed reflection.

'Yes.' She dropped her voice as if from guilt at revealing so much. 'His name is Karl Rainer Andor.'

Elliott hoped that the duty officer had had the wit to record the incoming call for later examination.

'How do you know?'

The girl was sure enough of his interest to answer with a laugh.

'I should know that better than anyone, Major Elliott. Your patient, Karl Rainer Andor, is my father.'

The answer came with such speed and finality that he feared she might put down the phone in a flourish of victory.

'Help us to help him,' he said quickly.

'No, Major Elliott. I regret I can do no more for you.'

'You could come and identify him, at least.' He was talking faster now, sensing that she was about to ring off. 'You might visit him.'

'I could not do that, Major Elliott. Not even if I wished.'

'Where are you?' he said abruptly.

'In Babelsberg,' she said with amused indifference.

'Babelsberg in the eastern zone?'

'In the German Democratic Republic, Major Elliott. If I am to identify my father for you, it would be necessary for you to bring him here.'

In Elliott's mind there rose the image of Colonel Rubin, prompting at Martina Hansen's side.

'No,' he said abruptly. 'You have told me far too little about the patient to make such a thing possible.'

'Then our reunion must be postponed a little, must it not, Major?'

'Give me the names of any other living relatives of Herr Andor.'

'He is Dr Andor,' said the young woman quietly. 'His sister, my aunt Sybille, was living in Dresden eight years ago. I have been married and divorced since then, when I last saw her. She may still be alive.'

Now she had begun to tease him by her indifference, as if in a flirtation.

'What was your father's profession?'

'He was an archivist, Major Elliott.'

'An archivist?'

'Yes,' said Martina Hansen plaintively. 'There is no reason why a man should not be an archivist by profession.'

In whatever time was left, Elliott decided, he must pin her to the truth.

'If your father is to visit you in Babelsberg, I shall need some means of getting in touch with you, Frau Hansen. An address, or better still a telephone number.'

'That will not be necessary, Major. I should prefer that you did not attempt to write or phone me. I have your number. I will telephone you again in a little while.'

'Before you do . . .' he said. But in the middle of the phrase he heard the line go dead. Whether Martina Hansen had put the phone down or whether the call had been interrupted by the eavesdroppers at the frontier was an open question. All the same, it would be useful to know whether she had called him at Rubin's suggestion or not.

Elliott gave his instructions to the duty officer and then began to dial Bonnell-Thornton's number. As he did so, the paradoxes of the divided city plagued him. East and west alike watched one another's television broadcasts. The workers of Pankow or Treptow toiled all day among industrial slogans of the Marxist-Leninist state. At night they luxuriated for several hours in the coloured dream-world of capitalist mythology. Most were divided for ever from the streets and people on the other side of the wall. Yet the telephone services ran between the forbidden zones without interruption.

The major sat on the edge of the desk, the receiver of the portable cordless phone in his hand. He sighed and waited without enthusiasm to impart the details of his conversation to Bonnell-Thornton.

It was late by the time that Elliott left the garrison headquarters and drove home through the little streets of Spandau to the Heer-Strasse crossing. The timbered and balconied houses, the unprepossessing shops of the narrower thoroughfares looked deserted in the long summer dusk.

Debby waited, as she always did, beyond the living-room of the maisonette, as if to conceal herself more easily in the presence of an intruder. She did not question the delay in his return. It occurred to Elliott that she must have grown used to such unpredictability in the case of Corporal Hoskins. That Hoskins deserted her casually and temporarily for other women was a matter of common knowledge among his fellow NCOs. Whether it was known to Debby herself was a question that Elliott had no desire to put.

It was not until they had eaten and sat together in an easy embrace that the girl made some allusion to his profession and its demands.

'What happens,' she asked, 'supposing that a man refuses to tell you what you want?'

Elliott smiled at the naïveté of the inquiry.

'He doesn't refuse. Not in the end.'

'How do you make him?'

'I don't. Not in the way you mean. The urge to confess – sooner or later – is one of the strongest human impulses. It's bravado – not conscience. The greater problem is to shut them up, not to make them talk.'

This seemed to satisfy her. Debby undressed, walked naked to the other room, and waited for her lover to follow. For much of the night, while she slept, Elliott lay awake and watched her. In the shadows of the bedroom he saw the uncertain shape of her face and head. Once, half sleeping, the images of Debby and the voice of Martina Hansen coalesced in his mind. By the time that the sky grew light, somewhere beyond the Tiergarten trees and the drab streets of the eastern city, he was ready to get up.

He woke Debby more than two hours later, just before he left for Spandau.

'I must go back,' she said. 'I need some things from the other apartment. Can you take me?'

'Not today.' He kissed her briefly as he sat on the bed. 'Soon. But not today. We'll have to be careful.'

The phone rang in the other room and he walked towards it, trying to remember the name of the duty officer who might be calling at this hour of the morning. But it was Corrigan.

'Can we meet, Sam, before you go to Spandau? I have a message for discussion with Bonnell-Thornton. I'd like to explain it to you first.'

'Where are you?'

'Parked in the Schloss-Strasse,' Corrigan said. 'I'll see you in the vestibule of the Egyptian Museum in half an hour. Best not meet in the avenue with the eyes of the world on us.'

Even at his most amiable, Corrigan never lost the tone of a prosecuting attorney. There was a puritanism in his nature which despised the social graces as hypocrisy and politeness as flattery.

'I can find us a quiet corner at Spandau.'

'Here, if you don't mind,' Corrigan said.

Elliott looked at his watch and hesitated. Corrigan spoke more softly.

'It's about a certain Karl Rainer Andor, Sam, presently in your care.'

'What about him?'

'He's been dead two months,' Corrigan said. 'He died in a fire in Argentina. That's official. The Ezeiza processing plant. Come on, get over here. I want to talk about it.'

Without waiting for a reply, Corrigan put the phone down, knowing that he had won the trivial skirmish of authority.

19

The Egyptian Museum at Charlottenburg was a monument to German archaeology of the Kaiser's era. It stood opposite the royal palace, among balconied terraces and the chestnut trees of the Schloss-Strasse. When Elliott arrived, Corrigan was waiting in the round marble vestibule. They went up the curve of the staircase with its black and gold rails to the exhibition floor above. In the grey-carpeted hall, the head of Nefertiti stared from its glass case. Elliott gave a moment's recognition to the painted brilliance of the sculpture with its flawed eye and pharaonic profile.

The museum had only just opened, so that the room was still empty, a single warder standing beyond earshot in the archway which led to the rest of the display.

'We got the details of Martina Hansen's call last night,' Corrigan said quietly. 'Thank you for those. We also got a message from CIA control at Langley. When the telecast went out, West German intelligence responded direct to them. If you believe the files of the BND in Cologne, three of their nationals died in a fire at Ezeiza, near Buenos Aires, a couple of months back. The plutonium processing plant. There was an accident in one of the laboratories. Two of the men who died were nuclear physicists on a long secondment from Karlsruhe. Vogel and Nunvar. The other was Karl Rainer Andor.'

Elliott touched the pale brown tie of his uniform, to check

if the knot had slipped.

'Then who the devil are we holding at the military hospital?'

'Karl Rainer Andor,' said Corrigan simply. 'An archivist at Ezeiza, presumably. The project that caused the fire wasn't known to Argentina or West Germany. The aim of the Argentines – perhaps the Germans – was to eliminate the three men. They thought they'd succeeded. We know they were wrong.'

'Our man is the real Andor?'

'Down to his very fingerprints and dental plate,' Corrigan said. 'When the fire was over, they simply divided the ashes into three piles and buried them in the Moreno cemetery as Walter Vogel, Reinhard Nunvar, and Karl Rainer Andor. Our private information is that the execution squad went up in flames at the same time. That's why no one knew that they'd missed killing Andor. By that time, this whole thing was in motion. They killed every man involved except Andor. But for him, the bomb would have gone off and no one would even have known why.'

'Could Vogel and Nunvar have constructed a device?'

'Easily,' Corrigan said. 'Not only *could* but, apparently, *did*.'

Elliott went across to the window of the grey-carpeted room and gazed out at the grand terraces of imperial Berlin.

'There are two things I don't believe in, Pat,' he said at last. 'The first is the belief that little old men like Andor could build bombs in their cellars – even if they happen to be nuclear physicists. The second thing I don't believe in is a scenario. Nazi scientists escape to Argentina in 1945 and build a bomb to avenge Hitler – forty years too late. You see?'

Corrigan shook his head, watching the museum warder cautiously.

'We're not talking about Hitler and 1945, Sam. Neither Nunvar nor Vogel was geriatric. This caper began in the 1960s. Check your own files at Ashridge. Since 1968 the

West German atomic research facility at Karlsruhe has supplied reprocessed fuel and reactors to Argentina. The reactor at Atucha – the MZFR – is identical to our own on the Savannah River. It's designed to yield weapons-grade plutonium. In return, the Argentines agreed to let West German scientists work on weapons technology at Ezeiza. By the end of 1982 the plant was producing enough plutonium for twenty bombs a year. The Argentines train at Karlsruhe – the Germans work on the production of nuclear weapons at Ezeiza. Perfect. The 1954 treaty forbids Germany from building nuclear weapons on its own territory. There's nothing to stop their scientists building them elsewhere. One thing you can bet on, Sam. If every other country in the world can get its hands on the damn things, these guys won't be left out.'

Another incoming jet, following the Tegel flight-path low over the western city, blotted out the rest of Corrigan's words.

'You think Andor and the other two were part of this?'

Corrigan shrugged.

'Vogel and Nunvar certainly were. Andor? I don't know. Word has it that Vogel and Nunvar were involved in the first test of an Argentine bomb. You won't need the MI6 files this time, Sam. Look up any major newspaper for October 1979. There was one hell of a flash and a bang in the South Atlantic on 22 September. Your government and ours put out a lot of heavy smoke about it being a South African test with the aid of the Israelis or a Soviet nuclear sub blowing up. As anyone at Langley knows, there was a surveillance satellite overhead at the time, watching the Argentines at play. The test went out of control and a few people died – then and after. It set back their programme by several years. Lucky for you, Sam, in a way. Just try and imagine how the Falklands war might have been, with nuclear weaponry on both sides.'

Elliott ignored this.

'Andor's plutonium,' he said. 'Was that from Argentina?'

'Knowing their level of security, Sam, it may well have been. Except that whoever Andor may be, he's not the man who burnt to death at Ezeiza back in May. Unless you believe in ghosts.'

'Not in ghosts, Pat. Nor in disembodied voices either. I'd like to see Martina Hansen, face to face. And I'd like to confront her with the man she says is her father.'

Corrigan shrugged and turned towards the stairs.

'Well, for God's sake don't take the old man over to the other side. They want him even worse than you do.'

'He's not going anywhere, Pat,' said Elliott firmly. 'Least of all to Colonel Rubin. What we do with him now is another matter. An archivist! He wouldn't know a nuclear warhead from a Christmas pudding.'

They went down the stairs and into the sunlight of the wide avenue of houses.

'What sort of an archivist?' Elliott said suddenly. 'Did you get anything on that?'

Corrigan looked across the street.

'We're working on it. I'll keep you informed.'

As he walked towards the car with Private Lucas reading at the wheel, Elliott's thoughts turned again to Martina Hansen. It was time to see what Colonel Rubin and his Soviet colleagues might yield.

20

In the glow of the standard lamp on carpet and polished wood, Elliott sat in his chair and felt the light, fragile pressure of the girl's shoulders against his knees. Debby had drawn her legs under her and was listening with more politeness than enthusiasm to the *Regenslieder* from the Brahms G major Sonata.

Presently she said, 'The man that Jimmy talked about – the prisoner – what will they do to him?'

'Nothing,' Elliott said casually. 'A confused old man.

He'll be taken to a hospital somewhere.'

'But he has to be questioned, surely?' Debby twisted her head round and looked at him.

'Of course,' he said.

'And you couldn't send him to a hospital until you knew that he was making up the story about the bombs?'

'No.' Elliott stroked her hair and looked down at her as she held his hand. Debby regarded the fingers and the palm as if she might be about to tell his fortune.

'You interrogate him,' she said, stating it as a fact. 'Him and people like him.'

'That's part of it,' he said.

Elliott knew perfectly well that her interest was not in Andor and the others. Debby was thinking of the hands which touched and caressed her. The same hands, to her, as those which bruised and broke their prisoner or strapped electrodes to cold perspiring flesh.

'You're wrong,' he contradicted her thoughts gently. 'It's done with words. In the last war, almost every spy who was caught – English and German – changed sides and operated as a double agent. Only the ones who wanted to be martyrs were carried out and shot at dawn.'

But she was not listening to him. The legend was what she chose to believe.

'Jimmy used to read,' Debby settled her back against his knees again, 'books about the Germans, Hitler and the rest. The ones that did the worst things loved their wives and children to the end.'

It fascinated her, he thought, that the caressing hands on her bare limbs at night could do such things as she imagined. There was no repulsion, no reproach in her voice. She would never plead with him on Andor's behalf. It was another world where she knew there was no place for her words.

'It's quite different,' he said. 'More like having an argument with someone. Much more like a court of law and the art of cross-examination. Lawyers make the best interrogators in time of war.'

'Would you ever do the other things?' Debby continued to read his palm with the same dispassionate curiosity.

'Yes.' If he lied, she would know at once. 'Should the choice be between the life of one terrorist and the life of one innocent person, then the terrorist must die. But it doesn't happen as neatly as that.'

'If one old man must die . . .'

'Then he must die,' Elliott said.

'Even in that way?'

'If it would save the innocent.'

Debby nodded, being now satisfied on the topic. She began to talk about Hoskins calmly, as if his death were merely a matter of record. A little while later she said, 'Jimmy never had a war, not a shot fired. He'd have seen more wounds and bodies if he'd been a nurse. But you've killed people. In Malaya and other places. He told me that.'

Hoskins, of course, was the sort of man to boast of deaths as trophies, even when they were the work of his commander. Elliott saw how easily the dead corporal would have drawn the girl into the same way of thinking.

'At such range and in such conditions, I couldn't tell you who was killed nor by whom the shots were fired – and nor could he.'

She had brought that other, separate part of his life into the privacy from which he habitually excluded it, the warm glow of the lamp on the tawny carpet and the mellow theme of the *Regenslieder*. The wraith of Andor seemed present in the soft air, mocking the girl's slim beauty and the flow of the violin. Elliott felt for the old man a bitterness that was brief but unbridled.

When they lay down together, the calmness of the previous evenings, the mutual consolation, enveloped them like a spell. It was relaxation and relief which held them rather than the intensity of their moment. Throughout it all however, Elliott knew instinctively that Debby pondered the mystery, the double life of her lover's hands.

21

The appointment with Colonel Rubin had been arranged, as usual, for the middle of the morning in Treptower Park. Elliott's driver followed the customary route through West Berlin to Checkpoint Charlie and there pulled over to one side, crossing by the lane reserved for military and diplomatic personnel. On such occasions the right of military vehicles belonging to the western powers to drive through the streets of East Berlin was a distinct convenience, Elliott thought. It was a right which had been challenged, begrudged, but at last conceded by the governments of the Soviet Union and the DDR. Nothing else remained of the fiction that Berlin was a single city jointly occupied by the four powers.

Even so, Elliott was still struck by the incongruity of seeing jeeps of the RAF Police or the RMP cruising among the Stalinist grandeur and red flags of the Karl-Marx Allee, the grand boulevard of a sovereign and hostile state.

On the western side of the checkpoint, he noticed that the sole British military presence was a sergeant in shirt-sleeve order, sitting in the sunlight of the control-room window with an open newspaper. On the far side he noticed as always the extreme youthfulness and the plump pallor of the DDR border guards.

Informal meetings with Rubin took place at the Soviet Memorial in Treptower Park. Like other members of his military intelligence, Rubin occupied an office in the KGB complex, built upon the old St Antonius Hospital at Karlshorst, a mile or so from the park.

The car passed down the restored imperial elegance of the Unter den Linden, the concrete towers and tourist shops of the Karl-Marx Allee. After the gaudy bustle of West Berlin, the empty stretches of pavement and silent sidestreets were like a quiet Sunday.

Treptow lay beyond the shabbier streets of brown buildings, dockside railways with barges and river steamers at the quays. The antiquated lorries of a Soviet troop convoy moved slowly across the Ost-Haven bridge towards the Warschauer-Strasse station and the trains to the east. Elliott noticed that the delay had been caused by the breakdown of the leading truck which was now pulled in at the side of the road with its engine cowl raised. It was part of his training to see and remember such things, the minutiae which went to make up the pattern of intelligence. A high rate of mechanical failure in Soviet transport had become an axiom of western military planning.

In the old bourgeois quarter of Treptow with its pleasure boats and cafés, the warm scent of pine from the thickly planted park filled the long suburban avenues. Elliott stopped the car at the gates and walked alone through the broad gravel paths with which the park had been laid since its transformation into a memorial.

Rubin was standing by the parapet at the top of the approach, beyond a broken arch of pink marble, embossed with hammer and sickle, and the two massive figures of Russian soldiers – father and son – bowed in grief. Like Elliott himself, Rubin was in uniform. A heavily built man, the square cut of the uniform, red tabs on khaki, and the wide flat hat unkindly exaggerated his bulk.

Punctilious in such matters, Elliott saluted first as the junior of the two officers. Rubin responded and then shook him by the hand. The cold impassive Russian of the propaganda cliché was a figure whom Elliott had never encountered in his dealings with the east. Rubin was a southerner, from the Crimea, yet even the Muscovite officers of the Berlin garrison had a warmth and frankness which Elliott sought in vain from some of his allies.

'I am so sorry, Mr Elliott, so sorry that I cannot come to Spandau today. So many people to see. It was impossible.'

Unlike the trainees of the KGB who cultivated American-accented English, Rubin spoke with the exaggerated Oxford intonation of the cultured Russian. As if it were a higher compliment, he always called Elliott by his civilian title rather than by his army rank.

'It was nothing,' Elliott said. 'No distance to speak of.'

They stood side by side at the balustrade. Below them the shallow valley of neat grass and concrete ran for several hundred yards to the white mausoleum and its figures on a mound of turf.

'I come here every two or three weeks,' said Rubin wistfully. 'I think of the five thousand men buried down there in their mass grave. The only place they could be put to rest in 1945. And I think that five thousand dead will be a small number compared to the worst that might happen. Tell me about your prisoner.'

Elliott felt the heat of the July morning draw perspiration under his tunic.

'I think you know all there is.' Though he had no intention of telling Rubin more than was necessary, there seemed no harm in repeating it. 'His name is Andor. Karl Rainer Andor. He has a sister living in Dresden and a daughter in Babelsberg. The device found in Dahlem was nothing more than an antique which opportunity put in his way. As for the plutonium, it remains a mystery.'

'You should not have pretended to be looking for a missing child at Staaken.' Rubin straightened up and faced him with a smile, shaking his head. 'Karen Silkwood! Did you think the KGB fellows would not check such a name? Had I been there, I should have taken your word as a friend. But you should not cross swords with the others. Did you find nothing more about Mr Andor?'

'No,' said Elliott, feeling his face grow warmer still.

'You did not know that he had worked in Argentina?' There was a light of unconcealed pleasure in Rubin's eyes as he watched his victim. 'You did not know that he had worked there and was thought to have died there?'

'No.' Elliott knew that there was nothing for it now but to cling to the lie, however discredited.

Rubin turned back and looked out over the mass grave again. He spoke gently, as if he might have believed Elliott after all.

'How remarkable. How remarkable that the Central Intelligence Agency should have passed their information to us and withheld it from you. You should be more careful in your choice of allies, Mr Elliott. In the end, you know, it is we Europeans – whatever our country – who share the closest interests.'

The smile had gone when Rubin looked round. Elliott's lie was unimportant to him now.

'I daresay the CIA will have informed London. There's no reason why the information should have reached me yet.'

Rubin appeared satisfied by this. The smile returned to his broad saturnine face.

'I expect that is what must have happened, Mr Elliott. Come with me. We will have some coffee and talk.'

Before they left, Rubin glanced back for a few seconds across the shallow enclosure in which the Red Army had buried its dead after the final battle for Berlin. Then he took Elliott's arm as they walked, like a long familiar friend. Rubin chuckled a little at what he was going to say next.

'I will tell you a story,' he said. 'It will amuse you, I think.'

'I'm sure it will,' Elliott said with distant politeness.

They walked down the broad gravel path between the warm odorous pine trees. Rubin began one of the anecdotes which he appeared to keep for Elliott's visits.

'There was an East German,' he said, smiling. 'A member of the Communist party. Most people in the DDR are not members and they try hard to recruit. You see?'

Elliott nodded, anxious to get the story done with. Rubin continued.

'One day the good German comrade came to the chairman of his branch and said that he had enlisted a new recruit. "Excellent," the chairman said. "As a reward, you are excused from attending party meetings." Such meetings are very tedious, Mr Elliott, and the good comrade was joyful to be excused them. You understand?'

Elliott nodded again, gently freeing his upper arm from Rubin's grip.

'So the good comrade went out and he found a second recruit. This time the chairman said, "You have done so well that we will reward you more richly still. You may now resign from the Communist party." The man was overjoyed at this. But though he was allowed to resign from the party he went on recruiting in the hope of further reward. Soon he brought his third recruit to the chairman. "Wonderful!" the chairman said. "How can we reward you this time? I know! We will give you a certificate to say that you never belonged to the Communist party." '

Rubin grinned more broadly, savouring the best moment of the joke.

'And so the good German comrade went out again. This time he came back with his fourth recruit. "Ah," said the chairman. "You have done an unprecedented thing and you shall have an unprecedented reward. It is an honour reserved for only our most diligent comrades. This time, we are going to give you back your original membership card of the Nazi party!" '

Rubin laughed loudly at his own story, looking at Elliott to see how he would take it. The major smiled courteously and forced a chuckle.

'You should be careful,' he said, as if joking. 'Stories like that might get you into trouble.'

Rubin's smile grew broader.

'Even if I tell you that I heard the story in Moscow from a member of the nomenclatura? Make no mistake, Mr Elliott, the DDR will fight for us, if that is necessary. But you cannot expect that the Soviet Union should forget so quickly the actions of Germany – East or West.'

The antipathy between many Soviet officers and their hosts was no secret to Elliott. Rubin had a relish for sharp-edged political humour. Despite the boast, it was unlikely that he had truly heard the story from a member of the nomenclatura.

They crossed the wooded boulevard of Alt Treptow to a

riverside café above the landing stage for the pleasure steamers.

'And your Mr Andor,' said Rubin as they went up the external stairs to the coffee room of the old picturesque building. 'Is he safe? You think he will not blow us all up? Eh?'

'I don't think he has the means,' said Elliott evasively. 'The plutonium flask and the bomb-casing were opportunist finds. If he had the means to blow us up, he would make more detailed demands by now. He does not make threats, Colonel, because he has not the means to enforce them. So runs the line of our reasoning in the matter.'

'Ah, reason!' said Rubin thoughtfully. 'One might trust British intelligence to be guided by reason.'

There was no mistaking the disappointment in his voice.

Elliott recognised the café as one which he and Rubin had visited before, normally reserved for tourists with hard currency and certain party members. Despite the summer morning outside the blinds were almost closed, the interior lit by a red glow. The low suspended ceiling of green formica, the yellow plastic moulding of the bar, even the tubular steel chairs, suggested a new and functional interior within the decayed walls of an older structure. Two girls, simply and cleanly groomed, served coffee behind the bar. Like so many of the young in the DDR, they seemed to Elliott excessively timid. It took an effort to identify this timidity as no more than a form of good manners long outmoded in the west. On a shelf behind the bar were a few bottles of spirit, for sale rather than consumption, and several souvenir rag-dolls. While Rubin got the coffee, the major bought himself a bottle of Bell's Scotch Whisky for a quarter of the price charged in West Berlin.

Elliott drank the bitter coffee with its odour of soft-soap in the dregs from the artificial cream which sank never to rise. The brightly coloured cake tasted only of sugar and the delicacy of a Cuban peach-segment with which it had been adorned.

Rubin ate and drank with relish.

'You know,' he said, 'it is good when friends work together. When our masters chose us to cooperate in this matter, did they know we had been friends so long?'

'I'm sure they did.' Elliott looked at Rubin's broad smile and tried not to show his reserve. The professions of friendship came only from the Russian. Yet it seemed as if Rubin's feelings in the matter were wholly sincere. Elliott put down his empty cup.

'Tell me,' he said. 'How do you distinguish between a friend and a comrade.'

Rubin laughed to himself and shook his head.

'I am your friend. Mr Corrigan is your comrade. You must work with him, be loyal to him, whether you find him *simpatico* or not. Mr Corrigan is not happy in Europe, I think. Berlin oppresses him and he dreams of Manhattan. You and I are closer to home. In a little while, you and I may fight each other in a war. But we shall still have been friends. In such circumstances one may have to shoot a friend, if the cause requires it, and yet still be his friend. One may not shoot a comrade – yet the cause does not require one to like him. You see?'

'Yes,' said Elliott. 'Perfectly.'

Rubin stood up.

'It is like your religion, Mr Elliott. You must love your neighbour. But you are not required to like him.'

He led the way down the exterior staircase. Holding the broad-topped cap of a Soviet staff officer under his arm, he presented a head whose weight suggested power and intelligence under the dark and carefully oiled hair. As they crossed the wooded avenue again his saturnine face was still set in its smile of amiability.

'Tell me how I may assist you.'

'You know Martina Hansen?'

Rubin nodded.

'I have had occasion to learn about her in the past few days.'

'I should like a meeting,' said Elliott delicately.

Rubin spread out his hands.

'Whenever you wish. You do not require my consent for such things.'

He ignored the car which had braked sharply to avoid them.

'With her father,' Elliott said patiently. 'With Andor.'

'That is not difficult. We shall accommodate him in Babelsberg and take good care of him.'

'Apart from his consent in the matter, which is doubtful, he is not fit to travel.'

The colonel nodded again as if he perfectly understood the problem.

'Consent, Mr Elliott. That is the root of the difficulty. You see, Martina Hansen will not consent to leave the DDR for the west. She is fearful.'

'I thought you might bring influence to bear.'

Rubin pulled a face of incredulity at the supposition.

'Mr Elliott! I am not a power in the DDR. Their own police have forcibly expelled subversives by locking them in trains bound for the west. But that is another matter. Imagine what would happen were I to deport one of their citizens against her will. Imagine for yourself. Suppose you were to seize a citizen of West Berlin and take him by force to the DDR. What do you think would happen to you? Be reasonable, my friend!'

'She has every guarantee of returning in a few hours.'

'Alas,' said Rubin, 'my comrades in the DDR do not think so. After a few hours in your company, they believe a message would come to say that she had sought political asylum in the Federal Republic. And that is the last they would see of her.'

'Do your German comrades know the story of Andor already?'

Elliott, sure that they would not have been informed, felt that he had thrown Rubin at last. But the colonel shrugged and would not discuss the matter further. Instead he smiled and laid his hand on Elliott's arm.

'You know what happened to Walter Ulbricht when he died?'

'No.' Elliott decided that this round of the battle was lost. Rubin was not to be moved.

'He went to heaven. Or at least to what you call the pearly gates. That is the phrase?'

'Yes.'

'St Peter came out and demanded what this man was doing there. An atheist! A persecutor of religion! Away with him to hell! A few days passed. Then there was another knocking at the gates, louder than ever before. St Peter opened them. You know what he found?'

'Yes,' said Elliott irritably. 'It was the devil asking for political asylum. You told me the story before. I sometimes think you make up all these anecdotes.'

Rubin laughed at this, as if it were a joke in itself.

'I have no need. In this country everyone tells such tales. You live on the wrong side of the wall, my friend. You think they are a subject race here. But they have far more spirit – *esprit* – than the Germans in the west.'

'Martina Hansen.' As they stood together near the park gates, about to part, Elliott repeated the name. Rubin spread out his hands again.

'She does not wish to leave Babelsberg, Mr Elliott. I will do what I can for you. But what can I do?'

'Thank you. And thank you for the coffee.'

Rubin smiled once more as they shook hands.

'Goodbye, Mr Elliott. Tell me if you hear any more about our friend and his plutonium. The harness has been laid upon our backs and we must pull together. Must we not?'

Elliott nodded. As military etiquette required, he stepped back two paces and saluted Rubin, his senior officer. The colonel returned the compliment with a salute like an abortive wave of the hand.

The major turned away with the familiar sense that a meeting with Rubin, which had promised so well, had ended in frustration. He saw that Private Lucas was waiting with some unease by the car.

'They want us back at the checkpoint, sir. Quick as

possible. Direct order from the commandant's office. Sounds like there's an almighty panic breaking out.'

22

The staff car moved slowly forward on the caged frontier lane for military and diplomatic personnel. Elliott put away the identity card which had just been scanned with chill courtesy by the young DDR lieutenant. In the distance was the long low pavilion on the western side of the checkpoint, the flags of France, the United States and Britain drooping in the airless heat.

Corrigan was standing by the guard-post of the US Military Police, having evicted the sergeant and two corporals who normally occupied it. Elliott got out of the car and walked across.

'You got the word?' Corrigan asked.

'A message to return, that's all. My driver reported it while I was talking to Rubin. What's happened?'

Corrigan led the way into the guard-post, the room empty and the windows closed.

'News from Buenos Aires. Most of it bad. Now that it's too late, they're chattering to us like a cage of monkeys.'

'There's not much encouragement from Comrade Rubin either. He's got no intention of letting Martina Hansen go. Not unless we can make him an offer.'

Corrigan ignored this.

'Did you get a briefing before you went over this morning? Anything about the fire at Ezeiza that killed Vogel and Nunvar?'

'No.'

'They now admit it was an accident involving investigation by so-called security police. That's the least of it from Buenos Aires.'

In the noon heat beyond the window the light glimmered pale on the monolithic structure of the former Luftwaffe building, now stranded in the eastern sector with a single red flag at its mast. Elliott turned to Corrigan.

'Why Buenos Aires?'

Corrigan closed the window.

'We've been screwed,' he said bitterly. 'You. Me. All of us. By Andor. And by this joke of Bonnell-Thornton's about old men building bombs in their kitchens and threatening the world with empty plutonium flasks. No one built a bomb. The Argentines have lost one. A single megaton warhead in perfect working order. Big enough to wipe this city off the map. Big enough to burn a hole in the middle of East Germany, the Soviet army, the Warsaw Pact. Ask your friend Rubin what that means!'

'Who says it's missing?' But the bravado died with his words.

'Four warheads left Ezeiza for Rio Gallegos air base.' Corrigan counted them on his fingers for emphasis. 'No fuss. No high-jack. A week ago, Andor's pet computer suggested to its masters the warheads should be checked. They brought them back to Ezeiza. Three were all right. One was a very convincing dummy. Just like that load of World War II scrap in Dahlem. Probably the same builder.'

'Not Andor, though?'

'Vogel or Nunvar. Perhaps both.'

'And the missing bomb?'

Corrigan shrugged.

'It probably left Ezeiza disguised as a routine shipment for a power station or a research institute. It's not like a suitcase full of heroin. Policemen don't take the lid off and look inside. In that form it could be sitting in Berlin now – at the Hahn-Meitner Institute or the Kraftwerk Reuter power station. But it isn't. Page insisted on a routine search but he won't find anything there.'

'Because?'

'Andor was no physicist but he could win a Nobel mathematics prize. He was the designing genius of the whole Ezeiza computer complex. Better still, he could hack his way into any other system with a bug on the phone junction-box and a modum on his own receiver. The big ones he didn't have to break into–because he built them. He and Vogel and Nunvar had access to the terminal wherever that warhead went. They could alter its designation, downgrade it, using the Ezeiza codes. By now it could be sitting in a warehouse labelled as a medical scanner or a television set.'

'Bombs travel in a forty-ton steel flask,' Elliott said.

'Not this one,' Corrigan shook his head. 'Andor and company don't give a damn about radiation hazards. Even the USAF bombs made at Amarillo in Texas would fit into a wash-basin.'

Elliott opened the window, drawing in a warm breeze. He said, 'Andor would only get clearance for his own files in the IBM-38. He'd need every other password and super-user code. How?'

The laughter of the MP corporals outside rose and then died.

'They found a bug at Ezeiza, three days back,' Corrigan said. 'A miniaturised FM mike, the size of a bean. It tapped the computer line in the phone junction-box. First they thought it was the Soviets. Their embassy beams in on every electronic signal. Then they traced it to Andor's own terminal. He used to dial from his office and pick up a short whistle on VHF. But the modum on his phone deciphered the microwaves and showed the information on the screen. In two days at most he saw all the super-users give their passwords or codes to his monster. After that, he owned Ezeiza. There was a search when Vogel and Nunvar died but they missed the FM mike. Andor was gone two weeks when they found it. And he's talked to the electronic brain ever since.'

'How?' Elliott sat on the table, his back to the window.

'Yesterday,' Corrigan explained, 'I hear the Ezeiza computer displayed some instructions in summary. Orders already sent to the warhead's circuits. To make quite certain that a hi-jacked bomb can't be set off–or that a lieutenant in a missile-silo can't set one off in a fit of pique – every warhead is equipped with PALS. Permissive Action Links. Until the right keys have been turned or signals programmed by half-a-dozen people, the bomb is about as lethal as a sack of potatoes. But in this case, the men who would set it off are the very ones who built the electronic circuitry. See? The system doesn't take account of German nationalists working in Argentine top security installations.'

Elliott nodded.

'Andor time-bombed the computer.'

'Right,' said Corrigan. 'Even while you had him under lock and key the damn thing was still obeying instructions he gave it weeks before. He time-bombed it all right. For a man with authorised access to the machine it was child's play. Save your admiration for the class of 1983. They penetrated the computers at the Pentagon, MIT, Digital Electric Corporation. At Pacific Telephone, they persuaded a Cosmos computer to give them the secret combinations of the locks so that they could burglarise the place. Andor had it easy compared to them.'

'Did the display suggest where the bomb might be?'

Corrigan shook his head.

'No. There's a whole file of encoded information which they turned up later from the computer data. That probably tells the entire story.'

'Can anyone read the code?'

'The National Security Agency at Fort Meade tried it. They can break almost any code in half a day. This one has a key about fifty digits long. Worse than that, it has a double key. You know what that means, Sam?'

'Not exactly.'

Corrigan loosened his tie and sat down.

'Imagine intercepting a message in Russian, when you don't know any Russian. The only dictionary you have is English into Russian. So for every word, you have to go through the entire book. It's a dictionary that comes in about two hundred volumes. The message also fills a number of volumes – stretching from here to Hamburg and back. That's about the scale of a double code like this. If anything it's worse in reality. The current reckoning is that advanced computers can break a double fifty-digit code in a length of time equivalent to the present age of the universe. In Andor's case, we don't have that leisure.'

'From what the computer did tell them, the bomb is definitely armed and despatched?'

Corrigan nodded.

'Then,' said Elliott, 'we can believe him about the fourteen-day timer?'

'Absolutely. And, it tells us, you can believe that it's in Berlin.'

Elliott seemed cheered by this.

'In that case, Pat, I go back to first principles. You and Fort Meade can try breaking the code if you choose to. I'm going to break Andor.'

23

A crowd of fifty or more young hitchhikers lined the side of the autobahn which ran south-west from the city. They waited patiently, holding out the squares of cardboard upon which their destinations were printed. Nürnberg, München, Stuttgart . . . The autobahn itself ran unmolested across the territory of the DDR for more than a hundred miles to the West German frontier. On either side the summer forest rose tall and dense. Elliott's driver turned on to the slip-road guarded by the concrete watch-tower above which the Soviet flag hung in an airless calm.

As within the city itself, the crossing was provided with a special lane for military and diplomatic traffic between east and west. Beside it six files of lorries waited at the row of concrete guard-posts for inspection and clearance by the grey-uniformed conscripts of the Volkspolizei. The compound was fenced in from the frontier strip by a tall barrier of wire mesh.

While his identity card was checked, Elliott looked across

the wide belt of level sand and the trees beyond, dividing the DDR from West Berlin. A single worker stripped to the waist was raking the sand. Behind him stood two vopos with machine pistols. Two more guards with rifles slung on their backs rode in circles round the group like siamese twins on a single motor-cycle. Elliott saw the point. If the man who was raking the sand had taken off at a run, he might have reached the trees and the frontier wall. The Soviet machine-gunner in the guard-tower could only have fired at the risk of spraying the bullets among the waiting lorries. The precaution of a double guard was logical enough. All the same, Elliott thought, the chronic economic ills of the DDR came as no surprise if it took five men to rake a single stretch of sand.

The young guard commander waved them on into the lanes and by-ways of the wooded countryside which divided Potsdam from Berlin. Beyond the mesh fencing another pair of guards on a single motor-cycle rode the sandy path of the frontier strip, glum and self-conscious.

On Elliott's instructions, the staff car skirted the old quarter of Babelsberg and followed the long boulevard of tramlines and cemeteries into the centre of Potsdam. Beyond the river bridge of the old town, the tall green dome of the Nikolaikirche and the municipal buildings, lay the Hegel-Allee. In the broad avenue, between the handsome balconied houses, the trees in full leaf formed a central reservation.

The Russian officers' club stood at the western end of the avenue, guarded by a single sentry, his shoulder inconspicuously resting against the lintel of the main door, his chin-strap hanging loose and his steel helmet at an angle on his head. The youth and immaturity of the Soviet conscripts was almost the first thing which Elliott had noticed on his arrival in Berlin. Despite the loud assertions of military advisers in the west, it was less the military arm of a super-power than a peasant militia.

Rubin was standing on the pavement in the strong noon sun, smoking a cigarette and with his cap still tucked under his arm. He raised a hand to forestall Elliott's descent from the Ford Sierra.

'Please!' he said genially, 'we will take your car. I will make it all right.'

He eased his bulk into the back seat beside the major.

'Where to?'

'The Cecilienhof Hotel. You will like that, I think. It is part of the old palace. Built for your English princess who married the Kaiser, so that she would not feel homesick. Built for the English!'

Rubin chortled with the good humour of one who takes as much enjoyment from giving pleasure as in receiving it. On his instructions, Private Lucas made an illegal U-turn and followed the line of the avenue towards the parkland palaces of the long-departed monarchy.

'Many tourists,' said Rubin disinterestedly, indicating the bulky middle-aged men with frumpish consorts, their cameras held expectantly but unused in their hands.

Elliott glanced aside. Even had he not recognised the build of the 'tourists' and their manner of looking about them, the tall square Zenith cameras would have identified the majority of strollers as Soviet officers and their wives making the most of a Potsdam posting.

Rubin spoke to Lucas again. They were following a grey wall beyond which, as Elliott was well aware, stretched the secluded housing-blocks of the Soviet army's married quarters. A Russian troop-carrier passed them, going in the opposite direction, and Rubin looked momentarily self-conscious.

The parkland with oaks and elms, surrounding the Cecilienhof palace, would have passed for one of the great English estates. They drew up by the main gate of the palace, which despite its title resembled the gabled and red-roofed English manor house that Rubin had promised. Within the courtyard the same cosiness prevailed, except that the round flowerbed at the centre had been laid out with red flowers in a huge star, the emblem of Rubin's army.

'You have been here before?' Rubin inquired, holding the car door for Elliott as he eased himself out. 'It is where they had their Potsdam conference in 1945. Your Mr Churchill and Major Corrigan's Mr Truman and my Mr Stalin.'

'I was here once before,' said Elliott blandly.

He followed Rubin through the main entrance, into the timbered hall whose waxed and polished wood had the very scent of England. It seemed to him implausible and, therefore, disquieting that Colonel Rubin should continue to act the part of a genial fool under the present circumstances.

They passed down a corridor connecting the palace to the hotel which had once been part of it. The wall was adorned with a propaganda montage of photographs, each showing a leader of West Germany shaking hands or hobnobbing with the Nazi leaders in the period of the Third Reich.

'You see?' said Rubin expansively. 'There are your friends, Mr Elliott! Beware! Beware!'

He smiled as he spoke.

'There's one missing,' said Elliott coldly.

Rubin stopped and looked.

'Which one is that?'

'The photograph of your Mr Molotov shaking hands with their Mr Hitler in Berlin in the autumn of 1940.'

He awaited the colonel's reaction. Rubin grinned broadly, without laughing, and put his arm round the major's shoulder.

'You will get me into trouble, Mr Elliott.' His face assumed a parody of wide-eyed alarm. 'Come. We shall go to our dinner.'

Beyond the damp-patched walls of the passageways, the dining-room of the hotel was large and its little tables crowded. Despite the brightness of the day outside, the dark oak panelling of the wall gave it a heavy and oppressive air. Rubin unfolded his napkin as they sat down and nodded at the bottle of Romanian sauvignon produced by the waitress for his approval.

'Eat, Mr Elliott! All shall by ready for you afterwards, but you must eat. I will tell you a story.'

'About the Democratic Republic?'

Rubin waved the suggestion aside.

'About my own country. A story my father told me. Once there was a husband whose young wife was to have a baby, you see? He went to a fortune teller for advice about the baby's future. If the child was a boy, the fortune teller said, all would be well. If it was a girl, the father would drop dead the moment it was born. You see?'

Elliott nodded and began to eat beetroot salad.

'The husband was very anxious. On the day when the child was born he waited in great fear. Imagine his alarm when the doctor came out and told him that the baby was a girl! But the moments went by and he did not drop dead. Ah, he thought, the fortune teller was a fraud, after all. But he was a good father and he sent at once for the priest to baptise the child, for the priest had been most kind in hearing his wife's confessions and in comforting her. The messenger came back alone. Alas, he said, the holy man cannot come to baptise your child. He dropped dead a quarter of an hour ago. You like that, I think, Mr Elliott? See how it is with these priests!'

'There's a similar joke in England,' Elliott took another forkful of beetroot. 'It has to do with the priest being red-haired.'

After the brightly coloured and almost tasteless gateau, they took their coffee out on to the little terrace overlooking the park and the lake. Elliott stared out across the water and saw a wooden barrier running into the distance down the centre of the water. While Rubin gave instructions to the driver, he had not realised how far they had turned back towards the fortified border zone.

Presently a young Russian lieutenant in civilian clothes, familiar to Elliott from a previous meeting, came out and spoke to Rubin in his own language. Elliott caught a few words of the exchange and knew that his journey to Potsdam was about to prove its worth.

'We should go upstairs,' said Rubin, when they were alone again. 'I believe you will find what you want. I shall be at hand, of course, but you may talk privately if you wish.'

Elliott followed his host up the stairs and along the uneven corridors where the walls smelt of new distemper and the grey paint of the doors was badly chipped. Despite the prestige of its name, he felt as if he were about to keep an assignation in a run-down commercial hotel, somewhere in provincial France or England. Outside one of the doors was a Soviet officer in civilian clothes. He stiffened to attention at Rubin's approach and opened the door. The uniformed lieutenant came out of the room, where he had been guarding the young woman, and saluted.

'You may go in alone and talk to her.' Rubin turned to Elliott. 'Perhaps that will be better. Then you will know that we have not influenced her decision.'

Elliott tried not to show his scepticism. He nodded, went through the doorway, and closed the door after him.

Martina Hansen was as unprepossessing as her name. Elliott had deduced that she was an actress, in part from information given to him and in part from the news that she lived at Babelsberg, the centre of the DDR film industry. The truth, however, was that she seemed more like a static ornament than an actress, painted and demure as a doll with her shock of blonde hair and inexpressive eyes.

She sat in a wicker chair, hands folded and head bowed as he introduced himself.

'I did not come here myself,' she said grudgingly, 'I was brought.'

Elliott sat on the side of the bed. More than ever, the room with its worn curtains and patched walls seemed like the mundane reality of a brothel.

'I'm sorry about that. I had no wish that you should be made to do anything against your will. My request was only to see you – to talk to you. About your father.'

Martina Hansen shrugged and her little mouth pouted slightly.

'There is nothing I can do for him now. I have not seen him for many years. If he wishes to visit me, I shall have no objection.'

'He is too ill for that,' said Elliott quietly. 'It would be necessary for you to go to him. He wants to see you very much. Surely you know that he has no one else in the world?'

She looked aside self-consciously but shrugged again.

'I cannot go to him in West Berlin. It would not be possible.'

'Colonel Rubin has no objection.'

'It would not be possible,' she repeated, 'I have work here. I am to have a film and a producer who will make it. If I do as you suggest, perhaps I should not be allowed back here. Perhaps by then the film would be made with someone else.'

There was no truth in her boast. Elliott was sure of that. He looked at the brightly painted doll-face. Already her attention had wandered back to her own body, the sole expression of her art. She was looking at the bare white feet from which she had removed the sandals. On each foot the nail of the big toe alone was varnished bright red.

'You see?' she said resentfully, 'I was brought here like that. No time even to finish getting ready.'

He looked in vain for some indication that she thought it a joke. But Martina Hansen frowned a little.

'One toe painted on each foot!' she said like a sullen child. 'I came here from West Berlin after he went abroad. If I go now, there will be others to take my place. I will not go. For almost ten years I have not seen him. He does not even write to me.'

'But you knew he was working as an archivist?'

'I was told.' The little doll looked up at him, woeful as if she might cry. 'They told me.'

Elliott was tempted to ask whether the news came from Rubin or Schroeder, but he knew that every word which passed between them was being monitored outside. Under the circumstances it seemed best to let the matter drop.

'What was your father doing when you saw him last?'

'I was a little girl. I did not notice such things.'

'You were not too little, or too young, to notice such things ten years ago.'

'He had lost his place as a teacher. He sold machinery.'

'I find that hard to believe.'

Martina Hansen shrugged. She turned her head and looked out of the window, swinging her feet slowly like a child.

'Your father is troubled. Please go to him.'

She shook her head without turning her face from the window. When she spoke it was in a curiously detached manner, as if she had been reciting a long remembered story about someone else. For the first time, Elliott wondered whether she could have been drugged.

'I came here when he left. There was work here in the studios at Babelsberg. I am well treated and looked after. I have no complaints.'

'You talk like a prisoner.'

She turned to face him at last.

'No. I am not a prisoner. I have worked hard to be successful and now that is going to happen. It has been promised. I am free, as I never was in West Berlin. There I had nothing. No work. Nothing but temporary jobs in shops and clubs. I am free here and I will not go back.'

Elliott had no need to ask in what her present freedom consisted. He knew well enough that as an artist of the state film industry it meant, for Martina Hansen, a flat which was luxurious by the standards of the monolithic grey blocks in the fields east of Potsdam. It included a pass to the hard-currency tourist shops where the imports from the west were available. There would be meals and entertainment at such hotels as this and even a Skoda car. He could well understand that she would refuse to put all this at risk even by a temporary return to West Berlin. Yet her story was false, of that he had no doubt. To see Martina Hansen and to hear her simple, self-indulgent patter was to know at once that she was not the stuff of which great actresses were made.

'Then you will not go to your father?' He spoke as if merely asking her to confirm her refusal.

'No.' She crossed her ankles and began to swing her feet again. 'You should ask my aunt Sybille. I'm sure she would be pleased to accept a visit to West Berlin. As for me, no.'

Elliott nodded and stood up, as if accepting his dismissal at her hands. Halfway to the door he turned round.

'Why did your father go to Argentina?'

'I did not know he had gone there.' The voice was dull and indifferent once more. 'He went there once, I think, for a little while when I was a child – to sell some machinery. When he left us, I did not know where he had gone. I was not told.'

'Us?'

'My aunt and I. We were the only two. My mother was dead long before then. My aunt brought me up. She came here with me and then went to Dresden after I was married.'

Elliott nodded, as if satisfied by this. He knew that he was now entering an area of interrogation in which Martina Hansen's answers would be well rehearsed, under the tutoring of Rubin or one of his colleagues. It seemed that the major was going to turn away again, but he paused a moment.

'If, as you say, you had no wish to see your father again – if you had no wish to be involved in any trouble which he might have brought upon himself – why did you phone the British Military Hospital in response to the television appeal?'

The dullness of the vain simpleton was replaced for an instant in her eyes by the glimmer of an intelligent woman's uncertainty. She was an actress, after all, Elliott thought, a much better one than he had given her credit for. Unfortunately for Martina Hansen, she was now thrown back upon a scene for which the lines had not been rehearsed – not by Colonel Rubin nor even by his subordinates.

'I thought I should,' she said, the dullness descending again. 'It wasn't much.'

'Even though you were so determined never to have dealings with West Berlin again?'

'There were no dealings.'

'And how did you see the appeal? Did someone tell you about it?'

'Of course not. No one knew who I was!'

Like a man setting his foot on a tightrope for the first time, Elliott took a deep breath.

'You certainly didn't get it from West Berlin television, I'm sure. Even if you were in the habit of watching it. Would it surprise you to know that I have it, on Colonel Rubin's authority, that you were otherwise occupied than in watching television – west or east – at the times in question?'

He thought at first that the bluff had failed. Then to his relief he saw once more the light of uncertainty in her glance.

'I must have lied to him,' she said, the sullen stupidity closing like armour round her.

'No, Frau Hansen.' He spoke as gently as if he might have crossed the room and stroked her hair. 'I am the one to whom you have lied. This afternoon. From first to last. I hope for your own sake that your masters will thank you for it.'

She looked up at him with the same defiant stupidity and, once more, he admired her for the actress that she was.

'I will not go to West Berlin.'

'No.' He stood with his hand on the doorknob. 'I don't suppose you will. Unless the time comes when the choice is made for you.'

He stepped into the corridor and held the door for the Soviet lieutenant who now entered the room in his place.

Rubin walked down with Elliott to the courtyard where the staff car was waiting. The heavy lines of his face creased again in a smile of friendship and wry self-depreciation.

'I do what I can.' His hands spread out philosophically.

'But what can I do? Now you have seen for yourself how it is.'

He watched the Sierra move slowly away towards the main drive and the road from Nauen to Potsdam which lay beyond the park. Then he turned and went back upstairs. By now the uniformed lieutenant had gone and only the officer in civilian clothes remained with the young woman. Martina Hansen was standing by the window, at once more alert and animated.

'You did well,' said Rubin appreciatively. 'It was good. Now, if you please.'

He moved behind her and took her wrists in a firm grasp. Her alarm was no more than a muted cry of intercession.

'It must be,' said Rubin softly. 'Once only. No more.'

He looked up at the plain clothes officer and nodded his head. The man's hand went back.

'Beware of the eye,' said Rubin quickly. 'Lower. The knuckles. Just below the cheekbone's point.'

He felt the young woman pull suddenly in his grasp and feared she might drop her head forward. But the menace of the fist held her gaze. The man brought it down hard, though with less than full force, in a heavy impact on the side of her face. Martina gave a retching cry of fear rather than pain, pulled away and dropped to the bed with her hands over her face.

'Two days,' said Rubin in the same quiet voice. 'Two days and even your father will believe you.'

The officer in civilian clothes said nothing, indifferent to the woman as to a chicken whose neck had been wrung. He took a handkerchief from his pocket and wiped from his knuckles the oily smear of face-cream.

24

Elliott turned over on to his side in the whiteness of early sun. Debby stirred beside him and he saw, through the spread veil of hair, the delicate bone-pattern of the vertebrae, the smoothness of her shoulders where his hand would run easily as a skate on ice.

This bed thy centre is, these walls thy sphere . . . Conditioned by his education and discovery of John Donne's verses at seventeen, all Elliott's experience of such intimacy had been enriched by the perspective of the great Elizabethan.

My face in thine eye, thine in mine appears . . . Waking, she turned and held him, smiling at the recollection of where she was and with whom. Naked in his arms, Debby was no longer the lost and frightened victim but his equal partner.

'Where can we find two better hemispheres?' he said, teasing as he held her. In the luxury of having woken early, they lay together in the sunlit world of the room, the light a yellow flush in the closed curtains, its thin gold colouring the pale polished wood of the dressing-table and wardrobe. It was a world quite separated from the dead cadences of Bonnell-Thornton, the shrewd professionalism of Corrigan, the plaintive self-righteousness of Andor. He drew her closer and turned her slightly in the familiar embrace.

It was three days since Elliott had committed one of the grosser follies of which his profession was capable. For the past two days he had reconciled himself to this totally. To be cashiered for his misconduct in concealing a suspect was the least that he could expect. Yet after so many years of solitude, a door stood open which he had believed was closed against him for ever until Debby's arrival. The sudden promise of what lay beyond was worth whatever it might cost him.

The little kingdom of their room seemed unconnected with the madness of the world outside it. He had a sense of safety and even of invulnerability. Seeing the girl's smile and feeling the smooth energy of her warm limbs he thought again of the poem first read in the school library. *She is all states . . . and all princes, I.* Far off he heard the sounds of that other world. An incoming jet on the Tegel flightpath. A radio voice from one of the nearby houses, the contrived bonhomie of a new day. Heavy gears of a military transporter on the Heer-Strasse.

Presently they drew apart and the exhilaration of certainty in Elliott's mind dwindled to hope. If the moment came, the private and public worlds would be simultaneously annihilated. Only the important few could be accommodated in deep shelter. Not wives, not children, not Debby. In the arithmetic of holocaust, one senior administrator was worth more than fifty dependent children. Were the chosen few to sneak away to their refuge without a word? Would they take leave of their families and consign them to their fate? Would they refuse to go, preferring to face annihilation with those they loved? In the politics of national insanity, such things were not debated. Elliott himself had given little thought to them until Debby's arrival.

As if sensing his thoughts, she turned on her stomach and said, 'What's going to happen to me – in the end?'

'Nothing,' he stroked her back lightly. 'This is the beginning and the end. You'll be safe here.'

She turned her head, brushing back the hair from her face as she looked up at him.

'But if it's true, about the man with the bomb, about Schroeder and the others? What then?'

'It doesn't matter,' he kissed the side of her face. 'Nothing will come of it all. I promise.'

But she knew the little world of their room was no sure refuge.

'You can't promise,' Debby kissed his hand, understanding and forgiving the lie. 'You don't know the outcome. No one does.'

As if reassured, she got up and walked with long naked strides to the dressing-table. Elliott watched her drawing the comb through the pale gold of her hair. She turned to him again.

'Who killed Jimmy?' she asked. 'It wasn't Schroeder, was it?'

The shadow of Corporal Hoskins fell between them for the first time in two days, sudden and cold.

'No,' he said gently. 'I shouldn't think it was Schroeder.'

'Did you do it? Order it, I mean.'

There was curiosity without accusation in her voice.

'No.' he walked across and put his arm round her. 'I wanted him alive, for every reason you can think of.'

'But it was our side who did it?'

'It wasn't counter-intelligence. The other people, the ones who penetrate DDR security, must have been on to him as well. If they did it, which they probably did, we'd be the last people to know. That's how the two British intelligence services work.'

'I thought so.' Debby's voice was hard and bright, triumph masking her anger and grief. 'Schroeder would have sent an Englishman to the shop to ask after Jimmy. He's got plenty working for him. The man I spoke to was German. I was stupid enough to fall for the trick and think that he must be from Schroeder because of that.'

'But you found out the trick,' he said touching her gently.

'Not really.' Debby put down the comb, resting her head on his shoulder. 'Only when it was too late. Only when your other people had killed Jimmy. I know it wasn't you, that's what matters. And even if it was you, perhaps it wouldn't matter now.'

She tightened her embrace upon him, like a child in danger.

25

Rubin's antipathy to West Berlin was always at its strongest in the summer. He knew its streets better than many of the citizens themselves, often choosing to walk from the military mission near Wilmersdorf to keep an evening appointment, the sun striking yellow on white and ochre blocks of offices or tenements. The heat of the central European summer brought out the crowds by that time of day, the young in all their loud boorishness and their elders in a slow and silent procession of resentment.

None of Rubin's superiors begrudged him such freedom. On the contrary, they encouraged it. Now, walking under the street arcading by the Bilka department store, he looked at the malevolent dullness in the eyes of his enemies' children. Was it their youth or their nationality which made them simultaneously mock and envy the world about them? He thought of Russian children of the same age, well dressed, courteous, subdued.

Because he had changed from his uniform into a grey suit, no one paid the least attention to him. Yet as he looked about him, Rubin felt no exultation over the moral decay of capitalism. His mind was filled by the pity and fascination of one who contemplates a mortal sickness. His eye caught the news-stands, the garish covers of what his mother used to refer to with knowledgeable disapproval as 'the literature of the boulevard'. What Elliott and Corrigan dismissed as the drab puritanism of the Soviet state was, to Rubin, more deeply rooted. It belonged to the old tradition in which husband and wife would draw a little curtain across the family ikon before they made love.

One day, Rubin supposed, a Soviet army of occupation must take over the few square miles of the western city. When that time came, it would be understanding rather than condemnation which determined the success of the mission.

He took a taxi from the stand just outside the Kranzler Café, where the street traders sat with their backs to the walls of the buildings. An old man paraded his furry clockwork animals on the paving stones. A Vietnamese refugee offered ivory figures in a little felt-lined tray. Despite his fascination with the streets and their people, the British Military Hospital was too far for Rubin to walk.

Half an hour later, in company with the uniformed figures of Elliott and Corrigan, Rubin entered the observation ward where Andor was still kept. The old man had been given a change of clothes, sitting on his upright chair in grey flannels and an open shirt. Deprived of the padding on his well-cut suit he appeared far more shrunken and frail. The flesh was looser on the round pale face.

Andor had the air of a man who had been carefully bathed and groomed for his interrogation by hands other than his own. His hair was neatly combed and yet it was not combed in its usual shape. His self-sufficiency as well as his physique seemed to have shrunk and withered. He looked up at the three men who came in, a quick blinking of his moist blue eyes the only evidence of apprehension. They set their chairs at a little distance before him with Corrigan forward slightly as the spokesman.

Before he sat down, Corrigan took out a packet of cigarettes, offered one to the old man, and lit it for him. Andor had never smoked before in their presence. He did so now in the manner of one reverting to a long abandoned habit. His interrogators watched this and congratulated themselves on having brought him to acknowledge such a need at their suggestion.

'You see?' Corrigan sat down and leant forward, as if to talk more privately to the old man. 'You have your wish, Dr Andor. The representatives of the three powers have come to you. This is Colonel Rubin of the Soviet high command in Berlin.'

Andor looked up and his lip quivered slightly before he spoke.

He is not in uniform. Why does he come in disguise?'

Rubin cocked his large head on one side, as if pretending to be a child caught in a trick.

'Perhaps, Herr Andor, it is because you too are in disguise.'

'I have disguised nothing! Concealed nothing!' The blue eyes grew rounder with neurotic indignation. 'You know my name, what I have done, where I come from. If you did not believe me at first, then the fault lies upon your side.'

Rubin shook his head in silence. He relaxed his grey-suited bulk and the little chair creaked under the shifting of his broad buttocks. When he looked at the old man again, the movement of his mouth was closer to a sneer than to a smile.

'No, my friend. It is you who employ the greater disguise. It matters little who you are, where you have come from, what you have done. Those are things we should discover for ourselves, as we discovered your daughter in Babelsberg and your sister Sybille in Dresden. But since your two accomplices, Vogel and Nunvar, are dead you alone can remove the most important disguise of all. The mask of death concealing a weapon which will destroy the people of this city.'

If this was intended as an appeal, it failed.

'You know my terms,' Andor said, 'and why I demand them.'

Corrigan intervened after a pause, resuming the questions.

'You worked at first on the Ezeiza copy of the United States computer, the VAX-782. What was your specific expertise?'

'Projectile guidance!' The old man shot back the answer with impatience and disdain.

'I know that,' Corrigan said coaxingly. 'The entire system is designed for missile guidance. Tell me in what area was your original expertise. Otherwise, I shall begin to doubt you.'

'In gyroscopic correction.' Andor's eyes moved shrewdly from one man to another as he spoke. Corrigan sighed.

'That tells us little more. I want you to be more specific.'

'I am not here to answer such questions.' There was no resentment in the voice, merely the sound of dryness in the old man's mouth. Corrigan seemed to pardon the refusal.

'Tell me at least what Vogel and Nunvar were to do.'

The cigarette hung disregarded from Andor's fingers.

'Only to see that the device was in working order. To ensure that the timer could be activated.'

'Where is that device now?'

'I cannot tell you.'

'Cannot or will not?'

'It does not matter which, Major Corrigan.'

'Are we not even to believe that it is in Berlin?'

'You know that it is in Berlin.'

Corrigan looked round at Rubin, passing the questions to him. Rubin wiped his mouth with a handkerchief, then folded the linen carefully.

'How big is this device of which you speak?'

'A little over eighty pounds. The Argentines can tell you.'

But Rubin shook his head, as if in slight reproof.

'I did not ask its weight, my friend. How big is it?'

'The size of a large television set.'

'No.' Rubin's denial was gentler still. 'You did not smuggle such a thing across oceans and frontiers on the authority of a mere computer.'

'Did I not?' For the first time during the questions a glint of hostility showed in Andor's eyes. 'How then do you account for the plutonium flask? The consignment was the same. The wooden horse is within the walls of Troy. Here and all over the world.'

'Explain that,' said Rubin quietly.

Andor shrugged with the manner of a teacher reiterating first principles to a class of backward children.

'Countries which possess such devices may despatch them piecemeal to their embassies or consulates all over the world. The diplomatic bag is immune from inspection. The poorest nation, without a single rocket to carry a warhead, may destroy the capital city of its most powerful enemy. That is merely an example of method. It is not the means employed in this case.'

Corrigan got up and poured himself a drink of water. Then he turned towards the others again.

'Major Elliott?'

But Elliott ignored the invitation to interrogate Andor. Instead he replied to Corrigan.

'I doubt if our questions can have much use at present. We have the authority to inflict certain forms of persuasion on a prisoner in these circumstances. I should prefer to keep my questions until he is in a more responsive mood.'

But Andor shrugged again, indifferent to the threat.

'Do as you please,' he said. 'By such methods, I shall

probably die at your hands. You would have to use more persuasion than I could bear. If I die, you condemn two million others.'

Still talking to Corrigan, Elliott seemed unmoved.

'A man will endure for himself,' he said casually. 'Whether he can endure the sufferings of his own daughter in his presence is another matter. Even if the process were carried to its limit, we should regard the death of one young woman as the necessary price of saving two million others.'

'You will not!' The anger brightened in the old man's eyes but his glance showed the first uncertainty of fear. At last Elliott spoke to him directly.

'The responsibility for her fate, Herr Andor, will be yours.'

The old man shook his head. Now it was he who took the initiative in the conversation.

'I do not seek the death of a single person, except that I am indifferent to my own. I have done all this only in order to demand justice and the fulfilment of promises made by your own nations. My country to be whole and free.'

He spread out his hands to show the simplicity of it all.

'Germany cannot be reunified in eight days,' said Elliott sharply. 'If you demand that, you demand two million deaths.'

Andor shook his head at the misunderstanding.

'I do not ask for such a thing in eight days. I ask only a beginning, that the barriers be removed in Berlin. It is what was agreed between you. It is what you practise yourselves when the vehicles of your armies travel freely through the streets of east and west. I demand nothing which you did not agree to. I ask it for the sake of your own nations as much as for mine.'

'In eight days?' Elliott looked at the others in exasperation.

'Do you not see?' Andor leant forward towards him earnestly. 'In the union of Berlin lies the union of

Germany. In the salvation of Germany – east and west – lies the salvation of Europe. In the peace of Europe lies the hope of the world!'

Elliott held the bright intensity of the old man's eyes. All that Andor had repressed during his earlier captivity burst from him now.

'Believe me, Major Elliott, I and my friends did not proceed to these lengths to pay homage to dead Nazism. But if you divide and demean my country, you divide and demean humanity. I have taken a terrible risk, I know that. I dread that I shall cause innocent deaths. I dread still more that your nations will cause the death of mankind.'

Corrigan took the cigarette butt from the old man's fingers.

'You are wrong, Dr Andor,' he said gently. 'Germany is evolving towards new unity. Such actions as yours will only impede it.'

Andor sat back and blinked. It was evident that the tears had gathered in his eyes, though he was too proud to shed them and his voice was firm.

'Major Corrigan, please do not talk to me of improvements. Suppose you could not walk from one street to another in your home town without written permission from the guards of a hostile power! Suppose you were forbidden to travel from one city to another in the United States to visit your mother or your daughter! Suppose that your children ignored this law and were butchered in cold blood! Would you talk of improvement and the need to be patient? I know what this means – and I know that the little favours extended by those who divide my city and my country may be withdrawn again as easily as they were granted. To be free is not a favour, Major Corrigan. It is a right. I would not harm the hair of one single head. Yet those who may die will die for freedom as surely as any soldier of your own armies. I ask nothing, except that I shall die with them.'

'Yours is the bomb which will destroy them,' said

Elliott sourly.

'Then you will evacuate them before the time comes,' said Andor placidly. 'When you do that, you will have to tell the world the truth of what has happened. Once men see that there are those prepared to go to any end in freedom's struggle, the death-knell of tyranny is sounded.'

Rubin, who had sat in silence during the outburst, shook his head wonderingly at the old man.

'No,' he said quietly. 'You know little of such things, my poor friend. It is the death-knell of the human race which will be sounded, once such people determine to use these means of attaining their ends.'

Half an hour later the three officers stood together outside the observation ward.

'An idealist!' Elliott buttoned his tunic. 'God save us from those. A psychopath with moral tendencies!'

But Corrigan seemed a good deal more content than when the interrogation had begun.

'We've opened the debate with him, Sam. That's what counts.'

'With eight days to go?'

Corrigan pulled on his gloves and looked down the corridor towards an approaching medical orderly.

'It's tight,' he conceded. 'Tighter than anyone in his senses would have chosen. But it's long enough. You can talk almost any fanatic out of a hi-jack or embassy siege in eight days. From now on, we keep the conversation going. Gently and lucidly. I don't doubt for one second that Andor has the means of letting off the big bang. All the same, when the moment comes, I don't think he'll do it. Any more than you will use the pliers on Martina Hansen.'

'I'll do what's necessary,' Elliott said.

'And what's permitted.' Corrigan buttoned his gloves. 'I don't think you'll find General Page in a hurry to be blown to Kingdom-Come because his daughter's cries have tipped Andor over the edge.'

26

By five o'clock the morning was bright but still cool, the waters of the Jungfern-See moving in a broad and sluggish swell. Where the land on either side came close, in two flat and wooded promentories, the lake was spanned by the iron-girder suspension of the Glienicker Bridge, which had once been the route of the direct road from Berlin to Potsdam. The crossing had long been closed. Standing by the little hut which served as a guard-post on the American side, Elliott shivered in the chill. The carriageway of the bridge was railed off, the tarmac stretch deserted up to the opposing barrier, beyond which two uniformed East German guards with machine-pistols performed a tireless and goose-stepping sentry-go.

Behind Elliott, on the allied side, was the parkland of the Schloss Glienicker, the fairy palace which had become a people's pleasure-ground with its tea-gardens and lakeside lawns. Further still the forest road ran back towards the city, skirting the frontier wall. The flags of the three western powers hung motionless in the morning cold outside the gates of the Berlin Golf and Country Club.

Elliott moved his legs impatiently, as if to restore circulation.

'Come on!' he said irritably. 'For God's sake!'

Tearing the silence of the early morning, a DDR patrol boat bore down towards the bridge, bow raised and double wake spreading astern. Without slackening speed, it passed between the stone pillars of the central span on the precise and imagined line of the frontier. Elliott watched it curve away, following the flat wooded shore of the lake towards Fahrland and the little villages north of Potsdam.

The water subsided into its tranquil swell again. Elliott went into the guard hut, from which the usual personnel of the West Berlin polizei had been temporarily evicted, and took the binoculars that Lieutenant Beresford was holding.

'Where the devil is Rubin?'

It was not a question which Beresford could be expected to answer. In Elliott's present mood it was scarcely a question at all. He went outside again and looked across the bridge through the glasses, under the arched girders of its twin towers. The East German sentries marched slowly and indefatigably to and fro, across and across the blocked carriageway. Behind them the royal castles of Potsdam were visible among the trees in full leaf. Indeed, from where he stood, Elliott could see directly into the heart of the town across the minefields of the flat pasture beyond the water.

'Get a move on!' he said to the invisible Rubin. 'For God's sake!'

It was still early, but as the morning grew warmer the first fishermen and campers, sunbathers and strollers would begin filling the lawns and woodland on the allied side. The Glienicker Bridge at the end of the long and wooded Koenig-Strasse was years ago closed by the DDR as a crossing point. It was used now, at such times of day or night, by the Soviet and western armies for the exchange of prisoners or transport of any kind which it was judged best for the world not to witness. First opened in 1962 for the exchange of the Russian Colonel Abel and the American U2 pilot Gary Powers, the bridge still had its white line painted across the tarmac at the halfway point, the exact place where such bargains were fulfilled.

Elliott was not in the business of making exchanges. He turned his glasses from Potsdam centre, the high green dome of the Nikolaikirche, and saw movement on the road beyond the bridge, where the parkland of the Hohenzollern palaces came down to the lake's edge.

It was a Soviet troop-carrier, distinguishable from the heavier and squarer western vehicles by its old-fashioned engine-bonnet and the curved wagon-roof of its body. As a rule, when such lorries entered West Berlin they were unmarked. It was a precaution against demonstrations or retaliation by the West Berliners. This one, however, bore its marking clearly. It was the black Volga staff car behind it which was unmarked.

Elliott watched a dozen steel-helmeted Soviet infantry drop down from the back of the troop-carrier and take up positions as the barriers on the far side of the bridge were moved aside. The disaffected burghers of Potsdam were to be given no chance of escape under cover of the staff car's crossing. Then the black car itself moved forward, one infantryman riding on either running-board until the halfway line. The Volga stopped briefly to let the men get down, then came slowly forward.

'Lift the barrier!' Elliott gave the command over his shoulder to the first of the accompanying corporals. On the allied side the road was blocked by nothing more than an ordinary striped pole which could be raised by pressing down the block on the end. It was Corporal Craig who brought the barrier upright and saluted as the black car passed through.

Colonel Rubin opened the door and got out. Elliott, rigorously observing military etiquette, was first to salute. The colonel replied with his customary casual wave.

'Mr Elliott, we are a little late. I apologise. *La ponctualité c'est la politesse des rois*. Is that right?'

'It would be,' Elliott humoured his guest laconically, 'if you had a monarchy.'

Rubin's broad face relaxed in an easy smile.

'The politeness of an English gentleman, then.' He put his hand on Elliott's arm and began to guide him towards the black car. 'Whatever our countries or politics, we should try to behave like English gentlemen.'

Martina Hansen was sitting, wide-eyed and apprehensive in the back seat, unobtrusively handcuffed to one of Rubin's female officers. Despite her captain's uniform, the woman had the air of an efficient middle-aged private secretary who might as well have worked in Wolverhampton or Milwaukee as in Karlshorst.

The two RMP motor-cyclists moved out ahead of them

on the long forest road, Lieutenant Beresford and Corporal Craig following the staff car in their jeep. By now the barriers had been replaced on the far side of the bridge and the Soviet infantrymen were standing easy. On the allied side the lawns and car park of the Schloss Glienicker were deserted. No one saw them go. At a little distance, the green and white police Mercedes waited to take the two German guards back to their post. Beyond it was a jeep belonging to the US Military Police. Elliott saw three white helmets but no sign of Corrigan. Though the Glienicker Bridge was in the American sector, Corrigan had persuaded his general to 'lend' it to British military intelligence for the period of time necessary.

There was no traffic on the road until they passed the lakeside resort of Wannsee in the cool light. Even the stadtring autobahn was well nigh deserted. Rubin observed a fastidious silence in the presence of his prisoner. Glancing aside at the girl, Elliott saw the brown suffusion of a bruise on her cheek, ill concealed by the white make-up. She looked to him even younger, more childish, and rather more stupid than on the occasion of their previous meeting.

Rubin's driver followed the two outriders, turning off the stadtring, circling the Theodor-Heuss-Platz with its store fronts still locked, its pavements empty. They followed the broad highway of the Heer-Strasse until the turning for the British Military Hospital. It was only as they passed the guard-post and entered the compound that Rubin broke his silence.

'I think you should let her rest for an hour or so first of all. I really think you should do that.'

Elliott nodded. He got out first and telephoned to the duty officer to ensure that the room next to Andor's had been prepared. He did not believe in such miracles as Rubin promised. However, there was no purpose in allowing Martina Hansen to see her father in her present confused state or at so early an hour. It was best that she should be left alone to accustom herself to the reality of deportation. He also guessed, from her apathetic response, that she had been drugged before the journey. In that case, it would be necessary to wait until the effects had fully dissipated.

Rubin waited without protest, drinking cup after cup of coffee in the office which Elliott had borrowed from the senior medical officer and telling a sequence of jokes, all of them at the expense of the East German regime. Corrigan arrived at nine o'clock and Bonnell-Thornton soon after. It was the brigadier, impatient to have done with the experiment, who said, 'Shall I do the honours?'

Rubin's understanding of colloquial English seemed to fail him and he watched in silence through the observation panel as the commandant went into Andor's room.

'You have a visitor,' said Bonnell-Thornton, watching Andor as the old man looked up from the table where he was reading. 'Someone who has made a very difficult journey to see you. Your daughter, Martina.'

No surprise or gratitude showed in Andor's expression.

'That is impossible. They would not let her come here unless it was a trick.'

'It is no trick,' Bonnell-Thornton shook his head. 'She has been transferred to the custody of the British occupying power in whose territory the investigation of your case is being carried out.'

'She is your prisoner?'

Bonnell-Thornton smiled at the sharpness of the old man's tone.

'No, Dr Andor. She is *your* prisoner. Martina Hansen is only in custody because she is your daughter and therefore her evidence may be relevant to your case. The moment you decide to cooperate with us in clearing up the matter, she will be set free. Whether she remains in West Berlin or returns to the east is entirely at her choice.'

'And if I refuse?'

The commandant shrugged.

'Then it is you who condemn her to be a prisoner.'

For the first time in their dealings, Andor looked at the commandant with a dry grimace of contempt.

'You think to move me by such threats?' His mouth worked as if he might spit at Bonnell-Thornton. 'I tell you that your conduct serves only to strengthen my beliefs in your unfitness to dictate my country's destiny.'

The brigadier touched the old man's shoulder in the gentlest reproof, resisting Andor's efforts to shake himself free.

'I hope that will not be your last word in the matter, Herr Andor. I sincerely hope not, for your sake most of all.'

He went across the room and unlocked the intercommunicating door beyond which Martina Hansen waited. Then, looking once more at Andor though without speaking, he left the father and daughter to their reunion.

Elliott watched with misgiving. Andor got wearily to his feet, supporting himself by his hands on the table as the young woman came in. She had been, Elliott supposed, a child of his middle age, born at a time when his enthusiasm for fatherhood had passed its zenith. They greeted one another politely and kissed formally. But intimacy failed in their words and gestures. In a moment more they were standing together like two strangers introduced by a well-meaning host and left to endure a shy and oppressive silence.

Presently Andor took his daughter's hand and led her to sit beside him on the edge of the bed.

'You must not believe it.' There was no hope in his tone, no expectation that she would do as he wished. 'You must not believe what they tell you about me. That is all that I ask.'

'They have told me little. They ask, that is all.'

It was now, in turning to her, that he saw the bruise discolouring her cheek under the make-up. He touched it lightly with his fingertips.

'And that? They did that? These men who ask the questions?'

'Yes.' She dropped her head a little and spoke as if ashamed of what had been done to her.

Andor made no reply. Instead he seemed to hunch

himself a little tighter, looking down at his hands folded in his lap. Then he began to cry.

The four officers watched from beyond the observation panel.

'That is enough,' said Rubin, just loudly enough for the others to hear. 'If you allow this to go too far, you will spoil everything.'

Unhindered by the others, he entered the adjoining room where Martina Hansen had been resting alone earlier in the morning. Elliott saw him open the communicating door and beckon the girl, who still sat beside her father, close to him and yet separated by their independent loyalties. She got up, walked slowly across to the door and went into the other room. Now it was Rubin who closed the door and came to the bed where the old man sat. He took Martina's place beside him. Elliott's sense of irony was stirred by the quietness of Rubin's sympathy for the prisoner, a display beyond anything which Martina had been able to pretend towards her father. Rubin seemed to be a willing substitute for the true child, behaving towards Andor almost like a son to an ailing father.

'I am sorry it has come to this, my friend,' he said gently. 'You think because I represent the nation and the army you hate most that I cannot share your feelings. I assure you that is not so.'

Andor shook his head without looking up.

'How can you share anything of mine? You who brought her here to be treated so?'

'It was not my decision.' The Russian spread out his broad hands in a gesture familiar to Elliott. 'You must blame yourself a little too. When you started on such a course of action – to promise the death of so many people – you cannot have thought that your daughter or any other person close to you would be immune from reprisals.'

Andor looked up at the word.

'Reprisals?'

Rubin nodded, slowly and mournfully.

'It is clear that she knows nothing of your plan, but that

will not save her. They will do these things to her in order that you will cooperate. The walls between these two rooms are thin enough. Can you not guess the sounds which you must hear, the shrillness in the night? They will kill her if they have to – as they would kill you – slowly and without compunction. What is your suffering – or hers – compared to the death and agony of thousands?'

Andor was looking up at Rubin now with the first sign of contempt.

'Then they must answer for it.'

Rubin shook his head and laid his hand briefly on Andor's shoulder.

'The true martyrs are not those who die by the bullet at the end of every failed hi-jacking or kidnapping. They are the men and women who survive, marched away to captivity by their enemies. There is no trial, no further reference to them. Their stations of the cross are a long and bitter progress to the final bullet in the back of the skull, somewhere in a cellar or a ditch. They exist in Israel and Arabia, Africa and the Latin states, even here in Germany. The martyrs of Entebbe, Our Lady of Mogadishu, the rich young German girl. Dead by now or living a life which would make death a blessing. You and your daughter must join the company of such saints and martyrs.'

Andor listened with a glimmer of uncertainty in his eyes. It was Rubin's skill that he could talk of such horrors as if he truly did not care whether they were believed or not. He knew them to be facts.

27

Elliott turned the car into the little road that led to the maisonette, parked it under the trees and turned off the engine. Oppression and frustration weighed upon him. The entire scheme of using Martina Hansen to break Andor's resistance had been a farce, from beginning to end. That it was a farce he had helped to engineer did nothing to lighten his mood. Short of extreme physical or mental suffering, Andor would not bc made to talk. That was the brief and clear reality.

He walked up the concrete stairs outside the building and thought of that other world within. The sunlight on the plain polished wood of the bedroom furniture; lamp-light on the carpet as the melody of the *Regenslieder* wove its evening spell. It was in this new dimension of his life with Debby that sanity and certainty survived.

So that she should not be seen at the door, he slid his key in quickly and opened it before she could walk across. Shadowed sunlight through the pine trees lit the silent sitting-room and he knew she must be in the kitchen. The taps were off, the stove cold, the kitchen freshly cleaned and empty. In the bedrooms, the beds had been made with clean sheets, the furniture dusted and polished. The rooms were empty.

In a cold apprehension, Elliott searched the maisonette. But Debby had gone. It was possible, he thought, that she had been taken. But it was not likely. Neither Rubin nor Schroeder had a use for her. Corrigan would not have risked the consequences. Perhaps she had made up her mind to go. Then she had cleaned the maisonette, room by room, polishing the floors and scrubbing the pans, as if discharging a debt to him. They were quits now.

He walked the length of the room and back, certainties and contradictions rivalling one another in his mind. What if Debby had been abducted? An amateur would have left the signs of a struggle behind him in his haste to get the girl out. The scrubbed pans and polished floors were a sign of the professional. Rubin, Schroeder, Corrigan? Perhaps there had been a visit from those who had eliminated Corporal Hoskins. At the thought of this, he felt the chill of perspiration down his spine and round his heart.

Looking at the mirror-glass chess-table, he thought for the first time that Debby might already have been killed.

Elliott walked across to the phone, hesitated, then picked it up and dialled Corrigan's home number.

'I want to know, Pat, what kind of surveillance your people have had on my apartment.'

'There is no surveillance,' said Corrigan bleakly. 'And even if there was, you know quite well we should tell you that there wasn't. Does that answer the question?'

'Pat,' Elliott tried to give the impression of patience at its limit, 'there has been an incident here. I want witnesses. That's all.'

'We don't have them,' Corrigan said. 'There was a moment when you roused our curiosity as to which woman you were keeping in your apartment. It now appears that it can't have been Andor's daughter or his sister. Apart from those, Sam, you are welcome to the rest of womankind so far as US intelligence is concerned. No one has the least need or desire to survey you. What you do to the maid is up to you.'

Elliott paused. During the last few minutes he had been constructing a plan in his mind quite separately from the telephone conversation.

'A few hours from now,' he said quietly, 'and I shall have the entire truth about Andor. Whoever wants it is going to have some questions to answer first.'

'We don't buy options on promises,' Corrigan said. 'I assume from all this that Hoskins' woman has disappeared. We haven't got her. We don't want her. There's a page every day in the *Berliner Zeitung*, between the household ads and the situations vacant. Ladies' names and telephone numbers. *Modell*, *diskret*, *gute Figur*. *Domina*, *travestie*, take your pick. Read it, Sam. You might find what you're looking for.'

Before Elliott could answer, Corrigan had put down the phone.

He dialled again and rang through to the duty lieutenant at the Entlastungs-Strasse RMP post.

'Major Elliott. I want an NCO and two men detailed to the checkpoint. It's possible that an attempt will be made in the next few hours to smuggle a British citizen into East Berlin against her will. I want any vehicle stopped and searched if there are the least grounds for suspicion. The subject is about twenty years old, slightly built, with long fair hair. I'll come down there myself as soon as I can. Until then, take charge of the operation yourself.'

Last of all he phoned Colonel Rubin at the Soviet Officers Club in Potsdam.

'Corporal Hoskins' girl has gone missing,' he said bluntly. 'We want to know where she is. It's possible that Schroeder knows something of the matter.'

'Ah,' said Rubin gently, 'the *petite amie*! So, if you have lost her, Mr Elliott, I deduce that you must have found her to begin with. She is, I think, a charming child. I would congratulate you upon the excellence of your taste, my friend, if that were appropriate.'

As on so many occasions Elliott sensed, under the courtesy of the speech, the mockery of the Soviet colonel.

'She is a witness. Our witness to certain events in West Berlin.'

'Alas, Mr Elliott, I have not got her. I cannot answer for Captain Schroeder. I do not believe that solemn little fellow would go to such trouble for the *petite amie*. What can she be to him? Is that not how we say it in England?'

'I'm putting a search on all vehicles crossing into East Berlin,' Elliott said sharply.

'You *must*.' Rubin spoke earnestly enough but his voice still betrayed the invisible smile. 'You can do no less, Mr Elliott. Had I the honour to be a British officer holding your command, I should do exactly the same.'

Controlling his anger, Elliott said, 'In a few hours more I shall be in possession of certain information about Andor. Information not otherwise available to anyone else. I want the girl returned wherever she may be.'

He heard Rubin's sympathetic sigh.

'Mr Elliott, I have seen more of life than you young fellows. Now you will never persuade me that the *petite amie* has not found a corner in your heart. Believe me, I do not reproach you. I will speak to Captain Schroeder. I will do what I can, but what can I do? I fear you have had a tiff– that is the word?–and that the young lady has left of her own accord.'

'She is a witness,' the major said coldly, 'nothing more.'

Rubin gave another sigh.

'Between men and women, Mr Elliott, there can be no such thing as "nothing more". Between men alone friendship is possible. You know, I laugh sometimes to myself after I talk with you. Because our countries have their differences, the world imagines you and I planning all the time to hate and fight. But all the while we are such good friends.'

At the limit of exasperation, Elliott ended the conversation. He had achieved nothing and had betrayed to both Rubin and Corrigan the nature of his feelings for Debby. The phone rang a few minutes later. He picked it up, knowing that he would hear her voice. It was Sadleir, the duty lieutenant at Spandau. Sadleir had the skilfully modulated voice of the public school salesman. Elliott imagined him selling water to drowning men and earning the gratitude of his victims.

'Last report for tonight, sir,' Sadleir said. 'You wanted to be told . . .'

'Save it,' Elliott glanced at his watch, 'I'm coming over. I want a search bulletin put out for a witness in the disappearance of Corporal Hoskins. I'll dictate the details when I get there. And I want to look at our prisoner.'

'He's been asleep an hour, sir.'

'Then I'll wake him,' Elliott said. 'It'll be no trouble. I shall need two reliable NCOs from the security wing. And a few bits and pieces. A scalpel, some swabs, and a small surgical bowl. Gowns and masks.'

Sadleir repeated the items, as if making a list.

'Amateur theatricals, sir?' he asked brightly.

Elliott thought of the leverage he might acquire in the search for Debby if he could break Andor unaided in the next few hours.

'Believe me,' he said quietly, 'there will be nothing amateur about this.'

28

Major Elliott came to him at night when the observation ward was lit only by the dim blue flush of the guard-light. Andor stirred in the artificial twilight, his mind between waking and sleeping. His first thought was that he heard no sound of Martina or the interrogators in the adjoining room. Then he moved his tongue and was aware of the musty sweetness which hung like a foul breath in his throat and mouth. A drug to make him sleep, that was the answer. Mixed in his food and drink, since he had not taken it otherwise.

If it was a drug, how had he woken so soon? Prompted at once by the thought, he felt the soreness of his upper arm and guessed that he had been injected with the antidote a few moments before. Was it merely an antidote – or something worse?

Elliott was standing at the foot of the bed, flanked by two men in aprons and caps who might equally have been butchers or surgeons. Andor knew instinctively that they were the interrogators. Unlike the torturers of the inquisition, they were neatly and hygenically dressed, as if to save bodies rather than souls. Yet the white surgical masks across their mouths and noses had all the brutal and dehumanised manner of the executioner's black hood.

The major spoke quietly to the two assistants. They gripped the old man's arms between them, strapping his wrists to the rail on either side of the bed. Elliott stooped over his prisoner. In the blue shadows of the lamp, the cold implacable anger of his eyes was just visible.

'The first questions will be of little consequence,' he said gently. 'You will lose nothing by answering them. A refusal to answer will be of great consequence – to you and Martina

Hansen.'

He straightened up again and nodded to his assistants. One man raised Andor's head while the other placed a white surgical bowl underneath so that, when his head was lowered again, it rested within the shallow enamel dish.

'We shall talk about Ezeiza,' Elliott sat down on the side of the bed, the shadow of his bulk darkening Andor's view, 'about the model of the VAX-786 and the copy of the IBM-38.'

'I will answer no more questions.'

'Forgive me.' Elliott's voice grew softer in a mockery of courteous dissension. 'You will answer whatever questions I choose to ask. Either before or after the use of the surgeon's knife. The choice is yours.'

Lying in blue twilight with his hands strapped to the bed-rails, Andor knew with the cold impulse of terror that the major meant every word in earnest.

'I want you to understand.' Elliott's voice was quiet, untiring, and pitiless. 'I want you to be under no illusion. You will not be subject to the ill-treatment of the police barracks here. No electrodes or batons. You might endure until you died. But have you any idea, Herr Andor, how simple a piece of surgery it is to cut out a man's eye?'

Andor gasped in his panic and pulled vainly at his bonds.

'A ruffian with his finger and thumb could remove an eye in a moment,' Elliott continued. 'A surgeon with a scalpel can do it in a few cuts. Believe me, when you have lost one eye you will answer any question put to you to save the other. How much more sensible to cooperate in the first place. Otherwise, as you will appreciate, our attentions to you will go far beyond your eyes. There will come a point, Herr Andor, where you know, even in blindness, that damage is being done to you – vital damage – which no surgery can repair. If you choose to be obstinate, I will bring you to such a condition that you will answer at last to obtain the blessing of a quick and easy death. Be in no doubt about it. When so many lives are at stake, no one here will pity you. It is by your own choice that these things must happen.'

Andor gave a sudden start of alarm as a light came on. It was not the dazzling beam of interrogation mythology but a white and steady glow which illuminated his face as the old man lay pale and blinking before his tormentors.

'Now,' said Elliott, 'your full name, if you please.'

'You know my full name!' What Andor had intended as a howl of defiance sounded, even in his own ears, like a wail of self-pity.

'Do you really intend to incur pain by refusing to reply to such a question?'

'My name is Karl Rainer Andor.'

'Good,' said Elliott encouragingly. 'And when did you first go to Ezeiza?'

'You already know!'

'Indeed. But you will tell me again, Herr Andor. Will you not?'

'It was eight years ago.'

One of the surgeons moved the light a little so that it fell more squarely on the round pale face.

'When were you given charge of the new computer project?'

'After three years.'

Now he was on the slope with nothing to stop him. Having begun to answer the questions which did not matter, how would he be able to determine the moment of refusal?

'What was your assignment?'

'The programming support environment of the IBM-38 copy.'

'What specifically?'

'The programming language of military systems.'

'Which language?'

Andor sensed the moment when the slope might become a precipice. He lay tense and still under the light without replying.

'CHILL,' said Elliott patiently. 'Argentine military systems use CHILL as their programming system. There is no secret about it. The language is commercially available in other forms. I beg you, Herr Andor, not to endanger your own well being or your daughter's by refusing to answer questions. Especially when some of the answers are known to us already. Why court martyrdom to no purpose?'

In this moment of respite from interrogation, Andor felt his courage revive a little.

'In a few more days, you and I and everyone who remains in this city will be dead. I am in fear of you, Major Elliott, but nothing you do can alter that truth.'

When Elliott contradicted the old man, his voice had the quiet tone of reassurance, as if setting Andor's misgivings aside.

'No,' he said gently, 'no. You will not die, Herr Andor. You may be sure that you are the last person whose death will be permitted in that fashion. When you have answered all the questions put to you, perhaps that will be another matter. Then we shall see.'

One of the masked surgeons touched a small white dish on the table and there was the rattle of a finely-honed blade.

'CHILL,' Elliott resumed the interrogation. 'Tell me. What were the functions of CHILL at Ezeiza?'

'If you know, it is foolish to ask.'

'I did not say that I knew, Herr Andor. Whether I do or not, you are going to tell me.'

Andor paused. It was certain that the development of CHILL by the British Ministry of Defence and their civilian contractors was advanced enough for Elliott to guess the answer if necessary.

'It was used in weapons guidance systems during the construction of warheads, and in controlling their military deployment.'

'Good.' The major touched the old man's shoulder lightly. 'You see how easily we shall get through our inquiry if you continue to answer sensibly. Your ultimate secret does not concern me tonight. I merely wish to be convinced that you were able to do the thing which you claim. How did you override the instructions for deployment in the case of one warhead?'

'By discovering one of the super-user codes. It was a matter of luck.'

'Which code was that?'

'I cannot tell you.'

Elliott assumed the tone of a disappointed teacher confronted with a difficult pupil.

'I thought, Herr Andor, we were agreed upon the foolhardiness of your refusing to answer questions which no longer mattered. You have accomplished what you set out to do. How can it matter which code you penetrated?'

'I cannot tell you because I do not remember it.'

Elliott shook his head.

'You cannot tell me because you never penetrated the codes. You are a thief, Herr Andor, but you were no petty pickpocket. To break a super-user code is a feeble explanation. It is like the thief who claims that he found the gold watch lying in the road. The method and the excuse are unworthy of you. You are the criminal who could empty an impenetrable vault of its bullion and leave no sign of how you came or went. Do you understand me?'

For a moment Andor's vision penetrated beyond the light which shone upon his face. It seemed that he had risen to a higher level of consciousness and that in the previous minutes he had not been fully awake. The room now appeared to be empty and the voice which had sounded in the blue twilight was silent. He struggled to move but his arms were still held fast. It occurred to him that he might be dreaming. Day after day and night after night he had rehearsed such interrogations, what he would say and what he would struggle to hold back as they dealt more brutally with him. Now, he thought, his imaginings had taken the form of a well-rehearsed drama in his own mind.

The sweet mustiness in his mouth and throat moved like a vapour in his breath, filling his head and blurring the clearer vision. Beyond the white light the room was dark again and he heard Elliott's voice.

'Tell me from the beginning how you overrode the instructions. Why was it that the super-users saw nothing amiss with the instructions?'

Whatever uncertainty Andor had felt about the value of his previous answers was now gone. Elliott had penetrated by his quiet skill to the secret which lay at the heart of Andor's strategy. In the dim blue flush of the observation ward, the enemy pressed against the fortress wall of the skull's truth.

'They were careless. Inept. Without the help of advisers they would never have mastered the most basic mathematical languages.'

'No.' The word was hardly more than a whisper in the darkness beyond the light. 'I will ask you once more. How did you conceal your manipulation of the weapon's deployment from those who could have called up the details at any time?'

'They were not competent to interpret the data.'

The frame of the bed creaked as Elliott stood up.

'If you choose to undergo a pointless martyrdom, I shall not prevent you.' One of the masked surgeons was carrying the white dish from the table. 'I shall not intervene. Indeed, I shall ask you no further questions until you have undergone the first ordeal.'

Andor's heart beat in his throat at the sound of the major going towards the door. Now he knew that they were in earnest. The surgeon with the bowl spoke to his colleague.

'Hold his head firmly. Draw the skin down a little further below the eyeball.'

Andor felt himself in the firm embrace of the surgeon's assistant in a sardonic parody of fondness. The tips of three fingers drew down the baggy skin beneath his eye, the thumb drawing the lid upwards. He cried out, the heartbeat almost choking him. With the skin pulled back, the eye bulged grotesquely, like a hanged man's. He was rushing down the slope towards the precipice of terror.

In the last moment he could not tell whether Elliott was still in the room nor whether he had cried out the major's name during these preliminaries. Nausea welled up in his gullet and he heard the light metallic contact of the hard blade with the side of the bowl.

'Hold him. Keep the swabs close to the cheek.'

His feet were free and he twisted them helplessly under the blanket but from the waist up his body was immobilised. The cold light shone on a hard polished surface and he saw the slim blade of the scalpel. It touched his face, following the lower contour of his left eye-socket, along the bone. The pain of the cut was so sharp as to numb him though he felt the wetness of blood. From his throat he vomited the cry of terror which alone might save him.

'ADA! ADA!'

At once their movements stopped and the blade was lifted clear of his face.

'That's enough,' said Elliott from the shadows. 'That's all I needed to hear.'

The arms which had been holding the old man now released him. His two masked tormentors stood back. Another needle seemed to pierce his arm again, though he scarcely felt it, and the black narcotic cloud weighed upon consciousness too heavily to be borne. His hands were free and he touched the wound below his eye. But now there was no cut and no blood. Only a smear of water that was colder than snow.

Waking at daylight, with sickness in his stomach and confusion in his mind, Andor tried to piece together the dialogue of nightmare. Perhaps, after all, it was the final dream rehearsal in his own mind for the encounter which must soon come. His ordered intelligence required the logic of the 'blade' of ice to explain his cry of betrayal.

He raised himself and saw on the table the small surgical bowl. Then he knew that his cry had been a reality, and that now the battle was moving towards its end.

ADA. Had they heard him? If they heard him, would they understand? There was no doubt of it. The flag still flew in all its bravado, but now the enemy was within the fortress wall.

29

'For that?' Corrigan's voice was dulled by incredulity. 'Any of our cybernetics people could have identified the computer language in half an hour! You might have killed him for nothing!'

'It'll take more than that to kill him,' Elliott said.

The two men, with Rubin and Bonnell-Thornton, sat round the briefing table.

'What's worse,' Corrigan said. 'you've tricked him to no purpose. That's all our chances gone!'

Rubin looked up, his broad-topped uniform cap on the table.

'What is ADA in relation to CHILL?'

'More complex,' Corrigan said. 'It takes a mathematical genius like Andor to control it. NATO abandoned it in 1984 as the most likely cause of World War III. The Defence Department named it after our first programmer. Ada Lovelace. Died 1852.'

'So,' said Rubin. 'Mr Andor's computer at Ezeiza talks two languages. But he is the only person who knows that it speaks ADA?'

'Right,' said Corrigan sharply. 'Like having a servant whom you order to obey commands in Russian. Unknown to you, someone else has taught him German and ordered him to give priority to any command spoken in that language. In this case it worked even better. If someone else stumbled across ADA they thought the machine was acting up. Call for good old Dr Andor.'

Rubin bowed his broad head in acknowledgement. Then he looked up again.

'But would it work in practice, Mr Corrigan,' he asked innocently.

'It would. It did. His pet computer would send three warheads to Rio Gallegos and one to Timbuctoo, while telling its masters that all four had gone to Rio Gallegos. Or it could list a completed warhead as still under construction. It could send a bomb to the docks at Buenos Aires for shipment to Germany under the description of nuclear fuel to be irradiated at Karlruhe or en route to the Hahn-Meitner Institute. It's what everyone in the game has dreaded. A computer with a secret life – and a secret lover.'

Bonnell-Thornton looked round at the others.

'What remedy is there, now that we know the method he used?'

This time it was Corrigan who answered him.

'There's no one in Ezeiza, no one in Argentina who can cope with ADA. In the last two hours we've made contact and given them instructions as to what to do until help arrives. They've done their best. So far as ADA is concerned, the machine seems to know only one word. *Vergesslichkeit*.'

'Meaning?'

'Oblivion. As we anticipated, he taught his creature to forget what it had been told and what it had done. The three men who pioneered ADA are being flown down from the Pentagon to Ezeiza. They don't hold out much hope. Interrogating Andor will be child's play by comparison with questioning his creation.'

The silence which settled on the room was broken only by the fading and surging of car engines at the traffic lights on the Gatower-Strasse. Bonnell-Thornton, the senior officer present, now resumed his authority.

'If Andor is to be believed, we have five days. In the next forty-eight hours, we must either break him or accede to his demands.'

'The Democratic Republic will not consent to a violation of its territorial integrity,' said Rubin suavely. 'I tell you that at once. Not as a policy which I dictate but a fact of which I am assured.'

'If the moment comes, I doubt the consent will be asked.'

Corrigan looked at Bonnell-Thornton, not Rubin, as he spoke, suggesting that they shared a joke at the Russian's expense. Rubin shrugged.

'In that case, gentlemen, you must break your prisoner or take the consequences. If the territory of the German Democratic Republic is violated by an attempt of the NATO powers to open its frontiers, then the treaty obligations of the Warsaw Pact are bound to be invoked. The piracy which this man has committed relates to your territory and your responsibilities.'

The face which had formed such lines of joviality and bonhomie during Elliott's visits to Potsdam or Treptow was now blank and implacable as a tribal war-mask.

'And if the West Berliners learn of the threat and begin a panic exodus across the frontier?'

Rubin looked quickly from Elliott to Corrigan on either side of him.

'It will be a matter for the immigration authorities of the Democratic Republic.'

'For God's sake!' In his exasperation, Corrigan got up and crossed to the window, staring out at the drab barrack blocks of Spandau. After a moment he turned to face the others.

'If Andor is to be broken, I have a request from General Page. To prevent a repetition of last night's incident, Andor is to be removed from the British Military Hospital to the hospital wing of the Wilhelm-Strasse military prison – under four-power protection.'

'Why?' Elliott, facing defeat in the matter, seemed resolved on forcing his opponent to the brink.

'So that by tomorrow morning our suspect's fingernails have not been removed with a pair of pliers.' Corrigan left no doubt that Page's 'request' was a command.

Bonnell-Thornton sat sullen and preoccupied for a moment.

'That means telling the French,' he said glumly.

30

'You are afraid,' said Corrigan reasonably. 'Of course you are. How could you fail to be? But yours is not the fear of cowardice, rather the apprehension that your plan will never work.'

He undid the tunic of his olive-green uniform, took it off and hung it on the back of the chair. Andor watched him, passive and without apprehension.

'Not fear of death.' Corrigan sat down again. 'Not that. Fear of betraying your country's cause and those two men who have died for it. Vogel and Nunvar. Vogel who assembled the remains of an antiquated weapons-mechanism in a cellar at Dahlem. And Nunvar who smuggled a laboratory flask contaminated by plutonium out of Ezeiza – and died for it. It was the flask that betrayed you to Argentine security, not the computer.'

It seemed that Andor was about to smile at the irony of it. Instead he shrugged his shoulders.

'It was a risk. We knew it was the greatest of the dangers.'

In the overheated ward, Corrigan felt the perspiration gather on his spine and down his ribs. He went to the basin again, drew two glasses of water, and handed one to the prisoner.

'Do you imagine that there is a single person in West Berlin – German, British, American, French – who does not want the same as you?'

Andor looked up and pulled a face.

'They want only what can be had without cost. It suits your country to have Germany divided, Major Corrigan. It suits you, for different reasons, as greatly as it does your friend Colonel Rubin. So long as Germany consists of two client-states, your battlelines are accurately drawn and the division of Europe is accomplished. If Germany were united and independent, there would be an end of the two great powers in Europe. The line would vanish and the deadlock would be broken. The truth is, major, that you and Colonel Rubin prefer the deadlock. You each know where you stand. That is the phrase, is it not?'

Looking at the old man, Corrigan felt further than ever from the success he had promised himself. But the time had not yet come. As the days passed, Andor would weaken. It was always the case with political blackmailers, in Corrigan's experience. Patiently he returned to the attack.

'A nuclear disaster in Berlin, the death of thousands or millions in central Europe, will do nothing to bring about Germany unity.'

Andor pulled the same sceptical face.

'No one will die. Either there will be agreement between us or you will evacuate those in danger.'

'How?'

'I do not know. It will be done.'

'The possibility of evacuating Berlin under such circumstances has been considered on many occasions,' said Corrigan softly. 'It is a logistical impossibility. It will not happen.'

He was gratified to see Andor's composure shaken again.

'There have been previous occasions?'

Corrigan looked at the old man, as if to console him.

'Surely you did not believe, Dr Andor, that you were the first? Like the others, your only hope is in realistic negotiation.'

'I should like a cigarette.'

Corrigan shook one from the packet, gave it to the old man and once again lit it for him.

'What can you offer me, major?' The words were blank of hope.

Corrigan sat back and pulled his tie loose at the neck.

'Almost everything you ask for – at the right moment. You want the union of your country beginning with reunion in Berlin? You want the opening of the frontier within the city as a token of this? Those things you demand will be conceded before long – with or without your intervention. The West Berlin government and the DDR are close to an agreement which would give all citizens of Berlin – east and west – a common form of identity card. For West Berliners, the frontier check would be as casual as the one which now applies to diplomatic and military personnel.'

'And for the east?'

'In exchange for economic assistance and technical expertise, the DDR will extend permission to travel – no longer confined to age-groups over sixty. Not to the entire population at first but gradually through categories of age and employment.'

'It will be too late.'

'No.' Corrigan leant forward towards the old man as if steering him back on to the paths of logic. 'Confidence must be built first. You will never move the DDR by threats. They have too much to be frightened of among their own people to care about you. You think they fear your bomb? Even if they believe you, they are much more alarmed about the possibility of an uprising among their own people. Let them move in their own way. Let them concede freedom by stages. They will do nothing otherwise, so long as they think that freedom of movement will be followed by a sudden exodus of skilled manpower.'

'You are deceived. Whatever they say to you, they will grant nothing in the end.'

But Corrigan listened to the tone of the old man's voice rather than to his words and knew that he could win. Not now, not this afternoon, but Andor's resistance would give way under such kindly persuasion long before the final days were over. He asked only to be convinced by the major that his scepticism about the intentions of the DDR was misplaced.

Corrigan stood up and touched the old man's shoulder.

'I'm not lying to you, Dr Andor. I wouldn't blame you for treating the DDR's negotiators as liars. That would be my own reaction. If you wish to treat me as your enemy too, you may. But you are wrong.'

Andor looked up and Corrigan nodded as if to reassure him.

'Don't you see it, Dr Andor? I want the very things which you demand. The United States and her allies have worked for Germany – through diplomacy – over many years. I don't pretend to want reunification as keenly as you – and those who have their homes here. How could I?'

'I would not expect that,' said the old man quietly.

'Of course not.' Corrigan was gentle as a nurse with a child. 'But you and I have identical aims. We differ in method and timing. That's all. Won't you listen to me, at least? If I thought I could accomplish those aims by planting in Berlin the biggest bomb ever built, I would do it. I hope I should have such courage and resolve as yours. But I know the ways of diplomacy as you know the laws of science. I know – surely know – that such an act must postpone all hope of achieving what you want. It may even destroy it for ever.'

Andor's lower lip moved as if to make a reply. But he said nothing. Corrigan laid a hand on his shoulder again.

'Please,' he said softly. 'Think of what I have said. I shall come to see you again tomorrow. But if you want me at any time – day or night – you have only to ask the duty warder. Whatever the time, I shall get the call in a few minutes and come straight here. If I said I was your friend, you would not believe me. But for the sake of millions of innocent men, women, and children, I beg you to believe that I understand what you want. Truly I do.'

There was no further response from the prisoner. Corrigan turned and walked from the hospital room, hearing the door lock with an hermetic click behind him.

Major Elliott was waiting in the corridor.

'I can't tell,' said Corrigan thoughtfully. 'I may have done some good. For a moment I thought the old fool was on the move. Once that happens, Sam, we've got him. He's on the brink. When he starts to fall he won't be able to stop himself, any more than a man who jumps from the roof can climb back half-way.'

Elliott ignored this, trumping Corrigan's hope with hard news.

'Rubin's bringing Martina Hansen over again.'

'It might be better if the old man saw no one but us,' Corrigan said. 'Being confronted with his daughter, it could go either way. I'd rather not take the risk.'

Elliott held up his hand.

'Rubin makes no conditions. I offered to have her held securely in Moabit. The women's wing. We've got an arrangement for prisoners to be held there under RMP guard.'

'What good will it do if Andor sees her?'

'Perhaps it would be better if he heard her, Pat.'

Corrigan turned away.

'Oh, God!' he said wearily, 'that's hopeless.'

'No, Pat,' said Elliott patiently. 'In the last resort it's not hopeless. Will you let a million people die rather than run a hundred volts through Frau Hansen's sensitive parts? Talk to Laplace. He was a lieutenant in Algeria, during the troubles. They never used a voltage which they hadn't tried on themselves. Torture's come a long way since the middle ages. Can you imagine the *bourreau* testing the hot iron on his own skin?'

'Try it,' said Corrigan grimly, 'and Page will have Bonnell-Thornton court-martial you!'

'Not unless we're going to discuss some of Page's own little japes as a military adviser. In any case, Pat, you'd have no evidence. Fear works faster than electrodes. This is the real world, not the Groton honour class or the Porcellian at Harvard.'

Corrigan said nothing. He walked to the main entrance of the building and called Bonnell-Thornton's office.

31

That evening Corrigan's car drew up at the grey doors filling the entrance arch of the British Military Prison in the Wilhelm-Strasse. The diminutive castle gate with its gothic towers in red brick stood among Spandau's suburban concrete. A strip of land with a wire fence surrounding it protected this last prison of the Nazi leaders from public curiosity.

The British guards had taken over from their Soviet predecessors for the next month. As a sergeant of the RMP checked his identity card, Corrigan glanced up at the tall perimeter wall of the brick prison. The Royal Fusiliers from the adjoining barracks now provided the guard. Where the concrete platforms had been perched at the wall's corners, the figures of the steel-helmeted sentries were just visible.

After a brief telephone call from the guard-room to the security control, the RMP sergeant waved Corrigan through. Within the surrounding wall, the prison complex consisted of a tall central block, its walls pierced by gothic windows, the long cell corridors running off in an arm to the north. Beyond this was the hospital block, its tall brick chimney rising beside it.

Corrigan left the car and walked to the door in the perimeter wall. He knew from previous visits that the door could only be operated by one of the guards on their platforms, when clearance was given at security control. As he stood and waited, the grey oblong of a television scanner was angled motionless above him. Two RMP corporals met him, saluted, and fell into step as they crossed the broad expanse of the exercise yard. The remaining Nazi leader was too far gone in senility to exercise any more. A tall poplar tree, planted in the prison garden by Grand Admiral Doenitz thirty years before was the only evidence of those who had long since been released or died.

At the entrance of the hospital block, the British Director, Colonel Forbes, had just begun his month's duty. Corrigan supposed it could have been worse, it could have been the turn of the French or the Russians to mount guard. He made polite and uninformative conversation with Forbes as the colonel led the way to the ward where Andor was being held. In the green distempered corridor, the old man's words were just audible through the intercom channel, whose volume control had been turned down.

'*Ein Hauch um nichts. Ein Wehn im Gott. Ein Wind.*'

'He's been doing that most of the while,' said Forbes disapprovingly. 'Chanting to himself. Like a litany of some sort.'

The old man was on his feet now. Intoning the lines, he walked as if his feet might be blistered from pacing the prison room.

'Rilke,' said Corrigan casually. 'He seems to have learnt most of the *Orpheus Sonnets* by heart. His fortress wall.'

Forbes shrugged, dismissing Andor and his eccentricities.

'Will you be long?'

'Yes,' said Corrigan dispassionately. 'A long, long time.'

The ward which he entered was scarcely distinguishable from the room Andor had occupied at the military hospital, except that the window was securely barred.

'*An aimless breath*,' Corrigan translated the line overheard, '*A stirring in the god . . .*'

The old man sat down, quiet and at ease.

'Rilke,' he said. 'The breath of true song. *Ein andrer Hauch.*'

Corrigan nodded.

'It's all over.' He sat down and faced Andor. 'You shall have what you ask for. By the authority of the United States government and with the reluctant consent of the Soviet Union. If such a battle can be won, you have won yours.'

He had expected Andor to receive the news with scepticism, indifference. In this he was right. But Corrigan persisted.

'You have no reason to hold back now. The Glienicker Bridge will be open for travellers in both directions from midnight tonight. Other crossings will be opened in the next week or two. Glienicker is easy but work needs to be done at the other checkpoints to clear the way.'

'Am I to believe you?'

'No.' Corrigan shook his head. 'Why should you? My instructions are to take you to Glienicker tomorrow so that you may see for yourself.'

'Is it true?' Andor appeared to direct the question to himself.

Corrigan leant forward.

'The demands you have made are those freedoms for which the western allies have argued and negotiated over many years. You did not believe me when I told you that the very things you demanded had already been agreed in principle? My orders are that you shall see for yourself.'

Andor shrugged.

'It would be an easy matter to close the Glienicker Bridge again.'

'No,' said Corrigan gently. 'The Soviets and the East Germans would not have given way at all if they meant to close it again.'

'If it is only the Glienicker Bridge, that is too little. It could be closed.'

'Glienicker is the pebble which will start the avalanche.' Corrigan scanned the old man's face for the first sign of yielding. 'There will be no going back. Everything you ask for will be conceded within a few weeks. Are you prepared to destroy your city, your country, perhaps the world, because every task cannot be done in the next three days?'

'How am I to know that it is not a trick?'

'By the evidence of your own eyes.' Corrigan counted off the possibilities on his fingers. 'You shall see the Glienicker Bridge open for travellers – east and west. I will bring any of the negotiators of the agreements here for you to talk to. If you wish to see the work beginning on other checkpoints, that can be arranged. Remember, though, how close the deadline is which you yourself have set.'

'There is time,' Andor nodded to reassure the major. 'Twelve hours will be enough for you to do all that is necessary. After Glienicker, we will see.'

Corrigan felt his throat tighten as he asked the final question.

'Glienicker – will that be enough for you?'

'If I believe.' Andor looked the major hard in the eye. 'If it is not a trick. Perhaps then.'

Despite his promise to Colonel Forbes of the length of time he would be with Andor, Corrigan knew better than to continue his questions. After Glienicker, it would be a different matter. He left the ward and went out into the green distempered corridor where Elliott was waiting.

'I hope to God you're right, Pat!' The gloom in Elliott's voice was heavy enough to sound like a physical affliction. 'I hope to God you're right, and I'm wrong. It's never going to work.'

Corrigan concealed his misgivings with a suavity he remained far from feeling.

'It'll work when he's on his own again, Sam. When he has nothing to think about but the fact that he may destroy everything for the sake of a couple of weeks' delay.'

'And meantime?'

'And meantime,' said Corrigan, 'Just be thankful for our friend Colonel Rubin and the serried ranks of the Soviet garrison at Potsdam.'

The two men walked together from the stale disinfectant odour of the prison hospital into the heat of the Berlin summer.

'If it doesn't work!' Elliott said for the second time.

Corrigan tightened the strap of his wrist-watch a little. He looked up at his companion with eyes whose gaze was a fine balance of amusement and contempt.

'In that case, Sam, I imagine you'll get your way. An hour or two of human carpentry. Eight fingernails and two thumbs.'

'I wonder, Pat,' said Elliott thoughtfully. 'Shall we be

able to hear the old man's cries above the splashing of our allies' hands being washed?'

Corrigan smiled without humour. The two majors turned and walked away in opposite directions.

32

By the time that the sun had risen above the sluggish waters of the lake with its fringe of trees, the scene resembled a badly organised film set. On the allied side of the bridge the car park was filled early by the Volkswagens and Audis of West Berlin. Few of the occupants showed any intention of crossing the bridge towards Potsdam. They stood in small groups on their own side of the bridge waiting for the first movements from the far bank. A US Army jeep was parked close to the first girder-arch of the Glienicker crossing. General Page perched on the back of the passenger seat and scanned the further shore through binoculars.

An olive-green helicopter appeared at insect-size over the woodland of the Wannsee shore. It dropped down and swooped in a low arc across the Glienicker Bridge and the invisible frontier.

'Corrigan,' said Elliott for Bonnell-Thornton's information. 'What the devil is Rubin playing at? He's late!'

'Everything in the DDR runs late,' said the commandant equably. 'Why should this be an exception?'

On the East German side of the bridge the troops had been withdrawn and only two volkspolizei stood by, as if to keep order when the crowd formed. A score of men and women, a few children, in family groups of four or five, appeared at the bend of the road. They walked towards the bridge, suspicious at first, as if showing a reluctance to believe what they had been told. One group carried suitcases and bundles, the rest seemed to have set out on foot for a day's excursion.

On the near side a bus appeared, a cream-painted service vehicle, down the Konig-Strasse from West Berlin. It stopped briefly at the approach to the bridge and then moved slowly forward on the Potsdam road. At the far side of the crossing it stopped again while the driver spoke briefly to one of the volkspolizei. Then it turned the corner and disappeared among the wooded roads.

'Come on!' said Elliott irritably to the invisible Rubin. 'Come on!'

The helicopter with Corrigan and Andor on board came in again, low on the allied side so that the parkland trees in full leaf stirred a little with the wash of its rotors.

'I hope your American friend knows what he's up to,' said Bonnell-Thornton coolly. 'If that damn thing crashes now with Andor on board . . .'

But Elliott was no longer attending to him, nor to the helicopter as it rose suddenly and pulled away towards the far shore.

'My God!' he said. 'Look at that!'

Down the road on the DDR side of the bridge came a disordered procession of men. Some were alone, some were accompanied by their women, a few led or carried their children.

'Hundreds of them!' said Elliott incredulously. 'They look more like a football crowd than political refugees.'

There was no doubting the holiday mood of the leaders as the crowd reached the bridge and began to tramp across, laughing and shouting. They carried few possessions, suggesting once more that they had taken advantage of the open frontier merely to spend a day in West Berlin or to test the reality of their new freedom.

Elliott watched the faces as they passed. The men were distinguished by a frankness and honesty in their blue eyes and strong features. The women were clean, attractive, and unglamorous. Their children had the healthy unspoilt look of east Europeans who had been uncontaminated by the modish self-abasement of the west.

As they reached the end of the bridge, most of them sat

down or stretched out on the lakeside grassland of the Schloss Glienicker pleasure gardens. A few were greeted by the owners of the parked cars – some with handshakes, the rest by embraces. The helicopter swung low again in an arc across the water.

'A picnic,' said Elliott disconsolately. 'That's all it looks like from the air. A damned great picnic party.'

Bonnell-Thornton waved towards the narrow stretch of water.

'Movement on the bridge, Sam. That's what counts.'

The helicopter came in once more and then turned away towards the landing pad of the garrison headquarters at Spandau. Andor was going back to safe keeping.

Now that the men and women on foot had crossed the narrow water, the bridge was deserted. A Volga staff car appeared and crossed slowly to the guard-post on the West Berlin side. Colonel Rubin, in full uniform, got out and saluted Bonnell-Thornton. He turned to the major.

'You see, Mr Elliott?' The smile of joviality clung to his broad face like a mask. 'I do what I can. Were my actors to your satisfaction?'

Elliott looked aside a little, across the Havel to the far shore.

'They should be, sir,' he said quietly. 'They've had the practice. Every time East Berlin receives a fraternal visit from a Warsaw Pact leader. The cheering crowds at the airport, the bouquets in the streets. Who else but the Soviet army and its ladies in civilian clothes? By the way, someone made a mistake when Todor Shiwkov and the Bulgarians came.'

'Really?' Rubin's smile was indestructible as granite and his question betrayed not the least misgiving.

'The television cameras picked up a German welcoming banner in Russian,' said Elliott lightly. 'Cyrillic script. I do think you ought to tell the comrades to get their act together.'

Rubin threw back his head and laughed enormously. He laid a hand on the major's arm.

'Mr Elliott,' he said, 'you will be the death of me. Is that not how we say it in England?'

A young American aide from General Page's party walked across and saluted the commandant.

'Chopper's down at Spandau, sir. Exercise Open Sesame is now called off.'

He marched away and Bonnell-Thornton turned to Rubin.

'I suggest, colonel, that you assemble your battalion again now. Before they all do a bunk into the centre of West Berlin and start painting the town red.'

He moved off, apparently unaware of the verbal faux pas.

'You see, Mr Elliott,' said Rubin with a confidential smile, 'I think my men know better. They know that on the Konig-Strasse, which is the only road from here to West Berlin, the frontier wall runs along it in two places. The Soviet army would not hide there to shoot deserters as they passed. But the East German comrades have a certain *rigeur*. They do not flinch from shooting in the back, either here or in the Soviet Union forty years ago.'

Elliott nodded.

'What it is to have allies,' he said impassively.

Rubin, uncertain of the implication, laughed again and walked away to give his orders. The picnic parties stood up and formed a military procession. The reunited families joined the rear of the column. In a long and orderly march they moved forward, crossing back over the bridge and turning the corner of the wooded road to the dispersal area where the lorries, buses and troop transports waited, concealed from overhead surveillance by the dense summer foliage. The volkspolizei replaced their barriers and uncoiled the barbed wire. General Page radioed for the removal of the two road blocks on the Konig-Strasse which had kept civilians at a distance for the duration of the exercise. By the time that Elliott and the commandant left, the cool serenity of a summer morning, silent and deserted, had settled again upon the lakeside scene.

33

'Why didn't he believe it?' In the observation room which adjoined Andor's prison ward, Bonnell-Thornton confronted Elliott as if the major had intended a personal affront to him. 'What more does he want?'

'He leaves that to us, sir.' Elliott put his cap and swagger stick on the table. Beyond the two-way mirror, Andor sat hunched in his chair, staring down at his folded hands as though he might be reading an invisible book. The major turned and faced the commandant once more.

'He doesn't disbelieve us,' Elliott said. 'He wants more proof, more evidence. Corrigan explained that it wasn't possible to put the helicopter down near the Glienicker Bridge. Andor wanted to talk to the people crossing from the east. He wants to see preparations for opening up the checkpoints.'

'We can't give him either.' Bonnell-Thornton picked up a memorandum and handed it to Elliott. 'Rubin and his masters make it quite clear that we shall have to be satisfied with what we've got. No interviews and no tampering with the other checkpoints. We'll work on him with what we've got until noon tomorrow.'

'And if he doesn't budge?'

'Then we'll dope him and try to get the truth that way,' Bonnell-Thornton said. 'Major Corrigan doesn't trust the medication but Page tells me he's ready to overrule the objection. So long as it's what we want. I want it, Sam. After that, there's only the old and rather nasty way of getting the story from him. I don't intend it to come to that.'

'I'll have one more try, sir.' Elliott watched the old man in the next room. 'First thing tomorrow. We'd better have the senior pharmacist briefed and the necessary authorisations signed. One medic in attendance. That should be enough. Once he's been doped, we shall have to confine the questioning to one interrogator.'

'And the questioning?'

'Corrigan,' the brigadier said. 'I daresay he doubts the use of it but he's the only man here with much experience of the technique.'

They went out together across the exercise yard to the main gate, now guarded by the Royal Fusiliers. Elliott began driving back to the Heer-Strasse, rehearsing in his mind the one last chance of orthodox questioning which was to take place in the morning. The imagined drama was interrupted from time to time by thoughts of the empty sitting-room and the space of a bed half-occupied. For the past day or two he had trained himself to expect no more of Debby, to think of her less and less. He knew of nowhere that she might be, except the old apartment by the Potsdamer-Strasse. Surely it was too dangerous a hiding place? Pride as well as discretion had held his curiosity in check. Now he felt the absurdity of such prohibitions. Glancing at his watch, he ignored the cul-de-sac and the maisonette, driving quickly eastwards along the broad axial road towards the Tiergarten.

Further still, he parked the car in the little street off the Potsdamer-Strasse and walked into the apartment-block. Going up by the bare concrete stairs with their iron rail, he found the door of the apartment, its dark brown paint chipped and scratched.

There was no answer when he pressed the bell. Trying the handle of the door, he found it unlocked. The civilian police as well as military intelligence would have checked the building long ago. It was pointless to wonder which of them had left the apartment open, or whether it was a casual thief.

Inside he found the shabby little rooms with their bare carpets undisturbed. There was no sign that Debby had been there since the day of Hoskins's death. In the bedroom a wardrobe had been improvised by hanging a curtain across an alcove. Elliott drew the curtain back. Whatever clothes belonged to Hoskins had been removed, no doubt by the first men to search the flat. There was nothing of Debby's but a black dress and a pair of red shoes in a cardboard box. He touched the dress, as if it might have been her living skin. The windows had been closed tight for more than a week in the heat of the Berlin summer, giving an oppressive dusty warmth to the room, an odour of the thin carpeting and the cheaply painted wood.

Elliott sat down on the edge of the bed. He looked at the blank mirrors which had held the girl's image so often, the dress which had moved on her young limbs, the carpet where her bare feet had walked and the bed which had borne the impress of her body. The warm enclosed air he breathed was the same that had caressed her.

It was Andor now, the image and the voice, which eluded him. Though he might never see the girl again, Elliott felt himself guilty of the last betrayal of duty. It was no longer Andor's image which interposed between him and his thoughts of her, but Debby's memory which lingered in every waking thought about Andor as the drama of annihilation moved towards its final hours.

34

'Nothing,' said Corrigan gently. 'You have nothing whatever to fear. No one will harm you. Least of all now that agreement between us is so close. None of us can force you to answer questions. You must respond of your own free will.'

But as he spoke, Corrigan saw the resentment and sense of degradation in the old man's eyes. Andor lay, fully-clothed in shirt and trousers on a high couch of hard green leather. At one end the surface had been raised to provide a support for his head. The blue eyes, watery though they were, appeared round and large with anger. Corrigan wondered if perhaps this was the effect of the injection which the senior American surgeon in the prison hospital had administered to Andor several minutes before. The last routine questioning had failed.

The surgeon was still standing by the raised examination couch. He held the subject's wrist lightly, checking the pulse-rate. It was slower now than at any time since Andor's arrest, if the charts were to be believed. With its distemper and tubular steel chairs, the examination room had been chosen as the scene of the final confession. Elliott and Rubin sat in attendance, as was their right. Corrigan, who doubted the need and the wisdom of interrogation under narcotics, was to ask the questions. He had protested privately to General Page against the whole procedure, and Page had overruled him. Corrigan had been permitted his hours of quiet and patient questioning. In turn, Elliott and Bonnell-Thornton were to be conceded the more sophisticated forms of interrogation.

Andor closed his eyes, not in sleep but as if to protect them against sunlight. The surgeon released the old man's wrist, though both arms were fastened to the sides of the couch by bands of soft rust-coloured rubber.

'Believe me,' said Corrigan softly. 'No one here wishes you ill.'

His voice rose and fell with the gentleness of understanding and affection. Alone among the three officers present, he had experience of questioning subjects under the sedation of a so-called truth drug. The first rule was that such drugs were unlikely to work without the patient having been reassured and relaxed.

'I'm truly sorry, Dr Andor, that you must tell us your story in this manner and under these circumstances.' His chair was three or four feet from the couch, the words spoken as if to accompany the intimacy of an understanding caress. 'When you think about it, you will appreciate the reason. I know that you will speak the truth. But there is too much at stake for the world to take you or I on trust. I know you understand that. Nothing has been done to you except to ease your anxiety. The injection you have been given is an atropine type to relax you. You will think more lucidly.'

As he watched Andor, Corrigan saw the eyelids flicker as if they might open. Then they were still again. The hyoscine was taking effect, lulling the patient into the state of 'twilight sleep', induced as a matter of routine in women during labour. Despite the reputation of the truth drug, it was primarily a sedative, useless without practised and sympathetic interrogation. A dozen western intelligence agencies had learnt this to their cost.

'I want to talk to you about language.' Corrigan's voice was so low that it scarcely seemed to carry beyond the man on the couch. 'The language of computer programming. Ada, the language of the computer at Ezeiza. You have nothing to fear in talking about it now. Your work is done. You have accomplished everything you set out to do. The frontier posts of Berlin are open now. If you had failed, it would have been another matter. As it is, the world will see you for what you are, a man of peace and idealism. For that I honour you.'

As he spoke, Corrigan was aware of Rubin sitting behind him, the good humour shielded by an impassive mask of disdain. Elliott's impatience was almost audible in every breath he drew.

'You are our ally.' Corrigan leant forward a little, as if Andor might otherwise miss his words. 'You have the peace you sought. We must preserve that peace by removing the threat of destruction from the innocent people of this city.'

It was like talking to a fractious child. Presently there was moisture under the lashes of Andor's eyes. But Corrigan looked for tears and saw none.

'Tell me first your instructions to the computer. The reference of the programme.'

At first it appeared that Andor would not reply. The pale round face was composed as if in death. Then he drew an uneven breath and spoke with an effort.

'Vergesslichkeit!'

Corrigan waited, but there was no more.

'It means *oblivion*,' said Elliott impatiently. 'Obliteration of instructions!'

Corrigan waved him to silence.

'The destination,' he said patiently to Andor, 'The destination which you chose. Surely that has not gone into oblivion. It exists in your own mind, if not in that of the computer.'

The moisture gathered more thickly on the lashes. Andor's mouth worked a little as if he might speak and saliva began to collect in the creases at its corners. Corrigan looked up quickly but the surgeon gave him a slow considered nod of reassurance.

'The destination.' Corrigan returned uneasily to the path of the interrogation. 'You have won the victories of peace and justice but they will count for nothing if you refuse to help us now.'

The old man's chest heaved with a deep spasmodic breath, released in a faint sob.

'Sybille!'

The name was spoken as exclamation and question. Andor seemed to see the image of his sister gathering in the drugged vision of his mind.

'She is safe,' Corrigan murmured. 'You need have no fear for her. In a little while you shall see her for yourself.'

But the prisoner was still striving to focus on the wraith of his inner vision. Corrigan heard the metallic squeak of Elliott's chair and frowned without turning his head. Use of the drug was carefully limited. Too much time had gone already. With a sense of futility, he gambled on the main question.

'To what destination was the warhead sent?'

'Berlin. To Berlin.'

'But tell me whereabouts in Berlin. West or east?'

It would have been easy for Andor to choose the west. His interrogators knew that much from previous questioning. But now he had begun to weep in his hyoscine drowsiness and Corrigan saw that illusion was replacing truth in the old man's mind. After days and hours of resolute self-reliance, Andor was overwhelmed by the luxury of tears.

'Please,' said Corrigan gently, 'I beg of you. Where was it sent?'

It was hopeless, of course. Corrigan knew that. Yet for the benefit of the other witnesses he followed the last fading light of comprehension in Andor's eyes.

The frame of Elliott's chair creaked again with those small echoes of impatience which had punctuated the interrogation.

'You've lost him, Pat. I doubt if you ever got through.'

'Please be quiet,' said Corrigan softly.

'He doesn't *want* to save Berlin – east or west,' Elliott persisted. 'Sodom and Gomorrah have been raised on the site of the holy city. If you remember Genesis, it was the destiny of such places to be consumed in iniquity – and fire.'

Corrigan turned in his chair, the anger behind his steel-rimmed spectacles under a chill control.

'Be quiet!' His voice was lowered but he held Elliott's gaze a moment more. 'Please be quiet until the questioning is over!'

It was Rubin who spread out his large hands pacifically.

'Gentlemen!' he said, mild in his reproof. 'Gentlemen!'

When Corrigan faced Andor once more, the prisoner began to talk without prompting. He was talking to his sister, Sybille, or to some other phantom of his brain.

'By my cowardice I sold my country!' Tears stood in his eyes and his words had the tone of incantation, formulae learnt long ago. 'I was a traitor to my people.'

His jaw trembled a little and he drooled as he wept. Corrigan leant forward and touched the old man's arm.

'Listen to me,' he said, gentle but imperious. 'Listen to me.'

'The houses were burning,' Andor whispered. 'The horses ran in flames. I ran with them. Away from you. The horses on fire and the children dead.'

He began to talk rapidly but indistinctly, using words they did not understand.

'Spanish,' said Rubin sadly. 'You see, Mr Corrigan, even

your drug cannot stipulate the language in which truth is spoken. Leave him for a moment. Let him purge this grief. Then try again.'

Despite his irritation at the advice, Corrigan knew it was correct. Sedatives of the atropine type were unpredictable. Phases of tranquillity and emotional release alternated in the subject's behaviour. Sybille and the griefs of forty years ago held sway at the moment. He waited, then tried again.

'Martina,' he said softly. 'Tell me of her.'

At the sound of the name, the old man sighed and grew calmer.

'Martina,' Corrigan repeated the name gently. 'Martina. The city where Martina lives. Peace and justice.'

The surgeon, who had been standing back during the questioning, came forward and listened with his stethoscope to the rhythms of Andor's heart, where the summer shirt was open at the neck. Corrigan waited impatiently. Then the surgeon stepped back and nodded.

'The city where Martina lives is in danger,' Corrigan persisted quietly. 'Tell me how it can be saved. What was the destination of the warhead? What instructions were given?'

'Vergesslichkeit!'

'No.' Corrigan's tone hardened a little. 'Memory, not oblivion. Memory. The memory which cannot be erased. Your memory.'

'Vergesslichkeit!'

'No!' Corrigan's exasperation was controlled and calculated. 'In oblivion the city will burn. In oblivion Martina must burn, quickly like straw or slowly like a moth. Women with their skin peeling like paper from them, children crawling in agony. I ask you again, Dr Andor. What was the destination?'

Andor was still crying, but his head lay a little to one side and, for the first time, Corrigan guessed that the old man had not heard him. He turned to the surgeon.

'How much did you give him?'

'Point six milligrams in fifteen of morphine.'

'It's a wonder he's not out cold,' said Corrigan ungratefully. 'What can you do to alert him a little more?'

'Nothing.' The surgeon checked the dilation of Andor's pupils.

'Choline of some sort.'

The surgeon shook his head.

'It's not medically feasible, as he is.'

'Feasible or not, I want it tried.'

'Then you'll need to administer it yourself, Major. I shall have to advise in a few more minutes that this questioning is terminated. Whatever you want from him, you won't get it this afternoon.'

'I want the truth!' said Corrigan angrily.

The surgeon took Andor's pulse again and nodded understandingly.

'The trouble with truth drugs, major, is they lack the subtlety to distinguish between various sorts of truth. The truth you wanted this man to tell you seems to have been unimportant by contrast with the truth he decided to tell himself. The best I can offer is another session tomorrow afternoon. Now that he's cleared a lot of lumber from the attic, he might be more inclined to respond.'

'It won't work, though,' said Corrigan firmly.

'It probably won't.' The surgeon tested a hypodermic and slid the needle into the vein of the old man's arm, administering the necessary dose to bring on a longer deeper sleep. He pressed a bell by the door and waited for the two orderlies with the trolley to fetch the patient and take him back to his ward.

Corrigan was aware that behind the observation panel the senior officers who witnessed the interrogation were taking their departure.

'Tomorrow will be late,' Rubin said doubtfully.

'Too late.' Elliott got up from his chair, pale and cold with fatigue. 'Too late, if it flops again. The problem in ethics is very simple, Pat. Will you allow two million people to die rather than inflict terror or agony – or both – on the man who promises to murder them? You think the cavalry will come riding in to rescue the ranch house from the Indians. I don't.'

Corrigan withdrew behind his bitter irony again.

'Ten fingernails and a pair of steel pliers! Or have you something more original in mind?'

'Ten fingernails, Pat. Against two million lives. Believe me, if it's done right, you wouldn't need more than the little fingernail of one hand. It's the drama, not the pain, that counts.'

'Please!' Rubin looked up at them from his chair. 'It is I who am the bourgeois moralist here, is it not? You would do those things to a criminal which make you as bad – or worse – than him. It is that, not the agony, which outlaws torture.'

'The death of one man is a tragedy,' Corrigan quoted at him. 'The death of a million is a statistic. Joseph Stalin.'

Rubin stood up, smiling a little in his coming triumph as he held Corrigan's gaze.

'A blasphemy against humanity, Mr Corrigan. But can you prove that he ever said it?'

35

That evening, just after nine o'clock, the phone rang in Elliott's room. When he picked up the receiver, there was a moment of silence at the other end. He knew that it was Debby.

'Where are you?' he said quietly.

'I'm all right.' Her voice had the formality, the courtesy of a stranger's. 'I'll be all right.'

'I'd like to see you again. To be with you.'

Elliott spoke with soft caution, the practised hunter stalking prey.

'No,' said Debby hesitantly. 'Not now.'

'At least tell me what happened. What was it that altered? What made you leave?'

The voice on the phone was the last tenuous thread between them, he thought. One sudden or angry inflection and it might snap for ever.

'It seemed wrong,' she said. 'The more I thought about it. I had time to think. All day. It seemed wrong, after Jimmy and that other girl who was killed. I know it wasn't you. But it was your side that did it.'

'I'm not sure that they did,' he said. 'It's possible. But they're not my side. My side is the two of us.'

'I wish it was.' For the first time during the conversation it seemed that her determination to separate herself from him had weakened.

'It is,' he said quietly. 'Surely you know that.'

This time there was no response. Like a prompter of her thoughts, Elliott spoke again.

'Wherever you want to meet. Wherever it is . . .'

'I'll have to see.' Now the voice grew tired with the effort of argument and negotiation. 'Perhaps later.'

'Is there someone else?'

'No,' she said wearily. 'No one.'

'Then why?'

'You don't see it,' Debby sighed. 'You don't. Do you?'

'Perhaps I don't. Are you all right for money and somewhere to live.'

'Yes,' she said simply. 'That's no problem.'

She was going to ring off soon, he guessed that.

'Listen to me,' Elliott said. 'In a few more days there may be some difficulties in Berlin. When that happens – if it does – you may need help. Remember that it's what I'm here for.'

'All right.' Elliott heard the listlessness in her voice again.

'Is there anywhere I can contact you,' he asked. 'Is there somewhere I could leave a message?'

'No,' she said. 'I'll call you again sometime. When I'm more certain.'

'Is that a promise?'

'Oh, yes,' she said vaguely. 'It's a promise. When I've

got something to tell you.'

She rang off. Elliott sat down in the chair. He saw himself now for what he was. The middle-aged major who had fallen for a girl of twenty, believing that his world of evening lamplight, the cadences of Brahms and Schumann, would hold a girl of Debby's background. Now, it seemed to him in a moment of self-dislike, he had got what he deserved.

36

'Three days, Sam. We'll have to put him through it again. Now.'

Bonnell-Thornton looked up doubtfully. He was sitting on the edge of the desk in the British Director's office of the military prison, swinging one leg and describing downward spirals with his swagger stick. The early morning sun was still cool and pale through the mist.

'We can start on him sharp at nine,' said Elliott philosophically. 'Corrigan thinks the drug can break him.'

'Dammit, the thing could still be at Ezeiza for all we know.' The commandant got up with a laugh of exasperation at the absurdity of it all.

'Not Ezeiza,' said Elliott evenly. 'Not a chance. It's either here or very close.'

Bonnell-Thornton nodded.

'In case he's not bluffing, and in case we don't get an answer today, the search begins tomorrow. One battalion of the Coldstreams flew in last night. Plenty of house-to-house experience in Northern Ireland. Also a detachment of the RAF regiment for more specialised installations. There's an RMP company on standby at Chichester and a battalion of the Suffolks flying out tonight. We can't accommodate any more even if we could find jobs for them.'

'Corrigan thinks they won't be needed.'

Bonnell-Thornton nodded and then his brow furrowed with bewilderment.

'What happens, Sam . . . What happens if the deadline comes and goes – and nothing explodes? It means the warhead is missing completely. Will it be found? Would it ever go off? Could the timer still be activated – even unintentionally? If a bunch of terrorists got hold of it, could they let it off?'

Elliott shook his head.

'Highly unlikely.' He touched the problems on his fingertips. 'An attempt to break into a warhead by force would disable it automatically. It's built in that way, for obvious reasons. Even if they didn't disable it, they wouldn't be able to operate the permissive action links to set it off. Andor and his friends could do it, because they built the links in the first place. Not so a gang of urban guerillas. Of course, they could get hold of the plutonium. But by the time they built another bomb round it, the core would have decayed too far to be of any use. And the people who tried it would probably be dead of radiation sickness anyway.'

The brigadier allowed one chin to sink into the fat of the other, duly approving the laws of science as Elliott described them.

'Well,' he said. 'I suppose that's something.'

'It's not much,' Elliott said. 'The odds of the device exploding on time are about a hundred-to-one. In its favour.'

The commandant pulled a face as the phone on the table rang.

'Tell the major to come in,' he said, then covered the mouthpiece with his hand and looked up at Elliott. 'Corrigan. With his shirt-tail on fire.'

Corrigan knocked and entered without awaiting an invitation. He stood in the doorway, looking at the other two men with a curiously distant gaze. It seemed that he was composing his message with difficulty, striving for the maximum effect and yet failing to find words that would convey it.

'How's our prisoner?' the brigadier said, with the air of one whose jaunty tone may ward off catastrophe.

Corrigan paused, then spoke to Bonnell-Thornton, as if Elliott had not been in the room.

'With your permission, sir, I must have a secure line to General Page. We'd all better prepare ourselves for some rather disagreeable developments.' He watched the commandant's eyes as he spoke. 'I've just seen Roach, the duty surgeon. Our prisoner is dead.'

Neither of them spoke.

'They found him this morning,' Corrigan said. 'It seems at the moment as if his heart gave out while he slept. The drug may have been more than he could withstand. We wound him up too far.'

Still the other two men said nothing, as if unwilling to lose a word of Corrigan's story. Corrigan himself went on talking in the quiet manner of a host who covers the lapse of conversation at a dinner party.

'In other words, gentlemen, the three individuals who planned this blackmail are all dead. Vogel. Nunvar. Andor. Now there's no one left who knows where the bloody thing is!'

Brigadier Bonnell-Thornton picked up the phone.

'I want lines to General Page,' he said, 'and to Sir Oliver Jupp at the Cabinet Office in Downing Street. Priority.'

3

The Day the Sun Rose Twice

37

Alexander Niculin, senior Washington correspondent of the Tass news agency gazed down from the press gallery at the long afternoon lethargy on the floor of the senate. The individual old-fashioned desks of reddish wood were ranged in semicircles before the speaker's leather chair on its rostrum. They were filling up now as the senators from the lobby came in through the double doors to join the dozen men who sat through the polite wrangling between majority and minority leaders over arrangements for the summer recess.

Niculin knew the chamber as well as any member present. He could tell the place of every bust of every president round the curving wall of the overhanging galleries. The grey marble pillars, the saffron yellow walls, the glass roofs and the white plasterwork seemed as familiar to him as his own study after fifteen years of duty.

As the house began to stir into life again, the clerks looked up from their green baize table below the rostrum. The page boys and girls, uniformly dressed in dark blue suits, ceased lounging on the rostrum steps and began to carry messages. On Niculin's first visit to the press gallery, it was the sight of these children lolling upon the carpeted steps which intrigued him most. They seemed like the abused yet pampered human toys at the throne of an oriental despot.

Niculin's interest was not in the afternoon's debate nor in the antics of the uniformed page children who laughed and lounged about with an air of self-conscious importance. He was waiting for Senator Praed to hand over the duties of acting speaker and walk out through the senate lobby.

At that moment Niculin had no idea why Praed should have sent a message asking to see him. Not that it came as a surprise. Niculin was not the most eminent of the press corps in Washington, despite his fifteen years service. Other men, the chief correspondents of *Pravda* or *Isvestia*, had won the prizes of the White House and the State Department – theirs were the front-page stories of crisis and resolution. Niculin provided background and comment. With his look of faded grey-haired diplomacy, he listened sympathetically to Wall Street wives on the hardships of affluence, and agreed earnestly with every suggestion from rising politicians on the need for Soviet-American understanding.

Much of the information which came Niculin's way was known in the business as non-attributable. He had never dishonoured a pledge in this matter. If he worked tirelessly, it was in the knowledge that the material which he supplied had more permanent value than all the stories and confidences in which his favoured colleagues traded.

The desks below him were almost full now, suggesting that a division was about to be called. Looking down on the members of the senate, Niculin saw them not as political parties but as two native tribes. Regardless of party, they were divided between men with silver hair in blue suits and striped ties and thrusting youngsters in grey flannel. Senator Praed belonged by age and rank to the former group, though he wore his clothes with the habitual untidy look of the fat man whom nothing fits and who has ceased to care about it. He was hidden from Niculin's gaze at the moment, under the press gallery, occupying his leather throne between the sergeant-at-arms and the secretary of the senate with the Stars and Stripes unfolded behind him like a cathedral tapestry.

Like the Wall Street wives and the retired military men who could afford at last to have unconventional opinions, Praed had received Niculin's courteous attention for more than ten years. From the Russian's point of view, the relationship had yielded little. Yet tolerance and patience were the tools of his trade. Better than any Washington commentator, he knew precisely the worth of the senator. Praed with his prairie origins and the economic theories of simple arithmetic had dreamt instead of embassies, diplomacy, and the world of foreign affairs. It was Niculin's duty to listen respectfully to the senator's increasingly resentful analysis of global politics, to applaud the brave hopes of franker exchanges between east and west, and to receive these sentiments as if from an ambassador-designate to the Soviet Union.

The vote was being taken on the floor of the chamber. Each senator's name was called by the clerk, with an inordinate interval between them, and the response of 'Aye' or 'No' given. Niculin had lost track of precisely what the motion was. Indeed, now that the debate was over the senate seemed more animated, its members wandering round among the desks, talking and laughing with each other. The young pages were lolling upon the carpeted steps again, as if awaiting the pleasure of their masters. At last the count was done.

Niculin put away his pencil and pad, stood up, and walked from the press gallery. Beyond the plush of the landings and the faint music of lift bells, he went down the stairs and into the ground floor corridors. With their low vaulted ceilings and richly painted scenes upon them, these windowless passageways under their bronze lamps seemed to him like the burial vaults of the czars or the pharaohs. He made his way to the wider approach which led to the larger of the committee rooms. He stood in the tiled vestibule before a finely inlaid double door marked 'Foreign Relations Committee'. Close by was the committee office allocated to John Stephen Praed.

He was not kept waiting there for long. In a few moments the senator appeared round the corner of the passageway, walking as jauntily as a boy released from school.

'Hi, Niculin!' He raised a hand, as if in agreeable surprise at finding the Russian there after all. Neither man in the years of their acquaintanceship had attempted to use the other's first name. Niculin preferred and respected that. It epitomised the static, predictable friendship between them. To Niculin the easy American use of first names had an unmanly familiarity. It belonged properly to women – or rather girls.

'Come on!' Praed opened the door of the office which he occupied near the committee room. 'While we have the place to ourselves.'

He passed through the doorway and the joviality vanished as if from the face of a mime. When he turned to his visitor the eyes in the coarse profile were cold and sceptical, the mouth thin as any cattle farmer resisting a suspect offer. He closed the door and gestured Niculin to a seat.

'Something I want to know.' Praed took the opposite chair. 'What the hell is going on in Berlin?'

Niculin shook his head.

'Nothing that I know of.'

'You know there's a Soviet division moved up on the Staaken airfield near the British checkpoint?'

Niculin shrugged the suggestion away.

'It's a frequent site for them. It means nothing.'

'There's a squadron of US Army tanks – M60s – marshalled less than half a mile from Checkpoint Charlie. And I have it on good authority that a Soviet unit with East German reserves moved up two days ago from Karlshorst to the Linden-Strasse area. Did you know that?'

'I had heard,' Niculin said. 'It means nothing. The British started some exercises near Staaken, on a small scale. None of this is big. It's a matter of routine for one side to match the moves of the other. You know that.'

'Damn the moves,' said Praed wearily. 'No one cares about them. I'm talking about why they happened. Do you know about that?'

'I don't think so.' From the way Niculin looked at him, Praed guessed it was the truth.

'Have you heard anything about a bomb in Berlin?'

'Nothing. What sort of bomb?'

Praed took his jacket off and hung it on the back of the chair. Despite the air conditioning, the sweat had plastered the white nylon shirt against his armpits and ribs.

'Listen,' he said. 'Listen carefully to this. I have been told by two members of the Foreign Relations Committee, independently, that rumours are beginning to fly about a nuclear warhead in Berlin . . .'

Niculin shook his head.

'It would be forbidden by the Four-Power agreement of 1971 and the Basic Relations Treaty between the two German states in 1973.'

Senator Praed dabbed the perspiration from his forehead.

'The rumours don't speak of powers or states. They describe a scenario in which the occupying forces are being held to ransom by an organisation with a hi-jacked Argentinian warhead.'

'Has there been a hi-jack?'

'Not that I know of. All the same, a lot of CIA specialists who were here in Washington two weeks ago are in Buenos Aires now. As far as I can trace the links in the chain of rumour they are reliable. And credible.'

'What demands have been made by the terrorists?'

'No one says.'

Niculin pursed his lips doubtfully under the line of his thin Douglas Fairbanks moustache.

'And what do you wish me to do?'

'Flush the story out,' Praed said. 'Ask the question outright at tomorrow's State Department press conference. Failing that, get someone else on your side to do it. There's something in this that has a ring of truth. What's more, the people concerned are acting like it's true. First time ever, General Page in Berlin won't talk to me – or anyone. I want this brought into the open.'

'And you wish me to make you no pledge of secrecy – of confidentiality – in the meantime?'

Praed looked up at Niculin still dabbing the perspiration.

'The hell with secrecy! I want the story to break. If you can do it at their press conference, okay. If there's some way of doing it before then, so much the better.'

The interest and animation in Niculin's eyes faded. It was like the drawing down of blinds, the moment at which the affable journalist returned to his first and purest loyalties. Praed knew the sign, having seen it as frequently in men from the *Washington Post* and the *New York Times* as in the correspondents of the Tass bureau.

Niculin nodded. When he spoke only the least trace of his own tongue betrayed itself in the inflections of American speech.

'I will see,' he said coolly. 'I will see what can be done.'

38

The pillared imperial palace, overlooking the grass and trees of Kleist Park, was still technically the headquarters from which the four nations of the Allied Control Commission governed Berlin. Since the end of agreements between the Soviets and the western allies, most of the tall rooms had been shuttered and dark, only a minimal guard from one of the World War II powers maintaining the victors' claim to the site. Yet the flags of the four occupying armies still hung above the Italianate balcony of the park entrance.

With a sense of their common discomfiture, General Page had chosen the commission building for his own press conference, which would forestall the public questioning of State Department officials by several hours. Geography favoured Page in this matter, though he acted on the orders of the President and with the knowledge of the Secretary of State.

'Look upon it as our chance to answer the questions here while the people who might ask them in Washington are still asleep,' he suggested to Bonnell-Thornton.

In this lay his advantage. At ten in the morning, when the Berlin correspondents of the world's press assembled under the chandeliers of the hall overlooking Kleist Park, it was only four in the morning in Washington. With Bonnell-Thornton, Rubin, and Colonel Léon of the French garrison, he watched the cars converging on the entrance to the underground garage. Forty years earlier the building had been set among the tree-lined cobbled streets of affluent suburbs. All that had changed. The area was one of kebab houses and the tenements of 'guest workers'. Rebuilt sites were filled by blocks of flats with shabby cement rendering, their forecourts a gravelled wasteland behind wire fencing. Verminous and grimy, the brown stucco of the older tenements faced the Florentine grandeur of the palace itself.

Though he was a few years older then Bonnell-Thornton, Page had the look of a younger man. He was a career soldier, the former Rhodes Scholar and oarsman who lacked a war to make his name. Even now he looked as if he might have come, freshly towelled, from working out on the Charles River or the Isis.

'Kennedy's long dead,' he had confided to Bonnell-Thornton, 'and the days are long gone when Middle America would get itself into a lather at the thought of Berlin being blown off the map.'

'It won't stop here.'

'They don't believe that. To most of them, West Berlin is a rather smartly painted whorehouse. A resort of decadent wimps who won't lift a finger to defend themselves but don't mind feeding off the Americans who do the job for them. If you want to get anything done about our problem, speak first and don't over-dramatise the truth. Not unless you want to scare them off.'

Before Bonnell-Thornton could reply, an aide appeared at the doors which separated them from the conference room and indicated to General Page that the journalists were in place.

Following Page, and followed in his turn by Rubin and

Léon representing their own commandants, Bonnell-Thornton made his way through to the platform where the long table and a dozen chairs had been set out. The American captain who acted as aide was down among the rows of chairs where the journalists sat.

'No photographs!' he said sharply. 'No cameras. This is a statement and questions. That's all.'

There were between thirty and forty correspondents representing the world's press, most of them the sort of men who would be sent to cover a routine assignment. Page rose to make his statement.

'In the light of certain rumours which have begun to circulate – and in order to alert the public to a state of affairs now existing in the city of Berlin – the four powers of the Control Commission have agreed to make available the following statement.'

He took up a sheet of paper and made a great show of reading from it with precision.

'A terrorist group, not identifiable as the Red Army Faction at this time, is believed to intend a bombing campaign in Berlin. Threats have been made on the basis that a considerable quantity of explosive material is concealed – possibly in the east as well as the western sectors of the city. The most vigilant efforts are currently being made by the four powers to ascertain the truth behind this threat and to track down the perpetrators of the outrage – or hoax.'

He looked up and, despite the captain's warning, a flashbulb split the room with its white pulse. Page ignored it.

'There is no cause for public alarm. However, it would be irresponsible to deny that danger to individual Berliners may be considerable in the next week or two. In consultation with the city government and that of the Federal German Republic, the following arrangements will be made.'

He glanced up again and waited for the pencils to stop.

'Firstly, all children of school age may be evacuated for

the next few weeks to schools in the Federal Republic where communal living accommodation will be made available.

'Secondly, all adults who can do so without undue inconvenience are urged to leave the city and go to family or friends in the Federal Republic for the next two weeks. Temporary accommodation in Swabia and Westphalia will be made available for those wishing to leave the city during this period but having no address to go to in the Federal Republic.'

By now the stirring among the correspondents almost drowned his words. Then there was stillness again.

'The occupying powers emphasise that these are measures designed as a precaution against the threatened acts of terrorism. There is no proof that the criminals have the means of putting such threats into practice.'

Again the flashbulb split the beams of sunlight from the park outside. This time the American staff captain moved towards the offender.

'Arrangements for those wishing to leave the city for a short period will be published in tomorrow's press and will be announced by the West Berlin television networks from six o'clock this evening. Every hour on the hour. The transportation of children, by schools, will take place by train from the Zoo station to Hamburg, their dispersal centre. Checkpoint Bravo and the motorway transit route to the west will be reserved for those with no present accommodation in the Federal Republic. Instructions will be given them either at the US checkpoint control there or upon arrival at the Federal Republic's control point of Helmstedt. Those with destinations already decided upon will leave the city by the Staaken checkpoint for Lauenberg.'

He waited once more for the pencils to stop.

'Normal rail and air services will run during this period. In addition to public transportation on the autobahns between the city and the Federal Republic, military buses will be run to take those without transport of their own. Allied military personnel will, of course, remain in the city to discharge their duties and to apprehend those responsible for the present outrage.'

He looked up and laid down the sheet of paper. There was a pause among the correspondents of such length that it seemed as if no questions were to be asked. It was a Berliner who rose first.

'How can it be necessary to evacuate the whole of Berlin because of a few terrorist bombs?'

Page looked at him bleakly.

'I have taken pains to avoid suggesting that it was necessary, Herr Lugand. However, we have some reason to take the threats seriously. If they materialised, Berlin would be subject to destruction on a wider scale than has occurred in bombing campaigns hitherto. It is the duty of the allied powers to inform the citizens of this and to suggest what course of action they might take. To take it or not must be a matter of individual choice.'

'You do not evacuate two million people because of the Red Army Faction,' the plump man persisted.

Page rubbed the back of one hand with the other in a motion of extreme patience.

'No one, Herr Lugand, suggests the evacuation of two million people. However, in the light of the threats which have been made, we feel it prudent that children should not be exposed to such danger here when they might be safer elsewhere. No one supposes that the industrial and commercial life of Berlin should come to a halt. However, if there are those who might conveniently leave the city for a week or two, it would seem prudent for them to do so.'

'And what if you have not caught your terrorists after a week or so?'

'We shall,' said Page confidently. 'It's a matter of days, perhaps.'

'How can you be sure?'

'No comment.'

The plump Berliner sat down and shook his head. He was followed by an American correspondent.

'General, your concern for the state of Berlin would not, I

suppose, be connected with rumours circulating in Washington press circles last night? Rumours that a nuclear warhead was on the loose?'

'I don't think I can usefully comment on that,' said Page smoothly. 'No rumours circulating in Washington press circles would surprise me, but I have no knowledge of such a story. It is precisely to put a stop to such rumours that I have made my statement this morning.'

Another newspaperman got up but the American refused to give way, waving him down again.

'In that case, General, can you be more specific about the size of the threat posed by these terrorist weapons?'

'I think it would serve no purpose.'

'Pardon me, General Page, but many of us would think it might serve a most useful purpose. You would not, I suppose, suggest this amount of evacuation for a bomb that was going to blow out half a dozen windows and take the tiles off a roof or two?'

'No.'

'Then I repeat my question. Are we talking about a bomb big enough to demolish a building.'

'Quite probably.'

'And how many of them?'

'That I can't tell you.'

'In other words,' said the American carefully, 'the threats suggest something on the scale of a World War II air raid?'

'If taken seriously.'

'But you are taking them seriously, General, aren't you?'

'We have no alternative, sir.'

Another of the Berliners stood up.

'You expect the people of this city to undertake an evacuation on this scale for a number of terrorist bombs?'

'I suggest it in *some* cases!' Page snapped. 'Children and those who have no pressing need to remain here–who could equally well be somewhere else for a few days. An attack of this sort might cost hundreds of lives. It might cost a thousand. If that happened and I had made no such suggestion – neither I nor any other authority – we should be held responsible for criminal negligence. And rightly so. I only want to put the facts before the people, with the aid of you ladies and gentlemen. The decision I leave to the common sense of the good people who live in this city.'

Another correspondent, whom Page recognised as the first lady of France-Presse, confronted him next.

'Do you know, sir, of any evacuation of this sort undertaken since 1945 for anything less than the threat of using a nuclear weapon?'

'I can't be expected to have details of all civilian evacuations since 1945 at my fingertips.' Page assumed a wan, tolerant smile. 'The question is, in this case, irrelevant, since the matter at issue does not involve nuclear weapons. There is no possibility known to us of a terrorist group being able to construct or even handle such a device.'

'Would you take it from me, General Page, that the only evacuation of civilians on this scale – begun or suggested – was during the Cuban missile crisis of 1962, in the United States and the Soviet Union?'

'If you tell me, I shall accept it. However, the purpose of this morning's statement is to put the truth before the people of this city and the world as plainly as we see it. In so doing we seek to prevent the spread of rumours, the alarm and uncertainty, to which your own questions can only contribute.'

For twenty minutes Page stuck to his brief. Elliott watched the proceedings on a television monitor in another room. He was surprised that Page stood firm for so long, alone among the interrogators, before he nodded to an aide who came forward and announced that the conference was over. Elliott reached out and turned off the monitor. There was something unusually enjoyable about the sight of the smooth lawns of Kleist Park just then, the beech trees in full and heavy leaf beyond the broad grass expanse where the imperial colonnades ran in parallel. He stared down from the tall window and watched the French guard in their dark blue uniforms. He knew quite well what made him savour the tranquillity of the scene. It was the moment of stillness before the breaking of the storm.

News replaced rumour at ten to six that evening on the Tagesschau of the television networks. It was followed on the hour by the regular Presseschau which consisted of an interview with General Page, no more informative than the morning's proceedings had been. He was followed at once by the Mayor of West Berlin, who corroborated the general's account and the arrangements to be made for the voluntary and partial evacuation of the city.

'Have they told him?' Elliott nodded at the grey-haired figure on the screen. 'Has anyone told him the truth?'

Corrigan shook his head.

'Page wanted to, until the intelligence chiefs showed him what that would mean. You can't tell anyone on the German side without the risk of a complete disclosure. He couldn't be expected to agree in advance to secrecy when the destruction of his entire city was at stake.'

Later in the warm sunlit evening, Elliott flew as observer in one of the helicopter patrols which both the British and American garrisons maintained to monitor traffic on the two transit autobahns from Berlin to the Federal Republic. From Staaken, across the flat plain with its village spires and red roofs, the carriageways carried less traffic than usual in the hour before sunset. On a random count there were as many vehicles entering West Berlin as leaving it.

'Traffic from the Republic should be stopped altogether,' Bonnell-Thornton said moodily when Elliott made his report. 'Easy enough to close the Lauenberg end of the autobahn. But you can't do that without telling the whole story. And you can't tell the whole story without starting international pandemonium.'

'Corrigan says they're much busier on the route from Checkpoint Bravo to Helmstedt.'

'Oh?' Bonnell-Thornton looked up from his desk. 'Why's that?'

'Corrigan attributes it to what he calls US civilian

personnel and dependants hauling ass.'

The commandant nodded.

'So one hears. General Page's wife and daughter flew out of Tegel for Frankfort this afternoon. Two seats on a scheduled flight. If I had people here, they'd be on the same plane. In another twenty-four hours there won't be a place available on any flight.'

Elliott sat down.

'They're full already, sir. You can't book a seat to anywhere by any airline. Even the black market seems to have given up.'

'You don't get the point, Sam.' Bonnell-Thornton slid some papers into a folder and put them on one side. 'There won't be civilian flights after today. All flights will come under allied military control. We decide who goes and who stays. The Americans and ourselves are taking over Tegel at midnight. Civilian staff continue to work under military direction. Two duty rotas of military police and a small detachment of the RAF Regiment from Gatow. That's our contribution.'

'They'll be under siege by tomorrow morning,' Elliott said gloomily.

'There's enough CS gas going out there to turn back the whole of Berlin. Dammit, Sam, if we don't take control of the place we shall have a riot on the tarmac. Anyone who wants to leave Berlin that badly can point himself towards the autobahn and *walk* to the Federal Republic.'

'I gather they've tried that, sir.' Elliott shielded his eyes against the late slant of sunlight filling the office with a warm yellow flush. 'Groups of boys and girls setting out with banners. The Vopos turned them back at the checkpoints before they could even get to the transit road. They tried again, without the banners. The Vopos still turned them back. Our treaty with the DDR does not give West Berliners the right to *walk* on the crossing of East Germany. As Rubin explains it, his Germans regard it as a threat to security. Anyone could walk off the motorway and into their territory.'

'Fiddlesticks!' said the commandant. 'The Vopo patrols would have them in ten minutes!'

Elliott shrugged.

'Even so. It's either car or nothing. When the people who haven't got cars get desperate enough, there's likely to be shooting at the checkpoints – on both sides. One way or another, Corrigan says, the transit autobahns from Berlin to the west will have been closed in another day or so. Either the East Germans will do it or else the traffic will block them solid. If that happens the Vopos will close them anyway.'

Bonnell-Thornton gave precise and equal weight to every syllable of his response.

'No one ever believed evacuation would be possible.'

'On the other hand, they can't very easily close the air corridors to military traffic. Not without the Russians shooting down our fighter escorts. Konstantin won't do that. He hasn't the authority to decide it for himself. The present inertia in the Moscow leadership makes it unlikely they would agree to sanction it in a hurry.'

The commandant opened the drawer of his desk and found a pipe.

'Transport Wing was there before you, Sam. They've got a full-scale operation from Gatow starting tomorrow. Group Captain commanding says he can fly out three thousand a day on a shuttle service to Lyneham. We can't use civilian airports in England without closing them to normal traffic and starting an even bigger panic. So far as the garrison is concerned I can have all dependants and non-essential personnel out of here before Andor's deadline. Two operational days. Three of the planes coming in tomorrow will bring new sappers and Royal Engineers for the search details. It's a long shot, but we may as well go on looking for the thing. What did Corrigan tell you?'

'Not much. The extra trains from the Zoo station will be reserved for children. Residential schools in the American sector go first. They're the easiest to organise. As for East Berlin, the poor sods don't know anything about all this –

except what they get from West Berlin television. Rubin says the East Berlin City Council will make its own arrangements. But they're not going to evacuate their part of the city just because a few conventional bombs have been planted by terrorists in the west.'

'The first mention of a nuclear device,' Bonnell-Thornton said, 'and they'll have scenes in the streets of East Berlin the like of which they haven't seen since 1953.'

He sat back, apparently refreshed by the thought.

Elliott drove down to the Heer-Strasse in the lingering summer dusk. He opened the door of his maisonette in the wooded cul-de-sac, walked straight across to the television and turned it on. The last of the news was coming over the SFB network. There was nothing different. Arrangements for the 'voluntary and partial evacuation of the city' were being summarised by the middle-aged announcer with bland reassurance. As if to emphasise the normality of the situation, this was followed by a brief and uninformative glimpse of the Washington press conference at the State Department. Berlin was not mentioned, either in the questions or the answers. There was much about Central America and the worsening situation in Mexico. The Secretary of State defended his country's right to intervene in a crisis where its territorial integrity was threatened, as much by infiltration as by invasion.

Ironically the Ost-Programm from the communist half of the city was in the last moments of a sombre discussion on the problems of terrorism in capitalist societies. Neither Colonel Rubin nor his superiors offered any comment on western plans for evacuation. Nothing was said to suggest that there might be immediate danger to either half of the city.

The radio alarm woke him at six with a preliminary jingle which announced the morning bulletin. Lying for a moment in bed, he recalled the events of the previous day. If Andor was to be believed, there was now one day and four hours before the ultimatum expired and the warhead exploded. Whatever the outcome, it seemed to Elliott unlikely that he would get much more sleep in that time. He thought of the last moments with Debby.

From the speaker in the corner of the room, a voice bland as a station announcer's began to read the news. Elliott heard the opening headlines and put down the coffee pot. He felt the dismay of a man caught in an ambush of his own devising.

Within the past two hours, a spokesman for the Defence Ministry in Buenos Aires has confirmed that a type EL205 warhead was unaccounted for a month ago at the Ezeiza weapons research centre. The spokesman emphasised that no actual weapon was missing. The error was one of internal computer accounting. In any case, the statement continued, such weapons were not armed at Ezeiza and the device contained no plutonium core. A further statement would be issued to the press and to foreign military attachés in a few hours. The present announcement was designed merely to counter rumours of a missing warhead which had given rise to public concern in Argentina.

Elliott drank his coffee in half a dozen gulps, picked up his case and went down the concrete stairs to the car. At Spandau he found no sign of Bonnell-Thornton. Only Corrigan was waiting there, having been sent by General Page with a briefing for the commandant.

'Did your people authorise that announcement in Buenos Aires?'

Elliott turned on Corrigan as soon as the two men were alone together. Corrigan took off his glasses and polished them.

'No one authorised it, Sam. I heard it was coming, about an hour ago. Someone had a query from the press corps. It was issued by the Argentines against the advice of our people working with them. As you'd suspect, Argentine security was leaking all over the floor. By this morning they expected to have a mob in the streets of Buenos Aires and every car in the city heading out for the pampas. We wanted to clamp down on the story – they wanted to reassure the public. After all, Sam, it's their public, not ours.'

He spread out his hands philosophically, the glasses dangling from his fingers. From time to time, Elliott had tried to envisage the state of affairs at the world's end. The panic, the terror and the human anguish had been easy to imagine. He had not anticipated that these ingredients should be so thickly spiced by incompetence and farce. Yet those friends who had served in Hitler's war had tried to enlighten him. Victory went by default to the side whose leaders made the fewest blunders. The arithmetic of disaster was all-prevailing.

Bonnell-Thornton's secretary came in.

'Major Elliott, sir. Will you take a call for the commandant? He's been delayed a few minutes.'

'Who is it?'

'Colonel Rubin, sir.'

Elliott went into the next room, overlooking the wide grey expanse of the barrack yard. He picked up the phone.

'Mr Elliott?' Rubin's voice had the tone of a friend at a family funeral. 'I have information to pass to Brigadier Bonnell-Thornton. May I tell you?'

'By all means. Are you sure an open line is the way to do it?'

'I have been instructed to issue a press release to the Ost-Programm radio and television news,' Rubin said reassuringly. 'Everyone will know it in half an hour.'

'What announcement?'

'Exactly,' Rubin said. 'Following the statement in Buenos Aires the people of the DDR will be told of the ransom demand in respect of a nuclear weapon hidden in West Berlin. It is necessary to begin precautions. We propose a *cordon sanitaire* of ten miles round West Berlin, from which all civilians of the DDR will be evacuated in the next twenty-four hours. We must tell our people the truth, Mr Elliott. Otherwise such an evacuation could not be justified.'

'I'm in favour of the truth,' Elliott said. 'On both sides.'

'Ah, Mr Elliott.' Rubin's sympathy deepened a shade. 'I have more freedom of movement just now than you have. There are D Notices issued by officials in London this morning to the press, to prevent wild stories about Berlin.'

'That's a matter for the Ministry of Defence,' Elliott said irritably. 'How did you come by it?'

'You know how it is, Mr Elliott,' said Rubin coaxingly. 'One gets to hear of such matters. Now you will excuse me. I shall look forward, as always, to our meeting this afternoon. At the commandant's briefing.'

Elliott went back to the room where Corrigan was still waiting.

'Rubin,' he said. 'They're putting out the whole story on East German radio and television to justify an evacuation of their sector.'

'I know.' Corrigan put his glasses back on. 'We had the same message from them. Earlier on. While we've got a minute, Sam, I thought you might care to look at these.'

He took several full-plate photographs from his briefcase and handed them to Elliott. Three of them showed Debby near the lakeside railway station of Wannsee. In the first she was sitting alone at a café table. In the second she was joined by Rubin. The third showed her handing to Rubin a well-filled envelope. Even as he looked at the prints, Elliott's mind spun a story to fit them. The truth no longer mattered. It was Corrigan now who threatened the private world, the sunlit bedroom with the light glowing on pale wood. There was a final photograph. It showed Debby against a background of grass and trees, unfastening clothes from a line.

'Every picture tells a story,' Elliott said casually. 'Where did you get these?'

'The first three we stole from the gentleman who took them,' Corrigan said. 'The last was all our own work. In the garden of your apartment.'

Elliott handed them back.

'So?'

Corrigan looked at him and spoke with the care of one who wishes not to be misunderstood.

'I want to know, Sam, why the late Corporal Hoskins' lady was passing documents to Rubin after Hoskins deserted. And I want to know why, after Hoskins died, she was living with you. I thought I'd ask you first, before I asked Bonnell-Thornton.'

A single inspired lie came to Elliott's mind.

'It's nothing to do with Bonnell-Thornton.'

'Sam!' Corrigan almost shouted with anger. 'It's to do with all of us! The girl in your apartment was passing information to Rubin! That's not private life, Sam!'

Elliott shook his head.

'You really don't get it, Pat. Do you? She was my way to Schroeder. All the time that Hoskins was selling useless bits of information. Then Schroeder killed Hoskins and for safety's sake I took her out of circulation fast.'

'Where is she now?'

'Safe,' Elliott said. 'Not in my apartment, however. I'll take you there and you can see for yourself.'

The first doubts were germinating in Corrigan's mind.

'Where, then?'

'That's not for your notebook, Pat. We were about to dynamite Schroeder's subversion exercise when Andor appeared. And that's still the aim. It's nothing to do with Bonnell-Thornton. Give me a couple of days to get clearance for you and you can have the whole story. See if it doesn't convince you.'

'I hope it does, Sam,' said Corrigan lightly. 'I hope it does. In two days.'

Elliott made no reply. He turned his back and crossed to the window again, imprisoned by his own sense of loss, the futility of risking so much for a girl he might never see again, and oppressed by Corrigan's carefully phrased suspicions.

In his mind he thought of another poet, anonymous and dead for many centuries. So far as Elliott knew, only two lines of the man's work survived. He was to think of them often in the time that remained.

'*O, western wind, when wilt thou blow that the small rain down may rain?*' Above the Gatower-Strasse the morning heat turned the sky to a silver burning-mirror. '*Christ, that my love were in my arms, and I in my bed again.*'

'You're not listening, Sam,' said Corrigan at his side. 'There's a call coming in on the other line.'

39

The first special train left the Zoo station for Hamburg with most seats empty. Scheduled rail services during the morning were busier than usual in mid-week but there seemed little urgency or even interest among most of the population. Elliott, on Bonnell-Thornton's suggestion, followed the RMP jeep patrol in an unmarked car. The established route was eastwards along the shopping avenue of the Kurfursten-Damm, past the Zoo station to the RMP post near the Soviet Memorial and the Brandenburg Gate.

Traffic was light, the grasshopper-green uniforms of polizei motorcycle patrols more in evidence, but every shop was open and the sunlit pavements were busy. Elliott watched the crowds, trying to pick out Debby's slim blonde image from the winding currents of shoppers. Brown-skinned daughters of Turkish or Yugoslav 'guest-workers' sauntered among red-awninged market tables of costume jewellery, assured in their youth and energy. Of Debby there was no sign. He had no idea whereabouts in Berlin she might be. The squatters' tenements of the Bulow-Strasse? The cheaper hotels in the little streets south of the Kurfursten-Damm itself? Or had she left the city altogether?

He turned the car, following the jeep at the corner which led past the Bilka department store to the square where the buses stopped, between the station and the gardens of the zoo. Did the crowds not know or not care about the promise of annihilation? Was it disbelief that the world could end on such a summer day? Tables were laid for lunch in the Kranzler Café and the Kempinski Hotel, on the Palmgarten terrace and outside the little restaurants of the leafy side streets.

There was a steady arrival of travellers at the station but nothing like a rush. Perhaps he was wrong. Andor's bomb was his article of faith. He had lived too close to it, for too long, to doubt its existence now, much less its efficacy.

In the warm sun, among the fresh green of the Hardenberg-Platz trees, the cream buses stood idle and empty, their drivers waiting at the wheel for the crowds who never came. The cool scepticism of the Berliners, however proverbial, began to set Elliott's nerves creeping. He had prepared himself for scenes of alarm and panic, even for riot and looting. In the summer calm of the June morning he felt that he had been let down.

The captain and the NCOs at the Entlastungs-Strasse police post seemed undismayed by the threat of terrorist bombs. If they guessed the whole truth, their knowledge was not betrayed to Elliott by word or expression.

'The Russians have withdrawn their guard of honour from the memorial,' the captain said with an air of pride in his discovery. 'About half an hour ago. Nothing said to us about it, of course. Bloody typical.'

Elliott went outside and walked through the Tiergarten trees to the final stretch of axial road approaching the Brandenburg Gate on the western side. The last few hundred yards were technically in the British zone, long ago fenced off to prevent conflict between West Berliners and the Soviet guard whose nation's memorial stood beyond their own sector.

Swinging himself over the low wire-mesh fence which closed off the road, Elliott walked down to the memorial, the massive figure of a cloaked Soviet soldier in black bronze atop the monolithic colonnade in white marble. The T34 tank of 1945 stood on its plinth, the olive-green paint lately renewed. Of the guards who had always been positioned at the centre of the memorial there was no sign.

Elliott walked further down towards the wall. A movement behind the glass of the concrete watch-tower, a hand raising binoculars, confirmed that the East German border police were still on duty. The withdrawal, it seemed, was as yet only a Soviet one.

Then it struck him that the DDR guards might have to stay. A regime as paranoid as that of East Germany would surely believe that to withdraw the guards on the wall would be to precipitate a rush by its own skilled workers to escape to the west – even a west under threat of nuclear attack.

He walked back and found the captain waiting for him.

'There's been another news bulletin from Buenos Aires, sir. Came over on the BBC just now. Corporal Rice got it on tape.'

Elliott listened and heard the same well-fed voice which had woken him that morning.

In a further statement, the Argentine government has categorically denied that a nuclear weapon or any part of one is missing from the weapons research establishment at Ezeiza. To prevent any misunderstanding of the press release last night, the foreign ministry this morning issued a clarifying document. The warhead in question, according to information released to foreign correspondents today, never left the Ezeiza installation nor even the area of criticality in which it was kept. The loss of the weapon was purely a computer error. An advanced IBM 38 computer failed to acknowledge the full number of weapons stored in the area of criticality. At no time was the warhead removed from its authorised bay.

Corporal Rice switched off the recorder.

'They want to make their minds up,' he said cheerfully.

It was the captain who led Elliott aside.

'There's a rumour from the American High Commission in Dahlem, sir. Regardless of what anyone else does, they're declaring a nuclear alert in Berlin from noon today.'

'Who told you?'

'Captain Clark from the post at Checkpoint Charlie.'

'Don't believe him,' said Elliott easily. 'He couldn't be further from the mark.'

In the office behind the main guard-room a phone began to ring. One of the corporals came to fetch Elliott. He took the receiver and before the commandant's secretary could finish her first sentence, he said, 'I'm coming back now.'

This time he was alone, with no RMP jeep to clear the way. Following the Tiergarten-Strasse and the streets beyond it, he entered the concrete shopping canyon of the Budapester-Strasse, approaching the Zoo station once more. Ahead of him the road was blocked by three vehicles.

Elliott pulled up and profferred his identity card. The motor-cycle patrolman in his bright green livery wagged a finger to and fro.

'You cannot go this way. The Hardenberg-Platz is closed. Westbound military traffic by the Kurfursten- Damm.'

'Closed by what?'

'People,' said the patrolman self-consciously. He waved his hand in the direction of the station. Elliott looked and saw them in the leafy space of the Hardenberg-Platz where the cream buses had stood deserted an hour earlier.

'You must go back – and round,' the patrolman said, moving off without waiting to see if Elliott obeyed the instruction.

The crowd which filled the Hardenberg-Platz had appeared from streets that were empty when Elliott last saw them. Now the men and women, some with children, were shifting and nudging against one another, filling the width of the square below the glass-walled Terrassen am Zoo and the station approach. They faced its entrances with a passive resentment, edging forward a little as each group at the front was admitted.

No one would ever know, Elliott supposed, whether the news from Argentine or merely the growing tension in Berlin itself had moved thousands of people at last to take advantage of the escape offered them. He reversed the car down an empty stretch of the Budapester-Strasse and turned aside into the approach to the Kurfursten-Damm, following the patrolman's instructions to go back and take the wider sweep of the the long central avenue. But ahead of him the width of the Ku-Damm was barricaded by the striped barber poles of a military checkpoint. Elliott drove closer and saw that the mile or more of tree-lined boulevard was almost deserted now, as if the crowd pressing towards the Zoo station consisted of those evicted from the smart shops and café terraces. There were uniformed guards from the British garrison on the nearer buildings, some at the main doors and some on the roofs.

At one of the earlier staff conferences, the impossibility of systematic searches had been agreed. Why start them now? Elliott felt a new irritation. It was not merely that the commandant had deliberately kept him in ignorance – had perhaps sent him to the Entlastungs-Strasse post to get him out of the way. Far more significant was the agreed futility of house-to-house searches without specific information to work upon. Page and Bonnell-Thornton had agreed, as Elliott was informed, that it was pointless to search the buildings of Berlin at random in the hunt for an object the size of a domestic washing machine. More futile still, when the placing of it might even now be a dead man's hoax.

He drew out his pass and displayed it once more, this time to the sergeant manning the barrier. The sergeant went to speak to a lieutenant, carrying Elliott's pass with him. The lieutenant walked off, in turn, to find a captain. It was the captain who came across to speak to Elliott and return the pass. He saluted self-consciously.

'If you'll drive straight on, sir,' he said, his face at the window. 'Turn right at the Leibnitz-Strasse. The way's clear to Spandau from there.'

'What the devil's going on?'

'Tip off.' The captain guarded the secret awarded him. 'A search of the Ku-Damm.'

'*All* of it?' Elliott looked at the flushed self-confident face. 'What for?'

'Couldn't say, sir.' The captain pulled himself up with the

air of one who could say but chose not to.

'All right,' Elliott put the car into gear again. 'Carry on.' He was tempted to tell the captain that, for the past three minutes, a nuclear alert had been in force for the American sector of the city. Discretion tempered the pleasure of doing so.

The way to Spandau was clear after this. He switched on the radio, tuning in to the RMP control room to see what sort of alarm might be developing in the rest of the zone. A jeep patrol, marooned somewhere on the transit autobahn to Lauenberg, was talking to the traffic controller.

'Foxtrot Bravo to control. We now have two – repeat two – civilian vehicles immobilised on the westbound carriageway. Thirteen miles west of Staaken checkpoint. One lane now closed. Present tailback of traffic estimated between four and five miles.'

'Spandau Control to Foxtrot Bravo. We are still trying to obtain clearance for two helicopters with lifting tackle to rendezvous and remove the immobilised vehicles. Please seek cooperation of DDR motorised patrols meanwhile for removal of any such vehicles from the carriageway.'

'Foxtrot Bravo. DDR authorities regard removal of vehicles from autobahn into their territory as unacceptable. Major Heine of the Volkspolizei has no authorisation for this.'

'Spandau Control to Foxtrot Bravo. Ask Major Heine if you can divert traffic by contraflow to the far side of the autobahn. We have *no* traffic coming from Lauenberg to Berlin.'

'Foxtrot Bravo. Major Heine already pointed out that it would violate transit agreements and constitute a hazard. DDR vehicles may still be using eastbound carriageway. Will you talk to him?'

'For God's sake! . . . Wait a minute . . .'

'Foxtrot Bravo to Spandau Control. Will someone please speak to him? There's almost nothing moving here. We're funnelling three lanes into one. There is now a tailback estimated six to seven miles long, towards the Checkpoint

Alpha at Staaken. Will you please talk to Major Heine?'

'Foxtrot Bravo, remain on listening watch. We will seek instructions and communicate as soon as possible.'

'Foxtrot Bravo to control. We have a *problem* here! Traffic is scarcely moving. The evacuation plan is effectively at a halt. We need instructions or negotiation *now*. One more collision will block the remaining carriageway. One more breakdown even . . .'

'Control to Foxtrot Bravo. Your message received. We will return to you as soon as possible.'

'We have Major Heine. Will you please talk to him and explain . . .'

Elliott turned off the radio. As he had anticipated, chaos was descending on the evacuation plan.

Ten minutes later he walked into the garrison offices at Spandau. The WRAC secretaries were busily packing files and emptying desk drawers.

'What's going on?' Elliott confronted the senior NCO.

'Nothing said, sir. Seems to be some sort of exercise.'

Elliott looked at the sergeant with suspicion. How on earth could anyone believe that it was an exercise? Perhaps they knew better but had decided to keep it to themselves.

He went into his own office and picked up the papers from the tray. Bonnell-Thornton knocked and entered, without waiting for an invitation.

'Ah, you're back, Sam,' he said buoyantly. 'Page and our American friends seem to have got overimpressed by Andor. You probably don't know it, but their sector of Berlin has been under a confidential nuclear alert since noon.'

'I heard,' Elliott said. 'By accident.'

Bonnell-Thornton nodded, as if in approval.

'In that case you'd better know the rest. All three command posts of the western powers in the city will be co-ordinated at the Allied Control Commission building. There's deep shelter there and all the facilities. We'll keep a skeleton staff in shelter here and make some arrangement at the military hospital for civilians. You'll be coming with us, of course, to the commission.'

'Who's staying in the city?'

'Half the civilian population, I should imagine,' the commandant said. 'The flotsam and jetsam who must be too far gone to recognise reality when it slaps them in the face.'

'And East Berlin?'

Bonnell-Thornton scowled.

'Odd thing, that. The line now is that the whole thing is a western hoax to compromise the frontiers of the DDR. It looks as if most of them are staying put.'

'And our own people?'

'Volunteers,' Bonnell-Thornton gestured at the office outside. 'Here, at the commission building, and at Gatow airfield. All in shelter. A few to police the hospital shelter, though that's for British civilians. Oliver Jupp made the position very clear as regards the front-line troops. The sappers and SAS can hunt for the bomb until four hours before the deadline. Then they pull out. Six Hercules transports from Gatow to Lyneham.'

Elliott looked past the brigadier at the sunlit drabness of urban Spandau. The threat of annihilation was numbed by the confusion around him. It was not evil but asininity which paved the road to Armageddon.

'Go home and pack, Sam,' said the brigadier gently. 'Enough to see you through the next two days or so.'

Elliott nodded. Presently he closed the window and turned to leave the room. Through the glass he noticed that a group of adolescent boys had begun to loot the first of the stucco apartment blocks on the Gatower-Strasse.

40

Elliott drove from Spandau to the cul-de-sac off the Heer-Strasse. He locked the car, knowing that it would only be a little while before the looters started on the deserted property of service personnel. He walked towards the concrete stairs outside the maisonette, thinking as he always did now of the first evening when Debby had been standing by the pine tree.

It was as he reached the foot of the stairs that he felt a chill of excitement and knew, before he turned, that she was standing there again.

'Sam!' She stood looking at him with uncertainty as to his reaction. Somehow, she had gone back to the Potsdamer-Strasse flat and retrieved the black dress and red shoes which she now wore.

'Where on earth have you been?' Even the banal phrasing of the question was that of a man who had expected her all this time. She ran forward and they put their arms round each other.

'Nowhere,' Debby said softly. 'Nowhere at all.'

He took her up to the apartment and they stood in the centre of the room, the one little world of security in the doomed city.

'Why?' he said again. 'Why?'

'I was frightened,' she said. 'More frightened here than wandering outside. I didn't know what you'd done. What you did to people. The old man with his bomb. Now I know it's all right.'

'He's dead,' Elliott said, standing back but still holding her hands. 'The city may well blow up by tomorrow. I daresay Colonel Rubin told you that.'

There was no accusation in his voice, merely a statement.

'I know you didn't kill him.' Debby tightened her grip on his hands. 'And Rubin told me nothing. Why should he?'

'Because you passed documents to him at Wannsee station café. The Americans have photographs of you doing it.'

'You fool!' she said, holding him tighter still. 'Don't you understand? Jimmy was still alive then and on the run. I did it for him. They were old papers that Schroeder already had copies of. RMP occurrence books and RTO orders at Tegel. Print-outs. Don't you think I'd do the same for you – and more?'

'Our leaders do not approve,' he said, teasing her.

'Leaders?' For the first time in their knowledge of each other he saw the wan young face convulsed by distaste. 'I can't imagine anyone who wouldn't betray them for love – or even friendship. No one owes anything to leaders – not the Russians, not the Americans, not us.'

'Debby's political testament,' he said kissing her. But she was not to be appeased.

'People in power stink,' she said bitterly. 'Worse than any others. People in America don't like capitalism, they just think communism's worse. The Russians don't like communism. But it's not as bad as what went before – and anyway they've guns trained on them so that there's no way out of it. Most of the people in England vote Labour because they hate the Tories and the businessmen or vote Tory because they can't stand the Labour party. The number of people who vote for a party because they like it – you can count almost on the fingers of one hand. And then they have the nerve to talk about a mandate from the people. Look how they've screwed the people – in every country. It doesn't matter if they're left-wing or right-wing, they're the ones who get the privileges, the houses, cars, flunkeys . . .'

'All right,' he said, stroking her hair and kissing her. 'We'll betray the lot of them between us, when the time comes . . .'

To find himself in a political argument a few minutes after their reunion was not at all how Elliott had imagined the reconciliation. He drew her to a chair, sat her down, and began to make arrangements.

'I'd like you to leave Berlin,' he said, picking up the phone.

'I'll leave with you.' Her tone was one of unconcern.

'I can't go,' he said simply.

'Then I don't need to go either.'

He put the phone down again and looked at her. Debby in this mood was a creature unfamiliar to him. Whatever had happened during their separation, she had formed a clear and irrefutable idea of what she wanted.

'In any case,' she said, 'everyone knows you can't get out. The roads are blocked. They're even saying that on the radio. The trains are struck at Wannsee because the signalling system has failed on the loop to the Zoo station. There's no air traffic except for military flights. There aren't any secrets any longer. I daresay I know as much as you do. That's why I'm staying.'

'You'll be on your own,' he said. 'I can't be here with you. In an hour or so I shall be on duty until whatever is going to happen happens.'

'I'll wait for you.'

Debby kicked off her shoes and curled her legs under her on the chair.

'You can't stay here.'

'Why not?'

'The looters have started on the houses.' Elliott picked up the phone again. 'And if a bomb did go off, you wouldn't stand a chance here.'

'What are you doing?'

'Dialling the British military hospital,' he said. 'They've got some shelter arrangements for our people. This time, I'm having my way. If I have to knock you cold and carry you over there, I will.' The facetiousness died as he spoke the words.

Debby shrugged as if indifferent to the outcome. She hugged his arm to her as Elliott telephoned the hospital and made the arrangements. She listened for a moment and then walked away across the room. As Elliott continued his conversation with the hospital administrator, he heard Debby's voice.

'A whole hour,' she said knowingly. 'Like a whole lifetime. They can blow us to pieces later, but they can't change what's happened now.'

She was referring, he supposed, to the presidents, prime ministers, and other objects of the girl's scorn. He finished the telephone call and promised to deliver the additional refugee on the way back to Spandau.

'Can they?' Debby asked, still referring to the spiritual impotence of the world's leaders.

Elliott turned, smiling as he saw where she stood waiting for him. In the white light of noon, Debby was nude as a ninepin.

In the last moments of their hour, she stretched her arm across the sheet and stroked his face.

'That's what they can't take away,' Debby said, referring to the time which had passed between them. 'That's the only thing. Shall I tell you what I'd like?'

'What would you like?' Elliott kissed the hand and saw the clock move to the hour.

'I'd like everyone to stand in a great crowd – everyone – just where the bomb is going off, and say to the owners of the bomb, "Destroy us if you dare." You and I and all the others standing there.'

He shook his head and touched her hair.

'The man who died – who stole the bomb – is the one. Not your presidents and prime ministers.'

Debby looked at him, her expression unsoftened.

'If they hadn't made it, he couldn't have stolen it.'

Elliott smiled and kissed her. He asked, 'Was that why you went off alone? Because of all that?'

'Partly.' Debby folded her hands behind her head and looked up at the ceiling. 'I was afraid of what was happening in the city – and of what you might have to do to that old man. But mostly I was afraid of the city. Not just the bomb but the looting and the other things. After a bit, I realised there was nowhere else except with you. Our room. Our life. That's all there is. I was still frightened of the men who wanted to destroy us but I began to feel angry too. That's when I came back. What right have those people in Washington or Moscow or London to decide that ordinary men and women must slaughter one another when they're told to?'

'None,' he said simply. 'Was that *all* there was to it?'

'One day,' Debby interrupted herself to kiss him, 'when

you've finished playing toy soldiers with little Corrigan and little Rubin, I'll tell you the rest.'

She slid from the bed. Elliott took a retributive swipe at her bottom and missed.

'Come on,' he said, 'I must get you booked in at the hospital shelter.'

'I'd sooner be above ground,' she said, brushing her hair and frowning, 'if that's where you're going to be.'

Elliott began pulling on his clothes.

'I'll be in deep shelter. Probably safer than you.'

'You'll be playing toy soldiers,' Debby turned and stuck her tongue out at him. 'With Corrigan and Rubin. I'd like to be there too.'

He dived at her in comic exasperation, seizing her bare waist. For a moment they tumbled on the bed again, laughing and breathless. It was true, of course, he thought. Men and women who knew that the shadow of doom stretched over them still teased one another like children, still laughed and tumbled in the sheets. At that moment, it seemed to him like the last hope for the world.

He held her firm and naked in his arms.

'From now on, little madam,' he said, 'you'll stop being perverse and obey orders.'

Despite the determination behind his laughter, he very much doubted that she would be so easily persuaded.

41

'There's a misunderstanding at the Friedrich-Strasse crossing.' Bonnell-Thornton was waiting for him as Elliott entered the commission at 10 pm, twelve hours before the deadline. 'We've got two corporals at the guard-post but they haven't the command of German needed for this. Nor the rank.'

'What sort of misunderstanding?'

'The Vopos on the other side want to close the road. Go

down and see what you can sort out. I gather that units of the American allies are already there in full fig. We need someone in authority.'

Elliott turned away and went to order a car from the duty sergeant. The streets of the shabby immigrant quarter were littered but deserted. There was little enough to loot in the cement-rendered blocks of apartments. Only a few of the little shops of the darkened Potsdamer-Strasse had suffered much damage in this area. Far off, along the more affluent shopping streets, the consumer treasure houses of the smart stores, Wertheim and Ka De We, were burning. A fire bell rang briefly in the distance and then stopped.

Two orderly lines of cars, one stretching down the Koch-Strasse and the other along the Friedrich-Strasse itself, converged on the western side of Checkpoint Charlie. It seemed to Elliott that they had been there for some time. Perhaps, turned back from the chaos at the autobahn controls, they hoped to find an escape through East Berlin itself.

The last of the American M60 tanks had been drawn up on one side of the western police posts, leaving the other carriageway clear for traffic. A row of steel-helmeted American infantry with rifles unslung faced a line of East German Alarm-Kommando across a vacant neutral stretch of the Friedrich-Strasse. There was no sign of the other M60 tanks which had waited three days in support and had then been withdrawn to the armoured depot in Zehlendorf. As he got out of the car Elliott noticed that the gun of the remaining tank appeared to be trained on the East German observation tower which rose like the bridge of a ship in white concrete at the centre of the street.

Another fire bell was ringing, just on the eastern side of the wall. The flames from a building in the Leipziger-Strasse burst erratically skywards and then subsided again. There was no sound of looting or gunfire.

At the far end of the Friedrich-Strasse, by the gap in the white concrete wall which provided a gateway to the DDR, several Vopos were shouting and gesturing, as if to turn back the queue of waiting cars. An American major was walking forward to remonstrate with the guards on the eastern side.

The line of the Alarm-Kommando watched him approach. None of the eyes under the rim of steel helmets betrayed so much as a movement of curiosity. With a screech-owl sound of rubber on tarmac a car pulled out of the line, accelerating towards the gap in the wall. A Vopo shouted and drew his pistol, then jumped aside from the path of the car. Several more engines surged and the line of cars began to move. The first car, safely through the gap, hit a concrete brace and slewed across the road. At the same time there was another shout on the East German side and a burst of automatic fire which sent a spray of burning metal into the night sky. Whether it was a spent round from the shots fired in the air, or a deliberate volley from the frontier guards behind the wall, Elliott could not see. Yet there was a sudden exhalation of flame and the wrecked car exploded.

The line of waiting cars began to reverse. Some of the drivers and their passengers scrambled from the vehicles and ran back for the cover of the western side. Across the dead street, the American infantry and the Alarm-Kommando faced each other, motionless in the confusion, capable only of mutual annihilation. Then the sky was torn by a flash and a crack from behind him which stunned Elliott's ears with the force of an unexpected blow. He thought of Andor's bomb and knew in an instant that if it had gone off he would be dead by now. Then he realised it was the 75 millimetre gun in the turret of the M60 tank.

The blackened buildings of the old Friedrich-Strasse shuddered and the earth seemed to move under his feet with the impact of the explosion. A sheet of flame erupted from the street, somewhere near the wall and a fire-coloured cloud obscured the scene at the DDR checkpoint. Elliott went down on hands and knees, partly from the impact and partly by instinct. The American major had thrown himself flat. Both the infantry and the Alarm-Kommando broke. They scattered to either side of the street and began taking up firing positions at the corners of the dilapidated buildings or behind concrete obstacles.

At last the cloud of smoke cleared and the survivors took in the scene. The East German observation tower had diminished to a pile of white-painted rubble. Of the DDR officers and their Soviet advisers there was no sound. Three of the Alarm-Kommando, at the centre of the roadway, lay motionless on the tarmac.

Elliott waited for the burst of small arms engagement. But now a silence settled upon East Germans and Americans alike. In the unfamiliar game of war, neither side was quite sure what should come next. The American major picked himself up and ran back. Elliott was the target of his fury.

'What the hell was that?' he shouted, flushed with shock and anger. 'Who authorised that? Who authorised it?'

He continued to run in the direction of the tank, in search of an explanation. As Elliott stared at the clearing smoke, the abandoned cars, the wreckage, the Vopos stunned and the infantry poised like the figures of a frieze, one man came forward from the eastern side. It was Colonel Rubin. As he walked up to Elliott, he moved slowly, wiping at the sides of his cheekbones as if to remove either stone dust or tears.

The English major saluted him.

'Mr Elliott,' said Rubin quietly, 'there has been an accident. Some men are trapped under the masonry. Perhaps you and your American friends would be so good as to help us in getting them out. We have only a few men here after the evacuation, most of them conscripts.'

Ten minutes later the infantry and the Alarm-Kommando began manhandling the blocks of white concrete.

'Mr Elliott,' said Rubin sadly, 'you know, of course, this cannot be the end of the matter. I wish that it could be, but the decision is not mine.'

42

The sky to the east, above the flat fields of Pomerania, had lightened to a pale duck-egg blue by the time that Elliott returned to the command post at the Control Commission building. General Page, his face pallid from lack of sleep, had formulated and despatched an official apology to General Konstantin for the incident at the Friedrich-Strasse checkpoint.

Elliott heard this and then retired to the small ground floor office with its two camp beds. Captain Morgan, who had volunteered to act as Bonnell-Thornton's aide-de-camp during the last hours of the crisis was nowhere to be seen. Had he slept earlier or not at all? Too tired to care, Elliott set his watch-alarm for two hours hence, and stretched out on the blankets.

It was less than half an hour later when he woke with the phone ringing. Outside the morning had broken into full sunlight.

'Sam?' For the first time there was a hint of apology in Bonnell-Thornton's voice. 'We've got something at last. Not much but worth following up. Can you come to the communications area in the basement and have a look?'

The underground area of the building was a legacy from Hitler's war, when it had been a ministerial headquarters during the allied blitz. Immediately below the building was a lime-washed corridor from which the map room and command post opened. Under this was the shelter, a broad and vaulted tunnel which extended fifty metres beyond the wall of the building beneath Kleist Park.

The communications area with its three computer terminals and phones of varying colours had a full view of the map room through the glass panel of their dividing wall.

The steel doors which flanked the staircase leading down

from the ground floor were still folded back and the machine-gun slit in the wall above was empty. By contrast with the elegance of the rooms above, the passageway at the foot of these stairs was lined by a mass of air-trunking and grey cables running along the yellow painted brick of its walls. The girders supporting the ceiling had been daubed pillar-box red.

The transformation of this Nazi bolt-hole to its present purpose was confirmed by a framed notice: 'Persons passing this point are notified that Military Police sentries have orders to examine ALL PASSES.' Elliott noticed that it was signed 'Charles Wesley Page, Commanding US Garrison, Berlin.'

The MP corporal glanced at Elliott's pass and confirmed its authority by phone. Beyond the sentries, the corridor seemed little altered since the building was taken over by the allies in 1945. The worn brown lino had been left, and the board for incoming mail. A hum of warm ventilation added to the oppressive stillness of the air, now drawn through new filters. Like chapels at either side were areas where bunks of wood and webbing had been arranged on the floor with their three-piece biscuit mattresses. Each door bore its wooden plaque: Officers' Mess, Waiting Room, Communications, Map Room, Commandant. A notice already stained by age proclaimed: 'There is to be no whistling or unnecessary noise in this passage.' On the door of the Communications Office another order had been pinned. 'No admission unless on Special List or by permission of the Duty Officer.'

It was the first time that Elliott had heard of the special list. Assuming that his name must be on it, he knocked and went in.

Two of the terminals were blank, the flickering grey light of their cathode tubes glimmering in the room's brightness. The third screen was filled with a list of numbers and figures, repeated at two-minute intervals.

Bonnell-Thornton leant across a table staring through the glass panel into the map room. He looked up as Elliott entered.

'Sorry to wake you up, Sam. We're having a last go at getting something new out of Andor's machine at Ezeiza. Or rather they're doing it from Langley and making the information available to us. It's not much, but whatever it is I want it. Those are my orders from General Page. Seems you're the only chap here they can rely on to deal with messages in ADA.'

Elliott sat down, tapped the keys, and watched the screen fill with a random pattern of 0's and 1's. Like most security services the Americans operated a binary code. What had once been bills of lading and schedules of freight was reduced to the scampering of green electronic digits.

He tapped in the receiver code and saw the green lettering spell out the sign for Ezeiza Terminal, Andor's operator code and the project number. Then he pressed the key for access to information in the 'bomb file'. The green letters began to sprint across the face of the glass tube.

BAS INTL 14714588 BLNTGL

He pressed another key to expand the information.

BUENOS AIRES INTERNATIONAL 14714588 TO BERLIN-TEGEL

'It's no use,' he said wearily. 'It's the same as before. Confirmation that it was sent. No indication of when.'

He felt the warmth of Bonnell-Thornton's plump face peering over his shoulder, watching the screen.

'A couple of hours from now,' he said sardonically, 'and it's all going to become rather academic.'

They were still watching the screen when a new set of lettering appeared. The CIA or its associates had intervened.

NSA FORT MEADE . . . BERLIN DESTINATION FOLLOWS

The two men waited. The screen cleared and filled again.

HAHN-MEITNER INSTITUT FUR KERNFORSCHUNG

'That's ridiculous!' Bonnell-Thornton straightened up and turned away. 'We've had every stick and stone of that place apart on three occasions. Every consignment directed there for the past two months has been vetted. Tell the CIA they're wrong!'

'They're not the CIA,' said Elliott patiently. 'It's the National Security Agency line at Fort Meade, just outside Washington. All they've got is the cover destination that Andor gave the computer, not the one he changed it to later. But it still confirms Berlin as the target.'

Bonnell-Thornton picked up the phone. It took him twenty minutes to establish a link with the computer terminal at the Tegel freight complex, by way of the Polizeipraesident building in the Tempelhofer-Damm.

With an oppressive sense of futility, Elliott began to tap out his questions to the Tegel computer. Neither Andor's original cargo reference nor the Hahn-Meitner codes provoked any response. He tried to reach the complex by phone. There was no reply.

'They've evacuated it,' said the brigadier, his irritation directed equally at Elliott and the missing guards. 'No one waits to be vaporised just so that he can look after other people's luggage.'

In the absence of its operators, the Tegel computer relayed the same pages of figures in endless repetition.

'Well,' Bonnell-Thornton asked at last, 'does it add up to anything?'

'Tegel has never heard of Andor's consignment, sir. But then it wouldn't have done. By the time it got there, all its codes and references would have been altered. I doubt if the package itself was any larger than a portable television set. To judge from the figures, there's complete chaos out there anyway. Some freight was allowed through, some held, and some turned back. They've been stopping all incoming cargo flights for the past three days.'

'So it could be on its way back to Buenos Aires?'

Elliott thought about this for a moment.

'If you were Andor, sir, wouldn't you want the bomb in place before you gave yourself up?'

Bonnell-Thornton eased himself on to the edge of the table.

'Probably, Sam. But I'd put a side bet on the idea of the bomb arriving in Berlin at the last moment. There's a certain logic in letting us search the city, street by street, for a bomb that hasn't yet arrived. Then let it slip through at the last moment in the general chaos.'

'Except that, in this case, it might well not slip through. According to these figures from the Tegel print-out, there was a final flight to Buenos Aires via Madrid due to leave yesterday afternoon. The plane was a cargo carrier. The last entry here says the flight was cancelled and some of the consignments transferred to another plane leaving at eleven last night.'

'Doesn't mean a damn thing,' said Bonnell-Thornton wearily. 'It may have started from Buenos Aires. But no one claims to know that it came to Berlin direct from there. If it was simply shipped back to its intermediate departure-point, it could be anywhere in the world by now.'

'But probably over the South Atlantic.'

'Probably. And even more probably right under our feet. Here in Berlin. You're right, Sam. If I was Andor, I'd have the bomb in place before I surrendered myself to the law. On the other hand, I would also arrange things just like this – to create absolute chaos in the end. You know, he was even smarter than we thought. There's not a single logical move we can make any more. Not a damn thing.'

'Can I switch out Tegel for the moment?'

'Yes.' The Brigadier slid down from the table. 'Did your friend Corrigan tell you where General Page was going to be?'

'On the phone to General Konstantin, talking nicely to the Soviet command. After last night's fracas at the checkpoint, it seems that our Russian allies will get us even if Andor's bomb fails.'

Before Elliott could reply, the lights went out like a stroke of blindness. The computer screens went blank and the air filters failed in a dying whine. Almost at once the lights sputtered on again in the dim yellow glow of emergency power from the underground generator. Bonnell-Thornton guessed Elliott's thoughts.

'Not the big bang,' he said. 'You'd notice far more if that happened. They warned us that Kraftwerk Reuter would shut down power production at eight. They're sending the morning shift to the shelters. No more power until noon, no pumping of water or sewage.'

Elliott looked up.

'They needn't bother going down to the shelters. Reuter West has an atomic reactor. A bomb at Tegel would set that off as well. If we were dealing with the real experts – the Red Army Faction rather than Andor – they wouldn't need a warhead. Just enough conventional explosive to smash the casing of the reactor. That alone might irradiate the whole of Berlin.'

The computer terminals were lit again but now the screens went blank, indicating the complete failure of the power supply at Tegel. From the speaker in the corner of the communications room, the voice of the duty officer delivered the first communal message of the crisis.

'All military units patrolling West Berlin will commence withdrawal at eight-thirty to deep shelter at Dahlem or Spandau. Shelters will be sealed at nine forty-five.'

'They can't do that,' Elliott said quietly. 'If the bomb is at Tegel, we must take a search detail out there and find it. At least there's a chance.'

Bonnell-Thornton shook his head.

'I doubt it, Sam. The bonded freight depots are in twenty or thirty warehouses all over the city. God knows what's in them now – or where Andor's consignment has gone. With the computer link to Tegel dead, we don't even know how to begin.'

'It's worth trying.' Elliott got up from the flickering screen.

'So it is, Sam, but not by you. Captain Morgan can organise half a dozen teams of volunteers from Spandau as the patrols come in. Most of the warehousing is in the Siemensstadt district so it won't be far. But you stay here. I need someone to hand who's not too confused about the spatial relationship of his arse and his elbow. Understand?'

Elliott nodded. He shared both Bonnell-Thornton's scepticism as to the finding of the warhead and the commandant's anxiety at being left without a reliable subordinate.

The phone linking the communications room with the commandant's office rang. Bonnell-Thornton picked it up. He listened, nodded, thanked his informant, and put the phone down again. When he turned to Elliott, his expression suggested that their part in the drama was over.

'General Page.' He sat down on the chair next to Elliott. 'Our friends in the east have a tap on the computer lines in and out of this building. Everything from Langley, the Pentagon, and Tegel is now common knowledge. I suppose there's still a point in sending Captain Morgan and his troops to search the bond warehouses. I'd rather not wait until one of the East German Alarm-Kommando units gets the order.'

Elliott looked at the clock and saw that it was a minute past eight. The patrols were withdrawing to deep shelter. In two hours more the world would know the location of Andor's bomb, if it was in Berlin. Otherwise, a cargo plane would merely disappear from the radar screens somewhere over the vast stretches of the South Atlantic. A seismic quiver, presumably in the ocean floor, would be registered by interested universities and geological institutes. Enhanced radiation might be recorded for a few weeks, perhaps on the West African coast. There would be rumours about South Africa's military research programme. More probably, the Argentines would be accused of carrying out another atmospheric nuclear test. Buenos Aires would deny it – would not be believed and would not care. In weeks – a few months at most – the incident would be forgotten. With luck, the crash of a cargo flight over a vast stretch of ocean would not be connected with the blast. If it was, then the recriminations might last a little longer. However, since the Argentines were the owners of both the bomb and the aircraft, interest in the matter would die before the year was out.

Even as he contemplated these possibilities, Elliott found it hard to believe that the crisis would resolve itself so easily. A routine, atmospheric test and a missing plane. Somewhere there still lurked a rogue factor, doomed to turn crisis into catastrophe.

He roused himself from these thoughts to find that Corrigan was standing by him.

'Sam,' he said casually. 'I tried to get you on the phone earlier on.'

'Why?'

'Just before the outside lines went dead, I felt minded to give your apartment a ring.'

Elliott stood up, guessing the sequel.

'On what authority?'

Corrigan shrugged. Light glinted on his angular spectacle frames.

'Intuition. Nothing stronger.'

They looked at one another. Then Corrigan said,

'Someone answered your phone. Wasn't that odd? A young woman. When this other business is over, Sam, us two intelligence officers will have to have a talk about your domestic situation.'

43

At five past eight, the first Alarm-Kommando in their field grey uniforms crossed a carefully prepared tract of the frontier death-strip between East German territory and the West Berlin enclave of Eiskeller. Before them went a bulldozer, whose ram demolished the grey concrete slabs of the roll-top frontier wall. Eiskeller, in the north-west of the British zone, was almost surrounded by East German territory, its few houses linked to the western city by a narrow wooded road. The buildings seemed deserted now and the British patrols had withdrawn to the deep shelter at Spandau.

The first of the East German troop-carriers followed, its outline distinguished by the curved roof and the flat square shape of the engine cowling. With the steel helmeted Kommando flanking it on either side, the carrier moved forward into the sunlit Spandau Forest.

At the same time a second Alarm-Kommando crossed the frontier several miles to the south, occupying another tiny western enclave at Steinstucken in the American sector. The jeep patrols of the US Military Police had withdrawn on the general order of their commandant. The Alarm-Kommando found no opposition and no sign of their counterparts.

The first Soviet crossing occurred a few minutes later by the Glienicker Bridge. An infantry convoy of half a dozen trucks moved forward, pausing only to decant a handful of men to assume guard duty at the deserted post on the American side of the bridge. The rest followed the long forest road to Wannsee, turned south, and took up positions round the Hahn-Meitner Institute. By nine o'clock the buildings were occupied. As yet, it seemed, none of the western allies was aware of what was happening.

The Red Oktober battalion of the 31st Brigade, complete with support vehicles and rocket launchers, crossed from the west at Staaken, occupying the deserted checkpoint. They advanced unopposed and almost unnoticed through the Spandau streets of brown stucco houses with balconies, survivors of the blitz of 1945. The battalion's objective was easily marked out, the three tall chimneys of Kraftwerk Reuter rising from the square power station block on the industrial bank of the Spree.

Here and there on the pavements of the Spandau shopping centre or by the open space of the railway goods yard, a few West Berliners watched the battalion pass, without enthusiasm or concern. The long arterial stretch of the Nunndamm-Allee divided the flat industrial wasteland between Spandau and Siemensstadt, a terrain of wire fences and lorry parks, withered grass and shacks in vacant lots. From this the battalion encircled the vast power station site on the river bank and began the process of occupying the buildings.

At the heart of the city the random gangs of young men from Charlottenberg or Moabit, the radical groups from the Bulow-Strasse, were still looting the remains of the fashionable stores on the Kurfursten-Damm and the Tauentzien-Strasse. Wertheim stood with windows smashed and doors open, now that the patrols had been withdrawn. Furs and costume jewellery were scattered on the pavement, snatched up by the looters who had started to fight among themselves for the booty. The oatmeal coloured stone of Ka De We, the greatest treasure house of all, was blackened by fire. Within the darkened building, the figures of the looters appeared briefly on the fine staircase with its art nouveau rails or among the glass fronted pillars.

A double drift of smoke from the city shops merged into a thin vaporous blur on the warm blue of the morning sky, like a malign blemish on the eye's perfection of vision. In the east, the cloud of ash particles was gone and the air above the Leipziger-Strasse seemed clear and still.

As the remaining military police details withdrew from the western control post at the Friedrich-Strasse crossing, the steel-helmeted Alarm-Kommando drawn up behind the drab buildings of the eastern perimeter moved into place. As soon as the street was empty they marched forward, goose-stepping in a manner more appropriate to the Wehrmacht of half a century earlier. Passing the smashed concrete of the observation tower destroyed the night before, they occupied the low chalets on the western side which the American, British, and French troops had just left. They moved no deeper into the western zone. The orders had been precise and unambiguous. The Alarm-Kommando was merely to occupy the buildings and assume the duties which the western allies had abandoned.

Where the Friedrich-Strasse crossed the broad avenue of the Unter den Linden in East Berlin, running northward through the diplomatic quarter, stood the vaulted glass terminus of the old main-line station. All other stations of the subway running from West Berlin under the eastern city had been closed many years earlier. Only at the Friedrich-Strasse did the trains still stop. As the Kraftwerk Reuter power supply was turned off, the first troops of the People's Militia began to move into the tunnels, securing them against illegal use from either side. By the light of tracked arc lamps they began the process of occupying the tunnels and stations under the streets and avenues of the western city. Safe from the immediate effects of an explosion, masked and protected by their overalls from contamination, their forward unit advanced slowly towards the Red Oktober battalion now in control of Kraftwerk Reuter itself.

By nine o'clock the honour guard of Soviet infantry had resumed duty at the war memorial in the British sector, just inside the Brandenburg Gate. The guard was company strength, one hundred and twenty officers and men. Its advance platoon, followed by two T-62 tanks, their 115 mm guns uncapped, surrounded the Royal Military Police Post on the Entlastungs-Strasse. The post had been evacuated almost an hour earlier.

At nine fifteen Captain Nikolai Tchernov hauled down the Union Jack and the RMP colours. He folded them respectfully, as if for future use. By nine twenty the red flag with its hammer and sickle in gold hung limply on the staff in the still air of the summer morning.

Several miles away on the western edge of the British enclave, Flight-Lieutenant Bradley, commanding a thirty-strong detachment of the RAF regiment at Gatow airfield, broadcast for the last time a message to Bonnell-Thornton.

'Soviet force now in command of airfield perimeter. No exchange of hostilities. Main runway blocked. Request instructions on rules of engagement.'

There was no reply. Following the orders already given, Bradley withdrew his men to the safety of deep shelter.

At the civilian air terminal of Tegel, Captain Daniel

Morgan had a simpler message to deliver.

'Major Simonov, Soviet forces, now in effective command of Tegel air terminal.'

44

'We've been screwed,' Corrigan said thoughtfully. He was sitting in the leather chair staring through the glass partition at the map room displays. 'Simply but very successfully screwed. By Colonel Rubin and his masters.'

He and Elliott were waiting for the commandants' meeting to end, half an hour before the expiration of Andor's ultimatum. Corrigan continued to stare at the display of maps, as if seeing the answer to a riddle. He said, 'Andor, Ezeiza, the warhead. One more Soviet subterfuge of quite unusual complexity. And we fell for it. We fell for it because for years we've been expecting this to happen. A bomb on the loose, in the hands of a fanatic. But never a Soviet fanatic.'

Elliott switched off the table light beside him.

'You're wrong, Pat. I don't see Andor as a Soviet agent. The last man to be one.'

'Andor may have been the puppet,' Corrigan said. 'Andor thought he was fighting for a united Berlin, a new Germany. But who was pulling the strings and opening the doors for him? This is likely to be the biggest Soviet propaganda and tactical victory for thirty years. Berlin and East Germany are threatened by a bomb of the imperialist powers. They're already saying that in their broadcasts. The western armies desert the city in the face of danger. So the brave Russian troops move in and take control.'

'They're certainly doing that.' Elliott conceded the truth of it.

'If the city survives, the Soviet army will be in control and no one will get them out! Without starting a full-scale war in Europe – without fighting through a hundred miles of East German territory – there's no way of dislodging them. Can't you see it, Sam? Rubin, Konstantin, even Romanov, shaking their heads sadly but wisely. Telling the world that the western powers have shown their unfitness as protectors of Berlin. They know where that bomb is, Sam! They must do. And that means the whole thing, even poor old Andor, was nothing but a Soviet plot from start to finish. Can you fault the argument?'

'Yes.' Elliott's swivel chair creaked as he turned. 'They were never going to evacuate East Berlin entirely. If that bomb goes off, the units remaining would be destroyed as easily in the east as in the west of the city. Why not take the gamble and put them in the west? I don't think Rubin or Konstantin – not even Romanov and the Kremlin – know any more about the warhead than you or I. But if those units survive, if perhaps the device doesn't explode, they've got Berlin in the palm of their hand. And all they need do is close the fist. It may be a rag-bag army, Pat, but their people die with fewer protests than ours.'

'And Andor?' Corrigan asked sceptically.

Elliott shrugged.

'Andor was exactly what he said he was. I don't believe in Soviet subtlety, Pat. They're effective but rarely subtle. They work by opportunism not by elaborate schemes. They used Andor, certainly. But they began using him when he surfaced in Berlin, not before. For a nation so opposed to capitalism, they know how to capitalise better than anyone in the world. It's the Americans who play poker, Pat, and the Soviets who play chess. The first move in chess doesn't much matter at all. It's the last move that counts. Rubin and his friends are playing their last move. Up above us, in the open air. With no opposition.'

Corrigan gave a perfunctory nod, as if he understood the argument without accepting its truth. They sat in silence for a moment. Then he said, 'Sam. Berlin may not be the worst of it. Suppose that damn thing isn't here any longer and the Russians know it. Suppose the detonation is somewhere else in the western world. You work that out. A single nuclear blast, casualties and damage on the most horrifying scale. An event like that would almost certainly destroy the nerve of the western nations to face a possible nuclear conflict with the Soviets – for whatever reason. That's the biggest prize of all for Rubin and his masters.'

But Elliott was thinking of Debby, the girl sitting in his apartment or perhaps occupying herself with domestic chores. He stood up and reached for his cap.

'When Bonnell-Thornton comes back, Pat, tell him that I've gone to find out what's happening. I'll be back as soon as I can.'

Corrigan showed not the least surprise.

'You won't get back,' he said flatly. 'This whole complex will have been sealed.'

'I'll try.'

'Would you care to tell me on what authority you're undertaking this sortie?'

'It doesn't need authority,' Elliott said. 'I want the truth.'

He walked back down the passageway and past the sentries who were already preparing to seal off the entrance to the shelter. At the rear of the building, where the grand façade overlooked Kleist Park, the staff cars had been parked in an orderly row. He took the key for the Ford Sierra and let himself into it.

In the new warmth of the summer morning, the city seemed still and deserted at last. The dusty little streets with their stunted trees were empty of movement. A plump rat ran across the cobbled way in front of him, a brown-grey grandfather, and it occurred to Elliott that as the power failed and the pumping of sewage ceased, a legion of plagues was bound to be released upon the western city. At the Bulow-Strasse crossing he hesitated, wondering whether to drive straight to Debby at the apartment or confront Rubin's emissaries at the RMP post. Staring at his watch he saw that it was too late to reach Spandau or the maisonette before the expiration of Andor's ultimatum. He glanced up and saw the curtain move behind a dusty window of the squatters' tenement as a hand let it fall. Elliott put the car into gear again and drove towards the parkland of the Tiergarten. Here and there a car had been overturned, looted and in some cases burnt out. Beyond the wall, in the eastern sector, the blank functional buildings of the Third Reich stood occupied by their new masters.

Still there was no sign of an invading army. Whatever sortie had been made by the Soviet or East German forces had not been in great strength. As it was, only a few men would be needed to take over the key installations of the western zone. He turned the car into the woodland avenue of the Entlastungs-Strasse and saw the white buildings of the RMP post just before the Reichstag building. A Soviet troop-carrier was parked outside the railings of the RMP complex and the red flag with its hammer and sickle in gold hung listlessly in the warm air.

Elliott parked on the far side of the road and walked across. The guard-room door was open, the lock broken, but there was no sign of the intruders. At that moment a young Soviet lieutenant came in through the communicating door. He looked not the least surprised to see Elliott. Indeed, he came to attention and saluted the major punctiliously. In the comedy of military etiquette, Elliott returned the salute.

'I am Major Elliott, Military Intelligence,' he said slowly in English. 'Who is in command here?'

'Lieutenant Second Class Tarasenkov,' the young man said, indicating his own identity.

'I wish to speak to Colonel Rubin.'

'I do not know Colonel Rubin, where he is.'

'Use your radio and find him. There is about to be a nuclear explosion in this city.'

'Colonel Rubin is not here.' Sincerity filled the young lieutenant's eyes, as if he implored Elliott to believe him.

'Then get him!' Elliott said. 'This is a British military post and so long as you are here, you will obey the orders given you by a senior officer!'

A look of reproach, even of sullenness, clouded the young man's face.

''Jah ni pani'maju vas,' he said. It was the standard tactic in such arguments. The Soviet representative would suddenly become unable to speak English, leaving his opponent silenced. Elliott, in the years that followed, had carefully cultivated the Russian idioms learnt at the Joint Linguists School in London and on Bodmin moor.

''Jah ni sa' glahsin,' he said, quickly continuing the argument in the lieutenant's own language. 'I think you understand me perfectly. I wish to see Colonel Rubin at once. He was reported as being here in the past twenty minutes.'

Confusion succeeded by resentment showed in the young lieutenant's eyes. Elliott drew his revolver.

'I also wish to know of any reason why I should not put you under close arrest for trespassing on Ministry of Defence property. This is a prohibited area within the meaning of the Official Secrets Act.'

Though there was no one but the lieutenant in sight, Elliott did not suppose that he and the young man were alone in the building. The time had come, however, to force an issue or two.

'Walk outside,' he said, moving the revolver barrel to indicate the direction, 'and get into the car on the far side of the road. I shall be walking behind you.'

The lieutenant seemed like an actor struck by stage-fright. He looked back over his shoulder quickly, as if seeking instructions. Elliott saw a movement in the shadows beyond the door. The bulk could only be Rubin's, he thought. At that moment the colonel himself appeared, his broad face opening in a smile of reassurance touched with just the slightest reproof. Elliott lowered the revolver and saluted.

'Mr Elliott!' Rubin spread out his hands to pacify the major. 'You must not blame my young friend. I was coming in through the back door and heard your voices. Please, Mr Elliott, look about you and you will see that everything here is in good order. We are looking after it well for you.'

Elliott had lowered the revolver but not put it away.

'You have no business to be here,' he said. 'None at all.'

'Mr Elliott!' Rubin stepped forward and stood so that if Elliott shot him he would have to do so while looking into the colonel's face at close range. 'Mr Elliott, see for yourself what is going on outside. Your army has withdrawn. The city is in anarchy. Shops burning. Cars destroyed. People have even been murdered in the street.'

'They were offered the chance of evacuation.'

But Rubin shook his head.

'By the treaties which our governments have signed, Mr Elliott, Berlin is one city under occupation by the four powers. You exercise the right to patrol the eastern sector. You have done it, several times a day or more, for many years. For us, it has not been essential to enter the western sectors, though our right to do so remained. Our troops have marched only to the Soviet memorial and to Spandau prison. But now the case has altered. Your armies have withdrawn from the city – some would say abandoned West Berlin and its people. We are the only power left to guarantee law and order. It is our right and our duty to do so.'

'Why are the airport runways blocked against incoming flights?'

Rubin shrugged.

'You must ask Major Simonov. They can easily be cleared when there is an understanding on the future of the western enclave.'

Elliott turned away and looked through the window at the Ford Sierra parked across the street.

'In other words, you intend a permanent occupation of West Berlin?'

Rubin laid a gentle hand on his shoulder.

'I know nothing of such things, Mr Elliott. However, it has been necessary that we should take up the administration of the western sectors during this crisis. Perhaps there will be an arrangement for the return of the western powers. But it cannot be as it was, Mr Elliott. Neither we nor the DDR can permit any situations which would ever allow again the kind of crisis you and I have seen. There will have to be discussions and new agreements.'

'While your army holds West Berlin?'

'That, Mr Elliott,' said Rubin blandly, 'is only a matter of geography. Friends should not quarrel over geography.'

The broad wooded avenue outside sounded to the whine of heavy vehicles moving past the Soviet memorial towards the commercial centre of West Berlin. There was no purpose in further argument, Elliott thought. Argument and discussion would come later, when the immediate crisis was over. For the time being, it was clear that General Konstantin's three divisions were systematically occupying the western zones. No confrontation with Rubin was going to prevent or delay the occupation.

'Mr Elliott,' Rubin's tone was that of an adult offering to indulge a disappointed child, 'I think it is too late now for you to join Mr Corrigan and our other good friends at the control commission. They will have locked themselves in by now, will they not?'

Elliott scanned the Soviet colonel's face for a hint of amusement at such precautions. He found none. Rubin said, 'I put myself at your disposal, Mr Elliott. Where you want to go, I will take you. If I cannot, I will give you a car and a driver. It is the least I can do. There is a shelter at the Karlshorst command centre, no more than ten minutes. You will be welcome there, I promise. Stay here, if you prefer, or wherever you wish. If your Mr Andor was right, however, time is very short. You would have to start for Karlshorst at once. I cannot accompany you there. I am posted to West Berlin. But a car with a driver is ready.'

Elliott shook his head. Now that there was no more to be done, he thought of Debby.

'I should like to go home.'

'Home, Mr Elliott?'

'To the apartment in Spandau.'

A look of genuine misgiving crossed Rubin's face.

'Will it be safe? If Mr Andor's device . . .'

'To tell you the truth,' Elliott said. 'I'd rather die there than here.'

Rubin nodded. He turned to his subordinate and spoke rapidly in Russian. Then he faced the English major once more.

'I will take you, Mr Elliott,' he said brightly. 'I will be your coachman. Is not that how we say it in England?'

'Chauffeur,' Elliott said. Rubin grinned and chuckled.

'Then I am your chauffeur.'

They walked outside into the summer morning and Rubin led the way to a black Volga staff car. Taking the main axial road westwards, Rubin drove at speed along the Bismarck-Strasse and the Kaiser-Damm. Several times he had to swerve round cars abandoned in the road. On the long post-war avenues there was less damage than Elliott had noticed elsewhere. However, even here several shop windows had been smashed and the contents scattered on the pavement as the looters withdrew. By now the pavements and the buildings themselves looked deserted.

Elliott glanced up at the heat of the blue sky beyond the car windshield. Somewhere, in the city or above the ocean, a fireball of destruction gathered malignant energy for its own extermination. Tiny worlds rushed to collide at a speed which rivalled that of light. The last image in a million eyes would be the silent beauty of its fireburst. Then tornado and darkness, the very stones bursting into sheets of fire from the contact of the air. As Rubin took the corner of the Kaiser-Damm at speed, Elliott thought of the mathematical inevitability, the exploding universes of a new alchemy.

Above them, the hot sky remained clear and still. The image of Debby rose in Elliott's mind, faded and imprecise, like the final echoes of an anthem in a cathedral dome. The spectre of beauty.

Without looking at Rubin, he said,

'The English gentleman, whom you admire so greatly, is a good loser. So they say. In that case, I should congratulate you.'

Rubin stared at the road ahead and smiled as if puzzled.

'History,' Elliott turned and looked with curiosity at the heavy head, the dark hair plastered flat on the broad skull, 'history will record this as one of the Soviet Union's great strategic triumphs. The taking of West Berlin. Possession in this case is more than nine points of the law. Without fighting their way through a hundred miles of Warsaw Pact territory – in other words without a major European war – there's nothing NATO or the west can do. They must start the fighting, and you don't think they will. They would resist if you attacked them, but they won't launch the first spearhead.'

Rubin shook his head and changed gear as they reached the Heer-Strasse.

'You are wrong, Mr Elliott. We are here to protect, not to conquer. To protect those whom others have abandoned.'

Elliott ignored the explanation.

'Corrigan thinks it was all a deep-laid Soviet plot, that Andor was your man all along, though perhaps without knowing it. Myself, I don't think Soviet strategy works like that. Andor was exactly what he appeared to be. But his appearance gave your people their chance – and they took it.'

Rubin shook his head again and spoke with a tone of soft sincerity.

'You are wrong, Mr Elliott. I regret to say it to you, but you are quite wrong. We did not take the chance. It is a duty which has been forced upon us by circumstances. If the western allies had resisted such blackmail, had held fast to their positions here, the assistance of the Soviet forces would not be necessary now.'

The car pulled over to the cul-de-sac. Elliott looked at his watch and saw that it was two minutes past ten. On every side, above the green feathering of the trees, the sky was blue and calm.

'The irony of it all,' he said, 'is that Andor's demands are conceded. Berlin's frontier is open between east and west, but not quite in the way he envisaged.'

Rubin smiled.

'You see, Mr Elliott? You are not angry. You make a joke of it.'

Elliott opened the car door. Before he got out, he turned to Rubin again.

'I do not make a joke of it. You knew that the bomb, wherever it went off, was not a threat to Berlin. That's why your army moved into the western sectors. You knew it was safe. There's only one explanation for that. You were in it from the start. You even had your agent. Andor.'

Rubin lowered his eyes, as if in embarrassment.

'We thought it was safe. There was a risk, but we were almost sure. And we had our agent, but he was not Andor.'

'Who then?'

Rubin looked up, the brown eyes gentle as they held the Englishman's gaze.

'You, Mr Elliott. You were our agent.'

Elliott stared back at him, not doubting that Rubin believed his own words, yet not understanding their use. The Soviet colonel rested his large arm on the steering wheel of the car.

'You are no traitor, Mr Elliott. No, my friend, you are a loyal officer of Her Majesty the Queen. Whatever our political differences, I honour you for that. I esteem a man who is honourable – because he is honourable. Yet you were our agent.'

'I doubt it,' Elliott said.

Rubin sighed.

'Mr Elliott. The great composer Tchaikovsky was once or twice a music critic. Do you know who were his greatest enemies? Not the singers he derided but the ones he did not mention at all. There is someone neither you nor I have mentioned at all.'

Elliott thought of the girl. Rubin smiled.

'No, Mr Elliott. Not the *petite amie*. It is Corporal Hoskins of whom you should think.'

'Hoskins was never permitted to pass anything of importance to Schroeder.'

'Mr Elliott!' Now the smile was broader in its wry

sympathy. 'Of course it was not important when you permitted him to pass the information. It became important later on. You see? That is how you were our agent. From those unimportant details it was possible to construct a computer profile of the Tegel air terminal. A tap on a junction box, which any workman could put in place, and one might read all that passed through Tegel for six months past. Because the two halves of our city are linked by a common telephone system, one could read the Tegel manifests while sitting in Karlshorst. You see?'

'Not entirely.'

Rubin leant forward.

'By following each consignment, its origin and destination, we concluded that Mr Andor's bomb was not in Berlin. We were not sure, of course. Perhaps it came by canal or road, yet that was not likely. We concluded that his plan was for the cargo to arrive at Tegel shortly before the deadline and to explode before it was even examined.'

Despite the warmth of the morning, a chill touched Elliott's heart.

'In that case,' he said, 'it was probably shipped out yesterday. All cargo flights were turned back.'

'We think so, Mr Elliott.'

'Why the devil didn't you share the information?'

Rubin shrugged.

'Had it been my decision, I would have done so. However, we could not believe that our western friends did not also have the same expertise. As General Konstantin put it, they had been less than candid with us in the matter of Mr Andor.'

'Where is the cargo now, by your calculations?'

Rubin looked at his watch.

'Ten minutes ago,' he said, 'it was about five hundred miles west of the Azores, high above the South Atlantic.'

Elliott looked at him as if in astonishment at Rubin's stupidity.

'You damn fool!' he said quietly. 'That was Buenos Aires via Madrid.'

'If our guess is right. Yes, Mr Elliott.'

Elliott got out of the car.

'It was cancelled,' he said bitterly, 'by written order. The freight went out on separate flights. It could be anywhere . . .'

He turned and began to run towards the concrete stairs of the maisonette.

45

The sky above the Atlantic mirror was as blue in its infinity as when Dr Andor had set out on his final journey a few weeks ago. At the controls of the 747 cargo flight, with his co-pilot Macbride, Captain Ralph Draycott could almost feel the warmer air of the early summer dawn. Prince Edward Island, the first Canadian landfall, was behind them now and they had turned out over the rippling glass of the August sea. The easy relaxed thoughts of a homeward voyage ran in Draycott's mind.

'Summertime, and the living is easy,' he glanced aside at MacBride without speaking. 'Fish are jumping and the cotton is high.'

Draycott smiled to himself at the thought of what he was going to do after their landing and clearance. A couple of weeks out of town.

On the radio he could hear Boston air traffic control talking down an Eastern Airlines Boeing, three hundred miles away. He listened for any message to his own flight PA 124/12788. There was nothing. Draycott had never expected that there would be. With its cargo hold well weighted down in the general evacuation of equipment from Berlin, the 747 rode the air currents smoothly.

They made good time, it seemed to Draycott. It was one of the best crossings ever. He looked at the cockpit dials. The westward crossing was always the easiest, landing only two or three hours later by the sun than take-off in Europe. This time it was moon rather than sun. Nothing more than a rather long night ending in summer dawn. Five to five in Newark, five to nine in London. Five to ten in Berlin.

Holding the stick firmly, Draycott put the heavy aircraft through a five degree turn, waiting clearance. Three minutes to the hour. The land below was still dark, the flats brown with a copper-tinted fog. By now the automatic control had locked on. Draycott relaxed and watched the altimeter. Then he glanced up with a frown as something, faster than a bullet and silver bright, came from the sun directly at the plane. It passed so close that he sensed the turbulence of the air about him.

'You see that?' he turned to MacBride. 'Going like a maniac! What the hell was it?'

'Phantom?' MacBride twisted round as if for a final view.

'They don't have Phantoms here.'

'Then I don't know.'

'Soon as we're down,' Draycott said, 'you report that. You see that you do. Make a note of the position and time. One minute and thirty seconds to the hour. Be exact.'

The 747 banked a little and settled down once more. At one minute to the hour with its flaps down and engine boosted it began to lose height over the flat waterlogged industrial desert, dropping into the bronze light of acid clouds. On one horizon, beyond a cold estuary, the sun through brown cloud lit a familiar silhouette. The two pillars of the World Trade Building, the clustering dwarfs about it, the old-fashioned elegance of Chrysler or the Empire State, familiar now as St Peters or Notre Dame.

As the clock moved without sound beyond fifty-nine minutes, the 747 skimmed a stagnant river winding through the flats. With the ease of automatic flying, it completed the last manoeuvre in the programme, bearing into the freight bay of Newark its rejected cargo from Berlin.

Author's Note

Author's Note

For the time being, the events of this novel remain fiction. But for how long? It is already said that there was an attempt in 1978 by terrorists in western Europe to contaminate a city centre by detonating radioactive material in the airshaft of a major building. The plan was foiled because the group was already under surveillance by the security services. Such threats are child's play by comparison with what may soon be possible.

To smuggle weapons-grade material out of major facilities is made all the easier because no one is quite sure how much should be there in the first place. An indeterminate amount of it is lost in processing. In 1976, the Government Accounting Office in Washington reported 11,000 pounds of plutonium and enriched uranium missing from government facilities. By 1980 the amount unaccounted for in privately owned facilities was over 15,000 pounds. Twenty pounds would provide a warhead powerful enough to destroy the major part of a city.

It is an open secret that some of the missing material found its way to Israel, with the tacit consent of the authorities. But the death of Karen Silkwood in 1974 raised unanswered queries as to how an individual could carry plutonium from the Kerr McGee facility at Cimmaron, Oklahoma, undetected by radiation checks. Elsewhere, security was so lax on occasions that the material of a plutonium core was locked away for the night in a desk drawer.

Such losses are discreetly and even soothingly reported.

On 5 November 1983 the London *Daily Telegraph* reported that six pounds of material – one third of a bomb – was missing from Dounreay and Sellafield. No one knew whether it had been lost in processing or by some more sinister means. However, four days later *The Times* reported that the containers for carrying this fuel were being withdrawn 'because of doubts about safety.'

The handling of such material by nuclear blackmailers would pose fewer problems than the authorities care to admit. The Royal Commission on Environmental Pollution in 1976 concluded that the equipment for making a warhead 'would not be significantly more elaborate than that already used by criminal groups engaged in the illicit manufacture of heroin.' Dr Kit Pedler put the matter more bluntly in the *Daily Express* on 18 May 1977. A solution of plutonium nitrate, dried and packed as crystals into two stainless steel mixing bowls, would probably set off a nuclear explosion if triggered by blocks of TNT.

The secret nuclear cooperation deal between West Germany and Argentina, agreed in 1968, has been public knowledge for some time. Such articles as 'Argentina's Nuclear Bomb,' *Listener* 22 April 1982 provide a general account of it. The mysterious nuclear flash in the South Atlantic occurred on 22 September 1979 and was withheld from the world's press until the following month.

Belatedly, in the summer of 1983, according to *The Times*, 'US fears junta is going ahead with scheme to test nuclear weapon.' However, on 19 August, the same paper was able to report 'US approves nuclear sale to Argentina.'

The security of computer systems – their vulnerability to 'computer hackers' – is another matter. Yet in 1983–4 alone the computer systems of the Pentagon, MIT, Digital Electric Corporation and Pacific Telephone were among the victims. Pentagon penetration was 'low-level', merely revealing what US security knew of the location of Soviet underground nuclear tests. In the case of Pacific Telephone, the Cosmos computer revealed the digital combinations of the company's security locks to the potential burglar with the price of a phone call.

In March 1984, Granada Television's 'Terror and the State' put a question to a number of leading politicians from the United States and Europe. What should be done if terrorists backed their demands by planting three conventional bombs capable of killing several hundred people? The politicians were united in saying that the demands must be resisted. No one was impolite enough to ask what would happen if one of the bombs proved to be nuclear.

The answer to that unasked question was given elsewhere by Dr Bernard Feld, Head of Nuclear and High-Energy Physics at MIT. His nightmare, as he called it, was a summons from the Mayor of Boston. Twenty pounds of plutonium is missing. A terrorist group has made its bomb and its demands. 'I would have to advise surrender.'

But suppose that the authorities would gladly 'surrender' because their political aims are those of the blackmailer. And suppose that a third party – in this case the Soviet Union and the DDR – makes 'surrender' impossible without a war in Europe between east and west.

That is the hypothesis of this fiction.